Shaking with the need to run, I forced myself to approach him. I waited for him to jump up and grab me the way they always do in the late-night movies, but he just lay there, smelling of blood and adrenaline.

A trail of liquid stretched out behind him as if he were a car that had blown a radiator hose and slung antifreeze all over the road – but the liquid that glistened under the street-lamp was blood.

Only then did it occur to me that I did not hear the thrum of his heart or the whisper of his breath.

I heard a car start up and took my eyes off the werewolf in time to see the black SUV squeal out of the parking lot and turn toward me.

By Patricia Briggs

The Mercy Thompson novels

Moon Called
Blood Bound
Iron Kissed
Bone Crossed
Silver Borne
River Marked
Frost Burned
Night Broken
Fire Touched
Silence Fallen

The Alpha and Omega novels

Cry Wolf
Hunting Ground
Fair Game
Dead Heat

Aralorn: Masques and Wolfsbane

MOON CALLED

PATRICIA BRIGGS

www.orbitbooks.net

ORBIT

First published in the United States in 2006 by Ace,
Penguin Group (USA) Inc.
First published in Great Britain in 2008 by Orbit
This paperback edition published in 2011 by Orbit

5 7 9 11 12 10 8 6

A CIP catalogue record for this book
is available from the British Library.

ISBN 978-0-356-50058-4

Typeset in Garamond 3 by Palimpsest Book Production Limited,
Falkirk, Stirlingshire
Printed and bound Great Britain by
Clays Ltd, St Ives plc

Papers used by Orbit are from well-managed forests
and other responsible sources.

MIX
Paper from
responsible sources
FSC
www.fsc.org   FSC® C104740

Orbit
An imprint of
Little, Brown Book Group
Carmelite House
50 Victoria Embankment
London EC4Y 0DZ

An Hachette UK Company
www.hachette.co.uk

www.orbitbooks.net

This book is for

Kaye's mom, Almeda Brown Christensen, who likes my books;
Alice and Bill Rieckman who like horses as much as I do;
and in memory of Floyd 'Buck' Buckner, a good man.

ACKNOWLEDGMENTS

As always, this book would not have happened without my personal editorial staff: Michael and Collin Briggs, Michael Enzweiler (who also draws the maps), Jeanne Matteucci, Ginny Mohl, Anne Peters, and Kaye Roberson. I'd also like to thank my terrific editor at Ace, Anne Sowards, and my agent, Linn Prentis. Bob Briggs answered a ton of questions about Montana wildlife and wolves. Finally, Mercedes owes a special debt to Buck, Scott, Dale, Brady, Jason, and all the folks who've worked on our VWs over the years. Thanks, everyone. Any mistakes found in this book are mine.

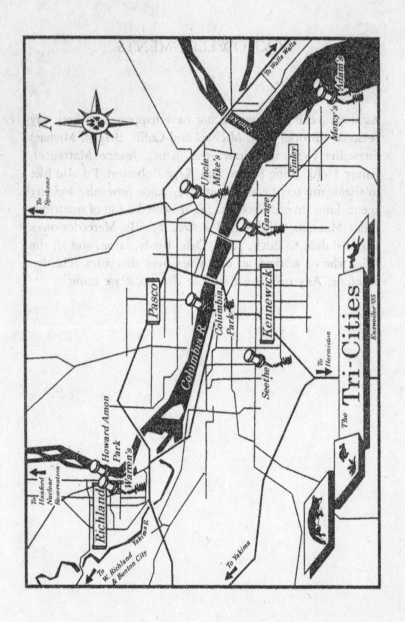

1

I didn't realize he was a werewolf at first. My nose isn't at
its best when surrounded by axle grease and burnt oil – and
it's not like there are a lot of stray werewolves running around.
So when someone made a polite noise near my feet to get
my attention I thought he was a customer.

I was burrowed under the engine compartment of a Jetta,
settling a rebuilt transmission into its new home. One of
the drawbacks in running a one-woman garage was that I
had to stop and start every time the phone rang or a customer
stopped by. It made me grumpy – which isn't a good way
to deal with customers. My faithful office boy and tool rustler
had gone off to college, and I hadn't replaced him yet –
it's hard to find someone who will do all the jobs I don't
want to.

'Be with you in a sec,' I said, trying not to sound snap-
pish. I do my best not to scare off my customers if I can
help it.

Transmission jacks be damned, the only way to get a
transmission into an old Jetta is with muscle. Sometimes
being a female is useful in my line of work – my hands are
smaller so I can get them places a man can't. However, even
weightlifting and karate can't make me as strong as a strong
man. Usually leverage can compensate, but sometimes there's
no substitute for muscle, and I had just barely enough to
get the job done.

Grunting with effort, I held the transmission where it
belonged with my knees and one hand. With the other I
slipped the first bolt in and tightened it. I wasn't finished,

but the transmission would stay where it was while I dealt with my customer.

I took a deep breath and smiled once brightly for practice before I rolled out from under the car. I snagged a rag to wipe the oil off my hands, and said, 'Can I help you?' before I got a good enough look at the boy to see he wasn't a customer – though he certainly looked as though *someone* ought to help him.

The knees of his jeans were ripped out and stained with old blood and dirt. Over a dirty tee, he wore a too-small flannel shirt – inadequate clothing for November in eastern Washington.

He looked gaunt, as though he'd been a while without food. My nose told me, even over the smell of gasoline, oil, and antifreeze permeating the garage, that it had been an equally long time since he'd seen a shower. And, under the dirt, sweat, and old fear, was the distinctive scent of werewolf.

'I was wondering if you had some work I could do?' he asked hesitantly. 'Not a real job, ma'am. Just a few hours' work.'

I could smell his anxiety before it was drowned out by a rush of adrenaline when I didn't immediately refuse. His words sped up until they crashed into one another. 'A job would be okay, too, but I don't have a social security card, so it would have to be cash under the table.'

Most of the people who come around looking for cash work are illegals trying to tide themselves over between harvest and planting season. This boy was white-bread American – except the part about being a werewolf – with chestnut hair and brown eyes. He was tall enough to be eighteen, I supposed, but my instincts, which are pretty good, pinned his age closer to fifteen. His shoulders were wide but bony, and his hands were a little large, as if he still

2

had some growing to do before he grew into the man he would be.

'I'm strong,' he said. 'I don't know a lot about fixing cars, but I used to help my uncle keep his Bug running.'

I believed he was strong: werewolves are. As soon as I had picked up the distinctive musk-and-mint scent, I'd had a nervous urge to drive him out of my territory. However, not being a werewolf, I control my instincts – I'm not controlled by them. Then, too, the boy, shivering slightly in the damp November weather, roused other, stronger instincts.

It is my own private policy not to break the law. I drive the speed limit, keep my cars insured, pay a little more tax to the feds than I have to. I've given away a twenty or two to people who'd asked, but never hired someone who couldn't appear on my payroll. There was also the problem of his being a werewolf, and a new one at that, if I was any judge. The young ones have less control of their wolves than others.

He hadn't commented on how odd it was to see a woman mechanic. Sure, he'd probably been watching me for a while, long enough to get used to the idea – but, still, he hadn't said anything, and that won him points. But not enough points for what I was about to do.

He rubbed his hands together and blew on them to warm up his fingers, which were red with chill.

'All right,' I said, slowly. It was not the wisest answer, but, watching his slow shivers, it was the only one I could give. 'We'll see how it works.

'There's a laundry room and a shower back through that door.' I pointed to the door at the back of the shop. 'My last assistant left some of his old work coveralls. You'll find them hanging on the hooks in the laundry room. If you want to shower and put those on, you can run the clothes you're wearing through the washer. There's a fridge in the laundry room with a ham sandwich and some pop. Eat, then come back out when you're ready.'

I put a little force behind the 'eat': I wasn't going to work with a hungry werewolf, not even almost two weeks from full moon. Some people will tell you werewolves can only shapechange under a full moon, but people also say there's no such things as ghosts. He heard the command and stiffened, raising his eyes to meet mine.

After a moment he mumbled a thank-you and walked through the door, shutting it gently behind him. I let out the breath I'd been holding. I knew better than to give orders to a werewolf – it's that whole dominance reflex thing.

Werewolves' instincts are inconvenient – that's why they don't tend to live long. Those same instincts are the reason their wild brothers lost to civilization while the coyotes were thriving, even in urban areas like Los Angeles.

The coyotes are *my* brothers. Oh, I'm not a werecoyote – if there even is such a thing. I am a walker.

The term is derived from 'skinwalker,' a witch of the Southwest Indian tribes who uses a skin to turn into a coyote or some other animal and goes around causing disease and death. The white settlers incorrectly used the term for all the native shapechangers and the name stuck. We are hardly in a position to object – even if we came out in public like the lesser of the fae did, there aren't enough of us to be worth a fuss.

I didn't think the boy had known what I was, or he'd never have been able to turn his back on me, another predator, and go through the door to shower and change. Wolves may have a very good sense of smell, but the garage was full of odd odors, and I doubted he'd ever smelled someone like me in his life.

'You just hire a replacement for Tad?'

I turned and watched Tony come in from outside through

the open bay doors, where he'd evidently been lurking and watching the byplay between the boy and me. Tony was good at that – it was his job.

His black hair was slicked back and tied into a short ponytail and he was clean-shaven. His right ear, I noticed, was pierced four times and held three small hoops and a diamond stud. He'd added two since last time I'd seen him. In a hooded sweatshirt unzipped to display a thin tee that showed the results of all the hours he spent in a gym, he looked like a recruitment poster for one of the local Hispanic gangs.

'We're negotiating,' I said. 'Just temporary so far. Are you working?'

'Nope. They gave me the day off for good behavior.' He was still focused on my new employee, though, because he said, 'I've seen him around the past few days. He seems okay – runaway maybe.' Okay meant no drugs or violence, the last was reassuring.

When I started working at the garage about nine years ago, Tony had been running a little pawnshop around the corner. Since it had the nearest soft drink machine, I saw him fairly often. After a while the pawnshop passed on to different hands. I didn't think much of it until I smelled him standing on a street corner with a sign that said WILL WORK FOR FOOD.

I say smelled him, because the hollow-eyed kid holding the sign didn't look much like the low-key, cheerful, middle-aged man who had run the pawnshop. Startled, I'd greeted him by the name I'd known him by. The kid just looked at me like I was crazy, but the next morning Tony was waiting at my shop. That's when he told me what he did for a living – I hadn't even known a place the size of the Tri-Cities would have undercover cops.

He'd started dropping by the shop every once in a while,

after that. At first he'd come in a new guise each time. The Tri-Cities aren't that big, and my garage is on the edge of an area that's about as close as Kennewick comes to having a high-crime district. So it was possible he just came by when he was assigned to the area, but I soon decided the real reason was he was bothered I'd recognized him. I could hardly tell him I'd just smelled him, could I?

His mother was Italian and his father Venezuelan, and the genetic mix had given him features and skin tone that allowed him to pass as anything from Mexican to African-American. He could still pass for eighteen when he needed to, though he must be several years older than me – thirty-three or so. He spoke Spanish fluently and could use a half dozen different accents to flavor his English.

All of those attributes had led him to undercover work, but what really made him good was his body language. He could stride with the hip-swaggering walk common to hand-some young Hispanic males, or shuffle around with the nervous energy of a drug addict.

After a while, he accepted I could see through disguises that fooled his boss and, he claimed, his own mother, but by then we were friends. He continued to drop in for a cup of coffee or hot chocolate and a friendly chat when he was around.

'You look very young and macho,' I said. 'Are the earrings a new look for KPD? Pasco police have two earrings, so Kennewick cops must have four?'

He grinned at me, and it made him look both older and more innocent. 'I've been working in Seattle for the past few months,' he said. 'I've got a new tattoo, too. Fortunately for me it is somewhere my mother will never see it.'

Tony claimed to live in terror of his mother. I'd never met her myself, but he smelled of happiness not fear when he talked of her, so I knew she couldn't be the harridan he described.

'What brings you to darken my door?' I asked.

'I came to see if you'd look at a car for a friend of mine,' he said.

'Vee-Dub?'

'Buick.'

My eyebrows climbed in surprise. 'I'll take a look, but I'm not set up for American cars – I don't have the computers. He should take it somewhere they know Buicks.'

'*She's* taken it to three different mechanics – replaced the oxygen sensor, spark plugs, and who knows what else. It's still not right. The last guy told her she needed a new engine, which he could do for twice what the car's worth. She doesn't have much money, but she needs the car.'

'I won't charge her for looking, and if I can't fix it, I'll tell her so.' I had a sudden thought, brought on by the edge of anger I heard in his voice when he talked about her problems. 'Is this *your* lady?'

'She's not my lady,' he protested unconvincingly.

For the past three years he'd had his eye on one of the police dispatchers, a widow with a slew of kids. He'd never done anything about it because he loved his job – and his job, he'd said wistfully, was not conducive to dating, marriage, and kids.

'Tell her to bring it by. If she can leave it for a day or two, I'll see if Zee will come by and take a look at it.' Zee, my former boss, had retired when he sold me the place, but he'd come out once in a while to 'keep his hand in.' He knew more about cars and what made them run than a team of Detroit engineers.

'Thanks, Mercy. You're aces.' He checked his watch. 'I've got to go.'

I waved him off, then went back to the transmission. The car cooperated, as they seldom do, so it didn't take me long. By the time my new help emerged clean and garbed in an

7

old pair of Tad's coveralls, I was starting to put the rest of the car back together. Even the coveralls wouldn't be warm enough outside, but in the shop, with my big space heater going, he should be all right.

He was quick and efficient – he'd obviously spent a few hours under the hood of a car. He didn't stand around watching, but handed me parts before I asked, playing the part of a tool monkey as though it was an accustomed role. Either he was naturally reticent or had learned how to keep his mouth shut because we worked together for a couple of hours mostly in silence. We finished the first car and started on another one before I decided to coax him into talking to me.

'I'm Mercedes,' I said, loosening an alternator bolt. 'What do you want me to call you?'

His eyes lit for a minute. 'Mercedes the Volkswagen mechanic?' His face closed down quickly, and he mumbled, 'Sorry. Bet you've heard that a lot.'

I grinned at him and handed him the bolt I'd taken out and started on the next. 'Yep. But I work on Mercedes, too – anything German-made. Porsche, Audi, BMW, and even the odd Opel or two. Mostly old stuff, out of dealer warranty, though I have the computers for most of the newer ones when they come in.'

I turned my head away from him so I could get a better look at the stubborn second bolt. 'You can call me Mercedes or Mercy, whichever you like. What do you want me to call you?'

I don't like forcing people into a corner where they have to lie to you. If he was a runaway, he probably wouldn't give me a real name, but I needed something better to call him than 'boy' or 'hey, you' if I was going to work with him.

'Call me Mac,' he said after a pause.

The pause was a dead giveaway that it wasn't the name he usually went by. It would do for now.

'Well then, Mac,' I said. 'Would you give the Jetta's owner a call and tell him his car is ready?' I nodded toward the first car we had finished. 'There's an invoice on the printer. His number is on the invoice along with the final cost of the transmission swap. When I get this belt replaced I'll take you to lunch – part of the wages.'

'Okay,' he said, sounding a little lost. He started for the door to the showers but I stopped him. The laundry and shower were in the back of the shop, but the office was on the side of the garage, next to a parking lot customers used.

'The office is straight through the gray door,' I told him. 'There's a cloth next to the phone you can use to hold the receiver so it doesn't get covered with grease.'

I drove home that night and fretted about Mac. I'd paid him for his work in cash and told him he was welcome back. He'd given me a faint smile, tucked the money in a back pocket, and left. I had let him go, knowing that he had nowhere to stay the night because I had no other good options.

I'd have asked him home, but that would have been dangerous for both of us. As little as he seemed to use his nose, eventually he'd figure out what I was – and were-wolves, even in human form, do have the strength they're credited with in the old movies. I'm in good shape, and I have a purple belt from the dojo just over the railroad track from my garage, but I'm no match for a werewolf. The boy was too young to have the kind of control he'd need to keep from killing someone his beast would see as a competing predator in his territory.

And then there was my neighbor.

I live in Finley, a rural area about ten minutes from my garage, which is in the older industrial area of Kennewick.

PATRICIA BRIGGS

My home is a single-wide trailer almost as old as I am that sits in the middle of a couple of fenced acres. There are a lot of small-acreage properties in Finley with trailers or manufactured homes, but along the river there are also mansions like the one my neighbor lives in.

I turned into my drive with a crunch of gravel and stopped the old diesel Rabbit in front of my home. I noticed the cat carrier sitting on my porch as soon as I got out of the car.

Medea gave me a plaintive yowl, but I picked up the note taped to the top of the carrier and read it before I let her out.

MS THOMPSON, it said in heavy block letters, *PLEASE KEEP YOUR FELINE OFF MY PROPERTY. IF I SEE IT AGAIN, I WILL EAT IT.*

The note was unsigned.

I undid the latch and lifted the cat up and rubbed my face in her rabbitlike fur.

'Did the mean old werewolf stick the poor kitty in the box and leave her?' I asked.

She smelled like my neighbor, which told me that Adam had spent some time with her on his lap before he'd brought her over here. Most cats don't like werewolves – or walkers like me either. Medea likes everyone, poor old cat, even my grumpy neighbor. Which is why she often ended up in the cat carrier on my porch.

Adam Hauptman, who shared my back fence line, was the Alpha of the local werewolf pack. That there was a werewolf pack in the Tri-Cities was something of an anomaly because packs usually settle in bigger places where they can hide better, or, rarely, in smaller places they can take over. But werewolves have a tendency to do well in the military and secret government agencies whose names are all acronyms, and the nuclear power plant complex close by the Hanford site had a lot of alphabet agencies involved in it, one way or another.

10

Why the Alpha werewolf had chosen to buy land right next to me, I suspect, had as much to do with the werewolf's urge to dominate those they see as lesser beings as it did with the superb riverfront view.

He didn't like having my old single-wide bringing down the value of his sprawling adobe edifice – though, as I sometimes pointed out to him, my trailer was already here when he bought his property and built on it. He also took every opportunity to remind me I was only here on his sufferance: a walker being no real match for a werewolf.

In response to these complaints, I bowed my head, spoke respectfully to his face – usually – and pulled the dilapidated old Rabbit I kept for parts out into my back field where it was clearly visible from Adam's bedroom window.

I was almost certain he wouldn't eat my cat, but I'd leave her inside for the next week or so to give the impression I was cowed by his threat. The trick with werewolves is never to confront them straight on.

Medea mewed, purred, and wagged her stub tail when I set her down and filled her food dish. She'd come to me as a stray, and I'd thought for a while that some abusive person had chopped her tail off, but my vet said she was a Manx and born that way. I gave her one last stroke, then went to my fridge to scrounge something for dinner.

'I'd have brought Mac home if I thought Adam would leave him be,' I told her, 'but werewolves don't take to strangers very well. There's all sorts of protocols they insist upon when a new wolf comes into someone else's territory, and something tells me that Mac hasn't petitioned the pack. A werewolf won't freeze to death sleeping outside, however bad the weather. He'll be all right for a little while.'

'Still,' I said, as I got out some leftover spaghetti to nuke, 'if Mac's in trouble, Adam might help him.' It would be better to introduce the subject gently when I knew what the boy's story was.

I ate standing up and rinsed out the dish before curling up on the couch and turning on the TV. Medea yowled and jumped on my lap before the first commercial.

Mac didn't come in the next day. It was a Saturday, and he might not know I worked most every Saturday if there were cars to fix. Maybe he'd moved on.

I hoped Adam or one of his wolves hadn't found him before I'd had a chance to break the news of his presence more gently. The rules that allowed werewolves to live undetected among humankind for centuries tended to have fatal consequences for those who broke them.

I worked until noon, then called to tell the nice young couple that their car was a lost cause. Replacing the engine in it would cost them more than the car was worth. Bad news calls were my least favorite job. When Tad, my old assistant, had been around, I'd made him do them. I hung up almost as depressed as the hapless owners of the shiny, decked-out, well-loved car now destined for a boneyard.

I scrubbed up and got as much of the gunk out from under my nails as was going to come and started in on the never-ending paperwork that had also fallen to Tad. I was glad he'd gotten the scholarship that allowed him to head to the Ivy League college of his choice, but I really missed him. After ten minutes, I decided there was nothing that couldn't be put off until Monday. Hopefully by then I'd have an urgent repair, and I'd be able to put off the paperwork until Tuesday.

I changed into clean jeans and a T-shirt, grabbed my jacket, and headed to O'Leary's for lunch. After lunch I did some desultory grocery shopping and bought a small turkey to share with Medea.

My mother called on the cell as I was getting into the car and tried to guilt me into driving up to Portland for Thanksgiving or Christmas. I weaseled my way out of both invitations – I'd had enough of family gatherings in the two years I'd lived with her to last a lifetime.

It's not that they are bad, just the opposite. Curt, my stepfather, is a soft-spoken, no-nonsense sort of person – just the man to balance my mother. I later found out he hadn't known about me until I showed up on his doorstep when I was sixteen. Even so, he opened his house to me without question and treated me as if I were his own.

My mother, Margi, is vivacious and cheerfully flaky. It's not difficult at all envisioning her getting involved with a rodeo rider (like my father) any more than it would be difficult imagining her running off to join the circus. That she is president of her local PTA is far more surprising.

I like my mother and stepfather. I even like all of my half siblings, who had greeted my sudden appearance in their lives with enthusiasm. They all live together in one of those close-knit families that television likes to pretend is normal. I'm very happy to know people like that exist – I just don't belong there.

I visit twice a year so they don't invade my home, and I make certain that it isn't a holiday. Most of my visits are very short. I love them, but I love them better at a distance.

By the time I hung up, I felt guilty and blue. I drove home, put the turkey in the fridge to thaw, and fed the cat. When cleaning the fridge didn't help my mood, though I'm not sure why I expected it to, I got back in the car and drove out to the Hanford Reach.

I don't go out to the Reach often. There are closer places to run, or, if I feel like driving, the Blue Mountains aren't too far away. But sometimes my soul craves the arid, desolate space of the preserve – especially after I get through talking with my mother.

I parked the car and walked for a while until I was reasonably certain there was no one around. Then I took off my clothes and put them in the small daypack and shifted.

Werewolves can take as much as fifteen minutes to shift shape – and shifting is painful for them, which is something to keep in mind. Werewolves aren't the most friendly animals anyway, but if they've just shifted, it's a good policy to leave them alone for a while.

Walkers' shifting – at least my shifting, because I don't know any other walkers – is quick and painless. One moment I'm a person and the next a coyote: pure magic. I just step from one form into the next.

I rubbed my nose against my foreleg to take away the last tingle of the change. It always takes a moment to adjust to moving on four feet instead of two. I know, because I looked it up, that coyotes have different eyesight than humans, but mine is pretty much the same in either form. My hearing picks up a little and so does my sense of smell, though even in human form I've got better senses than most.

I picked up the backpack, now stuffed with my clothes, and left it under a bunch of scrub. Then I shed the ephemera of my human existence and ran into the desert.

By the time I had chased three rabbits and teased a couple in a boat with a close-up glimpse of my lovely, furred self on the shore of the river, I felt much better. I don't have to change with the moon, but if I go too long on two feet I get restless and moody.

Happily tired, in human shape, and newly clothed, I got into my car and said my usual prayer as I turned the key. This time the diesel engine caught and purred. I never know from day to day if the Rabbit will run. I drive it because it is cheap, not because it is a good car. There's a lot of truth in the adage that all cars named after animals are lemons.

On Sunday I went to church. My church is so small that it shares its pastor with three other churches. It is one of those nondenominational churches so busy not condemning anyone that it has little power to attract a steady congregation. There are relatively few regulars, and we leave each other mostly alone. Being in a unique position to understand what the world would be like without God and his churches to keep the worst of the evil at bay, I am a faithful attendee.

It's not because of the werewolves. Werewolves can be dangerous if you get in their way; but they'll leave you alone if you are careful. They are no more evil than a grizzly bear or great white shark.

There are other things, though, things that hide in the dark, that are much, much worse – and vampires are only the tip of the iceberg. They are very good at hiding their natures from the human population, but I'm not human. I know them when I meet them, and they know me, too; so I go to church every week.

That Sunday, our pastor was sick and the man who replaced him chose to give a sermon based upon the scripture in Exodus 22: 'Thou shall not suffer a witch to live.' He extended the meaning to encompass the fae, and from him rose a miasma of fear and rage I could sense from my seat. It was people like him who kept the rest of the preternatural community in hiding almost two decades after the lesser fae were forced into the public view.

About thirty years ago, the Gray Lords, the powerful mages who rule the fae, began to be concerned about advances in science – particularly forensic science. They foresaw that the Time of Hiding was coming to an end. They decided to do damage control, and see to it that the human's realization of the world's magic was as gentle as possible. They awaited the proper opportunity.

When Harlan Kincaid, the elderly billionaire real estate magnate, was found dead near his roses with a pair of garden shears in his neck, suspicion fell upon his gardener Kieran McBride, a quiet-spoken, pleasant-faced man who had worked for Kincaid, a prize-winning gardener himself, for a number of years.

I saw bits of the trial, as most Americans did. The sensational murder of one of the country's wealthiest men, who happened to be married to a beloved, young actress, ensured the highest ratings for the networks.

For several weeks the murder occupied the news channels. The world got to see Carin Kincaid, with tears flowing down her California-tanned cheeks, as she described her reaction to finding her dead husband lying next to his favorite rosebush — which had been hacked to pieces. Her testimony was Oscar-quality, but she was upstaged by what happened next.

Kieran McBride was defended by an expensive team of lawyers who had, amid much publicity, agreed to work pro bono. They called Kieran McBride to the stand and skillfully baited the prosecuting attorney into asking McBride to hold the garden shears in his hand.

He tried. But after only an instant his hands began to smoke before dropping them. At his attorney's request he showed the blistered palms to the jury. He couldn't have been the murderer, the lawyer told the judge, jury, and the rest of the world, because Kieran McBride was fae, a garden sprite, and he couldn't hold cold iron, not even through thick leather gloves.

In a dramatic moment, McBride dropped his glamour, the spell that kept him appearing human. He wasn't beautiful, just the opposite, but anyone who has seen a Shar-pei puppy knows there is great charisma in a certain sort of ugliness. One of the reasons McBride had been chosen by the Gray Lords was because garden sprites are gentle folk and easy to look at. His sorrowful, overly large brown eyes made the covers of magazines for weeks opposite less-than-flattering pictures of Kincaid's wife, who was later convicted of her husband's death.

And so the lesser fae, the weak and attractive, revealed themselves at the command of the Gray Lords. The great and terrible, the powerful or powerfully ugly, stayed hidden, awaiting the reaction of the world to the more palatable among them. Here, said the Gray Lord's spin doctors who had been McBride's lawyers, here are a hidden people: the gentle brownie who taught kindergarten because she loved children; the young man, a selkie, who risked his life to save the victims of a boating accident.

At first it looked as though the Gray Lords' strategy would pay off for all of us preternaturals, fae or not. There were New York and L.A. restaurants where the rich and famous could be waited on by wood sprites or muryans. Hollywood moguls remade *Peter Pan* using a boy who could actually fly and a real pixie for Tinkerbell – the resulting film made box office records.

But even at the beginning there was trouble. A well-known televangelist seized upon fear of the fae to increase his grip over his flock and their bank accounts. Conservative legislators began making noise about a registration policy. The government agencies began quietly making lists of fae they thought they could use – or who might be used against them, because throughout Europe and parts of Asia, the lesser fae were forced out of hiding by the Gray Lords.

When the Gray Lords told Zee, my old boss, that he had to come out five or six years ago, Zee sold the garage to me and retired for a few months first. He'd seen what happened to some of the fae who tried to continue their lives as if nothing had happened.

It was all right for a fae to be an entertainer or a tourist attraction, but the brownie kindergarten teacher was quietly pensioned off. No one wanted a fae for a teacher, a mechanic, or a neighbor.

Fae who lived in upscale suburbs had windows broken and rude graffiti painted on their homes. Those who lived in less law-abiding places were mugged and beaten. They couldn't defend themselves for fear of the Gray Lords. Whatever the humans did to them, the Gray Lords would do worse.

The wave of violence prompted the creation of four large reservations for fae. Zee told me that there were fae in the government who saw the reservations as damage control and used fair means and foul to convince the rest of Congress.

If a fae agreed to live on a reservation, he was given a small house and a monthly stipend. Their children (like Zee's son Tad) were given scholarships to good universities where they might become useful members of society . . . if they could find jobs.

The reservations sparked a lot of controversy on both sides. Personally, I thought the Gray Lords and the government might have paid more attention to the innumerable problems of the Native American reservations – but Zee was convinced the reservations were only a first step in the Gray Lords' plans. I knew just enough about them to admit he might be right – but I worried anyway. Whatever ills it created, the reservation system had lessened the growing problems between the human and fae, at least in the US.

People like the visiting pastor, though, were proof that prejudice and hatred were alive and well. Someone behind me muttered that he hoped Pastor Julio recovered before next week, and a round of mumbled agreement cheered me a little.

I've heard of people who've seen angels or felt their presence. I don't know if it is God or one of his angels I sense, but there is a welcoming presence in most churches. As the pastor continued with his fear-driven speech, I could feel that spirit's growing sadness.

The pastor shook my hand as I left the building.

I am not fae, broad though that term is. My magic comes from North America not Europe, and I have no glamour (or need of it) to allow me to blend with the human population. Even so, this man would have hated me had he known what I was.

I smiled at him, thanked him for the service, and wished him well. Love thy enemies, it says in the scriptures. My foster mother always added, 'At the very least, you will be polite to them.'

2

Mac the werewolf was sitting on the step by the office door when I drove up Monday morning.

I kept my face impassive and showed none of the surprisingly fierce satisfaction I felt, just handed him a heavy sack of fast-food breakfast sandwiches so I could get my key out and open the door. I'd been raised around wild animals; I knew how to tame them. A hearty welcome would send him off faster than harsh words if I judged him aright, but food was always a good lure.

'Eat,' I told him as I set out for the bathroom to change into work clothes. 'Save me one – the rest are for you.'

All but one were gone when I came back.

'Thank you,' he told me, watching my feet.

'You'll work it off. Come on, help me get the garage doors up.' I led the way through the office and into the garage. 'There's nothing pending today so we can work on my project Bug.'

The Beetle was unprepossessing at the moment, but when I was finished it would be painted, polished, and purring like a kitten. Then I'd sell it for twice what I had put into it and find another car to resurrect. I made almost half my income refurbishing old VW classics.

We'd worked a few hours in companionable silence when he asked to use the phone to make a long-distance call.

'Long as it's not to China,' I said, coaxing a bolt held in place by thirty-odd years of rust.

I didn't sneak over to the office door to listen in. I don't make a practice of eavesdropping on private conversations. I don't have to. I have very good hearing.

'Hello,' he said. 'It's me.'

My hearing was not so good, however, that I could hear the person he was talking to.

'I'm fine. I'm fine,' he said quickly. 'Look I can't talk long.' Pause. 'It's better you don't know.' Pause. 'I know. I saw a news report. I don't remember anything after we left the dance. I don't know what killed her or why it didn't kill me.'

Ah, no, I thought.

'No. Look, it's better just now if you don't know where I am.' Pause. 'I told you, I don't know what happened. Just that I didn't kill her.' Pause. 'I don't know. I just want you to tell Mom and Dad I'm okay. I love them – and I'm looking for the ones who killed her. I have to go now.' Pause. 'I love you, too, Joe.'

There were a dozen stories that could account for the half of his conversation that I heard. Two dozen.

But the most prevalent of the cautionary tales werewolves tell each other is what happens the first time a werewolf changes if he doesn't know what he is.

In my head, I translated Mac's half of the conversation into a picture of a boy leaving a high school dance to make out with his girlfriend under the full moon, not knowing what he was. New werewolves, unless they have the guidance of a strong dominant, have little control of their wolf form the first few times they change.

If Mac were a new werewolf, it would explain why he didn't notice that I was different from the humans around. You have to be taught how to use your senses.

Here in the US, most werewolves are brought over by friends or family. There is a support structure to educate the new wolf, to keep him and everyone around him safe – but there are still the occasional attacks by rogue werewolves. One of the duties of a pack is to kill those rogues and find their victims.

Despite the stories, any person bitten by a werewolf doesn't turn into another werewolf. It takes an attack so vicious that the victim lies near death to allow the magic of the wolf to slip past the body's immune system. Such attacks make the newspapers with headlines like 'Man Attacked by Rabid Dogs.' Usually the victim dies of the wounds or of the Change. If he survives, then he recovers quickly, miraculously – until the next full moon, when he learns that he didn't really survive at all. Not as he had been. Usually a pack will find him before his first change and ease his way into a new way of life. The packs watch the news and read the newspapers to prevent a new wolf from being alone – and to protect their secrets.

Maybe no one had found Mac. Maybe he'd killed his date and when he'd returned to human shape he'd refused to believe what he'd done. What he was. I'd been operating under the impression that he had left his pack, but if he was a new wolf, an untaught wolf, he was even more dangerous.

I broke the rusted-out bolt because I wasn't paying attention. When Mac returned from his phone call, I was working on removing the remnant with an easy out, the world's most misnamed tool – there is nothing easy about it.

I hadn't planned on saying anything to him, but the words came out anyway. 'I might know some people who could help you.'

'No one can help me,' he replied tiredly. Then he smiled, which would have been more convincing if his eyes hadn't been so sad. 'I'm all right.'

I set down the easy out and looked at him.

'Yes, I think you will be,' I said, hoping I wasn't making a mistake by not pushing. I'd have to let Adam know about him before the next full moon. 'Just remember, I've been known to believe as many as six impossible things before breakfast.'

His mouth quirked up. 'Lewis Carroll.'

'And they say the youth today aren't being educated,' I said. 'If you trust me, you might find that my friends can help you more than you believed possible.' The phone rang, and I turned back to my work. 'Go answer the phone, please, Mac,' I told him.

That late in the year it was dark out when we finished at six. He stood and watched me as I locked up, obviously thinking about something. I deliberately fumbled with the lock to give him more time, but he didn't take advantage of it.

'See you tomorrow,' he said, instead.

'All right.' Then, impulsively, I asked, 'Do you have a place to sleep tonight?'

'Sure,' he said with a smile, and started off as if he had somewhere to be.

I could have bitten off my tongue because I pushed him into a lie. Once he started lying to me, it would be harder to get him to trust me with the truth. I don't know why it works that way, but it does – at least in my experience.

I kicked myself all the way home, but by the time I had fed Medea and made myself some dinner, I'd figured out a way around it. I'd take him a blanket tomorrow and unlock Stefan's VW bus, which was patiently awaiting brake parts from Oregon. I didn't think Stefan would mind Mac camping out for a night or two.

I called Stefan to make sure, because it's unwise to surprise vampires.

'Sure,' he said, without even asking who I wanted to let sleep in his van. 'That's all right with me, sweetheart. How long until my bus is roadworthy again?'

For a vampire, Stefan was all right.

'Parts are supposed to be in day after tomorrow,' I told him. 'I'll call you when they get here. If you want to help, we can get it done in a couple long evenings. Otherwise, it'll take me a day.'

'Right,' he said, which was apparently good-bye because the next thing I heard was a dial tone.

'Well,' I told the cat, 'I guess I'm headed out to buy a blanket.' It had to be a new blanket: mine would all smell like coyote – and a werewolf who hardly knew me wouldn't be comfortable surrounded by my scent.

I spent several minutes looking for my purse before I realized that I'd left it locked in the safe at work. Happily, my garage was on the way to the store.

Because it was dark, I parked my car on the street behind the garage where there was a streetlight to discourage any enterprising vandals. I walked through the parking lot and passed Stefan's bus, parked next to the office door, and gave it an affectionate pat.

Stefan's bus was painted to match the Mystery Machine, which said a lot about the vampire it belonged to. Stefan told me that he'd briefly considered painting it black a few years ago when he started watching Buffy, but, in the end, he'd decided the vampire slayer was no match for Scooby Doo.

I opened the office door, but didn't bother turning on the lights because I see pretty well in the dark. My purse was where I remembered leaving it. I took it out and relocked the safe. Out of habit, I double-checked the heat to make sure it was set low. Everything had been turned off and put away. All was as it should have been, and I felt the usual sense of satisfaction knowing it was mine – well, mine and the bank's.

I was smiling when I left the office and turned to lock the door behind me. I wasn't moving quietly on purpose, but having been raised by a pack of werewolves makes you learn to be quieter than most.

'Go away.' Mac's voice came from the other side of Stefan's bus. He spoke in a low, growling tone I hadn't heard from him before.

I thought he was talking to me and spun toward the sound, but all I saw was Stefan's bus.

Then someone else answered Mac. 'Not without you.'

The bus had darkened windows. I could see through them well enough to see the side door was open, framing the vague shadowy forms of Mac and one of his visitors. The second one I couldn't see. The wind was right, blowing gently past them to me, and I smelled *two* other people besides Mac: another werewolf and a human. I didn't recognize either one.

Although I know most of Adam's wolves by scent, it wouldn't be odd if he had gotten a new wolf without my hearing about it. But it was the human that told me something was up: I'd never known Adam to send a human out with one of his wolves on business.

Stranger yet was that no one showed any sign they knew I was around. I was quiet, but even so, both werewolves should have heard me. But neither Mac nor the other wolf appeared to notice.

'No,' said Mac, while I hesitated. 'No more cages. No more drugs. They weren't helping.'

Cages? I thought. *Someone had been keeping Mac in a cage?* There was no need for that, not with Adam around. Though some Alphas had to depend upon bars to control new wolves, Adam wasn't one of them. Nor did Mac's comments about drugs make sense: there are no drugs that work on werewolves.

'They were, kid. You just need to give them a chance. I promise you we can undo your curse.'

Undo his curse? There was no drug in the world that would undo the Change, and darn few werewolves who considered their state a curse after the first few months. Eventually most of them felt that becoming short-tempered and occasionally furry was a small price to pay for extraordinary strength, speed, and senses – not to mention the fringe benefit of a body immune to disease and old age.

Even if the werewolf belonged to Adam, I doubted he knew that one of his pack was telling wild stories. At least I *hoped* he didn't know.

Mac seemed to know these two, though, and I was beginning to feel that his story was more complicated than I had thought.

'You talk like you have a choice,' the third man was saying. 'But the only choice you have is how you get there.'

These weren't Adam's men, I decided. The mention of curses, cages, and drugs made them the enemy. If Mac didn't want to go with them, I wouldn't let them take him.

I took a quick glance around, but the streets were empty. After six the warehouse district is pretty dead. I stripped out of my clothes as quietly as I could and shifted into coyote form.

As a human I didn't stand a chance against a werewolf. The coyote was still not a match – but I was fast, much faster than a real coyote and just a hair quicker than a werewolf.

I jumped onto the railing and vaulted from there to the top of Stefan's bus for the advantage of the higher position, though I was giving up surprise. No matter how quietly I moved, a werewolf would hear the click of my nails on the metal roof.

I readied myself for launch, but paused. From atop the bus I could see Mac and the two men. None of them seemed to be aware of me. Mac had his back to me, but all the others would have had to do was look up. They didn't. Something wasn't right.

Behind the two strangers was a big black SUV, the kind of car you'd expect bad guys to drive.

'I don't believe there is any way to undo what you did to me,' Mac was saying. 'You can't give me back my life or give Meg back hers. All you can do is leave me alone.'

The human's hair was in a crew cut, but it was the big black gun I could see peeking out of his shoulder holster that first made me think military. Both of the strangers stood like military men – Adam had the posture, too. Their shoulders were just a little stiff, their backs a little too straight. Maybe they did belong to Adam. The thought made me hesitate. If I hurt one of Adam's wolves, there would be hell to pay.

'The moon's coming,' said the longer-haired man, the werewolf. 'Can't you feel it?'

'How're you planning on surviving the winter, kid?' It was Short-hair again. His voice was kindly. Fatherly. Patronizing even. 'It gets cold 'round December, even in this desert.'

I stifled a growl as I tried to determine the best way to help Mac.

'I'm working here,' Mac said, with a gesture at the garage. 'If it gets colder, I think she'll let me sleep in the garage until I find somewhere to live if I ask her.'

'Ask her?' Short-hair looked sympathetic. 'She kept you here for us. She's one of us, kid. How else do you think we found you?'

Mac smelled of shock first, then defeat. Emotions have a smell, but only in my coyote form is my nose good enough to distinguish more than the strongest feelings. My lips curled back over my teeth – I don't like liars, especially when they are lying about me.

The werewolf's voice was dreamy. 'When the moon comes, you can't stop the change.' He swayed back and forth. 'Then

27

you can run and drink the fear of your prey before they die beneath your fangs.'

Moonstruck, I thought, shocked out of my anger. If this wolf was so new that he was moonstruck, he certainly wasn't Adam's, and whoever had sent him out was an idiot.

'I'm not coming,' said Mac, taking a step away from them. He took another step back – putting his back against the bus. He stiffened, drew in a deep breath, and looked around. 'Mercy?'

But neither of the men paid attention when Mac caught my scent. The werewolf was still held in his moon dreams, and the human was drawing his gun.

'We tried to do this the easy way,' he said, and I could smell his pleasure. He might have tried the easy way first, but he liked the hard way better. His gun was the kind you find in military catalogues for wanna-be mercenaries, where what it looks like is at least as important as how well it performs. 'Get in the car, kid. I'm packing silver bullets. If I shoot you, you'll be dead.' He sounded like a thug from a fifties gangster movie; I wondered if it was deliberate.

'If I get in the car, I'll be dead anyway, won't I?' Mac said slowly. 'Did you kill the other two who were in the cages by me? Is that why they disappeared?'

None of them had noticed that the werewolf was starting to change, not even the werewolf himself. I could see his eyes gleaming brightly in the darkness and smell the musk of wolf and magic. He growled.

'Quiet,' snapped the human, then he looked. He paused, swallowed, and turned his gun, ever so slightly, toward his erstwhile partner.

As a human, the werewolf probably weighed in at about two hundred pounds. Werewolves, fully changed, weigh upward of two hundred and fifty pounds. No, I don't know where the extra weight comes from. It's magic, not science.

I'm a little large for the average coyote – but that meant that the werewolf was still five times my weight.

I'd been trying to figure out a way to turn my speed to advantage, but when the werewolf, his elongating jaws stretching around sharp, white fangs, focused on Mac and growled again, I knew I'd just run out of time.

I threw myself off the top of the car and onto the werewolf, who was still slowed by his ongoing change. I snapped at him to get his attention and caught his throat, still barren of the thick ruff designed to protect him from such an attack.

I felt my eyeteeth snag flesh, and blood spurted, pushed by his heart and the increased blood pressure that accompanies the change. It wasn't a mortal wound – werewolves heal too fast – but it should slow him down, giving me a head start while he bound the wound.

Only he didn't stop.

He was hot on my heels as I dashed past Stefan's bus, across the alley that allowed access to my garage bays, and leapt over the chain-link fence surrounding the Sav U More Self-Storage facility. If he'd been in full wolf form, he'd have cleared the fence easier than I did, but he was hampered by his awkward shape and had to stop and tear through the fence instead.

Spurred by hunting-rage, he was faster than I was, even on two legs. He shouldn't have been. I've outrun my share of werewolves, and I knew I was faster than they were; but no one had told him that. He was catching up to me. I jumped back over the fence because it had slowed him down the first time.

If there had been homes nearby, the impatient, frustrated whines the werewolf made as it was forced to stop and rip the chain-link fence again would have had the police on their way, but the nearest residences were blocks away. The thought reminded me that I needed to worry about innocent bystanders as well as Mac and myself.

I reversed my direction, running down the road back toward the garage, intent on leading the werewolf away from town rather than into it. But before I reached the garage, my pursuer tripped and fell to the street.

I thought at first that the change had taken him completely, but no werewolf rose on all fours to continue the chase. I slowed, then stopped where I was and listened, but all I could hear was my heart pounding with fear.

He was almost finished with the change, his face entirely wolf though his fur had not yet begun to cover him. His hands, lying limply on the blacktop, were distorted, too thin, with an inhuman distance between his fingers and his thumb. His nails were thickened and had begun to come to a point at the tips. But he wasn't moving.

Shaking with the need to run, I forced myself to approach him. I waited for him to jump up and grab me the way they always do in the late-night movies, but he just lay there, smelling of blood and adrenaline.

A trail of liquid stretched out behind him as if he were a car that had blown a radiator hose and slung antifreeze all over the road – but the liquid that glistened under the street-lamp was blood.

Only then did it occur to me that I did not hear the thrum of his heart or the whisper of his breath.

I heard a car start up and took my eyes off the werewolf in time to see the black SUV squeal out of the parking lot and turn toward me. The big car wobbled as the driver fought his speed and his turn. His headlights blinded me momentarily – but I'd already seen my escape route and took it blind.

He slowed a minute, as if he considered stopping by the body on the street, but then the V-8 roared, and the SUV picked up speed.

He narrowly avoided hitting the lamppost I'd dodged behind. I couldn't tell if Mac was in the car or not. I watched the SUV's taillights until it turned onto the highway and blended in with the traffic there.

I walked to the werewolf just to be certain – but he was well and truly dead.

I'd never killed anyone before. He shouldn't have been dead. Werewolves are hard to kill. If he had bothered to stanch the wound, or if he hadn't chased me, the wound would have healed before he could bleed out.

The taste of his blood in my mouth made me ill, and I vomited beside the body until the taste of bile overwhelmed anything else. Then I left him lying in the middle of the road and ran back to the garage. I needed to check on Mac before I took on the task of dealing with the dead werewolf.

To my relief, Mac was leaning on Stefan's van when I loped into the parking lot. He held a gun loosely in his hand, the barrel bent.

'Mercy?' he asked me, when I approached, as if he expected me to talk.

I ducked my head once, then darted around the front of the garage where I'd left my clothes. He followed me. But when I shifted back, and he saw that I was naked, he turned his back to let me dress.

I pulled on my clothing quickly – it was cold out. 'I'm decent,' I told him, and he faced me again.

'You have blood on your chin,' he said, in a small voice.

I wiped it off with the bottom of my T-shirt. I wasn't going shopping tonight, so it didn't matter if I got blood on my clothes. *Don't throw up again*, I told myself sternly. *Pretend it was a rabbit*. It hadn't tasted like rabbit.

'What are you?' he asked. 'Are you one of theirs? Where is . . . is the wolf?'

'He's dead. We need to talk,' I told him, then paused as

I collected my scattered thoughts. 'But first we need to get the dead werewolf out of the street. And before that, I guess we should call Adam.'

I led him back to the office – this time turning on the light. Not that either of us needed it for anything other than comfort.

He put his hand on top of mine when I reached for the phone. 'Who is Adam, and why are you calling him?' he asked.

I didn't fight his hold. 'The local Alpha. We need to get the body out of the road – unless you want both of us disappeared into some federal laboratory for science to pick over for a few years before they decide they can learn more from us dead than alive.'

'Alpha?' he asked. 'What's that?'

He *was* new.

'Werewolves live in packs,' I told him. 'Each pack has an Alpha – a wolf strong enough to keep the others under control. Adam Hauptman is the local Alpha.'

'What does he look like?' he asked.

'Five-ten, a hundred and eighty pounds. Dark hair, dark eyes. I don't think he has anything to do with your wolves,' I said. 'If Adam wanted you, he'd have you – and he'd have found you a lot sooner. He can be a jerk, but competence is his forte.'

Mac stared at me, his brown eyes looking yellowish in the fluorescent lighting of my office. Truth to tell, I was surprised he was still in human form because watching one wolf change tends to encourage others. I met his gaze calmly, then dropped my eyes until I was looking at his shoulder instead.

'All right,' he said, slowly removing his hand. 'You saved me tonight – and that thing could have torn you apart. I've seen them kill.'

I didn't ask when or whom. It was important to take action in the right order to avoid worse trouble. Call Adam. Remove body from the middle of the street where anyone could see it. Then talk. I punched Adam's number from memory.

'Hauptman,' he answered, with just a touch of impatience, on the fourth ring.

'I killed a werewolf at my garage,' I said, then hung up. To Mac's raised eyebrows I said, 'That will get a faster reaction than spending twenty minutes explaining. Come on, you and I need to get the body off the street before someone spots it.' When the phone rang, my answering machine picked it up.

I took Stefan's bus because loading something large into a bus is just easier than loading it into my little Rabbit. The bus smelled of Mac, and I realized he'd not lied to me when he said he had a place to spend the night. He'd been sleeping in it for a couple of nights at least.

The bus was without brakes until we fixed it, but I managed to get it to drift to a stop next to the body. Mac helped me get it in the bus, then dashed back to the garage while I drove. When I arrived, he had the garage open for me.

We set the dead man on the cement floor next to the lift, then I parked the bus back where it had been and pulled down the garage bay door, leaving us inside with the body.

I walked to the corner farthest from the dead werewolf and sat down on the floor next to one of my big tool chests. Mac sat down next to me, and we both stared across the garage at the corpse.

Half-changed, the body looked even more grotesque under the harsh lighting of the second bay than it had under the streetlight, like something out of a black-and-white Lon

Chaney movie. From where I sat I could see the slice in his neck that had killed him.

'He was used to healing fast,' I said, to break the silence. 'So he didn't pay attention to his wound. But some wounds take longer to heal than others. He didn't know any more than you do. How long have you been a werewolf?'

'Two months,' Mac said, leaning his head back against the tool chest and looking at the ceiling. 'It killed my girlfriend, but I survived. Sort of.'

He was lucky, I thought, remembering the suppositions I'd had while overhearing his phone call earlier. He hadn't killed his girlfriend after all. He probably wasn't feeling lucky though, and I wasn't going to tell him that it could be worse.

'Tell me about your life afterward. Where did those men come from? Are you from the Tri-Cities?' I hadn't heard of any suspicious deaths or disappearances in the last six months.

He shook his head. 'I'm from Naperville.' At my blank look, he clarified. 'Illinois. Near Chicago.' He glanced at the body, closed his eyes, and swallowed. 'I want to eat him,' he whispered.

'Perfectly natural,' I told him, though I have to admit I wanted to move away from him. Heaven save me, stuck with a new werewolf in a garage with fresh meat was not anyone's idea of safe. But we had to wait here until Adam came. It could have been worse: it could have been nearer the full moon, or he could have been as hungry as he'd been that first day.

'Deer not only tastes better, it's easier to live with afterward,' I said, then reflected that it might be better to talk about something other than food. 'What happened to you after that first attack? Did someone take you to a hospital?'

He looked at me a moment, but I couldn't tell what he was thinking. He said, 'After . . . after the attack, I woke up in a cage in someone's basement. There was someone in the room and when I opened my eyes, he said, "Good, you'll live. Leo will be happy to see it."'

'Wait,' I said. 'Leo. Leo. Chicago.' Then it came to me. 'Leo James? Looks as though he ought to be a Nordic skiing champion? Tall, long, and blond.'

Leo was one of the Chicago Alphas – there were two of them. Leo held territory in the western suburbs. I'd met him once or twice. Neither of us had been impressed, but then, as I said, most werewolves don't take kindly to other predators.

Mac nodded. 'That sounds right. He came down the stairs with the first guy and another man. None of them would talk to me or answer any of my questions.' He swallowed and gave me an anxious glance. 'This shit just sounds so weird, you know? Unbelievable.'

'You're talking to someone who can turn into a coyote,' I told him gently. 'Just tell me what you think happened.'

'All right.' He nodded slowly. 'All right. I was still weak and confused, but it sounded like Leo was arguing money with the third guy. It sounded to me like he sold me for twelve thousand dollars.'

'Leo sold you for twelve thousand dollars,' I said, as much to myself as to Mac. My voice might have been matter-of-fact, but only because Mac was right: it *was* unbelievable. Not that I thought he was lying. 'He had one of his wolves attack you and your girlfriend and when you survived, he sold you to someone else as a newly turned werewolf.'

'I think so,' said Mac.

'You called your family this afternoon?' I asked. I smiled at his wary look. 'I have pretty good hearing.'

'My brother. His cell phone.' He swallowed. 'It's broken. No caller ID. I had to let them know I was alive. I guess the police think I killed Meg.'

'You told him that you were after her killer,' I said.

He gave an unhappy laugh. 'Like I could find him.'

He could. It was all a matter of learning to use his new senses, but I wasn't going to tell him that, not yet. If Mac did find his attacker, chances were Mac would die. A new werewolf just doesn't stand a chance against the older ones.

I patted his knee. 'Don't worry. As soon as we get word to the right people – and Adam is the right people – Leo's a walking dead man. The Marrok won't allow an Alpha who is creating progeny and selling them for money.'

'The Marrok?'

'Sorry,' I said. 'Like I told you, except for the occasional rogue, werewolves are organized into packs under an Alpha wolf.'

It used to be that was as organized as werewolves got. But the only thing it takes to be Alpha is power, not intelligence or even common sense. In the Middle Ages, after the Black Plague, the werewolf population was almost wiped out along with real wolves because some of the Alphas were indiscreet. It was decided then that there would be a leader over all the werewolves.

'In the US, all the packs follow the Marrok, a title taken from the name of one of King Arthur's knights who was a werewolf. The Marrok and his pack have oversight of all the werewolves in North America.'

'There are more of us?' he asked.

I nodded. 'Maybe as many as two thousand in the US, five or six hundred in Canada, and about four hundred in Mexico.'

'How do you know so much about werewolves?'

'I was raised by them.' I waited for him to ask me why, but his attention had drifted toward the body. He inhaled deeply and gave an eager shudder.

'Do you know what they wanted with you?' I asked hurriedly.

'They told me they were looking for a cure. Kept putting things in my food – I could smell them, but I was hungry so I ate anyway. Sometimes they'd give me shots – and once when I wouldn't cooperate they used a dart gun.'

'Outside, when you were talking to them, you said they had others like you?'

He nodded. 'They kept me in a cage in a semitrailer. There were four cages in it. At first there were three of us, a girl around my age and a man. The girl was pretty much out of it – she just stared and rocked back and forth. The man couldn't speak any English. It sounded like Polish to me – but it could have been Russian or something. One of the times I was taking a trip on something they pumped in me, I woke up and I was alone.'

'Drugs don't work on werewolves,' I told him. 'Your metabolism is too high.'

'These did,' he said.

I nodded. 'I believe you. But they shouldn't have. You escaped?'

'I managed to change while they were trying to give me something else. I don't remember much about it other than running.'

'Was the trailer here in the Tri-Cities?' I asked.

He nodded. 'I couldn't find it again, though. I don't remember everything that happens when . . .' His voice trailed off.

'When you're the wolf.' Memory came with experience and control, or so I'd been told.

A strange car approached the garage with the quiet purr common to expensive engines.

'What's wrong?' he asked, when I stood up.

'Don't you hear the car?'

37

He started to shake his head, but then paused. 'I – yes. Yes, I do.'

'There are advantages to being a werewolf,' I said. 'One of them is being able to hear and smell better than the average Joe.' I stood up. 'It's turning into the parking lot. I'm going to look out and see who it is.'

'Maybe it's the guy you called. The Alpha.'

I shook my head. 'It's not his car.'

3

I slipped through the office and opened the outside door cautiously, but the smell of perfume and herbs hanging in the night air told me we were still all right.

A dark Cadillac was stretched across the pavement just beyond Stefan's bus. I pushed the door all the way open as the uniformed chauffeur tipped his hat to me, then opened the car's back door, revealing an elderly woman.

I stuck my head back in the office, and called, 'It's all right, Mac. Just the cleanup crew.'

Keeping the humans ignorant of the magic that lives among them is a specialized and lucrative business, and Adam's pack kept the best witch in the Pacific Northwest on retainer. Rumors of Elizaveta Arkadyevna Vyshnevetskaya's origins and how she came to be in the Tri-Cities changed on a weekly basis. I think she and her brood of grandchildren and great-grandchildren encouraged the more outrageous versions. All that I knew for certain was that she had been born in Moscow, Russia, and had lived in the Tri-Cities for at least twenty years.

Elizaveta rose from the depths of the big car with all the drama of a prima ballerina taking her bow. The picture she made was worth all the drama.

She was almost six feet tall and little more than skin and bones, with a long, elegant nose and gray, penetrating eyes. Her style of dress was somewhere between babushka and Baba Yaga. Layers of rich fabrics and textures came down to her calves, all covered with a long wool cape and a worn scarf that wrapped around her head and neck. Her outfit wasn't authentic, at least not to any period or place that I've heard of, but I've never seen anyone brave enough to tell her so.

'Elizaveta Arkadyevna, welcome,' I said, walking past the bus to stand by her car.

She scowled at me. 'My Adamya calls and tells me you have one of his wolves dead.' Her voice had the crispness of a British aristocrat, so I knew she was angry – her usual accent was thick enough I had to make a real effort to understand her. When she was really angry, she didn't speak English at all.

'Werewolf, yes,' I agreed. 'But I don't think it is one of Adam's.' Adamya, I had learned, was an affectionate form of Adam. I don't think she'd ever called him that to his face. Elizaveta was seldom affectionate to anyone likely to overhear her.

'I have the body in my shop,' I told her. 'But there is blood all over here. The werewolf chased me with a torn artery and bled from here over to the storage facility, where he tore up the fence in two places before he bled to death out on the street. The storage facility has cameras, and I used Stefan's bus' – I pointed to it – 'to move the body.'

She said something in Russian to her chauffeur, who I recognized as one of her grandchildren. He bowed and said something back before going around to open the trunk.

'Go,' she told me, and flung her arms in a pushing gesture. 'I will take care of the mess out here without your help. You wait with the body. Adam will be here soon. Once he has seen, he will tell me what he would have me do with it. You killed this wolf? With a silver bullet so I should look for casing?'

'With my fangs,' I told her; she knew what I was. 'It was sort of an accident – at least his death was.'

She caught my arm when I turned to go into the office.

'What were you thinking, Mercedes Thompson? A Little Wolf who attacks the great ones will be dead soon, I think. Luck runs out eventually.'

'He would have killed a boy under my protection,' I told her. 'I had no choice.'

She released me and snorted her disapproval, but when she spoke her Russian accent was firmly in place. 'There is always choice, Mercy. Always choice. If he attacked a boy, then I suppose it must not have been one of Adamya's.'

She looked at her chauffeur and barked out something more. Effectively dismissed, I went back to Mac and our dead werewolf.

I found Mac crouched near the body, licking his fingers as if he might have touched the drying blood and was cleaning them off. Not a good sign. Somehow, I was pretty certain that if Mac were fully in control, he wouldn't be doing that.

'Mac,' I said, strolling past him and over to the far side of the garage, where we'd been sitting.

He growled at me.

'Stop that,' I said sharply, doing my best to keep the fear out of my voice. 'Control yourself and come over here. There are some things you should know before Adam gets here.'

I'd been avoiding a dominance contest, because my instincts told me that Mac was a natural leader, a dominant who might very well eventually become an Alpha in his own right – and I was a woman.

Women's liberation hadn't made much headway in the world of werewolves. A mated female took her pack position from her mate, but unmated females were always lower than males unless the male was unusually submissive. This little fact had caused me no end of grief, growing up, as I did, in the middle of a werewolf pack. But without someone more dominant than he, Mac wouldn't be able to take control of his wolf yet. Adam wasn't there, so it was up to me.

I stared at him in my best imitation of my foster father and raised an eyebrow. 'Mac, for Heaven's sake, leave that poor dead man alone and come over here.'

He came slowly to his feet, menace clinging to him. Then he shook his head and rubbed his face, swaying a little.

'That helped,' he said. 'Can you do it again?'

I tried my best. 'Mac. Get over here right now.'

He staggered a little drunkenly over to me and sat at my feet.

'When Adam comes,' I told him firmly, 'whatever you do, don't look him in the eyes for longer than a second or two. Some of this should be instinct, I hope. It isn't necessary to cower – remember that you've done no wrong at all. Let me talk. What we want is for Adam to take you home with him.'

'I'm fine on my own,' Mac objected, sounding almost like himself, but he kept his head turned toward the body.

'No, you're not,' I said firmly. 'If there wasn't a pack, you might survive. But if you run into one of Adam's wolves without being made known to the pack, they'll probably kill you. Also, the full moon is coming soon. Adam can help you get control of your beast before then.'

'I can control the monster?' asked Mac, stilling.

'Absolutely,' I told him. 'And it's not a monster – any more than a killer whale is a monster. Werewolves are hot-tempered and aggressive, but they aren't evil.' I thought about the one who had sold him and corrected myself. 'At least not any more evil than any other person.'

'I don't even remember what the beast does,' Mac said. 'How can I control it?'

'It's harder the first few times,' I told him. 'A good Alpha can get you through that. Once you have control, then you can go back to your old life if you want. You have to be a little careful; even in human form you're going to have to deal with having a shorter temper and a lot more strength than you're used to. Adam can teach you.'

'I can't ever go back,' he whispered.

'Get control first,' I told him. 'There are people who can help you with the rest. Don't give up.'

'You're not like me.'

'Nope,' I agreed. 'I'm a walker: it's different from what you are. I was born this way.'

'I've never heard of a walker. Is that some sort of fae?'

'Close enough,' I said. 'I don't get a lot of the neat things that you werewolves have. No super strength. No super healing. No pack.'

'No chance you might eat your friends,' he suggested. I couldn't tell if he was trying to be funny, or if he was serious.

'There are some benefits,' I agreed.

'How did you find out so much about werewolves?'

I opened my mouth to give him the short version, but decided the whole story might better serve to distract him from the dead body.

'My mother was a rodeo groupie,' I began, sitting down beside him. 'She liked cowboys, any cowboy. She liked a Blackfoot bull-rider named Joe Old Coyote from Browning, Montana, enough to get pregnant with me. She told me that he claimed to come from a long line of medicine men, but at the time she thought he was just trying to impress her. He died in a car accident three days after she met him.

'She was seventeen, and her parents tried to talk her into an abortion, but she would have none of it. Then they tried to get her to put me up for adoption, but she was determined to raise me herself – until I was three months old, and she found a coyote pup in my crib.'

'What did she do?'

'She tried to find my father's family,' I told him. 'She went to Browning and found several families there with that last name, but they claimed they'd never heard of Joe. He was certainly Native American.' I made a gesture to encompass my appearance. I don't look pureblood; my features are too Anglo. But my skin looks tanned even in November, and my straight hair is as dark as my eyes. 'But otherwise I don't know much about him.'

'Old Coyote,' said Mac speculatively.

I smiled at him. 'Makes you think this shifting thing must have run in the family, doesn't it?'

'So how was it that you were raised by werewolves?'

'My great-grandfather's uncle was a werewolf,' I said. 'It was supposed to be a family secret, but it's hard to keep secrets from my mother. She just smiles at people, and they tell her their life stories. Anyway, she found his phone number and called him.'

'Wow,' said Mac. 'I never met any of my great-grandparents.'

'Me either,' I said, then smiled. 'Just an uncle of theirs who was a werewolf. One of the benefits of being a werewolf is a long life.' If you can control the wolf – but Adam could explain that part better than me.

His gaze was drawn back to our dead friend.

'Yes, well.' I sighed. 'Stupidity will still get you killed. My great-grandfather's uncle was smart enough to outlive his generation, but all those years didn't keep him from getting gutted by a moose he was out hunting one night.'

'Anyway,' I continued, 'he came to visit and knew as soon as he saw me what I was. That was before the fae came out and people were still trying to pretend that science had ruled out the possibility of magic. He convinced my mother that I'd be safer out in the hinterlands of Montana being raised by the Marrok's pack – they have their own town in the mountains where strangers seldom bother them. I was fostered with a family there who didn't have any children.'

'Your mother just gave you up?'

'My mother came out every summer, and they didn't make it easy on her either. Not overfond of humans, the Marrok, excepting their own spouses and children.'

'I thought the Marrok was the wolf who rules North America,' said Mac.

'Packs sometimes take their public name from their leader,' I told him. 'So the Marrok's pack call themselves the Marrok. More often they find some geographical feature in their territory. Adam's wolves are the Columbia Basin Pack. The only other pack in Washington is the Emerald Pack in Seattle.'

Mac had another question, but I held up my hand for him to be quiet. I'd heard Adam's car pull up.

'Remember what I said about the Alpha,' I told Mac and stood up. 'He's a good man and you need him. Just sit there, keep your eyes down, let me talk, and everything will be all right.'

The heavy garage door of bay one groaned, then rang like a giant cymbal as it was forced all the way open faster than it usually moved.

Adam Hauptman stood in the open doorway, stillness cloaking his body and for an instant, I saw him with just my eyes, as a human might. He was worth looking at.

For all his German last name, his face and coloring were Slavic: dusky skin, dark hair – though not as dark as mine – wide cheekbones, and a narrow but sensual mouth. He wasn't tall or bulky, and a human might wonder why all eyes turned to him when he walked into a room. Then they'd see his face and assume, wrongly, that it was the attraction. Adam was an Alpha, and if he'd been ugly he would have held the attention of anyone who happened to be nearby, wolf or human – but the masculine beauty he carried so unself-consciously didn't hurt.

Under more usual circumstances his eyes were a rich

chocolate brown, but they had lightened with his anger until they were almost yellow. I heard Mac gasp when the full effect of Adam's anger hit him, so I was prepared and let the wave of power wash off me like seawater on glass.

Maybe I should have explained matters better when I had him on the phone, but where's the fun in that?

'What happened?' he asked, his voice softer than the first snowfall in winter.

'It's complicated,' I said, holding his gaze for two full seconds before I turned my head and gestured toward the body. 'The dead one is there. If he belongs to you, he is new – and you haven't been doing your job. He was as deaf and blind as a human. I was able to take him by surprise, then he was too ignorant to realize that the wound wouldn't close as fast as usual if it was given by a preternatural creature. He let himself bleed out because he was too caught up in the chase to—'

'Enough, Mercedes,' he growled as he strode over to the dead wolfman and knelt beside him. He moved the body and one of the corpse's arms flopped down limply on the ground.

Mac whined eagerly, then bowed his head and pressed it against my thigh so that he couldn't see.

The sound drew Adam's attention from the body to the boy at my feet.

He growled. 'This one isn't one of mine – and neither is that.'

'So gracious,' I said. 'Your mother should be complimented on your manners, Hauptman.'

'Careful,' he whispered. It wasn't a threat, it was a warning.

Okay. He was scary. Really scary. He'd probably have been scary even when he was just a human. But it wouldn't do to let him know he intimidated me.

'Adam Hauptman,' I said politely to show him how it

was done. 'Allow me to introduce you to Mac – that's all of his name I know. He was attacked by a werewolf in Chicago about two moons ago. The werewolf killed his girlfriend, but he survived. He was taken by his attacker and put in a cage. A man who sounds a lot like the Chicago Alpha Leo sold him to someone who held him inside a cage in a semi-trailer and used him for what sounds like some sort of drug experiments until he broke free. Last Friday he showed up at my door looking for work.'

'You didn't inform me that you had a strange wolf on your doorstep?'

I gave him a put-upon sigh. 'I am not one of your pack members, Adam. I know this is difficult for you to fathom, so I'll speak slowly: I don't belong to you. I am under no obligation to tell you anything.'

Adam swore harshly. 'New werewolves are dangerous, woman. Especially when they are cold and hungry.' He looked at Mac, and his voice changed completely, the heat and anger gone. 'Mercy, come here.'

I didn't look down to see what he'd noticed in Mac's face. I took a step, but Mac was wrapped around my left leg. I stopped before I fell. 'Uhm. I'm a little stuck for the moment.'

'For a smart girl, you're pretty stupid sometimes,' he said, his voice rich and gentle so as not to startle the werewolf by my side. 'Locking yourself in a garage with a new wolf and a dead body isn't the smartest thing you could have done. I don't have a connection with him yet. It would help if you have his real name.'

'Mac,' I murmured. 'What's your name?'

'Alan,' he said dreamily, coming up to his knees so his face was pressed against my belly. 'Alan MacKenzie Frazier after my grandfather who died the year I was born.' The friction of his movement rucked my shirt up and he licked my bare skin. To an outsider it might have looked sensual, but the abdomen is a vulnerable spot on the body, a favorite of predators. 'You smell good,' he whispered.

He smelled like werewolf, and I was starting to panic – which wasn't a very useful thing to do.

'Alan,' said Adam, rolling the name on his tongue. 'Alan MacKenzie Frazier, come here to me.'

Mac jerked his head away from me but tightened his arms painfully on my hips. He looked at Adam and growled, a low rumble that caused his chest to vibrate against my leg.

'Mine,' he said.

Adam's eyes narrowed. 'I don't think so. She is mine.'

It would have been flattering, I thought, except that at least one of them was talking about dinner and I wasn't certain about the other. While Adam had Mac distracted, I reached behind me and grabbed my big crowbar from the shelf directly behind us. I brought it down on Mac's collar-bone.

It was an awkward hit because I didn't have much leverage, but the collarbone, even on a werewolf, is not hard to damage. I heard the bone crack and wrenched myself out of Mac's grip and across the garage before he recovered from the unexpected pain.

I didn't like hurting him, but he would heal in a few hours as long as I didn't let him eat me. I didn't think he was the kind of person who would recover from murder as easily as he would a broken bone.

Adam had moved almost as quickly as I had. He grabbed Mac by the scruff of his neck and jerked him to his feet.

'Adam,' I said, from the relative safety of the far end of the garage. 'He's new and untaught. A victim.' I kept my voice quiet so I didn't add to the excitement.

It helped that Mac wasn't looking particularly dangerous at the moment. He hung limply in Adam's grip. 'Sorry,' he said almost inaudibly. 'Sorry.'

Adam let out an exasperated huff of air and lowered Mac to the ground – on his feet at first, but when Mac's knees proved too limp to hold him up, Adam eased him all the way down.

'Hurts,' said Mac.

'I know.' Adam didn't sound angry anymore – of course, he was talking to Mac and not me. 'If you change, it'll heal faster.'

Mac blinked up at him.

'I don't think he knows how to do it on purpose,' I offered.

Adam slanted a thoughtful look at the body, then back at me. 'You said something about a cage and experiments?'

Mac didn't say anything, so I nodded. 'That's what he told me. Apparently someone has a drug that they are trying to get to work on werewolves.' I told him what Mac had told me, then gave him the details of my own encounter with the dead werewolf and his human comrade. I'd already told Adam most of the salient facts, but I wasn't certain how much information made it through his anger, so I just told him all of it again.

'Damn it,' said Adam succinctly when I'd finished. 'Poor kid.' He turned back to Mac. 'All right. You're going to be fine. The first thing we're going to do is call your wolf out so that you can heal.'

'No,' Mac said, looking wildly at me, then at the dead wolfman. 'I can't control myself when I'm like that. I'll hurt someone.'

'Look at me,' said Adam, and even though the dark, raspy voice hadn't been directed at me, I found myself unable to pull my eyes off him. Mac was riveted.

'It's all right, Alan. I won't allow you to hurt Mercy – much as she deserves it. Nor,' Adam continued, proving that he was observant 'will I allow you to eat the dead.'

When Mac hesitated, I walked back over and knelt beside

Adam so I could look Mac in the eye. 'I told you, he can control your wolf until you can. That's why he's Alpha. You can trust him.'

Mac stared at me, then closed his eyes and nodded. 'All right. But I don't know how.'

'You'll get the hang of it,' Adam said. 'But for right now I'll help you.' His knee nudged me away, as he got out his pocket knife. 'This will be easier without your clothing.'

I got up as unobtrusively as I could and tried not to flinch when Mac cried out.

The change is not easy or painless at the best of times, and it was worse without the aid of the moon's call. I don't know why they can't change like I do, but I had to close my eyes against the pained sounds that came from the corner of my garage. Certainly the broken collarbone didn't make the shift any easier for Mac. Some werewolves can change relatively quickly with practice, but a new werewolf can take a lot of time.

I slipped out of the garage through the office and walked out the door, both to give them some privacy and because I couldn't bear Mac's suffering anymore. I sat on the single cement step outside the office and waited.

Elizaveta returned, leaning on her grandson's arm about the same time that Mac's scream turned into a wolf's cry.

'There is another werewolf?' Elizaveta asked me.

I nodded and got to my feet. 'That boy I told you about,' I said. 'Adam's here, though, so it's safe. Did you clean Stefan's van?' I nodded at the bus.

'Yes, yes. Did you think you were dealing with an amateur?' She gave an offended sniff. 'Your vampire friend will never know that his van held a corpse other than his own.'

'Thank you.' I tilted my head, but I couldn't hear anything from inside the garage, so I opened the office door and called, 'Adam?'

'It's all right,' he said, sounding tired. 'It's safe.'

'Elizaveta is here with her chauffeur,' I warned him in case he hadn't noticed them when he'd stormed in.

'Have her come in, too.'

I would have held open the door, but Elizaveta's grandson took it out of my hand and held it for both of us. Elizaveta shifted her bony grasp from his arm to mine, though from the strength of her grip I was pretty certain that she didn't need help walking.

Mac was curled up in the far corner of the garage where I'd left him. His wolf form was dark gray, blending in with the shadows on the cement floor. He had one white foot and a white stripe down his nose. Werewolves usually have markings that are more doglike than wolflike. I don't know why. Bran, the Marrok, has a splash of white on his tail, as though he'd dipped it in a bucket of paint. I think it's cute — but I'd never had the nerve to tell him so.

Adam was kneeling beside the dead man, paying no attention to Mac at all. He looked up when we came in from the office. 'Elizaveta Arkadyevna,' he said in a formal greeting, then added something in Russian. Switching back to English, he continued, 'Robert, thank you for coming tonight, too.'

Elizaveta said something in Russian directed at Adam.

'Not quite yet,' Adam replied. 'Can you reverse his change?' He gestured to the dead man. 'I don't recognize his scent, but I'd like to get a good look at his face.'

Elizaveta frowned and spoke rapidly in Russian to her grandson. His response had her nodding, and they chatted for a few moments more before she turned back to Adam. 'That might be possible. I can certainly try.'

'I don't suppose you have a camera here, Mercy?' Adam asked.

'I do,' I told him. I work on old cars. Sometimes I work on cars that other people have 'restored' in new and interesting

51

fashions. I've found that getting a picture of the cars before I work on them is useful in putting them back together again. 'I'll get it.'

'And bring a piece of paper and an ink stamp pad if you have it. I'll send his fingerprints off to a friend for identification.'

By the time I returned, the corpse was back in human form, and the hole I'd torn in his neck gaped open like a popped balloon. His skin was blue with blood loss. I'd seen dead men before, but none that I was responsible for killing.

The change had torn his clothing – and not in the interesting way that comic books and fantasy artists always depict it. The crotch of his pants was ripped open along with his blood-soaked shirt's neck and shoulder seams. It seemed terribly undignified.

Adam took the digital camera from me and snapped a few pictures from different angles, then tucked it back in its case and slung it over his shoulder.

'I'll get it back to you as soon as I get these pictures off it,' he promised absently as he took the paper and ink stamp and, rather expertly, rolled the limp fingers in the ink, then on the sheet of paper.

Things moved rapidly after that. Adam helped Elizaveta's grandson deposit the body in the luxurious depths of the trunk of her car for disposal. Elizaveta did her mumbles and shakes that washed my garage in magic and, hopefully, left it clean of any evidence that I'd ever had a dead man inside. She took Mac's clothing, too.

'Hush,' said Adam, when Mac growled an objection. 'They were little more than rags anyway. I've clothes that should fit you at my house, and we'll pick up more tomorrow.'

Mac gave him a look.

'You're coming home with me,' said Adam, in a tone that brooked no argument. 'I'll not have a new werewolf running loose around my city. You come and learn a thing or two, then I'll let you stay or go as you choose – but not until I'm satisfied you can control yourself.'

'I am going now; it is not good for an old woman like me to be up this late,' Elizaveta said. She looked at me sourly. 'Don't do anything stupid for a while if you can help it, Mercedes. I do not want to come back out here.'

She sounded as if she came out to clean up my messes on a regular basis, though this was the first time. I was tired, and the sick feeling that killing a man had left in my stomach was still trying to bring up what little was left of my dinner. Her sharpness raised the hackles I was too on edge to pull down, so my response wasn't as diplomatic as it ought to have been.

'I wouldn't want that, either,' I said smoothly.

She caught the implied insult, but I kept my eyes wide and limpid so she wouldn't know whether I meant it or not. Insulting witches is right up there on the stupid list with enraging Alpha werewolves and cuddling with a new wolf next to a dead body: all of which I'd done tonight. I couldn't help it, though. Defiance was a habit I'd developed to preserve myself while growing up with a pack of dominant and largely male werewolves. Werewolves, like other predators, respect bravado. If you are too careful not to anger them, they'll see it as a weakness – and weak things are prey.

Tomorrow I was going to repair old cars and keep my head down for a while. I'd used up all my luck tonight.

Adam seemed to agree because he took Elizaveta's hand and tucked it into the crook of his elbow, drawing her attention back to him as he escorted her back to her car. Her grandson Robert gave me a lazy grin.

'Don't push the babushka too hard, Mercy,' he said softly. 'She likes you, but that won't stop her if she feels you aren't showing her proper respect.'

'I know,' I said. 'I'm going home to see if a few hours of sleep won't curb my tongue before it gets us into trouble.' I meant to sound humorous, but it just came out tired.

Robert gave me a sympathetic smile before he left.

A heavy weight leaned against my hip and I looked down to see Mac. He gave me what I imagined was a sympathetic look. Adam was still with Elizaveta, but Mac didn't seem to be having trouble. I scratched him lightly behind one pricked ear.

'Come on,' I told him. 'Let's lock up.'

This time I remembered to grab my purse.

4

Home at last, I decided that there was only one remedy for a night like this. My stash of dark chocolate was gone, and I'd eaten the last gingersnap, so I turned on the oven and pulled out the mixing bowl. By the time someone knocked at my door, I was pouring chocolate chips into the cookie dough.

On my doorstep was a sprite of a girl with Day-Glo orange hair that sprang from her head in riotous curls, wearing enough eye makeup to supply a professional cheerleading squad for a month. In one hand she held my camera.

'Hey, Mercy. Dad sent me over to give you this and to get me out of the way while he dealt with some pack business.' She rolled her eyes as she handed me the camera. 'He acts like I don't know enough to stay out of the way of strange werewolves.'

'Hey, Jesse,' I said and waved her inside.

'Besides,' she continued as she came in and toed off her shoes, 'this wolf was cute. With a little stripe here—' She ran her finger down her nose. 'He wasn't going to hurt me. I was just rubbing his belly and my father came in and had a *cow* – oh yum, cookie dough! Can I have some?'

Jesse was Adam's daughter, fifteen going on forty. She spent most of the year with her mother in Eugene – she must be in town to spend Thanksgiving with Adam. It seemed a little early to me for that, since Thanksgiving wasn't until Thursday, but she went to some private school for brilliant and eccentric kids, so maybe her vacations were longer than the public schools'.

'Did you dye your hair especially for your father?' I asked, finding a spoon and handing it to her with a healthy glob of dough.

'Of course,' she said, taking a bite, then continuing to talk as if her mouth weren't half-full. 'It makes him feel all fatherly if he can complain about something. Besides,' she said with an air of righteousness, 'everyone in Eugene is doing it. It'll wash out in a week or two. When I was tired of the lecture, I just told him he was lucky I didn't use superglue to put spikes in like my friend Jared. Maybe I'll do that next vacation. This is good stuff.' She started to put her spoon in the dough for another round, and I slapped her hand.

'Not after it's been in your mouth,' I told her. I gave her another spoon, finished mixing in the chips, and began dropping cookie dough on the pans.

'Oh, I almost forgot,' she said, after another bite, 'my father sent the camera with a message. It was needlessly cryptic, but I knew you'd tell me what it meant. Are you ready?'

I put the first pan in the oven and started loading the next one. 'Shoot.'

'He said, "Got a hit. Don't fret. He was a hired gun."' She waved her empty spoon at me. 'Now explain it to me.'

I suppose I should have respected Adam's need to protect his daughter, but he was the one who sent her to me. 'I killed a man tonight. Your father found out who he was.'

'Really? And he was a hit man? Cool.' She dropped the spoon in the sink next to the first one, then boosted herself up to sit on my counter and conducted a rapid question and answer session all by herself. 'Was that what you called him about earlier? He was fit to be tied. How come you called Dad? No wait. The man you killed was a werewolf, too, wasn't he? That's why Dad took off so fast. Who is the wolf he came back with?' She paused. '*You* killed a werewolf? Did you have a gun?'

Several. But I hadn't brought one with me to the garage.

She had paused, so I answered her last two questions. 'Yep and nope.'

'Awesome.' She grinned. 'Hey, how'dja do it?'

'It wasn't on purpose,' I told her repressively. I might as well have tried holding back a tidal wave with my bare hands, it would have had as much effect.

'Of course not,' she said. 'Not unless you were really pi—' I raised an eyebrow and she changed the word without slowing down. '—ticked off. Did you have a knife? Or was it a crowbar?'

'My teeth,' I told her.

'Ewwe—' She grimaced briefly. 'Nasty. Oh, I see. You mean that you took him on while you were a coyote?'

Most humans only know about the fae – and there are still a lot of people who think that the fae are just a hoax perpetrated by the government or on the government, take your pick. Jesse, however, as the daughter of a werewolf, human though she was, was quite aware of the 'Wild Things' as she called them. Part of that was my fault. The first time I met her, shortly after the Alpha had moved his family next to my home, she'd asked me if I were a werewolf like her father. I told her what I was, and she nagged me until I showed her what it looked like when I took my other form. I think she was nine and already a practiced steamroller.

'Yep. I was just trying to get his attention so he'd chase me and leave Mac – that's the striped werewolf—' I imitated her finger-down-the-nose gesture. 'He is pretty nice,' I told her. Then, feeling I had to play adult in fairness to her father, I said, 'But he's a newbie, and his control isn't terrific yet. So listen to your father about him, okay? If Mac bit you or hurt you, it would make him feel awful, and he's had a bad enough time of it already.' I hesitated. It really wasn't my business, but I liked Jesse. 'There are a few of your father's wolves that you really do need to stay away from.'

She nodded, but said confidently, 'They won't hurt me, not with *my* father. But you mean Ben, don't you? Dad told me to stay out of his way. I met him yesterday when he stopped by.' She wrinkled her nose. 'He's a snark — even if he has that cool British accent.'

I wasn't certain what a snark was, but I was certain Ben qualified.

We ate the cookies as they came out of the oven, and I gave her a loaded plate covered with tinfoil to take back with her. I went out to the porch with her and saw a sales-lot of cars parked at Adam's house. He must have called in the pack.

'I'll walk you home,' I said, slipping on the shoes I kept on the porch for when it was muddy.

She rolled her eyes, but waited for me. 'Really, Mercy, what'll you do if one of the pack decides to bother us?'

'I can scream really loud,' I said. 'That's if I don't decide to use my newly patented technique and kill him, too.'

'That's right,' she said. 'But I'd stick to screaming. I don't think that Dad would like it if you started killing his wolves.'

Probably none of them would harm a hair of her head, just as she thought. I was almost sure she was right. But one of the cars I could see was Ben's red truck. I wouldn't leave a fifteen-year-old alone if Ben was around no matter whose daughter she was.

No one bothered us as we walked through my back field.

'Nice car,' she murmured, as we passed the donor Rabbit's corpse. 'Dad really appreciates you setting it out here for him. Good for you. I told him the next time he annoyed you, you were likely to paint graffiti on it.'

'Your father is a subtle man,' I told her. 'I'm saving the

graffiti for later. I've decided that the next time he gets obnoxious, I'll take three tires off.' I held my hand out and canted it, like a car with one wheel.

She giggled. 'It would drive him nuts. You should see him when the pictures aren't hanging straight on the walls.' We reached the back fence, and she climbed cautiously through the old barbed wire. 'If you do decide to paint it – let me help?'

'Absolutely,' I promised. 'I'll wait here until you're safely inside.'

She rolled her eyes again, but grinned and sprinted for her back porch. I waited until she waved to me once from Adam's back door and disappeared inside.

When I took the garbage out before I went to bed, I noticed that Adam's place was still full of cars. It was a long meeting, then. Made me grateful I wasn't a werewolf.

I turned to go into my house and stopped. I'd been stupid. It doesn't matter how good your senses are if you aren't paying attention.

'Hello, Ben,' I said, to the man standing between me and the house.

'You've been telling tales, Mercedes Thompson,' he said pleasantly. As Jesse had said, he had a nifty English accent. He wasn't bad-looking either, if a trifle effeminate for my taste.

'Mmm?' I said.

He tossed his keys up in the air and caught them one-handed, once, twice, three times without taking his eyes off mine. If I yelled, Adam would hear, but, as I told him earlier, I didn't belong to him. He was possessive enough, thank you. I didn't really believe Ben was stupid enough to do something to me, not with Adam within shouting distance.

'"Stay here a moment, Ben,"' Ben said, with an exaggeration of the drawl that Adam's voice still held from a childhood spent in the deep South. '"Wait until my daughter has had a chance to get to her room. Wouldn't want to expose her to the likes of you."' The last sentence lost Adam's tone and fell back into his own crisp British accent. He didn't sound quite like Prince Charles, but closer to that than to Fagin in *Oliver*.

'I don't know what you think it has to do with me,' I told him with a shrug. 'You're the one who got kicked out of the London pack. If Adam hadn't taken you, you'd have been in real trouble.'

'It wasn't me that done it,' he growled ungrammatically. I refrained from correcting him with an effort. 'And as for what you have to do with it, Adam told me you'd warned him to keep Jesse out of my way.'

I didn't remember doing that although I might have. I shrugged. Ben had come to town a few months ago in a flurry of gossip. There had been three particularly brutal rapes in his London neighborhood, and the police had been looking in his direction. Guilty or not, his Alpha felt it would be good to get him out of the limelight and shipped him to Adam.

The police hadn't anything to hold him on, but after he'd emigrated the rapes stopped. I checked – the Internet is an amazing thing. I remembered speaking to Adam about it, and I warned him to watch Ben around vulnerable women. I'd been thinking about Jesse, but I didn't think I'd said that explicitly.

'You don't like women,' I told him. 'You are rude and abrasive. What do you expect him to do?'

'Go home, Ben,' said a molasses-deep voice from just behind my right shoulder. I needed to get more sleep, darn it, if I was letting everyone sneak up on me.

'Darryl,' I said, glancing back at Adam's second.

Darryl was a big man, well over six feet. His mother had been Chinese, Jesse had told me, and his father an African tribesman who had been getting an engineering degree at an American university when they met. Darryl's features were an arresting blend of the two cultures. He looked like someone who should have been modeling or starring in movies, but he was a Ph.D. engineer working at the Pacific Northwest Laboratories in some sort of government hush-hush project.

I didn't know him well, but he had that eminently respectable air that college professors sometimes have. I much preferred him at my back to Ben, but I wasn't happy being between two werewolves, whoever they were. I stepped sideways until I could see them both.

'Mercy.' He nodded at me but kept his eyes on Ben. 'Adam noticed you were missing and sent me to find you.' When Ben didn't respond, he said, 'Don't screw up. This is not the time.'

Ben pursed his lips thoughtfully, then smiled, an expression that made a remarkable difference to his face. Only for an instant, he looked boyishly charming. 'No fuss. Just telling a pretty lady good night. Good night, sweet Mercedes. Dream of me.'

I opened my mouth to make a smart comment, but Darryl caught my eye and made a cutoff gesture with his hand. If I'd had a really good comeback, I'd have said it anyway, but I didn't, so I kept my mouth shut.

Darryl waited until Ben started off, before saying brusquely, 'Good night, Mercy. Lock your doors.' Then he strode off toward Adam's.

Between the dead wolf and Ben's wish, I suppose I should have had nightmares, but instead I slept deeply and without dreams – none I remembered anyway.

I slept with the radio on, because otherwise, with my

hearing, all I did was catnap all night. I'd tried earplugs, but that blocked sound a little too well for my peace of mind. So I turned music on low to block the normal sounds of night and figured anything louder would wake me up.

Something woke me up that morning about an hour before the alarm, but though I turned down the music and listened, all I heard was a car with a well-muffled Chevy 350 driving away.

I rolled over to go back to sleep, but Medea realized I was awake and began yowling at me to let her out. She wasn't particularly loud, but very persistent. I decided it had been long enough since Adam's note that letting her run wouldn't make him feel like I was deliberately defying him. It would also buy me some quiet so I could catch that last hour of sleep.

Reluctantly, I got out of my warm bed and pulled on jeans and a T-shirt. Happy to have me up and moving, Medea stropped my shins and generally got in the way as I staggered blearily out of my room, across the living room to the front door. I yawned and turned the doorknob, but when I tried to open the door, it resisted. Something was holding it shut.

With an exasperated sigh, I put my shoulder against the door and it moved a reluctant inch or so, far enough for me to catch a whiff of what lay on the other side: death.

Wide-awake, I shut the door and locked it. I'd smelled something else, too, but I didn't want to admit it. I ran back to my room, shoved my feet in my shoes, and opened the gun safe. I grabbed the SIG 9mm and shoved a silver-loaded magazine in it, then tucked the gun into the top of my pants. It was cold, uncomfortable, and reassuring. But not reassuring enough.

I'd never actually shot anything but targets. If I hunted, I did it on four paws. My foster father, a werewolf himself, had insisted I learn how to shoot and how to make the bullets.

If this was werewolf business, and, after the previous night, I had to assume it was – I needed a bigger gun. I took down the .444 Marlin and loaded it for werewolf. It was a short rifle, and small unless you took a good look at the size of the barrel. The lipstick-sized silver bullets were guaranteed, as my foster father used to say, to make even a werewolf sit up and take notice. Then he'd put a finger alongside his nose, smile, and say, 'Or lie down and take notice, if you know what I mean.' The Marlin had been his gun.

The rifle was a comfortable, fortifying presence when I quietly opened my back door and stepped out into the predawn night. The air was still and cold: I took a deep breath and smelled death, undeniable and final.

As soon as I rounded the corner of the trailer I could see the body on my front porch, blocking my front door. He was on his face, but my nose told me who it was – just as it had when I first opened the door. Whoever had dumped him had been very quiet, wakening me only as they drove off. There was no one else there now, just Mac and me.

I climbed the four steps up to my porch and crouched in front of the boy. My breath fogged the air, but there was no mist rising from his face, no heartbeat.

I rolled him onto his back and his body was still warm to my touch. It had melted the frost off the porch where he had lain. He smelled of Adam's home; a fragrant mix of woodsmoke and the pungent air freshener favored by Adam's housekeeper. I couldn't smell anything that would tell me who had killed Mac and left him as a warning.

I sat on the frost-coated wood of the porch, set the rifle beside me, and touched his hair gently. I hadn't known him long enough for him to have a hold on my heart, but I had liked what I'd seen.

The squealing of tires pealing out had me back on my feet with rifle in hand as a dark-colored SUV shot away from Adam's house like the fires of hell were behind it. In the dim predawn light, I couldn't tell what color it was: black or dark blue or even green. It might even have been the same vehicle that the villains had driven last night at the shop – newer cars of a similar make all look alike to me.

I don't know why it had taken me so long to realize that Mac dead on my front porch meant that something bad had happened at Adam's house. I abandoned the dead in hopes of being of use to the living, tearing across my back field at a sprinter's pace, the rifle tucked under my arm.

Adam's house was lit up like a Christmas tree. Unless he had company, it was usually dark. Werewolves, like walkers, do very well in the dark.

When I came to the fence between our properties, I held the rifle away from my body and vaulted the barbed wire with a hand on top of the post. I'd been carrying the Marlin at quarter cock, but as soon as I landed on the other side of the fence, I pulled the hammer back.

I would have gone through the back door if there had not been a tremendous crash from the front. I shifted my goal and made it around the side of the house in time to see the couch land half-in and half-out of the flower bed that lined the porch, evidently thrown through the living room window and the porch rails.

The werewolf I'd killed last night notwithstanding, were-wolves are taught to be quiet when they fight – it's a matter of survival. Only with the broken window and the front door hanging wide open, did I hear the snarls.

I whispered the swear words I usually only bring out for rusty bolts and aftermarket parts that don't fit as advertised to give me courage as I ran. *Dear Lord*, I thought, in a sincere prayer, as I ran up the porch stairs, *please don't let anything permanent have happened to Adam or Jesse.*

I hesitated just inside the door, my heart in my mouth and the Marlin at the ready. I was panting, from nerves as much as exertion, and the noise interfered with my hearing.

Most of the destruction seemed to be concentrated in the high-ceilinged living room just off the entryway. The white Berber carpet would never be the same. One of the dining room chairs had been reduced to splinters against the wall, but the wall had suffered, too: broken plaster littered the floor.

Most of the glass from the shattered window was spread outside on the porch; the glass on the carpet was from a mirror that had been jerked off the wall and slammed over someone's head.

The werewolf was still there, a sizable chunk of mirror embedded in her spine. It wasn't a werewolf I knew: not one of Adam's because there were only three females in Adam's pack, and I knew all of them. She was near enough to truly dead that she wasn't going to be a problem for a while, so I ignored her.

I found a second werewolf under the fainting couch. (I liked to tease Adam about his fainting couch – How many women do you expect to faint in your living room, Adam?) He'd have to buy a new one. The seat was broken with splinters of wood sticking through the plush fabric. The second werewolf lay chest down on the floor. His head was twisted backward, and his death-clouded eyes stared accusingly at me.

I stepped over a pair of handcuffs, the bracelets bent and broken. They weren't steel or aluminum, but some silver alloy. Either they were specifically made to restrain a werewolf, or they were a specialty item from a high-ticket BDSM shop. They must have been used on Adam; he'd never have brought a wolf he had to restrain into his house while Jesse was here.

The noises of the fight were coming from around the corner of the living room, toward the back of the house. I ran along the wall, glass crunching under my feet and stopped just this side of the dining room as wood cracked and the floor vibrated.

I put my head around the corner cautiously, but I needn't have worried. The fighting werewolves were too involved with each other to pay attention to me.

Adam's dining room was large and open with patio doors that looked out over a rose garden. The floors were oak parquet – the real stuff. His ex-wife had had a table that could seat fifteen made to match the floor. That table was upside down and embedded in the far wall about four feet from the floor. The front of the matching china closet had been broken, as if someone had thrown something large and heavy into it. The result of the destruction was a fairly large, clear area for the werewolves to fight in.

The first instant I saw them, all I could do was hold my breath at the speed and grace of their motion. For all their size, werewolves still resemble their gracile cousin the timber wolf more than a Mastiff or Saint Bernard, who are closer to their weight. When weres run, they move with a deadly, silent grace. But they aren't really built for running, they are built for fighting, and there is a deadly beauty to them that comes out only in battle.

I'd only seen Adam's wolf form four or five times, but it was something you didn't forget. His body was a deep silver, almost blue, with an undercoat of lighter colors. Like a Siamese cat's, his muzzle, ears, tail, and legs deepened to black.

The wolf he was fighting was bigger, a silvery buff color more common among coyotes than wolves. I didn't know him.

At first, the size difference didn't bother me. You don't get to be the Alpha without being able to fight – and Adam had been a warrior before he'd been Changed. Then I realized that all the blood on the floor was dripping from Adam's belly, and the white flash I saw on his side was a rib bone.

I stepped out where I could get better aim and lifted the rifle, pointing the barrel at the strange werewolf, waiting until I could take a shot without risking hitting Adam.

The buff-colored wolf seized Adam just behind the neck and shook him like a dog killing a snake. It was meant to break Adam's neck, but the other wolf's grip wasn't firm, and instead he threw Adam into the dining table, sending the whole mess crashing onto the floor and giving me the opportunity I'd been waiting for.

I shot the wolf in the back of the head from less than six feet away. Just as my foster father had taught me, I shot him at a slight downward angle, so that the Marlin's bullet didn't go through him and travel on to hit anyone else who happened to be standing in the wrong place for the next quarter mile or so.

Marlin .444's were not built for home defense; they were built to kill grizzlies and have even been used a time or two to take out elephants. Just what the doctor ordered for werewolves. One shot at all but point-blank and he was dead. I walked up to him and shot him one more time, just to make sure.

I'm not usually a violent person, but it felt good to pull the trigger. It soothed the building rage I'd felt ever since I'd knelt on my porch next to Mac's body.

I glanced at Adam, lying in the midst of his dining table, but he didn't move, not even to open his eyes. His elegant muzzle was covered in gore. His silver hair was streaked dark with blood and matted so it was hard to see the full extent of his wounds. What I could see was bad enough.

Someone had done a fair job of gutting him: I could see pale intestines and the white of bone where the flesh had peeled away from his ribs.

He might be alive, I told myself. My ears were still ringing. I was breathing too hard, my heart racing too fast and loud: it might be enough to cover the sound of his heart, of his breath. This was more damage than I'd ever seen a werewolf heal from, far more than the other two dead wolves or the one I'd killed last night.

I put the rifle back on quarter cock, and waded through the remains of the table to touch Adam's nose. I still couldn't tell if he was breathing.

I needed help.

I ran to the kitchen where, in true Adam fashion, he had a tidy list of names and numbers on the counter just below the wall phone. My finger found Darryl's name with his work, home, and pager number printed in black block letters. I set my gun down where I could reach it fast and dialed his home number first.

'You have reached the home of Dr Darryl Zao. You may leave a message after the tone or call his pager at 543—' Darryl's bassy-rumble sounded intimate despite the impersonal message.

I hung up and tried his work number, but he wasn't there either. I'd started dialing his pager, but while I'd been trying to call him, I'd been thinking about our encounter last night.

This isn't the time,' he'd told Ben. I hadn't given it a second thought last night, but had there been a special emphasis in his voice? Had he meant, as I'd assumed: not after all the effort Ben had put into being on his best behavior since his banishment from London? Or had it been more specific as in: not now, when we have greater matters to deal with? Greater matters like killing the Alpha.

In Europe, murder was still mostly the way the rule of

the pack changed hands. The old Alpha ruled until one of the younger, hungrier dominant males decided the old one had grown weak and attacked him. I knew of at least one European Alpha who killed any male who showed signs of being dominant.

In the New World, thanks to the iron hand of the Marrok, things were more civilized. Leadership was mostly imposed from above – and no one challenged the Marrok's decisions, at least not as long as I had known him. But could someone have come into Adam's house and done this much damage without help from Adam's pack?

I hung up the phone and stared at the list of names, none of whom I dared call for help until I knew more about what was going on. My gaze dropped and rested on a photograph in a wooden frame set out beside the list.

A younger Jesse grinned at me with a baseball bat over her shoulder and a cap pulled a little to one side.

Jesse.

I snatched up my rifle and sprinted up the stairs to her room. She wasn't there. I couldn't tell if there had been a struggle in it or not – Jesse tended to live in a tumult that reflected itself in the way she kept her room.

In coyote form, my senses are stronger. So I hid both of my guns under her bed, stripped out of my clothes, and changed.

Jesse's scent was all over the room, but I also caught a hint of the human who'd confronted Mac at my garage last night. I followed the trail of his scent down the stairs because Jesse's scent was too prevalent to find a single trail.

I was almost out the door when a sound stopped me in my tracks. I temporarily abandoned the trail to investigate. At first I thought perhaps I had only heard one of the pieces of overturned furniture settling, but then I noticed Adam's left front paw had moved.

Once I saw that, I realized I could hear the almost imperceptible sound of his breathing. Maybe it was only the sharper senses of the coyote, but I would have sworn he hadn't been breathing earlier. If he was alive, there was a very good chance he'd stay that way. Werewolves are tough.

I whined happily, crawled over the wreckage of his table, and licked his bloody face once before resuming my search for his daughter.

Adam's house is at the end of a dead-end road. Directly in front of his house is a turnaround. The SUV I'd seen take off – presumably with Jesse – had left a short trail of burning rubber – but most cars have very little individual scent until they grow old. This one had not left enough behind for me to trail once the tang of burnt rubber faded from its tires.

There was no more trail to follow, nothing I could do for Jesse, nothing I could do for Mac. I turned my attention to Adam.

That he was alive meant I really could not contact his pack, not with him helpless. If any of the dominants had aspirations to become Alpha, they'd kill him. I also couldn't just bring him to my house. First, as soon as someone realized he was missing, they'd check my place out. Second, a badly wounded werewolf was dangerous to himself and everyone around him. Even if I could trust his wolves, there was no dominant in the Columbia Basin Pack strong enough to keep Adam's wolf under control until he was well enough to control himself.

I knew where one was, though.

5

A Vanagon resembles nothing so much as a Twinkie on wheels; a fifteen-foot-long, six-foot-wide Twinkie with as much aerodynamic styling as a barn door. In the twelve years that VW imported them into the US, they never put anything bigger in them than the four-cylinder *wasser-boxer* engine. My 1989 four-wheel-drive, four-thousand-pound Syncro's engine put out a whopping ninety horses.

In layman's terms, that means I was cruising up the interstate with a dead body and a wounded werewolf at sixty miles an hour. Downhill, with a good tailwind, the van could go seventy-five. Uphill I was lucky to make fifty. I could have pushed it a little faster, but only if I wanted to chance blowing my engine altogether. For some reason, the thought of being stranded by the roadside with my current cargo was enough to keep my foot off the gas pedal.

The highway stretched out before me in gentle curves that were mostly empty of traffic or scenic beauty unless you liked scrub desert better than I did. I didn't want to think of Mac, or of Jesse, scared and alone – or of Adam who might be dying because I chose to move him rather than call his pack. So I took out my cell phone.

I called my neighbors first. Dennis Cather was a retired pipefitter, and his wife Anna a retired nurse. They'd moved in two years ago and adopted me after I fixed their tractor.

'Yes.' Anna's voice was so normal after the morning I'd had, it took me a moment to answer.

'Sorry to call you so early,' I told her. 'But I've been called out of town on a family emergency. I shouldn't be gone long – just a day or two – but I didn't check to make sure Medea had food and water.'

'Don't fret, dear,' she said. 'We'll look after her. I hope that it's nothing serious.'

I couldn't help but glance back at Adam in the rearview mirror. He was still breathing. 'It's serious. One of my foster family is hurt.'

'You go take care of what you need to,' she said briskly. 'We'll see to things here.'

It wasn't until after I cut the connection that I wondered if I had involved them in something dangerous. Mac had been left on my doorstep for a reason – a warning to keep my nose out of someone's business. And I was most certainly sticking my whole head in it now.

I was doing as much as I could for Adam, and I thought of something I could do for Jesse. I called Zee.

Siebold Adelbertsmiter, Zee for short, had taught me everything I knew about cars. Most fae are very sensitive to iron, but Zee was a Metallzauber – which is a rather broad category name given to the few fae who could handle metal of all kinds. Zee preferred the modern American term 'gremlin,' which he felt better fit his talents. I wasn't calling him for his talents, but for his connections.

'*Ja,*' said a gruff male voice.

'Hey, Zee, it's Mercy. I have a favor to ask.'

'*Ja* sure, *Liebling,*' he said. 'What's up?'

I hesitated. Even after all this time, the rule of keeping pack trouble in the pack was hard to break – but Zee knew everyone in the fae community.

I outlined the past day to him, as best I could.

'So you think this baby werewolf of yours brought this trouble here? Why then did they take our *kleine* Jesse?'

'I don't know,' I said. 'I'm hoping that when Adam recovers he'll know something more.'

'So you are asking me to see if anyone I know has seen these strange wolves in hopes of finding Jesse?'

'There were at least four werewolves moving into the Tri-Cities. You'd think that someone among the fae would have noticed.' Because the Tri-Cities was so close to the Walla Walla Fae Reservation, there were more fae living here than was usual.

'Ja,' Zee agreed heavily. 'You'd think. I will ask around. Jesse is a good girl; she should not be in these evil men's hands longer than we can help.'

'If you go by the garage, would you mind putting a note in the window?' I asked. 'There's a "Closed for the Holidays" sign under the counter in the office.'

'You think they might come after me if I opened it for you?' he asked. Zee often ran the garage if I had to be out of town. 'You may be right. Ja, gut. I'll open the garage today and tomorrow.'

It had been a long time since Siebold Adelbertsmiter of the Black Forest had been sung about, so long that those songs had faded from memory, but there was something of the spirit of the *Heldenlieder*, the old German hero songs, about him still.

'A werewolf doesn't need a sword or gun to tear you to bits,' I said, unable to leave it alone, though I knew better than to argue with the old gremlin once he'd made up his mind. 'Your metalworking magic won't be much help against one.'

He snorted. 'Don't you worry about me, *Liebling*. I was killing werewolves when this country was still a Viking colony.' Many of the lesser fae talked about how old they were, but Zee had told me that most of them shared a life span similar to humankind. Zee was a lot older than that.

I sighed and gave in. 'All right. But be careful. If you're going to be there, I have a parts order that should be in.

Could you check it for me? I haven't ordered from this place before, but my usual source was out.'

'*Ja wohl.* Leave it to me.'

The next call I made was to Stefan's answering machine. 'Hey, Stefan,' I told it. 'This is Mercy. I'm headed to Montana today. I don't know when I'll be back. Probably late this week. I'll give you a call.' I hesitated, but there really wasn't a good way to say the next part. 'I had to haul a dead body in your van. It's fine; Elizeveta Arkadyevna cleaned it. I'll explain when I get back.'

Mentioning Elizaveta reminded me of something else I needed to do. Adam's house was on the end of the road, but it was clearly visible from the river. Someone would notice that the couch was sitting in the flowerbeds and call the police if the mess wasn't cleaned up soon.

I had her number on my phone, though I'd never had occasion to use it before. I got her answering machine and left a message telling her there was a mess at Adam's house, there had been a dead man on my porch, Jesse was missing, and I was taking Adam, who was wounded, somewhere he'd be safe. Then I closed the phone and put it away. I didn't know what happened at Adam's house, but that didn't stop me from feeling guilty and responsible. If I hadn't interfered last night when the two bullies came to find Mac, would everyone still be alive? If I'd sent Mac to Montana, to the Marrok, rather than letting Adam take him, what would that have changed?

Taking Mac to the Marrok had never even occurred to me. I hadn't contacted Bran since he'd sent me away from the pack, and he'd returned the favor. I took a quick glance behind my seat at the blue tarp concealing Mac's body. Well, I was bringing Mac to him now.

I found myself remembering the shy grin Mac had worn when I told him my name. I wiped my cheeks and fiercely blinked back further tears, but it was no use. I cried for him, for his parents and his brother who didn't even know he was dead. Doubtless they were all sitting beside their phones, waiting for him to call again.

I was coming down the grade into Spokane before more pressing worries distracted me from grief and guilt: Adam began stirring. My fear that Adam would die was instantly overwhelmed by the worry that he'd heal too fast.

I still had well over two hundred miles to go, most of it two-lane mountain highway meandering through dozens of small towns at twenty-five miles an hour. The last sixty miles was on a road marked 'other' on the state highway map – as opposed to highway or road. As I recalled, it was gravel most of the way. I figured it would take me at least four more hours.

Dominant wolves heal faster than the submissive wolves. By my rough estimate, it would be no more than two days before Adam was recovered enough to control his wolf – which would be capable of mayhem long before that. I needed Bran before Adam was mobile, and, if he was stirring already, I was going to be lucky if I made it.

When I hit Coeur d'Alene, where I'd have to leave the interstate for highway, I gassed up then drove to the first fast-food burger place I found and bought thirty cheese-burgers. The bemused teenager who started handing me bags through the service window peered curiously at me. I didn't explain, and she couldn't see my passengers because of the van's curtains.

I parked in the restaurant's parking lot, snatched a couple of the bags, stepped over Mac, and began stripping the buns off the meat. Adam was too weak to do more than growl at me and snatch the cheese-and-catsup-covered meat as fast as I could toss it to him. He ate almost twenty patties before he subsided into his previous comalike state.

The first few flakes of snow began falling on us as I took the highway north.

I drove into Troy, Montana, cursing the heavy wet snow that had distracted me so I missed my turnoff, which should have been several miles earlier. I topped off my gas tank, got directions, chained up, and headed back the way I'd come.

The snow was falling fast enough that the snow crews hadn't been able to keep up with it. The tracks of the cars preceding me were rapidly filling.

The gas station clerk's directions fresh in my mind, I slowed as I crossed back over the Yaak River. It was a baby river compared to the Kootenai, which I'd been driving next to for the past few hours.

I watched the side of the road carefully, and it was a good thing I did. The small green sign that marked the turnoff was half-covered in wet snow.

There was only one set of tracks up the road. They turned off at a narrow drive and, after that, I found my way up the road by driving where there were no trees. Happily, the trees were dense and marked the way pretty clearly.

The road twisted up and down the narrow river valley, and I was grateful for the four-wheel drive. Once, a couple of black-tailed deer darted in front of me. They gave me an irritated glance and trotted off.

It had been a long time since I'd been that way – I hadn't even had my driver's license then. The road was unfamiliar, and I began to worry I'd miss my turn. The road divided, one-half clearly marked, but the other half, the one I had to take, was barely wide enough for my van.

'Well,' I told Adam, who was whining restlessly, 'if we end up in Canada and you haven't eaten me yet, I suppose we can turn around, come back, and try again.'

I'd about decided I was going to have to do just that,

when I topped a long grade and saw a hand-carved wooden sign. I stopped the van.

Aspen Creek, the sign read in graceful script, carved and painted white on a dark brown background, *23 miles*. As I turned the van to follow the arrow, I wondered when Bran had decided to allow someone to post a sign. Maybe he'd gotten tired of having to send out guides — but he'd been adamant about keeping a low profile when I left.

I don't know why I expected everything to be the same. After all, I'd changed a good deal in the years since I'd last been there. I should have expected that Aspen Creek would have changed, too. I didn't have to like it.

The uninitiated would be forgiven for thinking there were only four buildings in Aspen Creek: the gas station/post office, the school, the church, and the motel. They wouldn't see the homes tucked unobtrusively up the draws and under the trees. There were a couple of cars in front of the gas station, but otherwise the whole town looked deserted. I knew better. There were always people watching, but they wouldn't bother me unless I did something unusual — like dragging a wounded werewolf out of my van.

I stopped in front of the motel office, just under the *Aspen Creek Motel* sign, which bore more than a passing resemblance to the sign I'd followed to town. The old motel was built the way the motor hotels had been in the middle of the last century — a long, narrow, and no-frills building designed so guests could park their vehicles in front of their rooms.

There was no one in the office, but the door was unlocked. It had been updated since I'd been there last and the end result was rustic charm — which was better than the run-down 1950s tacky it had been.

I hopped over the front desk and took a key marked #1.

Number one was the Marrok's safe room, specially designed to contain uncooperative werewolves.

I found a piece of paper and a pen and wrote: *Wounded in #1. Please Do Not Disturb.* I left the note on the desk where it couldn't be missed, then I returned to the van and backed it up to the room.

Getting Adam out of the van was going to be rough no matter what. At least when I dragged him into it, he'd been unconscious. I opened the reinforced metal door of the motel room and took a look around. The furnishing was new, but sparse, just a bed and a nightstand that was permanently fixed against the wall – nothing to help me get a werewolf who weighed twice what I did out of the van and into the room without hurting one or the other of us. There was no porch as there had been at Adam's house, which left almost a four-foot drop from the back of the van to the ground.

In the end I decided calling for help was better than hurting Adam worse. I went back to the office and picked up the phone. I hadn't called Sam's number since I'd left, but some things are just ingrained. Even though he was the reason I'd left here, he was the first one I thought to call for help.

'Hello,' answered a woman's voice that sounded completely unfamiliar.

I couldn't speak. I hadn't realized how much I'd been counting on hearing Samuel until I heard someone else's voice instead.

'Marlie? Is there something wrong at the motel? Do you need me to send Carl?' She must have caller ID, I thought stupidly.

She sounded frantic, but I recognized her voice at last, and felt a wave of relief. I don't know why Lisa Stoval was answering this number, but the mention of Carl and the sudden tension in her voice cued me in. I guess she had just never sounded cheerful when she talked to me.

Some things might have changed, but some things I had just forgotten. Aspen Creek had a population of about five hundred people, and only about seventy were werewolves, but I seldom thought about the human majority. Lisa and her husband Carl were both human. So was Marlie, at least she had been when I left. She'd also been about six years old.

'I don't know where Marlie is,' I told her. 'This is Mercedes, Mercedes Thompson. There's no one in the motel office. I'd really appreciate it if you'd send Carl down here, or tell me who else to call. I have the Alpha from the Columbia Basin Pack in my van. He's badly wounded, and I need help getting him into the motel room. Even better would be if you could tell me how to get ahold of Bran.'

Bran didn't have a telephone at his home — or hadn't when I left. For all I knew he had a cell phone now.

Lisa, like most of the women of Aspen Creek, had never liked me. But she wasn't one of those people who let a little thing like that get in the way of doing what was right and proper.

'Bran and some of the others have taken the new wolves out for their first hunt. Marlie's probably holed up somewhere crying. Lee, her brother, was one of the ones who tried to Change. He didn't make it.'

I'd forgotten. How could I have forgotten? The last full moon of October, all of those who chose to try to become werewolves were allowed to come forward. In a formal ceremony they were savaged by Bran, or by some other wolf who loved them, in the hopes that they would rise Changed. Most of them didn't make it. I remembered the tension that gripped the town through October and the sadness of November. Thanksgiving had a different meaning to the residents of Aspen Creek than it did for the rest of America.

'I'm sorry,' I said inadequately, feeling rawly incapable of dealing with more dead youngsters – I remembered Lee, too. 'Lee was a good kid.'

'I'll send Carl.' Lisa's voice was crisp, denying me the right to grieve or sympathize. She hung up without saying good-bye.

I avoided thinking – or looking at the tarp that covered Mac – while I sat in the van waiting for help. Instead, I fed Adam the remaining hamburgers while we waited. They were cold and congealed, but it didn't seem to bother the wolf. When they were gone, he closed his eyes and ignored me.

At long last, Carl pulled up next to me in a beat-up Jeep and climbed out. He was a big man, and had always been more of a man of action than words. He hugged me and thumped me on my back.

'Don't be such a stranger, Mercy,' he said, then laughed at my look of shock and ruffled my hair. I'd forgotten he liked to do that, forgotten the easy affection he showed to everyone – even Bran. 'Lisa said you have Adam here and he's in bad shape?'

Of course he'd know who the Alpha of the Columbia Basin Pack was. Adam's pack was closest to Aspen Creek.

I nodded and opened the back of my van so he could see what we were dealing with. Adam looked better than he had when I first put him in the van, but that wasn't saying much. I couldn't see the bones of his ribs anymore, but his coat was matted with blood and covered with wounds.

Carl whistled through his teeth, but all he said was, 'We'll need to tie his jaws shut until we get him in. I've got something we can use in the Jeep.'

He brought an Ace bandage and we wound it round and round Adam's muzzle. The wolf opened his eyes once, but didn't struggle.

It took a lot of grunting, a few swear words, and a little sweat, but the two of us managed to get Adam out of the van and into the room. Once we had him on the bed, I made Carl get back before I unwound the bandage and freed the wolf. I was fast, but even so, Adam caught my forearm with an eyetooth and drew blood. I jumped back as he rolled off his side and struggled to stand – driven to defend himself against the pain we'd caused him.

'Out,' Carl said, holding the door for me.

I complied and we shut the door behind us. Carl held it shut while I turned the key in the dead bolt. Unlike most motel rooms, this dead bolt operated by key from both sides – for just such situations. The windows were barred, the vents sealed. Number one served as prison and hospital on occasion: sometimes both.

Adam was safe – for now. Once he'd regained a little more strength things could still get problematical unless I tracked down Bran.

'Do you know where Bran took the new wolves?' I asked, shutting the back hatch of the van. Carl hadn't asked me about Mac – he didn't have a wolf's nose to tell him what was in the tarp – and I decided that Mac could ride with me for a while longer. Bran could decide what to do with his body.

'You don't want to go after him, Mercy,' Carl was saying. 'Too dangerous. Why don't you come home with me. We'll feed you while you wait.'

'How many wolves are left in town?' I asked. 'Is there anyone who could resist Adam's wolf?'

That was the downside of being dominant. If you did go moonstruck, you took everyone who was less dominant with you.

Carl hesitated. 'Adam's pretty weak yet. Bran will be back by dark.'

Something hit the door, and we both jumped.

'He took them up to the Lover's Canyon,' Carl told me, giving in to the obvious. 'Be careful.'

'Bran will have control of the new ones,' I told him. 'I'll be all right.'

'I'm not worried about them. You left enemies behind you, girl.'

I smiled tightly. 'I can't help what I am. If they are my enemies, it was not by my choice.'

'I know. But they'll still kill you if they can.'

The lovers were a pair of trees that had grown up twined around each other near the entrance to a small canyon about ten miles north of town. I parked next to a pair of old-style Land Rovers, a nearly new Chevy Tahoe, and a HumVee – the expensive version. Charles, Bran's son, was a financial genius, and the Marrok's pack would never be begging on street corners. When I left here, I'd had ten thousand dollars in a bank account, the result of part of my minimum wage earnings invested by Charles.

I stripped off my clothes in the van, jumped out into knee-deep snow, and shut the door. It was colder up in the mountains than it had been in Troy, and the snow had a crust of hard ice crystals that cut into the bare skin of my feet.

I shifted as fast as I could. It might have been safer to go as a human, but I didn't have the right kind of clothing on for a winter hike in Montana. I am not absolutely sure there *is* a right kind of clothing for a winter hike in Montana. Running as a coyote, I don't mind the cold all that much.

I'd grown used to city scents and sounds. The forest scents were no less strong, just different: fir, aspen, and pine instead of exhaust, fried grease, and humans. I heard the distinctive rat-a-tat of a woodpecker, and, faintly, the howl of a wolf – too deep to be that of a timber wolf.

The fresh snow, which was still falling, had done a fair job of hiding their tracks, but I could still smell them. Bran and his mate, Leah, both had brushed against the bough of a white pine. Charles had left tracks where the ground was half-sheltered by a boulder. Once my nose drew me to the right places, I could see where the old snow had been broken by paws before the snow had begun, and the tracks weren't difficult to follow.

I hesitated when the wolves' tracks began to separate. Bran had taken the new wolves – there seemed to be three of them – while his sons, Charles and Samuel, and Leah, Bran's mate, broke off, probably to hunt up game in the hopes of chasing it back to the rest.

I needed to find Bran to tell him what had happened, to get his help for Adam – but I followed Sam's trail instead. I couldn't help it. I'd been in love with him since I was fourteen.

Not that I am in love with him now, I assured myself, following his tracks down an abrupt drop and back up to a ridgetop where the snow wasn't as deep because the wind periodically swept it clean.

I was only a teenager when I last saw him, I thought. I hadn't spoken to him since then, and he hadn't tried to contact me either. Still, it had been his number I had called for help. I hadn't even thought about calling anyone else.

On the tail of that thought, I realized the forest had fallen silent behind me.

The winter woods were quiet. The birds, except for a scattering of nut hatches, cedar waxwings, and a few others like the woodpecker I'd heard, had gone south. But there was an ominous quality to the silence behind me that was too heavy to be only winter's stillness. I was being stalked.

I didn't look around, nor did I speed up. Werewolves chase things that run from them.

I wasn't really frightened. Bran was out there somewhere, and Samuel was even nearer. I could smell the earth-and-spice musk that belonged to him alone; the wind carried it to me. The tracks I was following had been laid several hours ago. He must have been returning the way he'd come; otherwise, he'd have been too far away for me to scent.

The new wolves were all with Bran, and the one following me was alone: if there had been more than one, I would have heard something. So I didn't have to be worried about the new wolves killing me by mistake because they thought I was a coyote.

I didn't think it was Charles stalking me either. It would be beneath his dignity to frighten me on purpose. Samuel liked playing practical jokes, but the wind doesn't lie, and it told me he was somewhere just ahead.

I was pretty sure it was Leah. She wouldn't kill me no matter what Carl had implied – not with Bran sure to find out – but she would hurt me if she could because she didn't like me. None of the women in Bran's pack liked me.

The wind carrying Samuel's scent was coming mostly from the west. The trees on that side were young firs, probably regrowing after a fire that must have happened a decade or so in the past. The firs were tucked together in a close-packed blanket that wouldn't slow me at all, but a werewolf was a lot bigger than I.

I scratched my ear with a hind foot and used the movement to get a good look behind me. There was nothing to see, so my stalker was far enough away for me to reach the denser trees. I put my foot down and darted for the trees.

The wolf behind me howled her hunting song. Instinct takes over when a wolf is on the hunt. Had she been thinking,

Leah would never have uttered a sound – because she was immediately answered by a chorus of howls. Most of the wolves sounded like they were a mile or so farther into the mountains, but Samuel answered her call from no more than a hundred yards in front of me. I altered my course accordingly and found my way through the thicket of trees and out the other side where Samuel had been traveling.

He stopped dead at my appearance – I suppose he was expecting a deer or elk, not a coyote. Not me.

Samuel was big, even for a werewolf. His fur was winter white, and his eyes appeared almost the same shade, an icy white-blue, colder than the snow I ran through, all the more startling for the black ring that edged his iris. There was plenty of room for me to dive under his belly and out the other side, leaving him between me and my pursuer.

Before he had a chance to do more than give me that first startled look, Leah appeared, a gold-and-silver huntress, as beautiful as Samuel in her own way: light and fire where he was ice. She saw Samuel and skidded ungracefully to a halt. I suppose she'd been so hot on the chase she hadn't been paying attention to Samuel's call.

I could see the instant he realized who I was. He cocked his head, and his body grew still. He recognized me all right, but I couldn't tell how he felt about it. After the space of a deep breath, he turned back to look at Leah.

Leah cringed and rolled onto her back – though as Bran's wife she should have outranked Samuel. Unimpressed by the show, he curled his lips away from his fangs and growled, a deep rumbling sound that echoed in my chest. It felt just like old times: Samuel protecting me from the rest of the pack.

A wolf howled, nearer than before, and Samuel stopped growling long enough to answer. He looked expectantly toward the north, and in a few minutes two wolves came into sight. The first one was the color of cinnamon with four black feet. He was a shade bigger even than Samuel.

The second werewolf was considerably smaller. From a distance he could have passed as one of the wolves that had only this decade begun to return to Montana. His coat was all the shades between white and black, combining to make him appear medium gray. His eyes were pale gold, and the end of his tail was white.

Charles, the cinnamon wolf, stopped at the edge of the trees and began to change. He was an oddity among werewolves: a natural-born werewolf rather than made. The only one of his kind that I have ever heard of.

Charles's mother had been a Salish woman, the daughter of a medicine man. She had been dying when Bran came across her, shortly after he arrived in Montana. According to my foster mother, who told me the story, Bran had been so struck with her beauty that he couldn't just let her die, so he Changed her and made her his mate. I never could wrap my imagination around the thought of Bran being overcome by love at first sight, but maybe he had been different two hundred years ago.

At any rate, when she became pregnant, she used the knowledge of magic her father had given her to keep from changing at the full moon. Female werewolves cannot have children: the change is too violent to allow the fetus to survive. But Charles's mother, as her father's daughter, had some magic of her own. She managed to carry Charles to term, but was so weakened by her efforts that she died soon after his birth. She left her son with two gifts. The first was that he changed easier and faster. The second was a gift for magic that was unusual in werewolves. Bran's pack did not have to hire a witch to clean up after them; they had Charles.

Bran, the smaller of the two wolves, continued on to

where I stood awaiting him. Samuel stepped aside reluctantly, though he was still careful to keep between Leah and me.

There was no sense of power about Bran, not like the one his sons and Adam carried — I'm not certain how he contained it. I've been told that sometimes even other werewolves, whose senses are sharper than mine, mistake him for a real wolf or some wolf-dog hybrid to account for his size.

I don't know how old he is. All I know is that he was old when he came to this continent to work as a fur trapper in the late eighteenth century. He'd traveled to this area of Montana with the Welsh cartographer David Thompson and settled to live with his Salish mate.

He padded up to me and touched his muzzle behind my ear. I didn't have to sink submissively to be lower than he, but I hunched down anyway. He took my nose between his fangs and released it, a welcome and a gentle chiding all in one — though I wasn't certain what he was chiding me for.

Once he released me, he stalked past Samuel and stared down at his wife, still lying in the snow. She whined anxiously and he bared his teeth, unappeased. It seemed that even though he'd once asked me to leave, I wasn't to be viewed as fair game.

Bran turned his back on her to look at Charles, who had completed his transformation and stood tall and human. Charles's features were pure Salish, as if the only thing that he'd gotten from his father was the ability to change.

I've been told that the Native Americans were shy about their bodies. It was certainly true of Charles. He'd used his magic to clothe himself and stood garbed in fur-lined buckskins that looked as if they had come out of another century.

I, like most shapeshifters, was nearly as comfortable naked as clothed — except in the middle of November, high up in the Rockies of Montana with a chill Canadian wind blowing from the northwest and the temperature beginning to drop as the snow quit falling at last. And as soon as Charles started to speak, I was going to have to become human so I could talk to him.

'My father bids you welcome to the territory of the Marrok,' Charles said, his voice carrying the flat tones of his mother's people with just a hint of the Welsh lilt Bran no longer spoke with unless he was really angry. 'He wonders, however, why you have chosen now to come.'

I took human form, quickly kicked snow away from me, then knelt to keep myself lower than Bran. I sucked in my breath at the chill of the wind and the snow under my shins. Samuel moved between me and the worst of the wind. It helped, but not enough.

'I came on pack business,' I told them.

Charles raised his eyebrows. 'You come smelling of blood and death.' Charles had always had a good nose.

I nodded. 'I brought the Columbia Basin Alpha here. He's been badly wounded. I also brought the body of another wolf, hoping someone here could tell me how he died and who killed him.'

Bran made a soft sound, and Charles nodded. 'Tell us what is necessary now. You can give us the details later.'

So I told them what I knew, as succinctly as possible, beginning with Mac's story, as he had told it to me, and ending with Mac's death, Adam's wounds, and Jesse's kidnapping. By the time I was finished, my teeth were chattering, and I could barely understand myself. Even when I shifted back into coyote form, I couldn't quite warm up.

Bran glanced at Samuel, who gave a woof and took off at a dead run.

'Bran will finish the hunt with the new ones,' Charles told me. 'It is their first hunt, and should not be interrupted. Samuel is going back to take care of Adam. He'll take a shorter route than the automobiles can manage, so he'll be there before us. I'll ride back with you and take care of your dead.'

On the tail end of Charles's words, Bran trotted off into the forest without looking at me again. Leah rose from her submissive pose, growled at me – like it was my fault she'd gotten herself in trouble – and followed Bran.

Charles, still in human form, strode off in the direction of the cars. He wasn't talkative at the best of times and, with me still four-footed and mute, he didn't bother to say anything at all. He waited politely on the passenger side of the van while I transformed again and dove into my clothes.

He didn't object to my driving as Samuel would have. I'd never seen Charles drive a car; he preferred to ride horseback or run as a wolf. He climbed into the passenger seat and glanced once behind him at the tarped body. Without commenting, he belted himself in.

When we got back to the motel, I pulled in at the office door. Carl was in the office with a red-eyed young woman who must be the missing Marlie, though I couldn't see the six-year-old I'd known.

'Mercedes needs a room,' Charles told them.

Carl didn't question him, just handed me a key. 'This is on the side away from the road, as far from #1 as we get.'

I looked down at the #18 stamped on the key. 'Don't you know that you're not supposed to put the room number on the key anymore?' I asked.

'We don't have much trouble with burglary,' Carl said, smiling. 'Besides, I know you spent a couple of years working here. Except for number one, there are only three different locks for all the rooms.'

I smiled at him and tossed the key up once and caught it. 'True enough.'

Charles opened the door for me as we left. 'If you'll get

your luggage and give me your car keys, I'll take care of the body.'

I must have looked surprised.

'Don't worry,' he told me dryly. 'I'll have Carl drive.'

'No luggage,' I told him. I pulled out my keys and gave them to him, but caught his hand before he pulled away. 'Mac was a good man,' I told him. I don't know why I said it.

Charles didn't touch anyone casually. I had always thought he rather despised me, though he treated me with the same remote courtesy he used with everyone else. But he put his free hand on the back of my head and pulled my forehead briefly against his shoulder.

'I'll take care of him,' he promised as he stepped back.

'His full name was Alan MacKenzie Frazier.'

He nodded. 'I'll see that he is treated well.'

'Thank you,' I told him, then turned and walked toward my room before I could start to cry again.

6

There was a pile of *National Geographics* and a paperback mystery stacked neatly on the nightstand. As I recall, the reading material was put there originally to make up for the absence of a TV. When I'd cleaned rooms here, you couldn't get reception so far in the mountains. Now there was a dish on top of the motel and a small TV positioned so you could watch it either from the bed or the small table in the kitchenette.

I wasn't interested in watching old reruns or soap operas so I flipped desultorily through the magazines. They looked familiar. Maybe they were the same stack that had been here when I'd last cleaned this room: the newest one was dated May of 1976, so it was possible. Or maybe random stacks of *National Geographics* have a certain sameness gained from years of appearing in waiting rooms.

I wondered if Jesse were lying in a hospital somewhere. My mind flashed to a morgue, but I brought it back under control. Panic wouldn't help anyone. I was doing the best that I could.

I picked up the lone book and sat on the bed. The cover was not prepossessing, being a line drawing of a Wisconsin-style barn, but I opened it anyway and started reading. I closed it before I'd read more than the first sentence. I couldn't bear sitting here alone, doing nothing.

I left the room. It was colder than it had been, and all I had was my T-shirt, so I ran to number one. I had the key in the pocket of my jeans, but when I tried the door, it opened.

Adam lay on top of the bed on his side, his muzzle wrapped with a businesslike strap. Samuel was bent over him wearing a pair of jeans, plastic gloves, and nothing else. It was a measure of my concern for Adam that my eyes didn't linger. Charles, leaning against the wall, glanced at me but said nothing.

'Shut the door,' Samuel snapped, without looking up. 'Damn it, Mercy, you should have set the break before you threw him in the car and drove all day – you of all people know how fast we heal. I'll have to rebreak his leg.'

Samuel had never yelled at me before. He was the least volatile male werewolf I'd ever met.

'I don't know how to set bones,' I said, wrapping my arms around myself. But he was right. I knew werewolves heal incredibly fast – I just hadn't thought about what that meant as far as broken bones were concerned. I hadn't even known his leg was broken. I'd been stupid. I should have just called Darryl.

'How much training does it take to set a leg?' Samuel continued with barely a pause. 'All you have to do is pull it straight.' His hands were gentle as they stretched out Adam's leg. 'He'd have had someone with medic training in his pack. You could have called for help if you didn't have the guts for it yourself.' Then to Adam he said, 'Brace yourself.' From my position by the door, I couldn't see what he did, but I heard a bone snap, and Adam jerked and made a noise I never want to hear again.

'I was worried that someone from his pack was involved in the attack,' I whispered. 'Adam was unconscious. I couldn't ask him. And they don't have anyone strong enough to control Adam's wolf.'

Samuel glanced back at me, then swore. 'If all you can do is snivel, then get the hell out of here.'

Despite his condition, Adam growled, swiveling his head to look at Samuel.

'I'm sorry.' I said, and left, closing the door tightly behind me.

I'd spent twenty minutes staring at the first page of the mystery when someone knocked on the door. My nose told me it was Samuel, so I didn't answer right away.

'Mercy?' His voice was soft, just as I remembered it, with just a touch of Celt.

If I left early in the morning, I could get a head start on looking for Jesse, I thought, staring at the door. Someone else could take Adam back when he was ready to travel. If I left early enough, I could avoid talking to Samuel altogether.

'Mercy. I know you're listening to me.'

I stared at the door, but didn't say anything. I didn't want to talk to him. He'd been right. I had been useless – subjecting Adam to a six-hour drive because of a chance remark of Darryl's, a remark that I was beginning to think meant nothing. Of course, as I'd told Samuel earlier, the pack would have had to bring Adam to Montana or at least send for a dominant until Adam could control himself – but they would have set his broken leg immediately. Darryl and the pack could be out looking for Jesse with Adam safely on the road to recovery if I hadn't been so stupid.

In my own world of engines and CV joints, I'd grown used to being competent. If Adam had been a car, I'd have known what to do. But in Aspen Creek, I'd always been not quite good enough – some things, it seemed, hadn't changed.

'Mercy, look, I'm sorry. If you didn't know first aid, and you couldn't trust his pack, there's nothing else you could have done.'

His voice was soft and sweet as molasses; but my mother once told me that you had to trust that the first thing out of a person's mouth was truth. After they have a chance to think about it, they'll change what they say to be more socially acceptable, something they think you'll be happier with, something that will get the results they want. I knew what he wanted, what he had always wanted from me, even if – while he had been working on Adam's injuries – Samuel, himself, had forgotten.

'Adam tore a strip off me for being so hard on you,' he said, his voice coaxing. 'He was right. I was mad because I don't like hurting someone unnecessarily, and I took it out on you. Can I come in and talk to you instead of the door?'

I rubbed my face tiredly. I wasn't sixteen anymore, to run away from difficult things, no matter how attractive that option was. There were, I thought reluctantly, things I needed to say to him as well.

'All right,' he said. 'All right, Mercy. I'll see you in the morning.'

He had turned around and was already walking away when I opened the door.

'Come in,' I said and shivered when the wind blew through my shirt. 'But you'd better hurry. It's colder than a witch's britches out there.'

He came back and stomped his feet hard on the mat, leaving behind clumps of snow before stepping inside my room. He took off his coat and set it on the table near the door, and I saw he'd found a shirt somewhere. They kept stashes of clothes around town, in case someone needed to dress quickly; unisex things mostly, like jeans, T-shirts, and sweats. The T-shirt he wore was a little small and clung to him like a second skin. If he'd had an extra ounce of fat or a little less muscle, it would have looked stupid, but he was built like a Chippendales' dancer.

His body was lovely, but I don't know if anyone else would have called him handsome. He certainly didn't have Adam's strikingly beautiful features. Sam's eyes were deeply set, his nose was too long, his mouth too wide. His coloring in human form was much less striking than his wolf: light blue-gray eyes and brown hair, streaked just a bit from the sun.

Looking at his face, I wasn't objective enough to decide how attractive he was: he was just Sam who had been my friend, my defender, and my sweetheart.

I glanced away from his face, dropping my own so that he couldn't read my anger – and whatever other emotion was hammering at me – until I'd gotten it under control. If he read the wrong thing into it, that wasn't my fault. I hadn't let him in to argue with him.

'I didn't think you were going to talk to me,' he said, with a shadow of his usual warm smile in his voice.

'Me either,' I agreed grimly to my shoes – I wasn't going to get through this if I had to look at him. 'But I owe you an apology, too.'

'No.' His tone was wary. Apparently he was too smart to believe my submissive gaze. 'You have nothing to be sorry for. I shouldn't have snapped your nose off earlier.'

'It's all right,' I told him. 'You were probably right. I found Mac dead and Adam almost in the same shape – and I panicked.' I walked to the bed and sat on it, because it was as far away from him as I could get in the motel room. Only then did I dare to look at him again. '*My* apology is years overdue. I should have talked to you before I left. I should have told you I'd decided to go to Portland.' *But I was afraid I might do something stupid like shoot you or, worse, cry* – but he didn't need to know that part.

The humor that usually touched his face leaked away, leaving behind neutral wariness, as if he were watching for a trap. 'My father told me he'd spoken to you and persuaded you to go to your mother's house instead of running off with me,' he said.

'How long did you wait for me?' After Bran had caught us necking in the woods and told me he was sending me to Portland, Samuel had decided that he'd take me away with him instead. I was supposed to sneak out and meet him in the woods a mile or so from my house. But the Marrok knew, he was like that. He told me why Samuel wanted to take me as his mate – and it hadn't been for any reason I could accept.

So while Samuel waited for me, Charles was driving me down to Libby to catch the train to Portland that morning instead.

Samuel looked away from me without answering.

In his own way, Samuel was the most honorable person I'd ever known – something that made his betrayal hurt worse because I knew that he'd never meant me to believe he loved me. He'd told me he would wait for me, and I knew he'd waited long after he'd realized I wasn't going to come.

'That's what I thought,' I said in a small voice. *Damn it, he shouldn't still affect me this way.* I found that I was taking deeper breaths than I normally did, just to breathe in his scent.

'I should have told you I'd changed my mind,' I told him, clinging by my fingernails to the threads of what I needed to tell him. 'I'm sorry for abandoning you without a word. It was neither right nor kind.'

'Father told you to go without talking to me again,' Samuel said. He sounded detached, but he'd turned his back on me and was staring at a damp spot on the rug near his boots.

'I am not of his pack,' I snapped. 'That has always been made perfectly clear to me. It means I didn't have to obey Bran then. I shouldn't have, and I knew it at the time. I'm sorry. Not for leaving, that was the right decision, but I should have told you what I was doing. I was a coward.'

'My father told me what he told you.' His voice started calmly enough, but there was a tinge of anger weaving itself through his words as he continued. 'But you should have known all of that already. I didn't hide anything.'

There was no defensiveness in his voice or in his posture; he really didn't understand what he'd done to me – as stupid as that made him in my eyes. It was still good, somehow, to know that the hurt he'd caused me had been unintentional.

He turned, his eyes met mine, and I felt the zing that had once been as familiar as his face. Part of it was attraction; but part of it was the power of a dominant wolf. The attraction brought me to my feet and halfway across the room before I realized what I was doing.

'Look, Samuel,' I said, coming to an abrupt halt before I touched him. 'I'm tired. It's been a rough day. I don't want to fight with you over things that are long past.'

'All right.' His voice was soft, and he gave a little nod to himself. 'We can talk more tomorrow.'

He put his coat back on, started for the door, then turned back. 'I almost forgot, Charles and Carl took the body—'

'Mac,' I told him sharply.

'Mac,' he said, gentling his tone. I wished he hadn't done that, because his sympathy brought tears to my eyes. 'They took Mac to our clinic and brought back your van. Charles gave me the keys. He would have returned them himself, but you left the room too quickly. I told him I was coming to deliver an apology, so he gave them to me.'

'Did he lock the van?' I asked. 'I've a pair of guns in there, loaded for werewolves—' Mention of the guns reminded me of something else, something odd. 'Oh, and there's a tranquilizer dart of some sort that I found near Adam when I moved him.'

'The van's locked,' he said. 'Charles found the dart and

left it at the lab because he said it smelled of silver and Adam. Now that I know where you found it, I'll make sure to look it over carefully.'

'Mac said someone was using him to experiment on,' I told him. 'They'd found some drugs that worked on were-wolves, he said.'

Samuel nodded. 'I remember you telling us that.'

He held out my keys and, careful not to touch his hand, I took them from him. He smiled as if I'd done something interesting and I realized I shouldn't have been so careful. If I had felt nothing for him, touching his hand wouldn't have bothered me. Living among normal humans, I'd forgotten how difficult it was to hide anything from werewolves.

'Good night, Mercy,' he said.

Then he was gone, and the room felt emptier for his leaving it. *I'd* better *go in the morning*, I thought, as I listened to the snow squeak under his feet as he walked away.

I was busy reading page fourteen for the third time when someone else knocked on the door.

'I brought dinner,' said a man's pleasant tenor.

I set the book down and opened the door.

A sandy-haired young man with a nondescript face held a plastic tray loaded with two plastic-wrapped sub sand-wiches, a pair of styrofoam cups of hot chocolate, and a dark blue winter jacket. Maybe it was the food, but it occurred to me that if Bran looked that much like the cliché of a delivery boy, it was probably on purpose. He liked to be unobtrusive.

He gave me a small smile when I didn't step away from the door right away. 'Charles told me that Adam is going to be fine, and Samuel made a fool of himself.'

'Samuel apologized,' I told him, stepping back and letting him into the room.

The kitchenette had a two-burner stove, six-pack-sized

fridge, and a small, Formica-covered table with two chairs. After tossing the coat on the bed, Bran set the tray on the table and rearranged the contents until there was a sandwich and cup on each side.

'Charles told me that you didn't have a coat, so I brought one. I also thought you might like something to eat,' he said. 'Then we can discuss what we're to do with your Alpha and his missing daughter.'

He sat down on one side and gestured for me to take the other seat. I sat and realized I hadn't eaten anything all day – I hadn't been hungry. I still wasn't.

True to his word, he didn't talk while he ate and I picked. The sandwich tasted of refrigerator, but the cocoa was rich with marshmallows and real vanilla.

He ate faster than I did, but waited patiently for me to finish. The sandwich was one of those huge subs, built to feed you for a week. I ate part of it and wrapped the rest in the plastic it had come in. Bran had eaten all of his, but werewolves need a lot of food.

My foster mother had liked to say, 'Never starve a were-wolf, or he might ask you to join him for lunch.' She'd always pat her husband on the head afterward, even if he was in human form.

I don't know why I thought of that right then, or why the thought tried to bring tears to my eyes. My foster parents were both of them almost seventeen years dead. She died trying to become a werewolf because, she'd told me, every year she got older and he didn't. There are a lot fewer women who are moon called, because they just don't survive the Change as well. My foster father died from grief a month later. I'd been fourteen.

I took a sip of cocoa and waited for Bran to talk.

He sighed heavily and leaned back in the chair, balancing it on two legs, his own legs dangling in the air.

'People don't do that,' I told him.

He raised an eyebrow. 'Do what?'

'Balance like that — not unless they're teenage boys showing off for their girlfriends.'

He brought all four legs back on the floor abruptly. 'Thank you.' Bran liked to appear as human as possible, but his gratitude was a little sharp. I took a hasty sip of cocoa so he wouldn't see my amusement.

He put his elbows on the table and folded his hands. 'What are your intentions now, Mercy?'

'What do you mean?'

'Adam's safe and healing. We'll find out how your young friend was killed. What are *you* planning to do?'

Bran is scary. He's a little psychic — at least that's what he says if you ask. What that means is that he can talk to any werewolf he knows, mind to mind. That's why Charles was able to be his spokesperson out in the woods. Bran uses that ability, among others, to control the North American packs. He claims it is all one way, that he can make people hear him but not the other way around.

The pack whisperers say he has other abilities, too, but no one knows exactly what they are. The most common rumor is that he really can read minds. Certainly he always knew who was responsible for what mischief around the town.

My foster mother always laughed and said it was his reputation for knowing everything that allowed him to appear infallible: all he had to do was walk through the room and see who looked guiltiest when they saw him. Maybe she was right, but I tried looking innocent the next time, and it didn't work.

'I'm leaving in the morning.' *Early*, I thought. *To get away without talking to Samuel again — but also to get started looking for Jesse.*

Bran shook his head and frowned. 'Afternoon.'

I felt my eyebrows rise. 'Well,' I said gently, 'if you knew what I was going to be doing, why didn't you just tell me instead of asking?'

He gave me a small smile. 'If you wait until afternoon, Adam will be ready to travel, and Samuel should know something about how your young man . . . Alan MacKenzie Frazier died. He's staying up tonight to perform the autopsy and run tests in the lab.'

He leaned forward. 'It's not your fault, Mercy.'

I spilled the cocoa all down the front of my T-shirt. 'Sh—' I bit off the word. Bran didn't approve of swearing. 'You *can* read minds.'

'I know the way your mind works,' Bran said, with a little smile that managed to be not quite smug. But he was quick enough retrieving a roll of paper towels stored under the sink and handed them to me as I held my shirt away from my body. The cocoa was still hot, though not scalding.

As I mopped myself up at the sink, he continued, 'Unless you've changed more than I can believe, if something happens, if someone gets hurt, it must be your fault. I had the story from Adam, as far as he knows it, and it had nothing to do with you.'

'Hah – you can read minds. He's in wolf form, and can't talk,' I said. I'd done the best I could with the shirt, but I wished I had an extra change of clothing.

Bran smiled. 'He's not now. Sometimes the change helps us heal faster. Usually we change from human to wolf, but the other way works as well. He was not happy with Samuel.' Bran's smile deepened. 'He spent his first words chewing him out. Told him that second-guessing the man in the field was an amateur's mistake. He said he'd rather not have someone who didn't know what they were doing "mucking about" with his wounds. He also said that you had more guts than sense sometimes.' Bran tipped his styrofoam cup in my direction. 'As it happens I agree – which is why I asked Adam to keep an eye on you for me when you moved into his territory.'

Ah, I thought and tried not to look as devastated as I felt. So Adam had been ordered to look after me? I had rather thought that the odd relationship we had was based on something else. Knowing that Bran had told him to watch me changed the shading of every conversation we'd ever had, lessened it.

'I don't like lies,' said Bran, and I knew I'd failed to keep the pain of his revelation from my face. 'Not even lies of omission. Hard truths can be dealt with, triumphed over, but lies will destroy your soul.' He looked as though he had personal knowledge of it. 'That distaste leads me to meddle where perhaps I should step back.'

He paused, as if to let me speak, but I had no idea where he was going with this.

He sat down and took another sip of cocoa. 'There were those who thought the truth of Bryan's death should be kept from you.' Bryan had been my foster father.

I remembered waking up shortly after Christmas to Bran's low-key voice in the kitchen. When I came out of my room. Bran told me that the police had found Bryan's body in the Kootenai River.

Suicide is difficult for werewolves. Even silver bullets don't always defeat the wolf's ability to heal itself. Decapitation is effective, but rather difficult to achieve in a suicidal situation. Drowning works very well. Werewolves are very densely muscled; they tend to have a difficult time swimming even if they want to, because, like chimpanzees, they have too much muscle and not enough fat to float.

'Some of the pack would have told you that Bryan had an accident.' Bran's voice was contemplative. 'They told me that fourteen was too young to deal with a suicide, especially on top of the death of Bryan's mate.'

'Her name was Evelyn,' I told him. Bran had a tendency to dismiss the humans around him as if they didn't exist. Samuel once told me that it was because humans were so fragile, and Bran had seen too many of them die. I thought that if I could handle Evelyn's death when I was fourteen, then, by hang, Bran could, too.

He gave me a quelling look. When I didn't look down as protocol demanded, his lips turned up before he hid them with the cup.

'Evelyn, indeed,' he said, then sighed. 'When you chose to live alone, rather than go to your mother, I agreed to that, too. You had proven your mettle to me; I thought you had earned the right to make your own choices.' His eyes roved around the room. 'Do you remember the last time you and I talked?'

I nodded and sat down finally. Even if he wasn't insisting on protocol tonight, it felt awkward to be standing while he was sitting in the chair.

'You were sixteen,' he said. 'Too young for him – and too young to know what it was that he wanted from you.'

When Bran had caught Samuel kissing me in the woods, he'd sent me home, then shown up the next morning to tell me that he'd already spoken with my real mother, and she would be expecting me at the end of the week. He was sending me away, and I should pack what I wanted to take.

I'd packed all right, but not to go to Portland; I was packed to leave with Samuel. We'd get married, he'd said. It never occurred to me that at sixteen, I'd have trouble getting married without parental permission. Doubtless Samuel would have had an answer for that as well. We'd planned to move to a city and live outside of any pack.

I loved Samuel, had loved him since my foster father had died and Samuel had taken over his role as my protector. Bryan had been a dear, but Samuel was a much more effective defense. Even the women didn't bother me as much once I had Samuel at my back. He'd been funny and charming. Lightheartedness is not a gift often given to werewolves, but Samuel had it in abundance. Under his wing, I learned joy – a very seductive emotion.

'You told me that Samuel didn't love me,' I told Bran, my mouth tasting like sawdust. I don't know how he'd found out what Samuel had planned. 'You told me he needed a mate who could bear his children.'

Human women miscarry a little over half of the children they conceive by a werewolf father. They carry to term only those babies who are wholly human. Werewolf women miscarry at the first full moon. But coyotes and wolves can interbreed with viable offspring, so why not Samuel and me? Samuel believed that some of our children would be human, maybe some would be walkers like me, and some would be born werewolves – but they all would live.

It wasn't until Bran explained it all to me that I understood the antagonism Leah had toward me, an antagonism that all the other females had adopted.

'I should not have told you that way,' Bran said.

'Are you trying to apologize?' I asked. I couldn't understand what Bran was trying to say. 'I was sixteen. Samuel may seem young, but he's been a full-grown adult as long as I can remember – so he's what, fifty? Sixty?'

I hadn't worried about it when I had loved him. He'd never acted any older than I. Werewolves didn't usually talk about the past, not the way humans do. Most of what I knew about Bran's history, I picked up from my human foster mother, Evelyn.

'I was stupid and young,' I said. 'I needed to hear what

you told me. So if you're looking for forgiveness, you don't need it. Thank you.'

He cocked his head. In human form his eyes were warm hazel, like a sunlit oak leaf.

'I'm not apologizing,' he said. 'Not to you. I'm explaining.' Then he smiled, and the resemblance to Samuel, usually faint, was suddenly very apparent. 'And Samuel is a wee bit older than sixty.' Amusement, like anger, sometimes brought a touch of the old country – Wales – to Bran's voice. 'Samuel is my firstborn.'

I stared at him, caught by surprise. Samuel had none of the traits of the older wolves. He drove a car, had a stereo system and a computer. He actually liked people – even humans – and Bran used him to interface with police and government officials when it was necessary.

'Charles was born a few years after you came here with David Thompson,' I told Bran, as if he didn't know. 'That was what . . . 1812?' Driven by his association to Bran, I'd done a lot of reading about David Thompson in college. The Welsh-born mapmaker and fur trader had kept journals, but he hadn't ever mentioned Bran by name. I wondered when I read them if Bran had gone by another name, or if Thompson had known what Bran was and left him out of the journals, which were kept, for the most part, more as a record for his employers than as a personal reminiscence.

'I came with Thompson in 1809,' Bran said. 'Charles was born in the spring of, I think, 1813. I'd left Thompson and the Northwest Company by then, and the Salish didn't reckon time by the Christian calendar. Samuel was born to my first wife, when I was still human.'

It was the most I'd ever heard him say about the past. 'When was that?' I asked, emboldened by his uncustomary openness.

'A long time ago.' He dismissed it with a shrug. 'When

I talked to you that night, I did my son a disservice. I have decided that perhaps I was overzealous with the truth and still only gave you part of it.'

'Oh?'

'I told you what I knew, as much as I thought necessary at the time,' he said. 'But in light of subsequent events, I underestimated my son and led you to do the same.'

I've always hated it when he chose to become obscure. I started to object sharply – then realized he was looking away from my face, his eyes lowered. I'd gotten used to living among humans, whose body language is less important to communication, so I'd almost missed it. Alphas – especially this Alpha – never looked away when others were watching them. It was a mark of how bad he felt that he would do it now.

So I kept my voice quiet, and said simply, 'Tell me now.'

'Samuel is old,' he said. 'Nearly as old as I am. His first wife died of cholera, his second of old age. His third wife died in childbirth. His wives miscarried eighteen children between them; a handful died in infancy, and only eight lived to their third birthday. One died of old age, four of the plague, three of failing the Change. He has no living children and only one, born before Samuel Changed, made it into adulthood.'

He paused and lifted his eyes to mine. 'This perhaps gives you an idea of how much it meant to him that in you he'd found a mate who could give him children less vulnerable to the whims of fate, children who could be born werewolves like Charles was. I have had a long time to think about our talk, and I came to understand that I should have told you this as well. You aren't the only one who has mistaken Samuel for a young wolf.' He gave me a little smile. 'In the days Samuel walked as human, it was not uncommon for a sixteen-year-old to marry a man much older than she. Sometimes the world shifts its ideas of right and wrong too fast for us to keep up with it.'

Would it have changed how I felt to know the extent of Samuel's need? A passionate, love-starved teenager confronted with cold facts? Would I have seen beyond the numbers to the pain that each of those deaths had cost?

I don't think it would have changed my decision. I knew that because I still wouldn't have married someone who didn't love me; but I think I would have thought more kindly of him. I would have left him a letter or called him after I reached my mother's house. Perhaps I'd even have gathered the courage to talk to him if I hadn't been so hurt and angry.

I refused to examine how Bran's words changed my feelings about Samuel now. It wouldn't matter anyway. I was going home tomorrow.

'There were also some things I didn't know to tell you.' Bran smiled, but it wasn't a happy smile. 'I sometimes believe my own press, you know. I forget that I don't know everything. Two months after you left, Samuel disappeared.'

'He was angry at your interference?'

Bran shook his head. 'At first, maybe. But we talked that out the day you left. He would have been more angry if he hadn't felt guilty about taking advantage of a child's need.' He reached out and patted my hand. 'He knew what he was doing, and he knew what you would have felt about it, whatever he tells himself or you. Don't make him out to be the victim.'

Not a problem. 'I won't. So if he wasn't angry with you, why did he leave?'

'I know you understand most of what we are because you were raised among us,' Bran told me slowly. 'But sometimes even I miss the larger implications. Samuel saw in you the answer to his pain, and not the answer to his heart. But that wasn't all Samuel felt for you – I doubt he knew it himself.'

'What do you mean?' I asked.

'He pined when you left,' Bran said, the old-fashioned wording sounding odd coming from the young man he looked to be. 'He lost weight, he couldn't sleep. After the first month he spent most of his time as a wolf.'

'What *do* you think was wrong with him?' I asked carefully.

'He was grieving over his lost mate,' said Bran. 'Werewolves aren't that different from our wild cousins in some respects. It took me too long to figure it out, though. Before I did, he left us without a word. For two years, I waited for the newspapers to report his body discovered in the river like Bryan's had been. Charles tracked Samuel down when he finally started to use the money in his bank account. He'd bought some papers and gone back to college.' Samuel had been through college at least once before that I knew of, for medicine. 'He became a medical doctor again, set up a clinic in Texas for a while, then came back to us about two years ago.'

'He didn't love me,' I said. 'Not as a man loves a woman.'

'No,' agreed Bran. 'But he had chosen you as his mate.' He stood up abruptly and put on his coat. 'Don't worry about it now. I just thought you ought to know. Sleep in tomorrow.'

7

I ventured out to the gas station the next morning in my borrowed coat and bought a breakfast burrito. It was hot, if not tasty, and I was hungry enough to eat almost anything.

The young man working the till looked as though he'd have liked to ask questions, but I cowed him with my stare. People around here know better than to get into staring contests. I wasn't a were-anything, but he didn't know that because he wasn't either. It wasn't nice to intimidate him, but I wasn't feeling very nice.

I needed to do something, *anything*, and I was stuck waiting here all morning. Waiting meant worrying about what Jesse was suffering at the hands of her captors and thinking of Mac and wondering what I could have done to prevent his death. It meant reliving the old humiliation of having Bran tell me the man I loved was using me. I wanted to be out of Aspen Creek, where the memories of being sixteen and alone tried to cling no matter how hard I flinched away; but obedience to Bran was too ingrained – especially when his orders made sense. I didn't have to be nice about it, though.

I'd started back to the motel, my breath raising a fog and the snow crunching beneath my shoes, when someone called out my name.

'Mercy!'

I looked across the highway where a green truck had pulled over – evidently at the sight of me, but the driver didn't look familiar. The bright morning sun glittering on the snow made it hard to pick out details, so I shaded my eyes with my hand and veered toward him for a better look.

As soon as I changed directions, the driver turned off the truck, hopped out, and jogged across the highway.

'I just heard that you were here,' he said, 'but I thought you'd be long gone this morning or else I'd have stopped in earlier.'

The voice was definitely familiar, but it didn't go with the curling red hair and unlined face. He looked puzzled for a moment, even hurt, when I didn't recognize him immediately. Then he laughed and shook his head. 'I forgot, even though every time I look in a mirror it still feels like I'm looking at a stranger.'

The eyes, pale blue and soft, went with the voice, but it was his laugh that finally clued me in. 'Dr Wallace?' I asked. 'Is that really you?'

He tucked his hands in his pockets, tilted his head, and gave me a wicked grin. 'Sure as moonlight, Mercedes Thompson, sure as moonlight.'

Carter Wallace was the Aspen Creek veterinarian. No, he didn't usually treat the werewolves, but there were dogs, cats, and livestock enough to keep him busy. His house had been the nearest to the one I grew up in, and he'd helped me make it through those first few months after my foster parents died.

The Dr Wallace I'd known growing up had been middle-aged and balding, with a belly that covered his belt buckle. His face and hands had had been weathered from years spent outside in the sun. This man was lean and hungry; his skin pale and perfect like that of a twenty-year-old – but the greatest difference was not in his appearance.

The Carter Wallace I'd known was slow-moving and gentle. I'd seen him coax a skunk out of a pile of tires without it spraying everything, and keep a frightened horse still with his voice while he clipped away the barbed wire it had become tangled in. There had been something peaceful about him, solid and true like an oak.

Not anymore. His eyes were still bright and kind, but there was also something predatory that peered out at me. The promise of violence clung to him until I could almost smell the blood.

'How long have you been wolf?' I asked.

'A year last month,' he said. 'I know, I know, I swore I'd never do it. I knew too much about the wolves and not enough. But I had to retire year before last because my hands quit working right.' He looked down, a little anxiously, at his hands and relaxed a bit as he showed me he could move all his fingers easily. 'I was all right with that. If there is anything a vet gets used to – especially around here – it is aging and death. Gerry started in on me again, but I'm stubborn. It took more than a little arthritis and Gerry to make me change my mind.' Gerry was his son and a werewolf.

'What happened?' I asked.

'Bone cancer.' Dr Wallace shook his head. 'It was too far gone, they said. Nothing but months in a bed hoping you die before the morphine quits working on the pain. Everyone has their price, and that was more than I could bear. So I asked Bran.'

'Most people don't survive the Change if they're already too sick,' I said.

'Bran says I'm too stubborn to die.' He grinned at me again, and the expression was beginning to bother me because it had an edge that Dr Wallace's, *my* Dr Wallace's, had never had. I'd forgotten how odd it was to know someone from both sides of the Change, forgotten just how much the wolf alters the human personality. Especially when the human wasn't in control.

'I thought I'd be practicing again by now,' Dr Wallace

said. 'But Bran says not yet.' He rocked a little on his heels and closed his eyes as if he could see something I didn't. 'It's the smell of blood and meat. I'm all right as long as nothing is bleeding.' He whispered the last sentence and I heard the desire in his voice.

He gathered himself together with a deep breath, then looked at me with eyes only a shade darker than the snow. 'You know, for years I've said that werewolves aren't much different from other wild predators.' Like the great white, he'd told me, or the grizzly bear.

'I remember,' I said.

'Grizzly bears don't attack their families, Mercy. They don't crave violence and blood.' He closed his eyes. 'I almost killed my daughter a few days ago because she said something I disagreed with. If Bran hadn't stopped by . . .' He shook his head. 'I've become a monster, not an animal. I'll never be able to be a vet again. My family never will be safe, not while I'm alive.'

The last two words echoed between us.

Damn, damn, and damn some more, I thought. He should have had more control by now. If he'd been a wolf for a full year and still couldn't control himself when he was angry, he'd never have the control he needed to survive. Wolves who can't control themselves are eliminated for the safety of the pack. The only question, really, was why Bran hadn't already taken care of it – but I knew the answer to that. Dr Wallace had been one of the few humans Bran considered a friend.

'I wish Gerry could make it back for Thanksgiving,' Dr Wallace told me. 'But I'm glad I got a chance to see you before you left again.'

'Why isn't Gerry here?' I asked. Gerry had always traveled on business for Bran, but surely he could come back to see his father before . . .

Dr Wallace brushed his hand over my cheek, and I realized I was crying.

'He's on business. He's in charge of keeping an eye on the lone wolves who live where there is no pack to watch them. It's important.'

It was. But since Dr Wallace was going to die soon, Gerry should be here.

'Livin's easier than dyin' most times, Mercy girl,' he said kindly, repeating my foster father's favorite saying. 'Dance when the moon sings, and don't cry about troubles that haven't yet come.'

His smile softened, and for a minute I could see the man he used to be quite clearly. 'It's cold out here, Mercy, and that coat isn't helping you much. Go get warm, girl.'

I didn't know how to say good-bye, so I didn't. I just turned and walked away.

When the clock in the motel room ticked over to noon, I walked out to the van, which Charles – or Carl – had parked just outside the door to number one. *If Adam isn't ready to go, he'll just have to find another ride. I can't stand another minute here.*

I opened the back to check my antifreeze because the van had a small leak I hadn't fixed yet. When I shut the back hatch, Samuel was just there, holding a bulging canvas bag.

'What are you doing?' I asked warily.

'Didn't my father tell you?' He gave me the lazy grin that had always had the power to make my heart beat faster. I was dismayed to see that it still worked. 'He's sending me with you. Someone's got to take care of the rogues who attacked Adam, and he's barely mobile.'

I turned on my heel, but stopped because I had no idea where to find Bran. And because Samuel was right, damn him. We needed help.

Happily, before I had to come up with something suitable to say in apology for my too-obvious dismay, the door to room one opened.

Adam looked as though he'd lost twenty pounds in the last twenty-four hours. He was wearing borrowed sweat-pants and an unzipped jacket over the bare skin of his chest. Most of the visible skin was bruised, mottled technicolor with purple, blue, and black touched with lighter spots of red, but there were no open wounds. Adam was always meticulous in his dress and grooming, but his cheeks were dark with stubble, and his hair was uncombed. He limped slowly onto the sidewalk and kept a tight grip on a cane.

I hadn't expected him to be walking this soon, and my surprise must have shown on my face because he smiled faintly.

'Motivation aids healing,' he said. 'I need to find Jesse.'

'Motivation aids stupidity,' muttered Samuel beside me, and Adam's smile widened, though it wasn't a happy smile anymore.

'I have to find Jesse,' was all that Adam said in reply to Samuel's obvious disapproval. 'Mercy, if you hadn't arrived when you did, I'd have been a dead man. Thank you.'

I hadn't figured out yet exactly what our relationship was, and knowing that Bran had told him to look after me hadn't helped. Even so, I couldn't resist the urge to tease him – he took life so seriously.

'Always happy to come to your rescue,' I told him lightly, and was pleased at the temper that flashed in his eyes before he laughed.

He had to stop moving and catch his breath. 'Damn it,' he told me, with his eyes shut. 'Don't make me do that.'

Samuel had stepped unobtrusively closer, but relaxed when Adam resumed his forward progress without toppling over. I opened the sliding door behind the passenger seat.

'Do you want to lie down?' I asked him. 'Or would you rather sit up on the bench seat? Sitting shotgun is out – you need something easier to get in and out of.'

'I'll sit up,' Adam grunted. 'Ribs still aren't happy about lying down.'

When he got close to the van, I backed out of the way and let Samuel help him up.

'Mercy,' said Bran behind my shoulder, surprising me because I'd been paying attention to the expression on Adam's face.

He was carrying a couple of blankets.

'I meant to get here sooner to tell you that Samuel was coming with you,' Bran said, handing the blankets to me. 'But I had business that took a little longer than I expected.'

'Did you know that you were sending him with me when you talked to me last night?' I asked.

He smiled. 'I thought it was probable, yes. Though I had another talk with Adam after I left you, and it clarified some things. I'm sending Charles to Chicago with a couple of wolves for backup.' He smiled wider, a nasty predatory smile. 'He will find out who is out trying to create new wolves without permission and see that it is stopped in such a way that we'll not see a problem like this again.'

'Why not send Samuel and give me Charles?'

'Samuel has too weak a stomach to handle Chicago,' said Adam, sounding breathless. I glanced at him and saw that he was sitting upright on the short middle bench seat, a sheen of sweat on his forehead.

'*Samuel* is a doctor and dominant enough to keep Adam from eating anyone until he gets better,' responded Samuel, climbing back out of the van and snatching the blankets out of my hands.

Bran's smile softened with amusement. 'Samuel was gone for a long time,' he explained. 'Other than Adam, I think that only Darryl, Adam's second, has ever met him. Until we know what is going on, I'd rather not have everyone know I'm investigating matters.'

'We think the time is coming when we will no longer be able to hide from the humans,' said Samuel, who had finished wrapping Adam in the blankets. 'But we'd rather control how that happens than have a group of murdering wolves reveal our existence before we're ready.'

I must have looked shocked because Bran laughed.

'It's only a matter of time,' he said. 'The fae are right. Forensics, satellite surveillance, and digital cameras are making the keeping of our secrets difficult. No matter how many Irish Wolfhounds and English Mastiffs George Brown breeds and crossbreeds, they don't look like werewolves.'

Aspen Creek had three or four people breeding very large dogs to explain away odd tracks and sightings – George Brown, a werewolf himself, had won several national titles with his Mastiffs. Dogs, unlike most cats, tended to like werewolves just fine.

'Are you looking for a poster boy like Kieran McBride?' I asked.

'Nope,' Adam grunted. 'There aren't any Kieran McBrides who make it as werewolves. Harmless and cute we are not. But he might be able to find a hero: a police officer or someone in the military.'

'You knew about this?' I asked.

'I'd heard rumors.'

'What we don't need right now is a murdering bastard running free around the Tri-Cities, using werewolves to kill people,' Bran said. He looked over my shoulder at his son. 'Find the blackguard and eliminate him before he involves the humans, Samuel.' Bran was the only person I knew who could use words like 'blackguard' and make them sound like swear words – but then he could have said 'bunny rabbit' in that tone of voice and weakened my spine with the same shiver of fear.

But I shivered more from the cold than fear. In the Tri-Cities it was still above freezing most days. It wasn't particularly cold for November in Montana – for instance, my nostrils weren't sticking together when I breathed, so it wasn't ten below zero yet – but it was considerably colder than I was used to.

'Where's your coat?' asked Bran, his attention drawn to my chattering teeth.

'I left it in the room,' I said. 'It's not mine.'

'You are welcome to it.'

'I'm out here now,' I said.

He shook his head. 'You'd better get going then, before you freeze to death.' He looked at Samuel. 'Keep me apprised.'

'Bran,' said Adam. 'Thank you.'

Bran smiled and brushed past me so he could reach in the van and take one of Adam's battered hands in a gentle grip. 'Anytime.'

When he stepped back he shut the sliding door with just the right amount of push so it didn't bounce back open. It had taken me three months to learn how to do it right.

He reached into the pocket of his coat and gave me a card. It was plain white with his name and two phone numbers in simple black lettering. 'So you can call me if you want to,' he said. 'The top number is my cell phone – so you won't have to risk talking to my wife.'

'Bran?' I asked him impulsively. 'What is it that Gerry is doing that is so important he can't come home to be with Dr Wallace?'

'Feeling sorry for himself,' snapped Samuel.

Bran put a hand on Samuel's arm, but spoke to me. 'Carter's case is tragic and unusual. Usually when a wolf lives through the Change but doesn't survive his first year, it is because the human cannot control the instincts of the wolf.'

'I thought it was always a matter of control,' I told Bran.

He nodded his head, 'It is. But in Carter's case it is not a lack of self-control, it is too much.'

'He doesn't want to be a werewolf,' said Samuel. 'He doesn't want to feel the fire of the killing instinct or the power of the chase.' For a moment the sun caught Samuel's eyes, and they glittered. 'He's a healer, not a taker of life.'

Ah, I thought, *that rankled, didn't it, Dr Samuel Cornick?* Samuel hadn't been given to in-depth talks – although that might have been as much a function of my age as his inclination – but, I remembered that he had trouble, sometimes, because his instinct to heal was not as strong as his instinct to kill. He told me that he always made certain to eat well before performing any kind of surgery. Did he think that Dr Wallace was the better man for choosing not to live with that conflict?

'Unless Carter allows the wolf to become part of him, he can't control it.' Bran's mouth turned down. 'He's dangerous, and he gets more dangerous every moon, Mercy. But all it would take was for him to compromise his damn hardheaded morals just once, so he can accept what he is and he'd be fine. But if it doesn't happen soon, it won't happen at all. I can't let him see another full moon.'

'Gerry's the one who talked him into Changing,' said Samuel, sounding tired. 'He knows that the time is coming when someone is going to have to deal with Carter. If he's here, it will be his duty – and he can't handle that.'

'I'll take care of it,' said Bran, taking a deep breath. 'I've done it before.' He moved the hand on Samuel's arm to his shoulder. 'Not everyone is as strong as you, my son.' There was a world of shared sorrow in his words and in his posture – and I remembered the three of Samuel's children who hadn't survived the Change.

'Get in the van, Mercy,' said Samuel. 'You're shivering.'

Bran put his hands on my shoulders and kissed me on the forehead, then ruined it by saying, 'Let the boys take care of this, eh, Mercedes?'

'Sure thing,' I said, stepping away from him. 'Take care, Bran.'

I stalked around the front of the bus. The only reason I wasn't muttering under my breath was because the werewolves would all hear what I was saying.

I started the van – it protested because of the cold, but not too much. I let it warm up while Bran said a few last words to Samuel.

'How well does Bran know you?' asked Adam quietly. The noise of the engine and the radio would most likely keep the others from hearing us.

'Not very well if he thinks that I'll leave things to you and Samuel,' I muttered.

'That's what I was hoping,' he said, with enough satisfaction that I jerked around to look at him. He smiled tiredly. 'Samuel's good, Mercy. But he doesn't know Jesse, doesn't care about her. I'm not going to be good for much for a while: I need you for Jesse's sake.'

The passenger door opened and Samuel pulled himself up into the seat and shut the door.

'Da means well,' Sam told me, as I started backing out, proving that he knew me better than his father did. 'He's used to dealing with people who listen when he tells them something. Mercy, he's right, though. You aren't up to dealing with werewolf business.'

'Seems to me that she's been dealing just fine,' Adam said mildly. 'She killed two of them in as many days and came out of it without a scratch.'

'Luck,' said Samuel.

'Is it?' In my rearview mirror, I saw Adam close his eyes

as he finished in almost a whisper. 'Maybe so. When I was in the army, we kept lucky soldiers where they would do us the most good.'

'Adam wants me to help find Jesse,' I told Samuel, putting my foot on the gas as we left Aspen Creek behind us.

The conversation went downhill from there. Adam dropped out after a few pointed comments, and sat back to enjoy the fireworks. I didn't remember arguing with Samuel much before, but I wasn't a love-struck sixteen-year-old anymore either.

After I pointedly quit talking to him, Samuel unbuckled his seat belt and slipped between the front seats to go back and sit next to Adam.

'Never argue with Mercy about something she cares about,' Adam advised, obviously having enjoyed himself hugely. 'Even if she stops arguing with you, she'll just do whatever she wants anyway.'

'Shut up and eat something,' growled Samuel, sounding not at all like his usual self. I heard him lift the lid on a small cooler and the sweet-iron smell of blood filled the van.

'Mmm,' said Adam without enthusiasm. 'Raw steak.'

But he ate it, then slept. After a while Samuel came back to the front and belted himself in.

'I don't remember you being so stubborn,' he said.

'Maybe I wasn't,' I agreed. 'Or maybe you didn't used to try to order me around. I'm not a member of your pack or Bran's pack. I'm not a werewolf. You have no right to dictate to me as if I were.'

He grunted, and we drove a while more in silence.

Finally, he said, 'Have you had lunch?'

I shook my head. 'I thought I'd stop in Sandpoint. It's grown since last time I drove through there.'

'Tourists,' said Samuel in disgust. 'Every year there are

more and more people.' I wondered if he was remembering what it had been like when he'd first been there.

We stopped and got enough fried chicken to feed a Little League team – or two werewolves, with a little left over for me. Adam ate again with restrained ferocity. Healing was energy-draining work, and he needed all the protein he could get.

When he was finished, and we were back on the road, with Samuel once again in the front, I finally asked, 'What happened the night you were attacked? I know you've told Bran and probably Samuel, too, already – but I'd like to know.'

Adam wiped his fingers carefully on the damp towelette that had come with our chicken – apparently he didn't think it was finger-lick'n good. 'I'd pulled the pack in to introduce Mac, and to tell them about your adventures with his captors.'

I nodded.

'About fifteen minutes after the last of them left, about three-thirty in the morning, someone knocked on the door. Mac had just managed to regain his human form, and he jumped up to answer the door.' There was a pause, and I adjusted the rearview mirror so I could see Adam's face, but I couldn't read his expression.

'I was in the kitchen, so I don't know exactly what happened, but from the sounds, I'd say they shot him as soon as he opened the door.'

'Which was stupid,' commented Samuel. 'They'd know you had to hear the shots – even a tranq gun makes a pretty good pop.'

Adam started to shrug – then stopped with a pained expression. 'Damned if – excuse me, Mercedes – I'll be darned if I know what they were thinking.'

'They didn't kill him on purpose, did they?' I said. I'd

been thinking, too. A gun with silver bullets is a much more certain thing than a dart full of experimental drugs.

'I don't think so,' Samuel agreed. 'It looked like a massive allergic reaction to the silver.'

'There was silver in the dart Mercedes found? Just like Charles thought?' asked Adam.

'Yes,' said Samuel. 'I've sent the dart off to the lab along with a sample of Mac's blood for proper analysis, but it looks to me as though they combined silver nitrate with DMSO and Special K.'

'What?' I asked.

'Special K is Ketamine,' Adam said. 'It's been used as a recreational drug for a while, but it started out as an animal tranquilizer. It doesn't work on werewolves. Silver nitrate is used to develop film. What's DMSO?'

'Silver nitrate is a convenient way to get silver in a solution,' Samuel said. 'It's used to treat eye infections, too – though I wouldn't recommend it for a werewolf.'

'I've never heard of a werewolf with an eye infection,' I said, though I understood his point.

He smiled at me, but continued to talk to Adam. 'DMSO – Dimeythyl Sulfoxide. It has a lot of odd properties, but the one of most interest here is that it can carry other drugs with it across membranes.'

I stared at the road ahead of me and put my right hand in front of the heater to warm it. The seals on my windows needed replacing, and the heater wasn't keeping up with the Montana air. Funny, I didn't remember being cold on the way over. No room for simple discomfort when you are trying to save someone, I guess.

'There was something in chem lab my freshman year,' I said. 'We mixed it with peppermint oil and put a finger in it – I could taste peppermint.'

'Right,' said Samuel. 'That's the stuff. So take DMSO and

mix it with a silver solution, and presto, the silver is carried throughout the werewolf's body, poisoning as it goes so that the tranquilizer, in this case, Ketamine, goes to work without interference from the werewolf metabolism that would normally prevent the drug from having any effect at all.'

'You think Mac died from the silver rather than an overdose of Ketamine?' asked Adam. 'They only shot him twice. I took at least four hits, maybe more.'

'The more recent exposure you have to silver, the worse the reaction,' said Samuel. 'I'd guess that if the boy hadn't spent the last few months in their tender care being dosed up with silver, he'd have made it just fine.'

'Obviously the silver nitrate and the Ketamine are relatively easily obtainable,' Adam said after a while. 'What about this DMSO?'

'I could get it. Good stuff is available by prescription – I'd bet you could buy it at any veterinary supply, too.'

'So they'd need a doctor?' I asked.

But Samuel shook his head. 'Not for the veterinary supply. And I'd expect you could get it fairly easily from a pharmacy, too. It's not one of the drugs they'd track carefully. I'd expect they could make as much of their cocktail as they wanted to without much trouble.'

'Great.' Adam closed his eyes, possibly envisioning an invading army armed with tranquilizer dart guns.

'So they killed Mac,' I said when it became apparent that Adam wasn't going to continue. 'Then what happened?'

'I came charging out of the kitchen like an idiot, and they darted me, too.' Adam shook his head. 'I've grown used to being damn near bulletproof – served me right. Whatever they gave me knocked me for a loop, and when I woke up, I was locked up, wrist and ankle in cuffs. Not that I was in any shape to do anything. I was so groggy I could barely move my head.'

'Did you see who they were?' I asked. 'I know one of them was the human who accompanied the werewolf I killed at the garage. I smelled him in Jesse's room.'

Adam shifted on the bench seat, pulling a little against the seat belt.

'Adam.' Samuel's voice was quiet but forceful.

Adam nodded and relaxed a little, stretching out his neck to release the build-up of tension. 'Thank you. It's harder when I'm angry. Yes, I knew one of them, Mercedes. Do you know how I became a werewolf?'

The question seemed to come from left field – but Adam always had a reason for everything he said. 'Only that it was during Vietnam,' I answered. 'You were Special Forces.'

'Right,' he agreed. 'Long-range recon. They sent me and five other men to take out a particularly nasty warlord – an assassination trip. We'd done it before.'

'The warlord was a werewolf?' I asked.

He laughed without humor. 'Slaughtered us. It was one of his own people who killed him, while he was eating poor old McCue.' He shut his eyes, and whispered, 'I can still hear him scream.'

We waited, Samuel and I, and after a moment Adam continued. 'All the warlord's people ran and left us alone. At a guess they weren't certain he was really dead, even after he'd been beheaded. After a while – a long while, though I didn't realize that until later – I found I could move. Everyone was dead except Spec 4 Christiansen and me. We leaned on each other and got out of there somehow, hurt badly enough that they sent us home: Christiansen was a short-timer, anyway, and I guess they thought I was mostly crazy – raving about wolves. They shipped us out of there fast enough that none of the docs commented about how quickly we were recovering.'

'Are you all right?' asked Samuel.

Adam shivered and pulled the blankets closer around himself. 'Sorry. I don't talk about this often. It's harder than I expected. Anyway, one of my army buddies who'd come back to the States a few months earlier heard I was home and came to see me. We got drunk – or at least I tried. I'd just started noticing that it took an awful lot of whiskey to do anything, but it loosened me up enough that I told him about the werewolf.

'Thank goodness I did because he believed me. He called in a relative and between them they persuaded me that I was going to grow furry and kill something the next full moon. They pulled me into their pack and kept everyone safe until I had enough control to do it myself.'

'And the other man who was wounded?' I asked.

'Christiansen?' He nodded. 'My friends found him. It should have been in time, but he'd come home to find that his wife had taken up with another man. He walked into his house and found his bags packed and his wife and her lover waiting with the divorce papers.'

'What happened?' asked Samuel.

'He tore them to pieces.' His eyes met mine in the rearview mirror. 'Even in that first month, if you get angry enough, it is possible to Change.'

'I know,' I told him.

He gave me a jerky nod. 'Anyway, they managed to persuade him to stay with a pack, who taught him what he needed to know to survive. But as far as I know he never did join a pack officially – he's lived all these years as a lone wolf.'

A lone wolf is a male who either declines to join a pack or cannot find a pack who will take him in. The females, I might add, are not allowed that option. Werewolves have not yet joined the twentieth century, let alone the twenty-first, as far as women are concerned. It's a good thing I'm not a werewolf – or maybe it is a pity. Someone needs to wake them up.

'Christiansen was one of the wolves who came to your house?' I asked.

He nodded. 'I didn't hear him or see him – he stayed away from me – but I could smell him. There were several humans and three or four wolves.'

'You killed two,' I told him. 'I killed a third.' I tried to remember what I'd smelled in his house, but I had only been tracking Jesse. There had been so many of Adam's pack in the house, and I only knew some of them by name. 'I'd know the man, the human, who confronted Mac and me earlier that night, but no one else for certain.'

'I'm pretty sure they intended I stay out until they'd done whatever they came for, but their whole plan was a botch job,' Adam said. 'First, they killed Mac. Obviously, from their attempt to take him at your shop, they wanted him, but I don't think they meant to kill him in my house.'

'They left him on my doorstep,' I said.

'Did they?' Adam frowned. 'A warning?' I could see him roll the thought around and he came up with the same message I had. 'Stay out of our business, and you won't end up dead.'

'Quick thinking for the disposal of a body they didn't know they were going to have,' I commented. 'Someone drove to my house to dump his body and was gone when I came outside. They left some people at your house who took off hell-bent-for-leather, probably with Jesse. I made it to your house in time to kill the last werewolf you were fighting.' I tried to think about what time that was. 'Four-thirty in the morning or thereabouts, is my best guess.'

Adam rubbed his forehead.

Samuel said, 'So they shot Mac, shot Adam, then waited around until Mac died. They dropped the body at your house

– then Adam woke up, and they grabbed Jesse and ran, leaving three werewolves behind to do something – kill Adam? But then why take Jesse? Presumably they weren't supposed to just die.'

'The first wolf I fought was really new,' I said slowly. 'If they were all that way, they might have just gotten carried away, and the others fled because they couldn't calm them down.'

'Christiansen isn't new,' said Adam.

'One of the wolves was a woman,' I told him. 'The one I killed was a buff color – almost like Leah but darker. The other was a more standard color, grays and white. I don't remember any markings.'

'Christiansen is red-gold,' Adam said.

'So did they come to kidnap Jesse in the first place or was her kidnapping the result of someone trying to make the best of a screwup?'

'Jesse.' Adam sounded hoarse, and when I glanced back at him I could see that he hadn't heard Samuel's question. 'I woke up because Jesse screamed. I remember now.'

'I found a pair of broken handcuffs on the floor of your living room.' I slowed the van so I didn't tailgate an RV that was creeping up the side of the mountain we were climbing. I didn't have to slow down much. 'Silver wrist cuffs – and the floor was littered with glass, dead werewolves, and furniture. I expect the ankle cuffs were around there somewhere.' I thought of something. 'Maybe they just came to get Mac and maybe punish Adam for taking him in?'

Samuel shook his head. 'Mercy, *you* they might leave warnings for – or try to teach a lesson. A pack of newbie werewolves – especially if they're headed by an experienced wolf – is not going to tick off an Alpha just to "punish" him for interfering in their business. In the first place, there's no better way I can think of to get the Marrok ticked off. In the second place there's Adam himself. He's not just the Columbia Basin Alpha, he's damn near the strongest Alpha in the US, present company excluded, of course.'

Adam grunted, unimpressed with Samuel's assessment. 'We don't have enough information to make an educated guess at what they wanted. Mac's dead, either accidentally or on purpose. They half killed me, and they took Jesse. The human you knew implies that it has something to do with Mac's story – and Christiansen's presence implies it has something to do with me. I'll be darned if I know what Mac and I have in common.'

'Mercy,' said Samuel.

'I forgot to tell you that I joined the secret society of villains while I was away,' I told Samuel, exasperated. 'I am now trying to put together a harem of studly, musclebound werewolves. *Please*. Remember, I didn't know Mac until he dropped in my lap sometime *after* the villains screwed up his life.'

Samuel, having successfully baited me, reached over and patted my leg.

I just happened to glance at Adam's face, and I saw his eyes lighten from chocolate to amber as his gaze narrowed on Samuel's hand before I had to return my eyes to the road to make sure the RV ahead of me hadn't slowed down again. There were four cars trailing slowly behind us up the mountain.

'Don't touch her,' whispered Adam. There was a shadow of threat in his voice, and he must have heard it, too, because he added, 'Please.'

The last word stopped the nasty comment I'd readied because I remembered that Adam was still hurt, still struggling to control his wolf, and the conversation we'd been having hadn't been designed to calm him.

But it wasn't my temper I should have been worried about.

Samuel's hand turned until his fingers spanned the top of my thigh, and he squeezed. It wasn't hard enough to hurt. I'm not certain Adam would have even noticed except that Samuel accompanied it by a throaty half growl of challenge.

I didn't wait to see what Adam would do. I yanked the wheel to the right and slammed on the brakes as soon as the van was on the shoulder of the road. I unsnapped my seat belt and twisted around to meet Adam's yellow gaze. He was breathing heavily, his reaction to Samuel's taunt tempered by the pain my jerky driving had caused.

'You,' I said firmly, pointing at him. 'Stay right there.' Sometimes, if you tell them firmly enough, even Alphas will listen to commands, Especially if you tell them to sit still while they're too hurt to move.

'You' – I turned my attention to Samuel – 'outside, right now.'

Then I jerked my leg out from under Samuel's hand and jumped out of the van, narrowly avoiding getting the door taken off as a truck passed by.

I wasn't certain either of them would listen to me, but at least I wouldn't have to try to drive with a pair of wolves trying to tear each other apart. However, Samuel opened his door as I stalked around the front of the van. By the time I walked a half dozen steps away from the van, he was beside me, and the van's doors were closed.

'Just what did you think you were doing?' I yelled at him, raising my voice over the passing cars. Okay, I was mad, too. 'I thought you were here to make sure no one challenged Adam until he was well – not challenge him yourself.'

'You don't belong to him,' he snapped back, his white teeth clicking together sharply.

'Of course not!' I huffed in exasperation – and a little in

desperation. 'But I don't belong to *you* either! For Pete's sake, Sam, he wasn't telling you that I belonged to him – just that he felt like you were invading his territory. He was asking you for help.' Someone should have awarded me a Ph.D. in werewolf psychology and counseling – surely I deserved something for putting up with this garbage. 'It wasn't a challenge, stupid. He's trying to control his wolf after nearly being killed. Two unmated male werewolves always get territorial in the presence of a female – you know that better than I do. You're supposed to be the one with all this control, and you're behaving worse than he is.' I sucked in air tainted by the traffic.

Samuel paused, then settled his weight on his heels – a sign that he was considering backing off from this fight. 'You called me Sam,' he said in an odd voice that frightened me as much as the violence I could still smell on him, because I didn't know what was causing him to act like this. The Samuel I knew had been easygoing – especially for a were-wolf. I was beginning to think that I wasn't the only one who'd changed over the years.

I didn't know how to respond to his comment. I couldn't see what my calling him Sam had to do with anything, so I ignored it. 'How can you help him control himself if your control isn't better than this? What is wrong with you?' I was honestly bewildered.

Samuel was good at calming the dangerous waters. One of his jobs had been teaching the new wolves control so they could be allowed to live. It is not an accident that most were-wolves are control freaks like Adam. I didn't know what to do with Samuel – except that he wasn't getting back into that van until he had a handle on whatever was bothering him.

'It isn't just that you are female,' he muttered at last, though I almost didn't hear him because two motorcycles blew past us.

'What is it then?' I asked.

He gave me an unhappy look, and I realized that he hadn't intended for me to hear what he'd said.

'Mercedes . . . Mercy.' He looked away from me, staring down the slope of the mountain as if the meadows below held some secret he was looking for. 'I'm as unsettled as a new pup. *You* eat my control.'

'This is all *my* fault?' I asked incredulously. It was outside of enough that he was scaring the bejeebers out of me – I certainly wasn't about to accept the blame for it.

Unexpectedly, he laughed. And as easily as that the smoldering anger, the bright violence, and the dominant power that had been making the air around us feel heavier than it could possibly be floated away. It was just the two of us and the warm scent of Samuel, who smelled of home and the woods.

'Stay out here and enjoy the diesel fumes, Mercy,' he said as a delivery van in need of a new engine chugged past us in a cloud of black smoke. 'Give me a few minutes to clear the air with Adam before you come back in.' He turned and took two steps back to the van. 'I'll wave to you.'

'No violence?' I said.

He put his hand over his heart and bowed. 'I swear.'

It took long enough that I got worried, but finally he opened the door and called me over. He hadn't rolled down the window because I had the keys and the windows were electric. For some reason I still hadn't tracked down, the windows only worked one at a time even with the car running.

I scooted in the driver's seat and gave Adam a cautious look – but his eyes were closed.

8

As soon as 'roaming' quit appearing on my phone, I called Zee.

'Who's this?' he answered.

'Mercy,' I told him.

'Didn't tell me the part was for the *vampire's* bus,' he said shortly.

I rubbed my face. 'I couldn't afford to pay them the percentage you were,' I explained, not for the first time.

In the Columbia Basin, which included Richland, Kennewick, and Pasco as well as the smaller surrounding towns like Burbank and West Richland, every business the vampires considered under their jurisdiction (meaning anyone touched by the supernatural who was too powerless to stand against them) paid them protection money. And yes, just like the mob, the vampires only protect you from themselves.

'They agreed I could repair their cars instead – and they pay me for parts. That way they save face, and I only have to repair Stefan's bus and an occasional Mercedes or BMW. Stefan's not bad for a vampire.'

There was a growl from the seat beside me.

'It's okay,' Adam told Samuel. 'We keep an eye on her. And she's right, Stefan's not bad for a vampire. Word is that he runs a little interference so she's not bothered.'

I hadn't known any of the vampires had *intended* to bother me – or that Stefan would care enough to stop them.

'I didn't know that,' said Zee, who'd obviously overheard Adam's comment. He hesitated. 'Vampires are bad news,

Mercy. The less you have to do with them the better – and writing a check and mailing it every month is safer than dealing with them face-to-face.'

'I can't afford it,' I told him again. 'I'm still paying the bank and will be until I'm as old as you are.'

'Well, it doesn't matter,' he said at last. 'I didn't have to deal with him, anyway. Your new supply house sent the wrong part. I sent it back to them and called with a word to their sales manager. The right part should be here on Friday – best he could do with Thanksgiving tomorrow. I called the number on the vampire's file and left a message. What kind of vampire plays the Scooby Doo song on his answering machine?' It was a rhetorical question, because he continued. 'And a woman came by and said your *Politzei* friend had sent her.'

I rubbed my forehead. I'd forgotten about Tony's girl. 'Did you figure out what's wrong with her car?'

'Mercy!' he snapped, insulted.

'No insult meant. Was it something worth fixing?'

'Wiring harness is bad,' he said. 'Mercy . . .'

I grinned because I'd seen the effect this woman had on 'I'm married to my job' Tony. 'You like her,' I told him.

Zee grunted.

'Did you give her a quote?'

'Haven't talked to her yet,' he said. 'She's got poor and proud written all over her. She wouldn't let me give her a lift, so she and her kids walked home. She doesn't have a phone number except a work phone.'

I laughed to myself. There was more than one reason that Zee didn't have the kind of money the older fae generally amass. Well, I'm probably never going to be rich either.

'Okay,' I said. 'What kind of deal are we talking about?'

'I called the *Politzei*,' Zee said. He knew what Tony's name was; he even liked him, though he did his best to hide it.

He just disapproved of letting the human authorities get too close. He was right, too – but I don't always follow the rules of wisdom. If I did, I wouldn't be hauling two werewolves in my van.

'What did he say?' I asked.

'He said that she has an older boy who's been looking for work after school.'

I let him say it; it was just too fun to listen to him squirm. He liked to play the gruff, nasty old man – but he had a marshmallow heart.

'With my Tad gone, you're short a pair of hands.'

And with Mac dead. I lost interest in teasing the old gremlin.

'It's fine, Zee. If you talk to her, you can tell her that her son can work off the bill. If he works out, I'll offer him Tad's job. I assume you've already fixed the car?'

'*Ja,*' he said. 'You'll have to talk to the lady yourself, though, unless you need me tomorrow, too. She works day shift.'

'No, I won't need you. Tomorrow is Thanksgiving. I'll leave the shop closed – if you would remember to put up a sign in the window.'

'No problem.' He hesitated. 'I might have a lead for you on Jesse. I was just getting ready to call you. One of the fae who is still in hiding told me she might be able to help, but she wouldn't tell me without talking to you.'

'Still in hiding' meant either that the Gray Lords hadn't noticed her yet, or that she was of the terrible or powerful sort.

This time it was Adam who growled. Such are the joys of trying to have a private phone call in the presence of werewolves. Somehow it didn't bother me so much when I was the eavesdropper.

'We're about an hour out of town,' I said. 'Could you set up a meeting tonight at a place of her choice?'

'All right,' he said, and hung up.

'You caught all of that?' I asked them.

'Adam can't go,' Samuel said firmly. 'No, Adam, you know it yourself.'

Adam sighed. 'All right. I even agree I'm not fit to be on my own – but I want Mercy there. We can call Darryl and—'

Samuel held up a hand. 'Mercy,' he said, 'what caused you to bring Adam all the way to Montana rather than calling on his pack for help?'

'It was stupid,' I said.

'Maybe, but tell us anyway.'

'I was trying to get in touch with Darryl, and I suddenly felt uneasy. I remembered a snippet of conversation between Ben and Darryl earlier that night, but in retrospect it wasn't much.'

'What were Ben and Darryl doing talking to you?' asked Adam in that mild voice he used to cozen people into thinking he wasn't angry.

'I can take care of myself, Adam,' I told him. 'I was taking the trash out and ran into them. All Darryl did was tell Ben to leave me alone. He said, "Not now." I don't know why I decided it meant he knew that something was going to happen.'

'First you felt uneasy,' said Samuel. 'Then you came up with this stupid reason.'

'Yes.' I felt my face flush.

'How do you feel about his pack now?'

I opened my mouth, then shut it again. 'Damn it. Something's wrong. I don't think Adam should go to the pack until he can defend himself.'

Samuel settled back with a small, smug smile.

'What?' I asked.

'You noticed something,' Adam said. 'A scent or something

135

at my house that makes you think someone from my pack is involved. Instincts.' He sounded grim. 'I thought it was odd that they came so soon after my wolves left.'

I shook my head. 'Look, I don't know anything.'

'We're not going to kill anyone,' said Samuel. 'Not on the basis of your instincts, anyway – but what's the harm in being careful? Call your friend back. We'll see to his information tomorrow, when Adam has enough control to be on his own.'

'No,' said Adam.

'Damned if I will.' It felt odd not to be arguing with Adam. 'The faster we find Jesse, the better.'

'I can't be in two places at once,' Samuel said. 'And I won't allow you to go out on your own and talk to who knows what kind of fae.'

'We need to find Jesse,' I said.

'My daughter comes first.'

Samuel twisted around to look at Adam. 'You have a dominant wolf in your pack that you trust? Someone not in line to be pack leader?'

'Warren.' Adam and I said his name in the same instant.

Warren was my favorite of Adam's pack, and the only wolf whose company I sought out. I met him shortly after I moved to the Tri-Cities, before I even knew there was a pack in town.

I hadn't met a werewolf since I'd left Montana, and I certainly hadn't expected to meet one working the night shift at the local Stop and Rob. He'd given me a wary look, but there were other people in the store, so he accepted my payment without a word. I accepted my change with a nod and a smile.

After that we'd mostly ignored each other, until the night a woman with a fresh shiner came into the store to pay for the gas her husband was pumping. She gave Warren the money, then took a firmer grip on the hand of the boy at her side, and asked Warren if he had a back door she could use.

He smiled gently at her and shepherded the two frightened people into a small office I'd never noticed before at the back of the store. He left me to watch the till and went out and had a short talk with the man at the pump. When he came back, he had two hundred dollars cash for her, and her husband drove away with a speed indicating either terror or rage.

Warren and I waited with the battered pair until the lady who ran the local women's shelter drove over to collect her newest clients. When they left, I turned to him and finally introduced myself.

Warren was one of the good guys, a hero. He was also a lone wolf. It had taken him a while to trust me enough to tell me why.

Perhaps in other ages, in other places, it wouldn't have mattered that he was gay. But most of the werewolves in power in the US had been born in a time when homosexuality was anathema, even punishable by death in some places.

One of my professors once told me that the last official act of the British monarchy was when Queen Victoria refused to sign a law that made same-sex acts illegal. It would have made me think more highly of her, except the reason she objected was because she didn't believe women would do anything like that. Parliament rewrote the law so it was specific to men, and she signed it. A tribute to enlightenment, Queen Victoria was not. Neither, as I have observed before, are werewolf packs.

There was no question of Warren's staying in the closet, either, at least not among other werewolves. As demonstrated by Adam and Samuel just a few hours ago, werewolves are very good at sensing arousal. Not just smells, but elevated temperature and increased heart rate. Arousal in werewolves tends to bring out the fighting instinct in all the nearby males.

Needless to say, a male wolf who is attracted to other male wolves gets in a lot of fights. It spoke volumes about Warren's fighting ability that he survived as long as he had. But a pack won't accept a wolf who causes too much trouble, so he'd spent his century of life cut off from his kind.

It was I who introduced Adam and Warren, about the time Adam moved in behind me. I'd had Warren to dinner and we'd been laughing about something, I forget what, and one of Adam's wolves howled. I'll never forget the desolation on Warren's face.

I'd heard it all the time when I was growing up – wolves are meant to run in a pack. I still don't understand it completely myself, but Warren's face taught me that being alone was no trivial thing for a wolf.

The next morning, I'd knocked on Adam's front door. He listened to me politely and took the piece of paper with Warren's phone number on it. I'd left his house knowing I'd failed.

It was Warren who told me what happened next. Adam summoned Warren to his house and interrogated him for two hours. At the end of it, Adam told Warren he didn't care if a wolf wanted to screw ducks as long as he'd listen to orders. Not actually in those words, if Warren's grin as he told me about it was an accurate measure. Adam uses crudeness as he uses all of his weapons: seldom, but with great effect.

I suppose some people might think it odd that Warren is Adam's best friend, though Darryl is higher-ranking. But they are heroes, both of them, two peas in a pod – well, except Adam isn't gay.

The rest of the pack weren't all happy when Warren came in. It helped a little that most of Adam's wolves are even younger than he, and the last few decades have seen a vast improvement over the rigid Victorian era. Then, too, none of the pack wanted to take on Adam. Or Warren.

Warren didn't care what the rest of the wolves thought, just that he had a pack, a place to belong. If Warren needed friends, he had me and he had Adam. It was enough for him.

Warren would never betray Adam. Without Adam, he would no longer have a pack.

'I'll give him a call,' I said with relief.

He picked up on the second ring, 'Warren, here. Is this you, Mercy? Where have you been? Do you know where Adam and Jesse are?'

'Adam was hurt,' I said. 'The people who did it took Jesse.'

'Tell him not to let anyone else know,' said Samuel.

'Who was that?' Warren's tone was suddenly cool.

'Samuel,' I told him. 'Bran's son.'

'Is this a coup?' Warren asked.

'No,' answered Adam from the backseat. 'At least not on Bran's part.'

'Excuse me,' I said. 'But this is *my* phone call. Would you all *please* pretend that it is a private conversation? That includes you, Warren. Quit listening to the other people in my van.'

'All right,' agreed Warren. Having heard Adam, his voice relaxed into its usual lovely south Texas drawl. 'How are you today, Mercy?' he asked sweetly, but as he continued his voice became gradually sharper. 'And have you heard the startling news that our Alpha's house was broken into and he and his daughter disappeared? That the only clue is the phone message left on the *damned* Russian witch's phone? A message that she has refused to let anyone else listen to? Rumor has it that the message is from you, and no one can find you either.'

Samuel leaned his head back, closed his eyes, and said, 'Tell him you'll explain when we get there.'

I smiled sweetly. 'I'm doing better all the time, Warren. Thank you for asking. Montana is nice, but I don't recommend a November vacation unless you ski.'

'Haven't put on skis for twenty years,' murmured Warren, sounding a little happier. 'Has Adam taken up skiing during this jaunt of yours to Montana?'

'He has skis,' I said, 'but his health wasn't up to it this time. I brought back a doctor, but the two of us found out that we need to go out tonight and were wondering if you were up for a little nursing.'

'Glad to,' said Warren. 'I don't work tonight, anyway. Did you say Jesse's been kidnapped?'

'Yes. And for right now, we need you to keep it under your hat.'

'I drove by your houses on the way back from work this morning,' Warren said slowly. 'There's been a lot of activity there. I think it's just the pack watching, but if you want to avoid them, maybe you all ought to spend the night at my place.'

'You *think* it's the pack?' asked Adam.

Warren snorted. 'Who'd call and talk to me about it? Darryl? Auriele called to tell me you were missing, but without you, the women are mostly left out of the business, too. The rest of the pack is supposed to be keeping their eyes out for you – all three of you – but that's all I know. How long do you need to keep them in the dark?'

'For a day or two.' Adam's voice was neutral, but the words would tell Warren all he needed to know.

'Come to my house. I don't think that anyone except you and Mercy even know where I live. I've got enough room for all of you – unless there are a couple of people who haven't spoken up.'

Each of the Tri-Cities has its own flavor, and it is in Richland that the frenzy of the dawn of the nuclear age has pressed most firmly. When the government decided to build weapons-grade plutonium here, they had to build a town, too. So scattered over the city are twenty-six types of buildings designed to house the workers for the nuclear industry. Each kind of house was given a letter designation beginning with A and ending Z.

I don't recognize them all, but the big duplexes, the A and B houses, are pretty distinctive. The A houses look sort of like Eastern farmhouses – two-story, rectangular, and unadorned. B houses are single-story rectangles. Most of them have been changed a little from what they once were, porches added, converted from duplexes to single-family dwellings – and back again. But no matter how much they are renovated, they all have a sort of sturdy plainness that overcomes brick facades, decks, and cedar siding.

Warren lived in half an A duplex with a big maple tree taking up most of his part of the front lawn. He was waiting on his porch when I drove up. When I'd met him, he'd had a sort of seedy I've-been-there-and-done-everything kind of look. His current lover had coaxed him into cutting his hair and improving his dress a little. His jeans didn't have holes in them, and his shirt had been ironed sometime in the not-too-distant past.

I was able to park directly in front of his home. As soon as I stopped, he hopped down the stairs and opened the van's sliding door.

He took in Adam's condition in one swift glance.

'You say this happened night before last?' he asked me.

'Yep.' His accent is thick enough that I sometimes found

myself falling into it – even though I'd never been to Texas.

Warren stuck his thumbs in his pockets and rocked back on the heels of his battered cowboy boots. 'Well, boss,' he drawled, 'I expect I ought to feel lucky you're alive.'

'I'd feel lucky if you could see your way to helping me up,' Adam growled. 'I wasn't feeling too bad this morning, but this thing's springs leave a lot to be desired.'

'We can't all drive a Mercedes,' I said lightly, having gotten out myself. 'Warren, this is Bran's son, Dr Samuel Cornick, who has come down to help.'

Warren and Samuel assessed each other like a pair of cowboys in a fifties movie. Then, in response to some signal invisible to me, Samuel held out a hand and smiled.

'Good to meet you,' he said.

Warren didn't say anything, but he shook Samuel's hand once and looked as if he took pleasure in the other man's greeting.

To Adam, Warren said, 'I'm afraid it'll be easier to carry you, boss. There's the front stairs, then the flight up to the bedrooms.'

Adam frowned unhappily, but nodded. 'All right.'

Warren looked a little odd carrying Adam because, while not tall, Adam is wide, and Warren is built more along the lines of a marathon runner. It's the kind of thing werewolves have to be careful not to do too often in public.

I opened the door for them but stayed in the living room while Warren continued up the stairs. Samuel waited with me.

Warren's half of the duplex had more square footage than my trailer, but between the small rooms and the stairways, my house always felt bigger to me.

He'd furnished the house comfortably with garage-sale finds and bookcases filled eclectically with everything from scientific texts to worn paperbacks bearing thrift-store price tags on the spines.

Samuel settled on the good side of the plush sofa and stretched out his legs. I turned away from him and thumbed through the nearest bookcase. I could feel his gaze on my back, but I didn't know what he was thinking.

'Oh, Mercy,' sighed a soft voice. 'This one is pretty. Why aren't you flirting with him?'

I looked at the kitchen doorway to see Kyle, Warren's current lover, leaning against the doorway of the kitchen in a typical Kyle pose designed to show off the toned body and tailored clothes.

The pose was deceptive; like Kyle's lowered eyelids and pouty, Marilyn Monroe expression, it was designed to hide the intelligence that made him the highest-paid divorce attorney in town. He told me once that being openly gay was as good for his business as his reputation as a shark. Women in the middle of a divorce tended to prefer dealing with him even over female lawyers.

Samuel stiffened and gave me a hard look. I knew what it meant: he didn't want a human involved in werewolf business. I ignored him; unfortunately Kyle didn't – he read the disapproval and mistook its cause.

'Good to see you,' I said. 'This is an old friend visiting from Montana.' I didn't want to get too detailed, because I thought it was up to Warren how much he told Kyle. 'Samuel, this is Kyle Brooks. Kyle, meet Dr Samuel Cornick.'

Kyle pushed himself off the doorframe with his shoulders and strolled into the living room. He stopped to kiss me on the cheek, then sat down on the sofa as close to Samuel as he could get.

It wasn't that he was interested in Samuel. He'd seen Samuel's disapproval and had decided to exact a little revenge. Warren usually retreated from the frowns of others or ignored them. Kyle was a different kettle of fish entirely. He believed in making the bastards squirm.

I'd like to say that he had a chip on his shoulder, but he had no way of knowing that it wasn't his sexual orientation causing Samuel's reaction. Warren hadn't told him he was a werewolf. It was strongly discouraged to discuss the matter with anyone other than permanent mates – and to werewolves that meant male and female pairings – and the punishment for disobedience was harsh. Werewolves don't have jails. The people who break their laws are either punished physically or killed.

To my relief, Samuel seemed more amused than offended by Kyle's blatant come-on. When Warren came down the stairs, he paused a little at the sight of Kyle's hand on Samuel's thigh. When he started down again, his movements were easy and relaxed, but I could smell the tension rising in the air. He was not pleased. I couldn't tell if he was jealous or worried for his lover. He didn't know Samuel, but he knew, better than most, what the reaction of most werewolves would be.

'Kyle, it might be a good idea to take a few days and check out the state of your house.' Warren's tone was even, but his drawl was gone.

Kyle had his own house, an expensive place up on one of the hills in West Richland, but he'd moved in with Warren when Warren had refused to move in with him. At Warren's words, he stilled.

'I'm hiding someone for a few days,' Warren explained. 'It's not illegal, but it won't be safe here until he's gone.'

Samuel might have turned invisible for all the attention Kyle paid him. 'Darling, if you don't want me around, I'm gone. I suppose I'll accept Geordi's invitation for Thanksgiving, shall I?'

'It's just for a couple of days,' said Warren, his heart in his eyes.

144

'This have something to do with what you've been so upset about the past couple of days?'

Warren glanced at Samuel, then nodded once, quickly.

Kyle stared at him for a moment, then nodded back. 'All right. A couple of days. I'll leave my stuff here.'

'I'll call you.'

'You do that.'

Kyle left, closing the door behind him gently.

'You need to tell him,' I urged. 'Tell him the whole thing or you're going to lose him.' I liked Kyle, but more than that, a blind person could have seen that Warren really loved him.

Warren gave a pained half laugh. 'You think he'd be over-joyed to hear that he was sleeping with a monster? Do you think that would make everything okay?' He shrugged and tried to pretend it didn't matter. 'He'll leave me one way or another anyway, Mercy. He graduated from Cornell and I work nights at a gas station. Hardly a match made in Heaven.'

'I've never seen that it bothered him,' I said. 'He bends over backwards to keep you happy. Seems to me that you might give him a little something back.'

'It's forbidden,' Samuel said, but he sounded sad. 'He can't tell him.'

'What do you think Kyle'd do,' I said indignantly. 'Tell everyone that Warren's a werewolf? Not Kyle. He didn't get where he is by shooting off his mouth – and he's not the kind of person to betray anyone. He's a lawyer; he's good at keeping secrets. Besides, he's got too much pride to allow himself to be just another tabloid headline.'

'It's all right, Mercy.' Warren patted me on my head. 'He hasn't left me yet.'

'He will if you have to keep lying to him,' I said.

The two werewolves just looked at me. Warren loved Kyle, and he was going to lose him because someone had decided you had to be married before you told your spouse what you were — as if that wasn't a recipe for disaster.

I was pretty certain Kyle loved Warren, too. Why else would he live at Warren's when he had a huge, modern, air-conditioned monstrosity with a swimming pool? And Warren was going to throw it all away.

'I'm going for a walk,' I announced, having had enough of werewolves for one day. 'I'll come back when Zee calls.'

I wasn't as civilized as Kyle. I slammed the door behind me and started off down the sidewalk. I was so mad, I almost walked right past Kyle who was just sitting in his Jag, staring straight ahead.

Before I could think better of it, I opened the passenger door and slid in.

'Take us to Howard Amon Park,' I said.

Kyle gave me a look, but his lawyer face was on, so I couldn't tell what he thought, though my nose gave me all sorts of information on what he was feeling: angry, hurt, and discouraged.

What I was about to do was dangerous, no question. It wasn't just a werewolf's obligation to obey his Alpha that kept Warren's mouth shut. If Kyle did start telling everyone about werewolves, he would be silenced. And like me or not, if Adam or Bran found out I was the one who told him, they'd silence me, too.

Did I know Kyle well enough to trust him with our lives?

The Jag slid through the sparse Wednesday-after-work traffic like a tiger through the jungle. Neither Kyle's driving, nor his face, gave any sign of the anger that had raised his pulse rate, or the pain that fueled his anger — but I could smell them.

He pulled into Howard Amon near the south end and parked the car in one of the empty spaces. There were a lot of empty parking slots: November is not a time when most people decide to head to a river park.

'It's cold,' he said. 'We could talk in the car.'

'No,' I said, and got out. He was right, it was chilly. The wind was mild that day, but the Columbia added moisture to the air. I shivered in my cocoa-stained T-shirt – or maybe with nerves. I was going to do this and hope I wasn't wrong about Kyle.

He opened the trunk of his car and pulled a light jacket out and put it on. He took out a trench coat, too, and handed it to me.

'Put this on before you turn blue,' he said.

I wrapped myself in his coat and in the smell of expensive cologne. We were much of a size, so his coat fit me.

'I like it,' I told him. 'I need to get one of these.'

He smiled, but his eyes were tired.

'Let's walk,' I said, and tucked my arm in his, leading him past empty playground equipment and onto the path that ran along the river.

Warren was right, I thought. Having Kyle know he was a monster might not help matters between them at all – but I had the feeling that today would be the final straw if someone didn't clue Kyle in.

'Do you love Warren?' I asked. 'Not the good sex and great company kind of love. I mean the I'll-follow-you-to-death-and-beyond kind.'

It made me feel better that he paused before he answered. 'My sister Ally is the only one of my family I still talk to. I told her about Warren a few months ago. I hadn't realized, until she mentioned it, that I'd never told her about any of my other lovers.'

He put his hand over mine where it rested on his arm, warming it. 'My parents denied what I was for years. When I finally confronted them about it after my mother set me up with yet another young woman with a good pedigree, my father disinherited me. My sister Ally called as soon as she heard — but, after that first conversation, we avoid talking about my being gay. When I talk to her, I feel as if I have a scarlet letter sewn on my chest, and we are both trying to pretend it's not there.' He gave a bitter, angry laugh that changed subtly at the end. When he spoke again his voice was subdued. 'Ally told me to bring him to visit.' He looked at me and shared what that invitation meant to him.

We'd set out at a fast pace, and the park had narrowed to a strip of lawn on either side of the path. The riverbank exchanged its well-groomed look for a more natural growth of bushes and winter-yellowed, knee-high grass. There was a metal porch-type swing set on the top of a rise, set to look out over the river. I tugged him to it and sat down.

It was so important to get this right. Now that the time had come, I was afraid I'd ruin everything.

Swinging lazily, we watched the water flow past us, almost black in the growing shadows of the overcast sky. After a moment he rubbed his face briskly to warm it — and to wipe away incipient tears.

'God,' he said, and I flinched. I'm not a vampire, who can't bear to hear His name, but I don't like it used in vain. When he continued, though, I thought perhaps it hadn't been in vain at all.

'I love him.' It sounded as though the words were ripped from his throat. 'But he won't let me *in*. People call in the middle of the night, and he leaves without telling me where he's going.'

A lone bicyclist, wearing the skintight uniform of the die-hard enthusiast, appeared from the way we'd come. He passed us in a blur of spokes and Superman blue lycra.

'Nice legs,' said Kyle.

It was an old game. Kyle and I comparing notes on men while Warren pretended exasperation.

I leaned my head against Kyle's shoulder. 'Too small. I don't like it when I outweigh my men.'

Kyle leaned back until he was looking at the sky rather than the river. 'When we were in Seattle last month, he drove away a group of drunken, redneck gay-bashers, just scared them off with a few words. But that Darryl treats him like . . . like dirt, and Warren just puts up with it. I don't understand. And this stuff tonight . . .' He sucked air in to steel himself. 'Is he involved with drug dealers?'

I shook my head quickly. 'No. Nothing illegal.' Not yet anyway.

'Is he a fae, then?' he asked, as if it wouldn't bother him much.

'The fae all came out years ago.'

He snorted. 'You're not that dumb. I know a few doctors and teachers who are still in the closet about being gay – and all they have to worry about is losing their jobs, not having a group of idiots burn their houses down.' I could feel him deciding Warren was fae, and his agitation dropped appreciably. 'That would explain some things, like how strong he is and how he knows who's coming before he answers the door.'

Well, I thought feeling hopeful, being fae wasn't quite the same as being a werewolf. But if he could accept the one, maybe the other wouldn't be too big a stretch.

'He's not fae,' I said. I started to tell him just what Warren was, but the words caught in my throat.

'Warren should be the one telling me this,' said Kyle.

'Right,' I agreed. 'But he can't.'

'You mean he won't.'

'No. Can't.' I shook my head. 'I don't have many friends,' I said. 'Not "come over and eat popcorn and watch a stupid movie" friends. You and Warren are sort of it.' I don't have many girlfriends. My work isn't conducive to meeting other women.

'Pretty sad,' Kyle commented. Then he said, 'You and Warren are the only people I eat popcorn with, too.'

'Pathetic.' The banter helped. I drew in a breath and just said it. 'Warren's a werewolf.'

'A what?' Kyle stopped the swing.

'A werewolf. You know. The moon-called, run-on-four-feet-with-big-fangs kind of werewolf.'

He looked at me. 'You're serious.'

I nodded. 'And you're not going to breathe a word of it.'

'Oh?'

'That's why Warren couldn't tell you. That and because Adam – the pack Alpha – forbade it. If you go out now and talk to the authorities or the papers, even if they don't believe you, the pack will kill you.' I knew I was speaking too fast, but I couldn't seem to slow down. In Warren's house, with only Samuel and Warren, it hadn't seemed so dangerous. Samuel and Warren might care for me, but there were plenty of werewolves right here in town who would be happy to see me – and Kyle – dead for what I had just told him. 'Warren will fight them, but there are too many of them. He'll die, and you'll die with him.'

Kyle held up a hand. 'Hold on. It's a little soon for you to have Warren and me dead, don't you think?'

I took a deep breath. 'I hope so. You have to believe me on this – they take their secrecy very seriously. How do you think they've remained undetected for so long?'

'Mercy.' He caught my hand – his own felt cold, but that might have been from the wind. 'A werewolf?'

He didn't really believe me – that might be more dangerous. 'Twenty years ago no one believed in the fae, either. Look, I can prove it to you.'

I looked at a thicket of leafless bushes. They weren't really thick enough for me to strip and shift in, but there weren't any boats out on the water, and as long as we didn't get another biker at the wrong moment . . . I could just shift in my clothes – I get smaller, not bigger – but I'd rather be given a ticket for indecent exposure. A coyote in human clothes looks ridiculous.

'Wait here.' I gave him the trench coat so it wouldn't get dirty, then hopped off the swing and waded through the old grass into the bushes. I took off my clothes as fast as I could and shifted as soon as I dropped the last piece of clothing.

I stopped on the path and sat down, trying to look harmless.

'Mercy?' Kyle had his lawyer face on, which told me how shocked he was. He really hadn't believed me.

I wagged my tail and made a crooning noise. He got out of the swing like an old, old man and approached me.

'A coyote?' he asked.

When I went down to get my clothes, he followed me. I shifted right in front of him – then scrambled back into my clothes as I heard another bicycle coming along.

'I'm not a werewolf,' I told him, running my fingers through my hair. 'But I'm as close as you're going to get until you talk Warren into changing for you.'

Kyle made an impatient sound and pulled my hands away, rearranging my hair himself.

'Werewolves are bigger,' I said, feeling as though I ought to warn him. 'A lot bigger. They don't look like wolves. They look like really, really big wolves who might eat you.'

'Okay,' he said, stepping back. I thought he was talking about my hair, until he continued. 'Warren's a werewolf.'

I looked at his lawyer face and sighed. 'He couldn't tell you. If I tell you, and you don't do anything stupid – you and he are both safe. But if he told you, no matter how you reacted, he would have disobeyed a direct order. The penalty for that is brutal.'

He still wasn't giving anything away. He was so closed off, I couldn't sense what he was feeling. Most humans don't have that kind of control over themselves.

'Won't his pack—' He stumbled over that word a little. 'Won't they think he told me?'

'A lot of werewolves can smell a lie,' I said. 'They'll know how you found out.'

He went back to the swing, picked up the trench coat, and held it out to me. 'Tell me about werewolves.'

I was in the middle of trying to explain just how dangerous a werewolf could be and why it wasn't a good idea for him to flirt with Samuel – or Darryl – when my cell phone rang.

It was Zee.

'Business?' Kyle asked when I hung up.

'Yes.' I bit my lip.

He smiled. 'It's all right. I think I've heard enough secrets for one day. I take it you need to go back to Warren's?'

'Don't talk to him yet,' I said. 'Wait for it to sink in. If you have other questions, you can call me.'

'Thanks, Mercy.' He wrapped an arm around my shoulder. 'But I think I need to talk the rest out with Warren – after his business is finished.'

9

Samuel and Warren were seated on opposite sides of the living room when I walked in, and the air smelled thick with anger. I couldn't tell, just by looking at them, whether they were angry with each other or something else. But then, werewolves are always ready to be angry about something. I'd forgotten what it was like.

Of course, I wasn't the only one with a nose. Warren, sitting closest to the door, took a deep breath.

'She's been with Kyle,' he said, his voice flat. 'She smells like the cologne I gave him. You told him.' He swore at me, but there was more pain than anger in it. I felt a sharp twinge of guilt.

'*You* weren't going to tell him,' I said. I was *not* apologizing. 'And he deserved to know that all the crap he has to put up with is not all your doing.'

Warren shook his head and gave me a despairing glance. 'Do you have a death wish? Adam could have you and Kyle executed for it. I've seen it done.'

'Just me, not Kyle,' I said.

'Yes, damn it, Kyle, too.'

'Only if your lover decides to take it to the news or police.' Samuel's voice was mild, but Warren glared at him anyway.

'You risked too much, Mercy,' said Warren, turning back to me. 'How do you think I'd feel if I lost both of you?' All the anger left him suddenly, leaving only misery behind. 'Maybe you were right. It was still my job. My risk. If he was going to know, it should have been me telling him.'

'No. You are pack and sworn to obedience.' Adam swayed

at the top of the stairs, leaning a little on his cane. He was wearing a white shirt and jeans that fit. 'If you'd told him, I'd have had to enforce the law or risk a rebellion in the pack.'

He sat down on the top stair more abruptly than he meant to, I think, and grinned at me. 'Samuel and I both can witness that Warren didn't tell Kyle anything, you did. Despite Warren's objections, I might add. And, as you keep insisting, you are not pack.' He looked over at Warren. 'I'd have given you permission a long time ago, but I have to obey orders, too.'

I stared at him a moment. 'You knew I was going to tell Kyle.'

He smiled. 'Let's just say that I thought I was going to have to come down and order you not to tell him so you would storm out the door before Kyle drove off.'

'You manipulative bastard,' I said, with a tinge of awe. That was it, three tires were going to come off that old Rabbit.

'Thank you.' He gave me a modest smile.

And when we got Jesse back, she could help me with the graffiti.

'How did he take it?' asked Warren. He'd gotten off the couch and stood staring out his window. His hands hung loose and relaxed by his side, giving nothing of his feelings away.

'He's not gone running to the police,' I told Adam and Samuel. I searched for something more hopeful to tell Warren, but I didn't want to raise his expectations in case I was wrong about Kyle.

'He said he'd talk it over with you,' I told him at last. 'After this business is finished.'

He raised his hands to his face abruptly, in a gesture very like the one Kyle had used. 'At least it's not over, yet.'

He wasn't talking to any of us, but I couldn't stand the bleakness of his voice. I touched his shoulder, and said, 'Don't screw it up anymore and I think he'll be okay with it.'

Samuel and I headed out to meet with Zee and his informant, and I was still trying to figure out if I should have been mad at Adam for manipulating me like that. Except that he actually hadn't done any manipulation, had he? All he'd done was claim credit for my actions afterward.

The light turned red, and I had to stop behind a minivan a little closer than I usually did. Samuel's hand braced itself on my dash and he sucked in his breath. I made a face at the kid in the backseat of the van who had twisted around in his seat belt to look at us. He pulled his lower eyelids down and stuck out his tongue.

'It's not that I object to being in a car wreck,' Samuel said. 'I just prefer to have them on purpose.'

'What?' I glanced over at him, then looked in front of us. The back of the other van made an all-encompassing wall about two feet from our windshield. Sudden comprehension made me grin. 'Vanagons have no nose,' I said gently. 'Our bumper is about a foot from your toes. You could walk between our cars.'

'I could reach out and touch that boy,' he said. The boy had made another face, and Samuel made one back, sticking his thumbs in his ears and spreading his fingers out like moose antlers. 'You know, one of Adam's jobs was to make sure you didn't run around telling the world about werewolves.'

The light turned green, and the kid waved sadly as his van accelerated onto the interstate ramp. We were accelerating, too, but the ramp curled around in an uphill slant so it would take us a while to get to interstate speed.

I snorted. 'Kyle's not the world.' I glanced at him. 'Besides, you knew what I was going to do as well as Adam did. If you'd really objected, you could have stopped me before I left.'

'Maybe I think Kyle is trustworthy.'

I snorted. 'Maybe the moon is made of green cheese. You don't care. You think the werewolves need to come out in public like the fae.' Samuel had never been afraid of change.

'We aren't going to be able to hide much longer,' Samuel said, confirming my guess. 'When I went back to school, I realized just how far forensic medicine has come. Ten years ago, when it was just the military and the FBI labs we had to worry about, having a few wolves in the right places was sufficient. But there aren't enough wolves to infiltrate every small-town police laboratory. Since the fae came out, the scientists are paying closer attention to abnormalities they used to attribute to lab equipment failure or specimen contamination. If Da doesn't pick his time soon, it'll pick him.'

'You're the reason he's considering it at all.' That made sense. Bran had always given close consideration to Samuel's advice.

'Da's not stupid. Once he understood what we faced, he came to the same conclusion. He has a meeting scheduled for all the Alphas this coming spring.' He paused. 'He considered using Adam – the handsome Vietnam war hero.'

'Why not you?' I asked. 'The handsome, selfless doctor who has been keeping people alive for centuries.'

'That's why Da's in charge and you're just a minion,' he said. 'Remember, popular culture holds that all you need to become a werewolf is to have one bite you – not unlike AIDS. It will be a while before they're comfortable rubbing elbows up close and personal. Better to leave them thinking that all the wolves are in the military and the police. You know – "To Serve and Protect".'

'I'm not a minion,' I objected hotly. 'Minions have to be followers.' He laughed, pleased at having gotten my goat again.

'You don't mind that I told Kyle early?' I asked after a while.

'No, you were right. He has too much to lose by going to the tabloids, and he's the kind of people we need behind us – to keep the mobs under control.'

'Educated, well-spoken, well-bred lawyer?' I tried. Yes, that all fit Kyle. 'But he's not exactly mainstream.'

Samuel shrugged. 'Being gay has a certain cachet today.'

I thought of the story Kyle had told me about his family and thought Samuel was mistaken, at least in some quarters. But all I said was, 'I'll tell Kyle he has a certain cachet with you.'

Unexpectedly, Samuel grinned. 'I'd rather you didn't. He'll just flirt with me some more.'

'Speaking of uncomfortable,' I said, 'what had you and Warren so uptight?'

'It was mostly Warren,' he said. 'I'm a stranger, a dominant wolf in his territory – and he was already upset because he thought he was losing the love of his life. If I'd realized how dominant he was, I'd have taken myself elsewhere for the night. We'll manage, but it won't be comfortable.'

'He's Adam's third.'

'Would have been nice if someone had seen fit to tell me that,' Samuel groused good-naturedly. 'With Adam wounded and the second not there, that sticks Warren in the Alpha role – no wonder he was so wound up. I was ready to go out and take a walk myself when you showed up.' He gave me a sharp look. 'Odd how you showing up let him back down. Just as if Adam's second were there – or his mate.'

'I'm not pack,' I said shortly. 'I'm not dating Adam. I have no status in the pack. What I did have was a long overdue conversation with Kyle – which is what distracted Warren.'

Samuel continued to watch me. His mouth was quirked up, but his eyes were full of things I couldn't read, as he said, 'Adam's staked his claim on you before his pack. Did you know that?'

I hadn't. It made me suck in an angry breath before I realized why he might have done that. 'He had to keep his pack from killing me somehow. Wolves kill coyotes who are in their territory. A formal claim of me as his mate would keep me safe. I understand that was something Bran asked him to do. It doesn't make me pack, it doesn't make me his mate. The first is out because I'm a coyote, the second because somebody has to ask me before he can claim me for a mate.'

Samuel laughed, but there was no amusement in it. 'You can think as you please. How much time do we have before we find this bar?'

'It's in the far side of Pasco,' I said. 'We'll be there in ten minutes.'

'Well,' he said, 'why don't you tell me about Zee and this fae we are supposed to meet?'

'I don't know a lot,' I told him. 'Not about the fae. Just that she's got some information we might be interested in. As for Zee, he's a gremlin. He gave me my first job out of college, and I bought the garage from him when he retired. He still helps out when I need him – or when he gets bored. He likes to take things apart and see what's wrong with them, but he usually lets me put them back together again.'

'There's a fae reservation near here.'

I nodded. 'About forty miles away. Just outside of Walla Walla.'

'Adam says that having so many lesser fae around has attracted more of the greater fae.'

'I don't know about that,' I said. 'I can smell their magic, but I can't tell how strong they are.'

'He thinks that's also why there are more vampires, ghosts, and whatnot around the Tri-Cities than, say Spokane, which is a larger city.'

'I try to stay out of the other species' business,' I told him. 'I can't avoid the werewolves, not with Adam living right next door, but I try. The only fae I associate with are Zee and his son Tad.'

'The fae are willing to talk to you.' Samuel stretched his legs out and clasped his hands behind his neck, sticking his elbows out like wings. 'Adam says your old boss is one of the oldest of the fae – and, just so you know, the metal-smiths – gremlins – are not included with the lesser fae. Also, Warren told me that Stefan the vampire visits you quite often. Then there's this human police officer. Drawing the attention of the police is dangerous.'

It did sound as if I had my finger in all sorts of pies.

'Zee was forced public by the Gray Lords,' I said. 'So someone considers him to be one of the lesser fae. Stefan loves his bus, and I let him help me fix it.'

'You *what*?'

I forgot he'd never met Stefan. 'He's not like most vampires,' I tried to explain. Even though Stefan was the only vampire I'd ever met, I knew how they were supposed to act: I went to movies just like everyone else.

'They are *all* like most vampires,' Samuel said darkly. 'Some of them are just better at hiding it than others.'

It wouldn't do any good to argue with him – especially since I agreed with him in principle.

'And the police officer wasn't my fault,' I muttered, taking my exit into Pasco. It seemed like a good time to change the subject, so I said, 'The Fairy Mound in Walla Walla is the bar where tourists go to see the fae. The fae who don't want to be gawked at mostly hang out at Uncle Mike's here in Pasco. Zee says there's a spell on it that makes humans avoid it. It doesn't affect me, but I don't know about werewolves.'

'You aren't going in without me,' he said.

'Fine.' *Never argue with werewolves before you need to*, I reminded myself.

Uncle Mike's was across the Columbia River from my garage, which put it near Pasco's Industrial Park. The old building had once been a small warehouse, and there were warehouses on either side, both heavily tagged by the local kids. I wasn't sure if magic kept the kids away, or someone with a lot of paint and a brush, but Uncle Mike's exterior was always pristine.

I pulled into the parking lot and turned off my lights. It was about seven, still a little early for the regular crowd, and there were only four other cars in the lot, one of which was Zee's truck.

Inside, the bar was dark enough that a human might stumble over the stairs that led from the entry to the bar proper. Samuel hesitated in the doorway, but I thought that it was a tactical thing and not a reaction to a spell. The bar took up all of the wall to our right. There was a small dance floor cleared in the center of the room, with clusters of small tables scattered around the outside.

'There they are,' I told Samuel, and headed for the far corner, where Zee sat looking relaxed next to a moderately attractive woman in conservative business dress.

I've never seen Zee without his glamour; he told me he'd worn it so long that he was more comfortable in human guise. His chosen form was moderately tall, balding, with a little potbelly. His face was craggy, but not unattractively so — just enough to give it character.

He saw us coming and smiled. Since he and the woman already had the defensive seats, setting their backs against the wall, Samuel and I sat across from them. If having the rest of the room behind him, mostly empty as it was, bothered Samuel, I couldn't tell. I hitched my chair around until I could at least get a glimpse of the rest of the room.

'Hey, Zee,' I said. 'This is Dr Samuel Cornick. Samuel, meet Zee.'

Zee nodded, but didn't try to introduce his companion. Instead, he turned to her, and said, 'These are the ones I told you about.'

She frowned and tapped the table with long, manicured nails. Something about the way she used them made me think that beneath the glamour she might have claws. I'd been trying to pin down her scent, but finally was forced to conclude that either she didn't have one or that she smelled of iron and earth just like Zee.

When she looked up from contemplating her nails, she spoke to me and not to Samuel. 'Zee tells me there is a child missing.'

'She's fifteen,' I said, wanting to be clear. The fae don't like it if they think you've lied to them. 'The local Alpha's human daughter.'

'This could be trouble for me,' she said. 'But I have talked to Zee, and what I have to tell you has nothing to do with the fae, and so I am at liberty to share it. I would not usually help the wolves, but I do not like those who take their battles to the innocents.'

I waited.

'I work at a bank,' she said at last. 'I won't tell you the name of it, but it is the bank that the local seethe of vampires uses. Their deposits follow a regular pattern.' Meaning that most of their victims' payments were monthly. She sipped her drink. 'Six days ago, there was an unexpected deposit.'

'Visitors paying tribute,' I said, sitting up straighter in my chair. This sounded promising. A single fae or wolf or whatever wouldn't have paid a tribute high enough to catch anyone's eye.

'I took the liberty of speaking to Uncle Mike himself before you came,' said Zee quietly. 'He's heard of no new visitors, which means these people are keeping very quiet.'

'We need to talk to the vampires,' said Samuel. 'Adam will know how to do it.'

'That will take too long.' I took out my cell phone and dialed Stefan's number. It was early for him to be up, but he'd called me not much later than this.

'Mercy,' he said warmly. 'Are you back from your trip?'

'Yes. Stefan, I need your help.'

'What can I do for you?' Something changed in his voice, but I couldn't worry about that.

'Tuesday night or early Wednesday morning, a group of people including out-of-territory werewolves kidnapped the Alpha's daughter. She's a personal friend of mine, Stefan. Someone told me that your seethe might know of a visiting pack.'

'Ah,' he said. 'That's not in my area of responsibility. Do you want me to inquire for you?'

I hesitated. I didn't know much about the vampires except that smart people avoid them. Something about the formality of his question made me think it was a bigger question than it sounded.

'What does that mean, exactly?' I asked suspiciously.

He laughed, a cheerful unvampire-like sound. 'Good for you. It means that you are appointing me your representative and that gives me certain rights to pursue this that I might not otherwise have.'

'Rights over me?'

'None that I will take advantage of,' he said. 'I give you

my word of honor, Mercedes Thompson. I will force you to do nothing against your will.'

'All right,' I said. 'Then yes, I would like you to inquire for me.'

'What do you know?'

I glanced at the woman's expressionless face. 'I can't tell you everything — just that I've been told that your seethe knows of visitors to the Tri-Cities who might be the group I'm looking for. If that group doesn't have any werewolves, then they're the wrong ones. They might be doing something experimental with medicines or drugs.'

'I'll inquire,' he said. 'Keep your cell phone at hand.'

'I'm not certain that was wise,' said Zee, after I hung up.

'You said she deals with the werewolves.' The woman curled her upper lip at me. 'You didn't tell me she also deals with the undead.'

'I'm a mechanic,' I told her. 'I don't make enough money to pay off the vampires in cash, so I fix their cars. Stefan has an old bus he's restoring. He's the only one I've ever dealt with personally.'

She didn't look happy, but her lip uncurled.

'I appreciate your time,' I said, narrowly skirting an outright thank you — which can get you in trouble. The wrong kind of fae will take your thanks as an admission that you feel obligated to them. Which means that you must then do whatever they ask. Zee had been very careful to break me of that habit. 'The Alpha will also be happy to recover his daughter.'

'It is always good for the Alpha to be happy,' she said; I couldn't tell if she was being honest or sarcastic. She stood up abruptly and smoothed down her skirts to give me time to move my chair so she could exit. She stopped by the bar and spoke to the bartender before she left.

'She smells like you,' Samuel said to Zee. 'Is she a metal-smith, too?'

'Gremlin, please,' said Zee. 'It may be a new name for an old thing, but at least it is not a bad translation. She is a troll – a relative, but not a close one. Trolls like money and extortion, a lot of them go into banking.' He frowned at me. 'You don't go into that nest of vampires alone, Mercy, not even if Stefan is escorting you. He appears better than most, but I have been around a long time. You cannot trust a vampire. The more pleasant they appear, the more dangerous they are.'

'I don't plan on going anywhere,' I told him. 'Samuel is right, the wolves don't pay tribute here. Likely they are people who have nothing to do with taking Jesse.'

My phone rang.

'Mercy?'

It was Stefan, but there was something about his voice that troubled me. I heard something else, too, but there were more people in the bar and someone had turned up the music.

'Wait a moment,' I said loudly – then lied. 'I'm sorry I can't hear you. I'm going outside.' I waved at Samuel and Zee, then walked outside to the quieter parking lot.

Samuel came with me. He started to speak but I held up a finger to my lips. I didn't know how good a vampire's hearing was, but I didn't want to risk it.

'Mercy, can you hear me now?' Stefan's voice was overly crisp and even.

'Yes,' I said. I could also hear the woman's voice that said sweetly, 'Ask her, Stefan.'

He sucked in his breath as if the unknown woman had done something that hurt.

'Is there a strange werewolf with you at Uncle Mike's?' he asked.

'Yes,' I said, looking around. I couldn't smell anything

like Stefan nearby, and I was pretty certain I'd have noticed. The vampires must have a contact at Uncle Mike's, someone who could tell Samuel was a werewolf and who knew Adam's werewolves.

'My mistress wonders that she was not informed of a visitor.'

'The wolves don't ask permission to travel here, not from your seethe,' I told him. 'Adam knows.'

'Adam has disappeared, leaving his pack leaderless.' They spoke together, his words so tight on the end of hers that he sounded like an echo.

I was relatively certain she didn't know I could hear her – though Stefan did. He knew what I was because I'd shown him. Apparently he hadn't seen fit to inform the rest of his seethe. Of course, someone as relatively powerless as I was of little interest to the vampires.

'The pack is hardly leaderless,' I said.

'The pack is weak,' they said. 'And the wolves have set precedent. They paid for permission to come into our territory because we are dominant to Adam's little pack.'

Samuel's eyes narrowed, and his mouth tightened. The vampire's contributors were the people who'd killed Mac, the people who had Jesse.

'So the new visitors have werewolves among them,' I said sharply. 'They are not Bran's wolves. They cannot be a pack. They are less than nothing. Outlaws with no status. I killed two of them myself, and Adam killed another two. And you know I am no great power. Real wolves, wolves who were pack, would never have fallen to something as weak as I.' That was the truth, and I hoped they both could hear it.

There was a long pause, I could hear murmuring in the background, but I could not tell what they said.

'Perhaps that is so,' said Stefan at last, sounding tired. 'Bring your wolf and come to us. We'll determine if he needs a visitor's pass. If not, we see no reason not to tell you what we know of these outlaws who are so much less than pack.'

'I don't know where your seethe is,' I said.

'I'll come and get you,' said Stefan, apparently speaking on his own. He hung up.

'I guess we're going to visit the vampires tonight,' I said. Sometime during the conversation, Zee had come out as well. I hadn't noticed when, but he was standing beside Samuel. 'Do you know vampires?'

Samuel shrugged. 'A little. I've run into one a time or two.'

'I'll go with you,' the old mechanic said softly, and tossed back the last of the scotch in the shot glass he'd brought out with him. 'Nothing I am will help you – metal is not their bane. But I know something of vampires.'

'No,' I said. 'I need you for something else. If I don't call you tomorrow morning, I want you to call this number.' I pulled an old grocery receipt out of my purse and wrote Warren's home number on the back of it. 'This is Warren's, the wolf who's Adam's third. Tell him as much as you know.'

He took the number. 'I don't like this.' But he shoved the note into his pocket in tacit agreement. 'I wish you had more time to prepare. Do you have a symbol of your faith, Mercy, a cross, perhaps? It is not quite as effective as Mr Stoker made it out to be, but it will help.'

'I'm wearing a cross,' Samuel said. 'Bran makes us all wear them. We don't have vampires in our part of Montana, but there are other things crosses are good for.' Like some of the nastier fae – but Samuel wouldn't mention that in front of Zee – it would be rude. Just as Zee would never mention that the third and fourth bullets in the gun he carried were silver – I made them for him myself. Not that he couldn't do it better himself, but if he got tangled up with were-wolves, I figured it would be because of me.

'Mercy?' asked Samuel.

I don't like crosses. My distaste has nothing to do with the metaphysical like it does for vampires; when I lived in Bran's pack, I wore crosses, too. I have a whole spiel about how sick it is to carry around the instrument of Christ's torture as a symbol for the Prince of Peace who taught us to love one another. It's a good spiel, and I even believe it.

Really though, they just give me the willies. I have a very vivid memory of going to church with my mother on one of her rare visits when I was four or five. She was poor and living in Portland; she just couldn't afford to come very often. So when she could come, she liked to do something special. We went to Missoula for a mother-daughter weekend and, on Sunday, picked a church to attend at random – more, I think, because my mother felt she ought to take me to church than because she was particularly religious.

She stopped to talk to the pastor or priest, and I wandered farther into the building so I was alone when I turned the corner and saw, hanging on the wall, a bigger-than-life-size statue of Christ dying on the cross. My eyes were just level with his feet, which were tacked to the cross with a huge nail. It wouldn't have been so bad, but someone with talent had painted it true to life, complete with blood. We didn't go to church that day – and ever since then, I couldn't look at a cross without seeing the son of God dying upon it.

So, no crosses for me. But, having been raised in Bran's pack, I carried around something else. Reluctantly, I pulled out my necklace and showed it to them.

Samuel frowned. The little figure was stylized; I suppose he couldn't tell what it was at first.

'A dog?' asked Zee, staring at my necklace.

'A lamb,' I said defensively, tucking it safely back under my shirt. 'Because one of Christ's names is "The Lamb of God."'

Samuel's shoulders shook slightly. 'I can see it now, Mercy holding a roomful of vampires at bay with her glowing silver sheep.'

I gave his shoulder a hard push, aware of the heat climbing up my cheeks, but it didn't help. He sang in a soft taunting voice, 'Mercy had a little lamb . . .'

'I've been told it's the faith of the wearer that matters,' Zee said, though he sounded doubtful, too. 'I don't suppose you've ever used your lamb against a vampire?'

'No,' I said shortly, still huffy over the song. 'But if the Star of David works, and Bran says it does, then this should, too.'

We all turned to watch a car drive into the parking lot, but its occupants got out and, after the driver tipped an imaginary hat at Zee, walked into Uncle Mike's. No vampires in that lot.

'Is there anything else we should know?' I asked Zee, who seemed to be the most informed of us. All I knew for certain about vampires came under the heading of 'Stay Away From.'

'Prayer doesn't work' he said. 'Though it seems to have some effect on demons and some of the oldest of the dark fae. Garlic doesn't work—'

'Except like insect repellent,' said Stefan, just appearing between two parked cars behind Zee. 'It doesn't hurt, but it smells bad and tastes worse. If you don't irritate one of us, and make sure you bring a friend who hasn't eaten garlic, it'll at least put you last on the menu.'

I hadn't heard him come, hadn't seen him or sensed him at all until he spoke. From somewhere, Zee drew a dark-bladed dagger as long as my arm and stepped between me and the vampire. Samuel growled.

'I'm sorry,' Stefan apologized humbly, as he noticed how badly he'd startled us. 'Moving unseen is a talent of mine, but I usually don't use it on my friends. I've just had an unpleasant episode, and it left me with my guard up.'

Stefan was tallish, but he always seemed to take up less space than he should, so I seldom thought of him as being a big man unless he was standing next to someone else. He was, I noticed, just exactly the same height as Samuel and nearly as broad in the shoulders, though he lacked some of the werewolf's bulk.

His face had regular features and in repose he might be handsome, I suppose. But his expressions were so big that I lost the shape of his features for the bright engagement of his grin.

Just then, though, he frowned at me. 'If I am to take you before the Mistress, I'd rather you had dressed up a bit more.'

I looked down and realized I was wearing the clothing I'd had on when I'd gone over to check out Adam's house. It seemed like a week ago, rather than the night before last. The T-shirt was one Stefan himself had given me for teaching him how to correct the timing on his bus. It read 'Happiness is German engineering, Italian cooking, and Belgian chocolate' and bore a large stain from the cocoa I spilled on it. Thinking about how long I'd been wearing it made me realize that it smelled a little bit stronger than it usually did – and not of detergent and fabric softener either.

'We just came back into town late this afternoon,' I apologized. 'I haven't had a chance to go home and change yet. But you're not much better.'

He looked down at himself, rocking back on his heels and spreading his hands like a vaudeville comic exaggerating his motions for an audience. He was wearing a casual black long-sleeved shirt unbuttoned over a plain white T-shirt, and jeans with a hole over one knee. I've never seen him wearing anything more formal, but for some reason his casual clothes always looked . . . wrong somehow, as if he were wearing a costume.

'What, this?' he asked. 'This is my best down-at-the-heels vampire look,' he said. 'Maybe I should have worn black jeans and a black shirt, but I hate overdoing it.'

'I thought you were picking us up.' I looked around pointedly. 'Where's your car?'

'I came the fast way.' He didn't explain what that was, but continued, 'I see you have your van. There should be plenty of room for the four of us.'

'Zee's staying here,' I said.

Stefan smiled. 'To bring in the troops.'

'Do you know where the people who attacked Adam are?' I asked, rather than commenting on Stefan's observation.

He shook his head regretfully. 'The Mistress didn't see fit to tell me any more than I conveyed to you.' His face grew still for a moment. 'I'm not even certain what she told me was truth. She may know nothing. You might want to find an excuse for not going, Mercy.'

'These visitors have already killed one man and made a mess of Adam's house,' I told him. 'If your Mistress knows where they are, we need to go ask.'

He gave me an oddly formal bow and turned to look at Samuel, giving him a wide smile that managed to keep from displaying his fangs. 'I don't know you. You must be the new wolf in town.'

I made introductions, but it was obvious that Samuel and Stefan were not going to be instant friends – and it wasn't Stefan's fault.

I was a little surprised. Both men shared the easygoing charm that usually had other people smiling. But Samuel's manner was unusually grim. Obviously, he didn't like vampires.

I hopped in my van and waited while Stefan and Samuel

had a very polite argument about where they would sit. Both of them wanted the backseat. I was willing to believe that Stefan was trying to be considerate, but Samuel didn't want the vampire sitting behind him.

Before he dropped his politeness and told Stefan so, I broke in. 'I need Stefan in front so he can tell me where we're going.'

Zee knocked on my window and, when I turned on the power to roll it down, he gave me the dagger he'd pulled when Stefan first emerged from the shadows, along with a handful of leather that looked to be a sheath and belt.

'Take this,' he said. 'The belt ties so you can adjust it to fit you.'

'May I?' Stefan asked diffidently, as he settled himself in the front seat. When Zee gave a curt nod, I handed it over.

The vampire held the blade up and turned it back and forth under the van's dome light. He started to hand it back to me, but Samuel reached between the seats and took it from him. He tested the sharpness of the edge, pricking himself lightly on the thumb. Sucking in his breath, he jerked his hand away and put his thumb in his mouth.

For a moment nothing happened. Then power washed through the van, not like the power the Alphas could call, nor did it feel like the magic Elizaveta Arkadyevna used. It was akin somehow to the fae power of glamour and tasted like metal and blood in my mouth. After a bare moment, the night was quiet again.

'I would suggest that feeding old blades your blood is not a good idea,' said Stefan mildly.

Zee laughed, a full-throated openmouthed sound that made him throw his head back. 'Listen to the vampire, Samuel Bran's Son. My daughter likes the taste of you a little too well.'

Samuel handed the dagger and its accouterments back to

me. 'Zee,' he said, then, as if he'd just realized something he continued in German, '*Siebold Adelbertkrieger aus dem Schwarzenwald.*'

'Siebold Adelbertsmiter from the Walla Walla Fae Preserve,' Zee said mildly.

'Siebold Adelbert's Smiter from the Black Forest,' I translated, using my required two years of a foreign language course for the first time ever. It didn't matter; in German or in English, the words, which Sam made sound like a title of honor, still meant nothing to me.

Go to any Irish village and they'll tell you the names of the fae who interacted with their ancestors. There are rocks and ponds that bear the names of the brownies or kelpies that live there. The German stories tended to concentrate on the heros. Only a few of the German fae, like Lorelei and Rumpelstiltskin, have stories that tell you their names and give you fair warning about the fae you might be dealing with.

Samuel, though, knew something about Zee.

Zee saw the look in my eye and laughed again. 'Don't you start, girl. We live in the present and let the past take care of itself.'

I have a degree in history, which is one of the reasons I'm an auto mechanic. Most of the time, I satisfy my craving for the past by reading historical novels and romances. I'd tried to get Zee to tell me stories before, but like the werewolves, he would not say much. The past holds too many shadows. But armed with a name, I was going to hit the Internet as soon as I finally got to go home.

Zee looked at Stefan, and the laughter faded from his eyes. 'The dagger probably won't help a great deal against vampires, but I'll feel better if she has something to defend herself.'

Stefan nodded. 'It will be allowed.'

The dagger lay on my lap just like any other blade, but I remembered the caress of power and slid it carefully into its sheath.

'Don't look them in the eyes,' Zee told me abruptly. 'That means you, too, Dr Cornick.'

'Don't play dominance games with vampires,' said Samuel. 'I remember.'

The second half of that old wolf aphorism is 'just kill them.' I was happy that he'd left it out.

'Do you have any other warnings, vampire who is Mercy's friend?' Zee asked Stefan.

He shrugged. 'I wouldn't have agreed to this if I truly thought the Mistress had harm in mind. Mostly she just grows bored. Mercy is very good at soft answers that don't promise anything. If the wolf can manage the same, we should all be safe in our beds before dawn.'

10

I don't know where I expected the vampires to live. I suppose I'd been influenced by all those late night flicks and imagined a large Victorian mansion in a disreputable part of town. There are a few along the downtown area in Kennewick, most of them polished and painted like old opera stars. And, while there are a few run-down neighborhoods around, they tend to be populated with houses too small to house even a small seethe.

It shouldn't have surprised me to be driving along a street with Mercedes, Porsches, and BMWs in every elegant cobbled driveway. The road had been cut into the side of a hill that overlooked the town, and for thirty years, doctors, lawyers, and CEOs had been building their four-thousand-square-foot homes on the steeply sloped lots. But, as Stefan told us, the vampires had been there first.

At the end of the main street, a smaller gravel road broke off and cut between a pair of two-story brick edifices. It looked almost like it might be a driveway, but continued past the houses and into the undeveloped area behind them.

We drove through about a quarter mile of the usual eastern Washington scrub – cheat grass, sagebrush, and tackweed mostly – and then up over a small ridge that was just large enough to hide a two-story, sprawling hacienda surrounded by an eight-foot wall. As the road came down the hill our view of the house was limited to what we could see through the double, wrought-iron gates. I thought the sweeping Spanish arches that graced the sides of the building did a wonderful job of disguising the scarcity of windows.

At Stefan's direction, I parked just outside the walls, where the ground had been leveled. The vampire jumped out and was around to open my door before Samuel got out of the van.

'Should I leave this?' I asked Stefan, holding up Zee's dagger. On the way, I'd decided that since it was too big to be hidden without fae glamour – which I don't have – it might be a good thing not to take it in at all.

Stefan shrugged, his hands patting lightly on his thighs as if he heard music I didn't. It was a habitual thing with him; he was seldom absolutely still.

'Carrying an artifact this old could make them respect you more,' said Samuel, who'd come around the van. 'Wear it.'

'I was worried about setting the wrong tone,' I explained.

'I don't expect things to get violent tonight,' said Stefan. 'The dagger is not going to start anything.' He grinned at me. 'It is illegal in this state, though. You'll have to remember to take it off when you leave.'

So I wrapped the leather belt around my hips a few times. There was a handmade buckle without a pin on one end, and I wove the other end of the belt through and tied it off.

'It's too loose,' said Stefan, reaching for it – but Samuel got there first.

'Tighten it around your waist,' he said, adjusting it for me. 'Then pull it over your hips so the weight of the blade doesn't slide the whole thing down around your ankles.'

When he was satisfied, he stepped away.

'I'm not the enemy,' Stefan told him mildly.

'We know that,' I said.

Stefan patted my shoulder, but continued, 'I am not your enemy, Wolf. I've risked more than you know by taking both of you under my protection. The Mistress wanted to send others for you – and I don't think you'd have enjoyed that.'

'Why take the risk?' Samuel asked. 'Why take us under

your protection? I know something of what that means. You don't know me – and Mercy is just your mechanic.'

Stefan laughed, his hand still on my shoulder. 'Mercy is my friend, Dr Cornick. My mother taught me to take care of my friends, didn't yours?'

He was lying. I don't know how I was so certain of it, but I was.

Some werewolves can tell if a person is lying. I can only do it if it is someone I know really well, *and* I'm paying attention. It has to do with the change in the normal sounds a person makes – breathing and pulse, things like that. Usually I'm not paying that much attention. I've never been able to tell a thing about Stefan, not even the usual emotions that carry such distinctive smells. And Stefan's pulse and breathing tended to be erratic. I sometimes thought he only breathed because he knew how uncomfortable he made people when he didn't.

Nonetheless, I knew he had lied.

'You just lied to us,' I told him. 'Why *are* you helping us?' I pulled out from under his hand so I could turn and face him, putting Samuel at my back.

'We don't have time for this,' Stefan said, and some of the usual liveliness faded from his face.

'I need to know if we can trust you,' I told him. 'Or at least how far we can trust you.'

He made one of those grand stage magician gestures, throwing his hands up and tossing his head – but I felt a fine cloak of real magic settling around us. Like Zee, it tasted of earth, but there were darker things in Stefan's spell than anything the gremlin had done around me.

'Fine,' he said. 'Just don't blame me when she's in a rotten mood because we kept her waiting. You called me tonight with a question.'

'What did you just do?' asked Samuel quietly.

Stefan let fall an exasperated sigh. 'I made certain that the three of us are the only ones participating in this conversation, because there are things that hear very well in the night.'

He turned his attention back to me. 'When I called our accountant she put me right through to our Mistress — which is not standard procedure. Our Mistress was obviously more interested in your Dr Cornick than she was with your question. She came to me and had me call you back — she didn't intend me to escort you. She didn't want you to have even that much protection, but once I offered, she could not contradict me. I am here, Mercy, because I want to know what is going on that stirs my Mistress from the lethargy that has been her usual state since she was exiled here. I need to know if it is a good thing, or something very bad for me and my kind.'

I nodded. 'All right.'

'But I would have done it for friendship's sake,' he added.

Unexpectedly, Samuel laughed a little bitterly. 'Of course. We all do things for our Mercy for friendship's sake,' he said.

Stefan didn't take us through the front gates, which were large enough to drive a semi through, but led the way around the side to a small, open door in the wall.

In contrast to the undeveloped scrub outside the gates, the interior grounds were elaborate. Even in November, the grass, under the moon's waxing light, was dark and luxurious. A few roses peeked out from protected areas near the house, and the last of the mums still had a few blooms. It was a formal French-style garden, with organized beds and meticulous grooming. Had the house been a Victorian- or Tudor-style home, it would have looked lovely. Next to a Spanish-style adobe house it just looked odd.

Grapevines, bare in their winter guise, lined the wall. In

the moonlight they looked like a row of dead men, hanging arms spread wide and crucified on the frames that supported them.

I shivered and moved closer to Samuel's warmth. He gave me an odd look, doubtless scenting my unease, but set his hand on my shoulder and pulled me closer.

We followed a cobbled path past a swimming pool, covered for the winter, around the corner of the house to a broad swath of lawn. Across the lawn there was a two-story guest-house almost a third the size of the main house. It was to this smaller building that Stefan led us.

He knocked twice at the door, then opened and waved us into an entry hall decorated aggressively in the colors and textures of the American Southwest, complete with clay pots and kachina dolls. But even the decor was overwhelmed by the smell of mostly unfamiliar flowers and herbs rather than the scents of the desert.

I sneezed, and Samuel wrinkled his nose. Perhaps all the potpourri was designed to confuse our noses – but it was only strong, not caustic. I didn't enjoy it, but it didn't stop me from smelling old leather and rotting fabrics. I took a quick, unobtrusive look around, but I couldn't see anything to account for the smell of rot; everything looked new.

'We'll wait for her in the sitting room,' Stefan said, leading the way through the soaring ceilings of a living room and into a hall.

The room he took us to was half again the size of the biggest room in my trailer. From what I'd seen of the house, though, it was cozy. We'd left behind the Southwest theme for the most part, though the colors were still warm earth tones.

The seats were comfortable, if you like soft fluffy furniture. Stefan settled into a chair with every sign of relaxation as the furniture swallowed him. I scooted toward the front edge of the love seat, which was marginally firmer, but the cushions would still slow me down a little if I had to move quickly.

Samuel sat in a chair that matched Stefan's, but rose to his feet as soon as he started to sink. He stalked behind my love seat and looked out of the large window that dominated the room. It was the first window I'd seen in the house.

Moonlight streamed in, sending loving beams over his face. He closed his eyes and basked in it, and I could tell it was calling to him, even though the moon was not full. She didn't speak to me, but Samuel had once described her song to me in the words of a poet. The expression of bliss on his face while he listened to her music made him beautiful.

I wasn't the only one who thought so.

'Oh, aren't you lovely?' said a voice; a throaty, lightly European voice that preceded a woman dressed in a high-cut, semiformal dress of gold silk that looked rather odd combined with jogging shoes and calf-high athletic socks.

Her reddish blond curls were pulled up with elegant whimsy and lots of bobby pins, revealing dangling diamond earrings that matched the elaborate necklace at her throat. There were faint lines around her eyes and mouth.

She smelled a little like Stefan, so I had to assume she was a vampire, but the lines on her face surprised me. Stefan looked scarcely twenty, and I'd somehow assumed that the undead were like the werewolves, whose cells repaired themselves and removed damage of age, disease, and experience.

The woman padded into the room and made a beeline for Samuel, who turned to regard her gravely. When she leaned against him and stood on tiptoe to lightly lick his neck, he slid a hand up around to the base of her skull and looked at Stefan.

I shifted a little farther toward the edge of my seat and twisted so I could watch them over the back of the love seat.

I wasn't too worried about Samuel – he was poised to break her neck. Maybe a human couldn't have managed it, but he wasn't human.

'Lilly, my Lilly fair.' Stefan sighed, his voice puncturing the tension in the room. 'Don't lick the guests, darling. Bad manners.'

She paused, her nose resting against Samuel. I gripped the hilt of Zee's dagger and hoped I didn't have to use it. Samuel could protect himself, I hoped, but he didn't like hurting women – and Stefan's Lilly looked very feminine.

'She said we had guests for entertainment.' Lilly sounded like a petulant child who knows the promised trip to the toy store is about to be delayed.

'I'm sure she meant we had guests for *you* to entertain, my sweet.' Stefan hadn't moved from his chair, but his shoulders were tight, and his weight was forward.

'But he smells so good,' she murmured. I thought she darted her head forward, but I must have been mistaken because Samuel didn't move. 'He's so warm.'

'He's a werewolf, darling Lilly. You'd find him a difficult meal.' Stefan got up and walked slowly around my couch. Taking one of Lilly's hands in his, he kissed it. 'Come entertain us, my lady.'

He pulled her gently off Samuel and escorted her formally to an upright piano tucked into one corner of the room. He pulled out the bench and helped her settle.

'What should I play?' she asked. 'I don't want to play Mozart. He was so rude.'

Stefan touched her cheek with the tips of his fingers. 'By all means, play whatever you wish, and we will listen.'

She sighed, an exaggerated sound with an accompanying shoulder droop, then, like a marionette she straightened from head to toe and placed her hands just so on the keys.

I don't like piano music. There was only one music teacher

in Aspen Creek when I grew up, and she played piano. For four years I banged out tunes for a half hour a day and hated the piano more each year. It hated me back.

It took only a few measures for me to realize I'd been wrong about the piano – at least when Lilly played it. It didn't seem possible that all that sound came from the little upright piano and the fragile woman sitting before us.

'Liszt,' whispered Samuel, stepping away from the window and sitting on the back of my seat. Then he closed his eyes and *listened*, just as he'd listened to the moon.

Stefan stepped away from the piano once Lilly was focused on her music. He drifted back to stand beside me, then he held out a hand.

I glanced at Samuel, but he was still lost in the music. I took Stefan's hand and let him pull me to my feet. He took me to the far side of the room before releasing me.

'It isn't being a vampire that made her this way,' he said, not whispering, exactly, but in low tones that didn't carry over the music. 'Her maker found her playing piano at an expensive brothel. He decided he wanted her in his seethe, so he took her before he understood that she was touched. In the normal course she would have been mercifully killed: it is dangerous to have a vampire who cannot control herself. I know the werewolves do the same. But no one could bear to lose her music. So she is kept in the seethe and guarded like the treasure she is.'

He paused. 'But usually she is not allowed to wander about at will. There are always attendants who are assigned to keep her – and our guests – safe. Perhaps our Mistress amuses herself.'

I watched Lilly's delicate hands flash across the keys and produce music of power and intellect that she didn't possess herself. I thought about what had happened when Lilly had come into the room.

'If Samuel had reacted badly?' I asked.

'She'd have no chance against him.' Stefan rocked back on his heels unhappily. 'She has no experience at taking unwilling prey, and Samuel is old. Lilly is precious to us. If he had hurt her, the whole seethe would have demanded retribution.'

'Shh,' said Samuel.

She played Liszt for a long time. Not the early lyrical pieces, but the ones he composed after hearing the radical violinist Paganini. But, right in the middle of one of his distinctively mad runs of notes, she switched into a blues piece I didn't recognize, something soft and relaxed that lazed in the room like a big cat. She played a little Beatles, some Chopin, and something vaguely oriental in style before falling into the familiar strains of *Eine Kleine Nachtmusik*.

'I thought you weren't going to play Mozart,' said Stefan when she'd finished the song and begun picking out a melody with her right hand.

'I like his music,' she explained to the keyboard. 'But he was a pig.' She crashed her hands on the keys twice. 'But he is dead, and I am not. Not dead.'

I wasn't going to argue with her. Not when one of those delicate fingers broke the key beneath it. No one else said anything either.

She got up from the piano abruptly and strode through the room. She hesitated in front of Samuel, but when Stefan cleared his throat, she trotted up to him and kissed him on the chin. 'I'm going to eat now,' she said. 'I'm hungry.'

'Fine.' Stefan hugged her, then directed her out of the room with a gentle push.

She hadn't once so much as looked at me.

'So you think we're being set up?' asked Samuel, with lazy geniality that seemed somehow out of place.

Stefan shrugged. 'You, I, or Lilly. Take your pick.'

'It seems like a lot of trouble to go to,' I ventured. 'If Samuel died, Bran would tear this place apart. There wouldn't be a vampire left in the state.' I looked at Stefan. 'Your lady may be powerful, but numbers matter. The Tri-Cities isn't that big. If there were hundreds of you here, I'd have noticed it. Bran can call upon every Alpha in North America.'

'It is nice to know how we are esteemed by the wolves. I'll make certain our Mistress knows to leave the wolf alone because she should fear them,' said a woman from just behind me.

I jumped forward and turned, and Stefan was suddenly between me and the new vampire. This one was neither ethereal nor seductive. If she hadn't been a vampire, I'd have put her age somewhere around sixty, every year etched in the lines of grim disapproval that traversed her face.

'Estelle,' said Stefan. I couldn't tell if it was a greeting, introduction, or admonition.

'She has changed her mind. She doesn't want to come up to visit with the wolf. They can come to her instead.' Estelle didn't seem to react to Stefan at all.

'They are under my protection.' Stefan's voice darkened in a way I'd never heard it before.

'She said you may come, too, if you wish.' She looked at Samuel. 'I'll need to take any crosses or holy objects you are wearing, please. We do not allow people to go armed in the presence of our Mistress.'

She held out a gold-embossed leather bag, and Samuel unhooked his necklace. When he pulled it out of his shirt, the necklace didn't blaze or glow. It was just a bit of ordinary metal, but I saw her involuntary shudder when it brushed close to her skin.

She looked at me and I pulled out my necklace and showed her my sheep. 'No crosses,' I said in a bland voice. 'I didn't expect to be out speaking to your Mistress tonight.'

She didn't even glance at Zee's dagger, dismissing it as a weapon. After pulling the drawstring tight, she let the bag dangle from it. 'Come with me.'

'I'll bring them down in a minute,' Stefan said. 'Go tell her we are coming.'

The other vampire raised her eyebrows but left without a word, carrying the bag with Samuel's cross in it.

'There's something more happening than I thought,' Stefan said rapidly. 'Against most of those here, I can protect you, but not the Mistress herself. If you'd like, I'll get you out of here and see if I can find the information without you.'

'No,' said Samuel. 'We're here now. Let us finish this.'

Samuel's words slurred a little, and I saw Stefan give him a sharp glance.

'Once more I offer you escort away from here.' This time Stefan looked at me. 'I would have no harm come to you and yours here.'

'Can you find out where the other wolves are, if she doesn't want you to?' I asked him.

He hesitated, which was answer enough.

'We'll go talk to her, then,' I said.

Stefan nodded, but not like he was happy about it. 'Then I find myself echoing your gremlin. Keep your eyes away from hers. She'll probably have others with her, whether she allows you to see them or not. Don't look at anyone's eyes. There are four or five here who could entangle even your wolf.'

He turned and led the way through the house to an alcove sheltering a wrought-iron spiral staircase. As we started down, I thought we were going to the basement, but the stairway went deeper. Small lights on the cement wall surrounding the stairs turned on as Stefan passed them. They allowed us to see the stairs – and that we were traveling down a cement tube, but they weren't bright enough to do much more. Fresh air wafted out of small vents that kept the air moving, but it also kept me from smelling anything from deeper down.

'How far down are we going?' I asked, trying to fight off the claustrophobic desire to run back the way we'd come.

'About twenty feet from the surface.' Stefan's voice echoed a little – or else something below us made a noise.

Maybe I was just jumpy.

Eventually the stairway ended in a pad of cement. But even with my night vision, the darkness was so absolute I could see only a few yards in any direction. The smell of bleach danced around several scents I'd never encountered before.

Stefan moved and a series of fluorescent lights flickered to life. We stood in an empty room with cement floors, walls, and ceilings. The overall effect was sterile and empty.

Stefan didn't pause, just continued through the room and into a narrow tunnel that sloped gently upward as we walked. Steel doors without knobs or handles lined the tunnel at even intervals. I could hear things moving behind the doors and scooted up until I could touch Samuel's shoulder for reassurance. As I passed the last door, something slammed against it, ringing with a hollow boom that echoed away from us. Behind another door someone – or something – began a high-pitched hopeless cascade of laughter that ended in a series of screams.

By the end of it, I was all but crawling up on top of Samuel, but he was still relaxed, and his breathing and pulse hadn't even begun to speed up. Damn him. I didn't take a deep breath until we'd left the doors behind.

The tunnel took a narrow turn, and the floor became a steep upward set of twelve stairs that ended in a room with curved plastered walls, wooden floors, and soft lighting. Directly opposite the stairway was a sumptuous mocha leather couch whose curves echoed the walls.

A woman reclined on two overstuffed tapestry-covered pillows braced against one of the couch's arms. She wore silk. I could smell the residue of the silkworms, just as I could smell the faint scent I was learning to identify with vampire.

The dress itself was simple and expensive, revealing her figure in swirling colors ranging from purple to red. Her narrow feet were bare except for red and purple toenail polish. She had them braced so her knees came up and provided backing to support the paperback she was reading.

She finished the page, dog-eared one corner, and set it carelessly on the floor. She swung her legs off the couch and shifted so that her face was toward us before she raised her gaze to look at us. It was so gracefully done that I barely had time to drop my own eyes.

'Introduce us, Stefano,' she said, her voice a deep contralto made the richer by a touch of an Italian accent.

Stefan bowed, a formal gesture that should have looked odd with his torn jeans, but somehow came out gracefully old-fashioned instead.

'*Signora* Marsilia,' he said, 'may I introduce you to Mercedes Thompson, auto mechanic extraordinaire and her friend Dr Samuel Cornick, who is the Marrok's son. Mercy, Dr Cornick, this is Signora Marsilia, Mistress of the Mid-Columbia Seethe.'

'Welcome,' she said.

It had been bothering me how human the two women upstairs had seemed with their wrinkles and imperfections. Stefan, himself, had a touch of otherness that I could see. I had known him for inhuman the first time I'd seen him, but, except for the distinctive scent of vampire, the other two women would have passed for human.

This one would not have.

I stared at her, trying to nail down what was making the hair on the back of my neck rise. She looked like a woman in her early twenties, evidently having died and become vampire before life had marked her. Her hair was blond, which was not a color I associated with Italy. Her eyes were dark, though, as dark as my own.

Hastily, I jerked my gaze from her face, my breath coming more rapidly as I realized how easy it was to forget. She hadn't been looking at me though. Like the other vampires, her attention was on Samuel, and understandably so. He was the son of the Marrok, Bran's son, a person of influence rather than a VW mechanic. Then, too, most women would look at him rather than me.

'I have said something to amuse you, Mercedes?' Marsilia asked. Her voice was pleasant, but there was power behind it, something akin to the power the Alphas could call upon.

I decided to tell her the truth and see what she made of it. 'You are the third woman tonight who has virtually ignored me, Signora Marsilia. However, I find it perfectly understandable, since I have trouble taking my attention off Dr Cornick, too.'

'Do you often have such an effect on women, Dr Cornick?' she asked him archly. See, her attention was still really on him.

Samuel, unflappable Samuel, stuttered. 'I-I haven't . . .' He stopped and sucked in air, then, sounding a little more like himself, he said, 'I expect that you have more luck with the opposite sex than I do.'

She laughed, and I realized finally what it was that bothered me. There was something off about her expressions and her gestures, as if she were only aping humans. As if, without us here to perform for, she would not appear human at all.

Zee told me that modern advances in CGI allowed film-makers to create computer-animated people who seemed very nearly human. But they found that after a certain point, the closer the characters looked to real, the more they repelled their audience.

I knew now exactly what he meant.

She had everything *almost* right. Her heart beat, she breathed regularly. Her skin was flushed slightly, like a person who has just finished walking in the cold. But her smiles were just slightly wrong: coming too late or too early. Her imitation of a human was very close, but not quite close enough to be real – and that small difference was giving me the creeps.

Generally, I don't have the control problems that the were-wolves do – coyotes are adaptable, amiable beasts. But at that moment, if I had been in coyote form, I'd have been running away as fast as I could.

'My Stefano tells me that you want to know about the visitors who paid me so nicely to leave them alone.' She had gone back to ignoring me again – something I wasn't really unhappy with.

'Yes.' Samuel kept his voice soft, almost dreamy. 'We will eventually find them ourselves, but your information would help.'

'After I give you this information,' her voice rumbled in her throat like a cat's, 'we shall talk a little about the Marrok and what he will give me for cooperation.'

Samuel shook his head. 'I am sorry, Signora, I do not have authority to discuss this matter. I will be happy to forward any messages you might have to my father.'

She pouted at him, and I felt the impact of her intent upon him, could smell the beginnings of his arousal. The scary things making noise behind steel doors hadn't caused his pulse to increase, but the Mistress of the seethe could. She leaned forward, and he closed the distance between them until her face was only inches from his groin.

'Samuel,' said Stefan quietly. 'There is blood on your neck. Did Lilly cut you?'

'Let me see it,' suggested the Signora. She breathed in deeply, then made a hungry noise that sounded like the rattle of old dry bones. 'I will take care of it for you.'

That sounded like a really bad idea somehow. I wasn't the only one who thought so.

'They are under my protection, Mistress,' Stefan said, his voice stiffly formal. 'I brought them here so you could speak to the Marrok's son. Their safety is my honor – and it was almost lost earlier when Lilly came to us unescorted. I should hate to think your wishes were opposed to my honor.'

She shut her eyes and dropped her head, resting her forehead on Samuel's belly. I heard her take in another deep breath, and Samuel's arousal grew as if she called it from him as she inhaled.

'It has been so long,' she whispered. 'His power calls to me like brandy on a winter night. It is difficult to think. Who was in charge of Lilly when she wandered into my guests?'

'I will find out,' Stefan said. 'It would be my pleasure to bring the miscreants before you and see you once more attend your people, Mistress.'

She nodded, and Samuel groaned. The sound made her open her eyes, and they were no longer dark. In the dimly lit room, her eyes gleamed red-and-gold fire.

'My control is not as good as it once was,' she murmured. Somehow I'd expected her voice to harshen with the heat of the flames in her eyes, but instead her voice softened and deepened seductively, until my own body was reacting – and I don't care for other women that way as a rule.

'This would be a good time for your sheep, Mercy.' Stefan's attention was so focused upon the other vampire it took me a moment to realize he was speaking to me.

I'd been edging closer to Samuel. Five years of study in the martial arts had given me a purple belt, the muscles to heft car parts around almost as well as a man, and the understanding that my paltry skills weren't worth a damn thing against a vampire.

I'd debated the wisdom of knocking Samuel away from her, but something my senses had been trying to tell me for a while had finally kicked in: there were others here, other vampires I couldn't see or hear – only scent.

Stefan's advice gave me something better to do. I pulled out my necklace. The chain was long enough that I could tug it over my head, and I let it dangle from my hand just as Marsilia moved.

I grew up with werewolves who ran faster than greyhounds, and I am a little faster yet – but I never saw Marsilia move. One moment she was pressed against the front of Samuel's jeans, and the next her legs were wrapped around his waist and her mouth was on his neck. Everything that followed seemed to happen slowly, although I suppose it was only a few seconds.

The illusion hiding the other vampires dissipated in the frenzy of Marsilia's feeding, and I saw them, six vampires lined up against the wall of the room. They were making no attempt to appear human, and I gathered a hurried impression of gray skin, hollow cheeks, and eyes glittering like backlit gemstones. None of them moved, though Stefan had wrapped himself around Marsilia and was trying to pull her off. Nor did they interfere when I closed the distance between Samuel and me, the silly necklace wrapped around my wrist. I suppose they didn't consider either of us a threat.

Samuel's eyes were closed, his head thrown back to give Marsilia better access. So scared I could barely breathe, I pressed the silver lamb against Marsilia's forehead and said a hurried, but fervent prayer, that the lamb would work the same way a cross did.

The little figure pressed into her forehead, but Marsilia,

as absorbed in the feeding as Samuel, paid me no mind. Then several things happened almost at the same time – only afterward did I put them in their probable order.

The sheep under my hand blazed up with the eerie blue flame of a well-adjusted Bunsen burner. Marsilia was suddenly crouched on the back of the couch, as far from my necklace – and Samuel – as she could get. She shrieked, a high-pitched noise just barely within the range of my hearing, and made a gesture with her hands.

Everyone dropped to the floor, Samuel, Stefan, and Marsilia's guards, leaving me standing, my little sheep aglow like an absurdly small blue neon sign, facing the Mistress of the nest. I thought at first that the others had fallen voluntarily, reacting to some secret sign I hadn't seen. But Marsilia jerked her chin, a quick, inhuman motion, and screamed again. The bodies on the floor twisted a little, as if something hurt, but they could not move to alleviate it – and I finally realized that it was magic as well as fear that was stealing my breath. Marsilia was doing something to hurt them all.

'Stop it,' I said, with all the authority I could muster. My voice came out thin and shaky. Not impressive.

I cleared my throat and tried again. Surely if I could face down Bran after the time I ran his Porsche into a tree without either a driver's license or permission to drive it, I could steady my voice so it didn't squeak. 'Enough. No one has harmed you.'

'No harm?' she hissed, tossing her head so her mane of hair fell away from her forehead to reveal a nasty-looking burn vaguely in the shape of my necklace.

'You were feeding upon Samuel without his permission,' I said firmly, as if I knew that her action had given me the right to defend him – I wasn't certain it was true, but bluffing worked with the wolves. And vampires seemed to be big on manners.

She raised her chin but didn't reply. She took a deep breath, and I realized she hadn't been breathing since I'd driven her off Samuel. Her eyelids fluttered as she took in the smell of the room — I could smell it, too: fear, pain, blood, and something sweet and compelling brushed with the scents of those present.

'It has been a long time since I had such presented for me,' she said. 'He was bleeding and half-caught already.' Her tone wasn't apologetic, but I'd settle for mere explanations if it only got us all out of here alive.

Stefan managed to get out a single word. 'Trap.'

She drew a quick circle in the air and dropped her hand out and away. In response, all the men on the floor went limp. Samuel, I noticed with relief, was still breathing.

'Explain, Stefan,' she said, and I took a deep, relieved breath at having her attention somewhere else.

'A trap for you, Mistress,' Stefan said, his voice hoarse like a man who has been screaming. 'Bleed the wolf and present him to you as if he were gift-wrapped. They were good. I didn't notice that he was under thrall until I saw the blood.'

'You may be right,' she said. She gave me an irritated look. 'Put that thing away, please. You don't need it now.'

'It's all right, Mercy,' said Stefan, his voice still whisper-thin. He hadn't raised himself off the floor, but lay with his eyes closed, as if he'd come to the end of his strength.

I hid the necklace again, and the room looked even dimmer in the remaining, more mundane, lighting.

'Tell me about this trap, Stefano,' she said briskly as she climbed from the back of the couch and into her seat. If her eyes dwelled a moment too long upon Samuel, who was still limp, at least their inhuman flames had died to flickers.

The vampires were all showing signs of life, but only

Stefan was moving. He groaned as he sat up and rubbed his forehead as if it hurt. His movements were jerky, inhuman.

'Lilly was sent to us without her attendant. I thought she was sent to create an incident. If Samuel had killed her, it would be war between our seethe and the Marrok. But perhaps it was more than that. I thought we got him away before she marked him, but looking back, I believe he was in thrall from that moment on. They sent him down here bleeding like a rare steak and presented him to you. If you had killed Samuel – and I think it likely, half-starved as you've been keeping yourself—' I could hear the disapproval in his voice. 'If you had killed Samuel . . .' He let his words trail off.

She licked her lips as if there was still a trace of blood left. I saw a flash of regret on her face as she stared at Samuel, as if she wished no one had stopped her.

'If I had killed him, there would have been war.' She looked away from Samuel and met my eyes – but nothing happened. She frowned at me, but seemed less surprised than I was. But maybe the little sheep who must have protected me from her magic was still at work. She tapped her long, manicured nails together, looking as if she were considering something.

'We would be badly outnumbered,' Stefan said, when she said no more. He gathered himself visibly before getting to his feet. 'If war broke out, we would be forced to leave this country.'

She stilled, as if his words were of great significance. 'To leave this cursed desert and return *home*' – she closed her eyes – 'now that is a prize that many here might risk my wrath to gain.'

The other vampires were stirring by then. I moved between them and Samuel, trusting Stefan to keep his mistress off us. As they rose, they seemed to be more focused on Samuel than on Marsilia. Like most everyone else tonight, they ignored me as they slowly began closing in.

'Wake up, Sam.' I nudged him with the heel of my foot.

Stefan said something in liquid tones with the unmistakable cadence of Italian. Like they were in a peculiar game of 'Swing the Statue,' the other vampires simply stopped moving, though it left some of them in awkward poses.

'What's wrong with Samuel?'

I asked the question of Stefan, but it was Marsilia who answered. 'He is bespelled by my bite,' she said. 'Some do die of the Kiss, but it will probably do no permanent harm to a werewolf. If I were less, then he would not have succumbed.' She sounded pleased.

'Then how did Lilly manage?' asked Stefan. 'It wasn't a full Kiss, but he was in thrall.'

She crouched by my feet and touched Samuel's neck. I didn't like the way she just kept appearing places, especially when she did it near Samuel who couldn't defend himself.

'That is a good question,' she murmured. 'He is a dominant, this son of Bran?'

'Yes,' I answered. I knew that humans had trouble telling a dominant from a submissive wolf. I hadn't thought the same would be true of a vampire.

'Then Lilly could not enthrall him. But . . . perhaps she could have been loaned the power.' She brought her fingers to her lips and licked Samuel's blood off them. Her eyes were glowing again.

I reached into my shirt and started to draw out the sheep, but a pale hand wrapped around my wrist and jerked me against a body, all cold bone and sinew.

By the time I realized I'd been grabbed, I'd already thrown him. If I'd had time to think, I'd never have tried to throw a vampire the way I would a human, but it was a reflexive thing born of hundreds of hours in the dojo.

He landed right on top of Samuel because Marsilia had gotten out of the way. The creature twisted, and I thought he was coming at me again, but he was after Samuel instead. He struck at Samuel's bleeding neck.

Marsilia jerked her vampire off, leaving torn skin where his fangs had already locked onto flesh. Without visible effort or emotion, she tossed him into the nearest wall. Plaster flew, but he bounced to his feet with a snarl that died as soon as he saw who had thrown him the second time.

'Out, my dears.' I noticed that the burn mark on her forehead was healing. 'Out before we lose all honor, overcome by such sweetness as is laid out here before us like a tempting feast.'

I'd gotten my sheep out finally, but before it started glowing we were alone, Stefan, Samuel, and I.

11

There was an elevator hidden behind one of the doors in the corridor. Stefan leaned wearily against the wall; he carried Samuel, who was bloodstained, limp, but still breathing.

'You're sure he's all right?' I asked, not for the first time.

'He'll not die of it,' he said, which was not quite the same thing.

The elevator came to a smooth stop, and the doors slid open to reveal a kitchen. Bright lights gleamed on bird's-eye maple cabinetry and creamy stone countertops. There were no windows, but a clever use of mirrors and backlit stained-glass panels made up for the lack. Next to the refrigerator was something I was a lot more interested in, an outside door. I didn't wait for Stefan, but opened the door and ran out to the manicured lawn. As I sucked in a shaky breath of air that smelled of dust and exhaust rather than vampires, I realized that I'd come out of the main house.

'The houses are connected by the tunnels,' I said, as Stefan came down the back steps.

'There's no time to talk,' grunted Stefan.

I looked at him and saw that he was struggling with Samuel's weight.

'I thought vampires were strong enough to upend trees,' I said.

'Not after Marsilia gets finished with them,' said Stefan. He shifted Samuel, trying to get a better grip.

'Why not a fireman's carry?' I asked.

'Because I don't want to be carrying him that way when he starts waking up – he's not going to be a happy wolf.

This way I can put him down and get out of the way if I need to.'

'I'll carry him,' said a stranger's voice.

Stefan turned with a snarl and, for the first time ever, I saw his fangs, white and sharp in the night.

Another vampire stood near us, wearing jeans and one of those white, piratey shirts, open to the waist, that you see at Renaissance Fairs and Errol Flynn movies. It didn't look good on him. His shoulders were too narrow, and his flat stomach just looked cadaverous rather than sexy – or maybe I'd just had enough of vampires that night.

'Peace, Stefan.' The vampire held up a hand. 'Marsilia thought you could use some help.'

'You mean she didn't want Dr Cornick to be here when he came out of the Kiss's hold.' Stefan relaxed a little. 'All right.'

They transferred Samuel from one vampire to the other – the newcomer apparently wasn't suffering from Stefan's worries because he lifted the werewolf over his shoulder.

The night was quiet, but there was a waiting quality to it that I recognized from the hunt. Someone was watching us – big surprise. None of us talked as we made our way through the garden and out the main gates, which someone had propped open while we had been inside.

I slid the door of the van open and pointed to the long bench seat. The pirate-clad vampire pulled Samuel off his shoulder and put him on the far backseat. I decided that much strength was creepier in vampires than it was in were-wolves – at least the wolves looked like people who should be strong.

With Samuel safely stowed, the vampire turned directly to me.

'Mercedes Thompson,' he said. 'My mistress thanks you for your visit, which has allowed us to discover problems that otherwise might have gone unnoticed. She also thanks you for allowing her to keep her honor and that of her vassal, Stefano Uccello.' He saw the skepticism on my face and smiled. 'She said that she'd never been repulsed by a sheep before. Crosses, scriptures, and holy water, but not a sheep.'

'The Lamb of God,' explained Stefan. He was looking almost like his usual self, with one elbow propped against the door of the van. 'I didn't think it would work either. Otherwise, of course, I would have told her to give it to Estelle.'

'Of course.' The other vampire gave me another quick, charming smile. 'In any case, I am to extend Signora Marsilia's apologies for any discomfort you or yours experienced this night and we hope that you will extend our apologies also to Dr Cornick. Please explain that the Mistress intended him no hurt, but that her recent indisposition has allowed some of her people to become . . . obstreperous. They will be punished.'

'Tell the Signora that I find her apologies gracious and that I, too, regret any trouble she suffered this night,' I lied. But I must have done it well, because Stefan gave me a half nod of approval.

The vampire bowed, then, holding it gingerly by its chain, handed me Samuel's cross and a small sheet of paper, the thick handmade kind. It smelled of the same herbs that scented the house and upon it, written in a flourishing hand that had learned to write with a quill, was a Kennewick address.

'She had intended to give this to you herself, but has asked me to tell you more. The wolves paid us just under ten thousand dollars for the rights to live at this address for two months.'

Stefan straightened. 'That's too much. Why did she charge them so much?'

'She didn't. They paid us without any negotiation. I

expressed my concerns about the oddity of the transaction to the Signora, but . . .' He glanced at Stefan and shrugged.

'Marsilia has not been herself since she was exiled here from Milan,' Stefan told me. He looked at the other vampire, and said, 'It is a good thing that happened tonight. To see our Mistress potent with her hunger again is wondrous, Andre.'

'Wondrous' was not the word I'd have chosen.

'I hope so,' said the other harshly. 'But she has been asleep for two centuries. Who knows what will happen when the Mistress awakens? You may have outsmarted yourself this time.'

'It was not I,' murmured Stefan. 'Someone was trying to stir up trouble again. Our Mistress has said I might investigate.'

The two vampires stared at each other, neither of them breathing.

At last Stefan said, 'Whatever their purpose, they have succeeded in awakening Her at last. If they had not put my guests in danger, I would not willingly hunt them.'

Vampire politics, I thought. *Humans, werewolves, or, apparently, vampires, it doesn't matter; get more than three of them together and the jockeying for power begins.*

I understood some of it. The older wolves pull away from the world as it changes until some of them live like hermits in their caves, only coming out to feed and eventually even losing interest in that. It sounded as if Marsilia suffered from the same malady. Evidently some of the vampires were happy with their Mistress's neglect while Stefan was not. Andre sounded as if he didn't know which side he was on. I was on whichever side meant that they left me alone.

'The Mistress told me to give you something, too,' Andre told Stefan.

There was a sound, like the crack of a bullet, and Stefan

staggered back against the van, one hand over his face. It wasn't until the faint blush of a handprint appeared on Stefan's cheek that I realized what had happened.

'A foretaste,' Andre told him. 'Today she is busy, but tomorrow you will report to her at dusk. You should have told her what Mercedes Thompson was when you first knew. You should have warned the Mistress, not let her find out when the walker stood against her magic. You should not have brought *her* here.'

'She brought no stake or holy water.' Stefan's voice gave no indication that the blow bothered him. 'She is no danger to us – she barely understands what she is, and there is no one to teach her. She does not hunt vampires, nor attack those who leave her in peace.'

Andre jerked his head around faster than anyone should and looked at me. 'Is that true, Mercedes Thompson? You do not hunt those who merely frighten you?'

I was tired, worried about Samuel, and somewhat surprised to have survived my encounter with Signora Marsilia and her people.

'I don't hunt anything except the occasional rabbit, mouse, or pheasant,' I said. 'Until this week, that was it for me.' If I hadn't been so tired, I'd never have uttered that last sentence.

'What about this week?' It was Stefan who asked.

'I killed two werewolves.'

'You killed two werewolves?' Andre gave me a look that was hardly flattering. 'I suppose you were defending yourself and just happened to have a gun at hand?'

I shook my head. 'One of them was moonstruck – he'd have killed anyone near him. I tore his throat out and he bled to death. The other one I shot before he could kill the Alpha.'

'Tore his throat out?' murmured Stefan, while Andre clearly didn't know whether to believe me or not.

'I was coyote, and trying to get his attention so that he'd chase me.'

Stefan frowned at me. 'Werewolves are fast.'

'I know that,' I said irritably. 'I'm faster.' I thought about the wild chase with Bran's mate, and added, 'Most of the time anyway. I didn't intend to kill—'

Someone screamed, and I quit talking. We waited, but there were no more sounds.

'I had better attend the Signora,' said Andre, and was gone, just gone.

'I'll drive,' Stefan told me. 'You'll need to ride in the back with Dr Cornick so he has someone he trusts with him when he wakes up.'

I gave him the keys and hopped in the back.

'What's going to happen when he wakes up?' I asked as I settled onto the backseat, lifting Samuel's head so I could scoot underneath it and sit down. My hands smoothed over his hair and slid over his neck. The marks of the vampires were already scabbed over, rough under my light touch.

'Maybe nothing will happen,' Stefan said, getting in the driver's seat and starting the van. 'But sometimes they don't react well to being Kissed. Signora Marsilia used to prefer wolves to more mundane prey – that's why she lost her place in Italy and was sent here.'

'Feeding off of werewolves is taboo?' I asked.

'No.' He turned the van around and started back up the drive. 'Feeding off the werewolf mistress of the Lord of Night is taboo.'

He said Lord of Night as if I should know who that was, so I asked, 'Who is the Lord of Night?'

'The Master of Milan – or he was last we heard.'

'When was that?'

'Two hundred years, more or less. He exiled Signora Marsilia here with those who owed her life or vassalage.'

'There wasn't anything here two hundred years ago,' I said.

'I was told he stuck a pin in a map. You are right; there was nothing here. Nothing but desert, dust, and Indians.' He'd adjusted the rearview mirror so he could see me, and his eyes met mine as he continued. 'Indians and something we'd never encountered before. Mercy. Shapeshifters who were not moon called. Men and women who could take on the coyote's form as they chose. They were immune to most of the magics that allow us to live among humans undetected.'

I stared at him. 'I'm not immune to magic.'

'I didn't say you were,' he answered. 'But some of our magics pass you by. Why do you think you stood against Marsilia's rage when the rest of us fell?'

'It was the sheep.'

'It wasn't the sheep. Once upon a time, Mercedes, what you are would have been your death sentence. We killed your kind wherever we found them, and they returned the favor.' He smiled at me, and my blood ran chill at the expression in those cool, cool eyes. 'There are vampires everywhere, Mercedes, and you are the only walker here.'

I'd always thought of Stefan as my friend. Even in the heart of the vampires' seethe I hadn't questioned his friendship, not really. Stupid me.

'I can drive myself home,' I told him.

He returned his gaze to the street in front of him and laughed softly as he pulled the van over. He got out and left it running. I loosened my grip on Samuel's shoulder and forced myself away from the safety of the back bench seat.

I didn't see Stefan or smell him when I got out of the van and moved to the driver's seat, but I could feel his eyes on my back. I started to drive off, then pulled my foot off the gas and stomped on the brakes.

I rolled down the window and spoke to the darkness. 'I know you don't live there – you smell of woodsmoke and popcorn. Do you need a ride home?'

He laughed. I jumped, then jumped again when he leaned in the window and patted my shoulder.

'Go home, Mercy,' he said, and was gone – for real this time.

I chugged along behind semis and Suburbans and thought about what I'd just learned.

I knew that vampires, like the fae, and werewolves and their kindred were all Old World preternatural creatures. They'd come over for the same reasons most humans did: to gain wealth, power, or land, *and* to escape persecution.

During the Renaissance, vampires had been an open secret; being thought one added power and prestige. The cities of Italy and France became havens for them. Even so, their numbers were not great. Like werewolves, humans who would become vampires died more often than they accomplished their goal. Most of the princes and nobles believed to be vampires were just clever men who saw the claim as a way to discourage rivals.

The Church saw it differently. When the Spanish invasion of the New World filled the coffers of the Church so they no longer had to depend upon the favor of the nobles, they went after the vampires as well as any other preternatural creature they could find.

Hundreds of people died, if not thousands, accused of vampirism, witchcraft, or lycanthropy. Only a small percentage of those who died actually were vampires, but those losses were still severe – humans (lucky for them) breed much faster than the undead.

So vampires came to the New World, victims of religious persecution like the Quakers and the Puritans – only different.

Werewolves and their moon-called kindred came to find new territory to hunt. The fae came to escape the cold iron of the Industrial Revolution, which followed them anyway. Together these immigrants destroyed most of the preternatural creatures who had lived in the Americas, until at last, even the bare stories of their existence were mostly gone.

My people, apparently, among them.

As I took the on-ramp onto the highway to Richland, I remembered something my mother once told me. She hadn't known my father very well. In my mostly empty jewelry box was a silver belt buckle he'd won in a rodeo and given her. She told me his eyes were the color of sunlit root beer, and that he snored if he slept on his back. The only other thing I knew about him was that if someone had found his wrecked truck sooner, he might have lived. The wreck hadn't killed him outright. Something sharp had sliced open a big vein, and he bled to death.

There was a noise from the back of the van. I jerked the rearview mirror around until I could see the backseat. Samuel's eyes were open, and he was shaking violently.

Stefan hadn't told me what the bad reaction to the Kiss might be, but I was pretty sure I was about to find out. I was already passing the exit for Columbia Park, but I managed to take it without getting rear-ended.

I drove until I came to a small parking lot next to a maintenance shed. I parked, killed the lights, then slipped between the seats of the van and approached Samuel cautiously.

'Sam?' I said, and for a heartbeat his struggles slowed down.

His eyes gleamed in the shadows of the van's depths. I smelled adrenaline, terror, sweat, and blood.

I had to fight not to flee. Part of me knew that so much fear must have a cause. The rest of me figured out why some werewolves had a bad reaction to the vampire's Kiss – waking up unable to move, his last memory being something sucking his blood was bound to hit every panic button in a werewolf's arsenal.

'Shhh,' I said, crouching in the space between the second seat and the sliding door. 'The vampires are gone. What you are feeling is something they can do with their bite. It makes their victims passive so they can feed without drawing attention. It's wearing off now – Stefan said it will leave no ill effects.'

He was beginning to listen to me. I could see it in the softening of his shoulders – then my cell phone rang.

I answered it, but the sudden noise had been too much. The van bumped and bobbed as Samuel scrambled over the backseat and into the luggage space behind the seat.

'Hey,' I said, keeping my voice soft.

'Mercy.' It was Warren, his voice urgent. 'You need to come here as soon as you can – and bring Samuel.'

Samuel was making harsh noises behind the seat. Changing was painful for the wolves at the best of times – when they are comfortable and eager to hunt. Changing when the air is thick with fear and blood would not be good. Not good at all.

'Samuel is indisposed,' I said, as he screamed, a roar of agony and despair. He was fighting the change.

Warren swore. 'Tell me this then. Is Adam afraid someone in the pack betrayed him?'

'That's my fault,' I said. 'Warren, is the pack coming to your house?'

He grunted. I assumed it was a yes.

'Tell Adam.'

'I made steaks and fed him about an hour ago, and he's sleeping it off. I tried to wake him up before I called, but he's shut down hard in a healing sleep. I don't know what it would take to wake him up.'

'Dr Cornick would,' I muttered, wincing at the noises Sam was making in the back of the van. 'But he's not available to come to the phone right now.'

'It's all right, Mercy.' He sounded suddenly calm. 'I'll take care of it. If that's Samuel in the middle of an involuntary change, you need to get away from there and give him time to calm down.'

'What? And leave Samuel to go hunting in the middle of Kennewick? I don't think so.'

'He won't know you, not if he's changing like that. It won't be Samuel Bran's son, it will be only the wolf.'

The sounds behind the seat were becoming more canid and less human.

'Mercy, get out of there.'

'It's all right, Warren,' I said, hoping I was right.

Wolves, the real wolves, are not usually vicious animals unless they are frightened, hurt, or cornered. Werewolves are always vicious, always ready for the kill.

'If this doesn't work – tell him the vampires got me,' I said. 'I don't think he'll remember. It'll be true enough. The vampires are what forced this change. You tell him that.' I hung up the phone.

It was already too late to run, but I wouldn't have anyway. Leave Samuel to deal with the aftermath of his wolf's rampage? Samuel was a healer, a defender of the weak. I wasn't certain that he would live with innocent blood on his hands.

I'd deserted him once, a long time ago. I wouldn't do it again.

The sounds died down until all I could hear was the harsh panting of his breath, but I could smell his rage. I didn't bother undressing before I shifted – it would have taken too long. When Samuel's white head appeared over the top of the seat, I was backing out of my T-shirt and bra.

I stopped what I was doing and crouched on the floor of the van, tail tucked between my legs. I didn't look up, but I felt the springs give way as he climbed slowly over the back and stood on the seat.

I was so scared it was hard to breathe. I knew what I had to do next, but I wasn't certain I could manage it. If some part of me weren't absolutely convinced that Sam, my Sam, could never hurt me, I wouldn't have been able to do the next part.

He was utterly silent. In Montana, on a hunt, the wolves howl and cry, but in the city all hunting is done soundlessly. Growls, whines, and barks are all bluffing tools – it is the quiet wolf that will kill you.

With Samuel perched silently on the backseat, I rolled over onto my back and exposed my belly to his jaws. I stretched my chin so that my neck was vulnerable to him as well. It was one of the hardest things I'd ever done. It wasn't as if he couldn't kill me as easily if I were lying on my belly, but there was something worse about exposing my unprotected underside. Being submissive is a bitch.

The van dipped again as he jumped down, landing almost on top of me. I could smell his anger – the sour smell of his fear had faded all away with his humanity, leaving only the wolf. Hot breath moved my fur as he sniffed his way upward, his nose parting my hair as he went. Slowly the anger faded along with the intensity that had allowed me to know what he was feeling.

I tilted my head and risked a glance. Samuel filled the space between the short bench seat and the sliding door. Caught beneath him, one front paw on either side of my shoulders, I felt a sudden claustrophobia and instinctively tried to roll over.

I stopped the movement as soon as it began, but Samuel lunged forward with a warning growl and a snap of teeth in

my face. I tried to take comfort from the growl, since theo-
retically, if he was growling he wasn't likely to kill me –
but I was too aware of the volatile nature of the werewolves.

He moved suddenly, closing his mouth over my throat –
but too wide for a jugular strike. I could feel his teeth through
the fur on my neck, but they stopped as soon as they touched
my skin.

I prayed then that Bran was right, and Samuel's wolf
looked upon me as his mate. If he was wrong, then both
Samuel and I would pay the price.

I held very still as my heart tried desperately to pound
its way out of my rib cage. He released me, nipped gently
at my nose, then slipped soundlessly away.

I rolled to my feet and shook my fur to resettle it, shed-
ding my bra at last. Samuel was stretched along the backseat,
watching me with his beautiful white eyes. He blinked at me
once, then resettled his muzzle on his front paws and closed
his eyes, saying, as clearly as he could without words, that the
two halves of his soul were together again.

I heard the quiet purr of a big engine coming down the
park road. I shifted to human as quickly as I could and
began scrambling for clothes. My underwear was pale green
and I found them first. The sports bra went on easier than
it had come off, and I found my T-shirt when my foot
touched it.

The car slowed as it approached, its headlights glinting
through the window of my van.

'Pants, pants, pants,' I chanted as I brushed my hands
over the floor. My fingers found them as tires crunched gravel
and the car parked behind us. They also found Zee's dagger.
I shoved it under the rubber mat near the side of the van
farthest from the sliding door.

Feverishly, I jerked my pants up, zipped, and buttoned
them as the driver's side door of the other car opened. Shoes.

Luckily they were white and I snatched them up and pulled them on over my bare feet without untying them.

I gave the hulking brute stretched across the full length of the van's backseat a frantic look. Samuel wouldn't be able to change back for a while yet, probably a few hours. A forced change takes time to recover from, even for a wolf of Samuel's power, and it was too late to try to hide him.

'You're a good dog, Samuel,' I told him sternly. 'Don't scare the nice police officer. We don't have time to be escorted down to the station house.'

A flashlight found me, and I waved, then slowly opened the sliding door.

'Jogging, Officer,' I said. The flashlight kept me from picking out a face.

There was a long pause. 'It's one in the morning, ma'am.'

'I couldn't sleep.' I gave him an apologetic smile.

'Jogging alone at night isn't safe, ma'am.' He lowered the flashlight, and I blinked rapidly, hoping the residual after-images would fade soon.

'That's why I always take him,' I said, and jerked a thumb toward the back of the van.

The policeman swore. 'Sorry, ma'am. That's just the biggest damn dog I've ever seen – and I grew up with Saint Bernards.'

'Don't ask me what he is,' I said, sliding through the door so I stood beside the policeman rather than below him. 'I got him from the pound when he was a puppy. My vet says he might be an Irish Wolfhound cross of some sort, maybe with something with a little wolf like a Husky or Samoyed.'

'Or Siberian Tiger,' he muttered, not intending me to hear. In a louder voice, he said, 'Why don't you let me see your license, registration, and insurance, ma'am.' He was relaxed, now, not expecting trouble.

I opened the front passenger door and retrieved my purse

from the jockey box, where I'd tucked it when we'd stopped at Uncle Mike's. Right next to the registration, insurance cards and my SIG.

Life would be much easier if the nice police officer didn't see that – or the .444 Marlin in the far back. I had a concealed carry permit, but I'd rather keep this low-key. Especially since, according to Stefan, Zee's dagger was not legal.

I gathered the insurance card and registration, then shut the jockey box – gingerly, so the SIG didn't rattle. I needn't have worried. When I looked for him, the police officer was sitting on the floor of the van petting Samuel.

Any other werewolf of my acquaintance I'd have been worried about – they aren't pets, and some of them resent being treated like one. Samuel canted his face so that the policeman's fingers found just the right spot behind his ear and groaned with pleasure.

Samuel liked humans. I remember him coming down to play with the elementary-school kids – all human – at recess. Most werewolves avoid children, but not Samuel. They all knew who he was, of course, and when they saw him as a man they called him Dr Cornick and treated him as they would have treated any other adult. But when he came to school as a wolf, they put him to work playing pony, runaway dog, and ferocious, but loyal, wolf-friend. He did it with the same fierce enjoyment as the children.

'He's beautiful,' the policeman said, getting out of the van at last and taking my paperwork. 'How big is he when he's standing up?'

I clicked my fingers. 'Samuel, come.'

He stood up on the bench seat, and the top of his back brushed the roof of the van. Then he stretched and hopped off the seat and onto the gravel road without touching the floor of the van. He deliberately moved like a big dog, a little clumsy and slow. His thick winter coat and the night provided some camouflage of the differences that no amount of mixed breeding could account for.

Werewolves' front legs are built more like a bear's or a lion's than a timber wolf's. Like the former two, werewolves used their claws to rip and tear flesh, and that means their musculature is different, too.

The policeman whistled and walked around him. He was careful to keep the flashlight out of Samuel's eyes. 'Look at you,' he murmured. 'Not an ounce of fat and every bit of two hundred pounds.'

'You think so? I've never weighed him,' I said. 'I know he's heavier than I am, and that's good enough for me.'

The policeman gave me back my license and assorted papers without actually looking at any of them. 'I'd still be happier if you ran in the daylight, ma'am. In any case, this park is closed at night — safer for everyone.'

'I appreciate your concern for my safety,' I said earnestly, patting the werewolf lightly on the head.

The police officer moved his car, but he waited while I closed Samuel back into the van and followed me out of the park as far as the on-ramp to the highway — so I couldn't stop to put my socks on. I hate going barefoot in leather tennis shoes.

Samuel levered his bulk up on the front passenger seat and stuck his head out the window, flattening his ears against the tear of the wind.

'Stop that,' I chided him. 'Keep all your body parts in the van.'

He ignored me and opened his mouth, letting his tongue get swept back like his ears. After a while, he pulled his head in and grinned at me.

'I've always wanted to do that,' I confessed. 'Maybe when this is all over, you can drive, and I'll stick my head out the window.'

He turned toward me and let his front paws rest on the floor between our seats. Then he stuck his nose in my midriff and whined.

'Stop that!' I shrieked, and slapped his muzzle. 'That's just rude.'

He pulled his head back and gave me a quizzical look. I took the opportunity to glance at my speedometer and make sure I wasn't speeding.

'You're going to cause a wreck, Samuel Llewellyn Cornick. Just you keep your nose out of my business.'

He snorted and put one paw on my knee, patted it twice – then stuck his nose in my belly button again. He was quicker than my slap this time, withdrawing all the way back onto his seat.

'My tattoo?' I asked, and he yipped – a very bassy yip. Just below my navel I had a pawprint. He must have seen it while I was scrambling into my clothes. I have a couple on my arms, too.

'Karen, my college roommate, was an art major. She earned her spending money giving people tattoos. I helped her pass her chemistry class, and she offered to give me one for free.'

I'd spent the previous two years living with my mother and pretending to be perfect, afraid that if I weren't, I'd lose my place in my second home as abruptly as I had the first. It would never have occurred to me to do something as outrageous as getting a tattoo.

My mother still blames Karen for my switching my major from engineering to history – which makes her directly responsible for my current occupation, fixing old cars. My mother is probably right, but I am much happier as I am than I would have been as a mechanical engineer.

'She handed me a book of tattoos that she had done and about halfway through was a guy who'd had wolf tracks tattooed across his back from one hip to the opposite shoulder.

I wanted something smaller, so we settled on a single pawprint.'

My mother and her family had known what I was, but they'd asked no questions, and I'd hidden my coyote self from them, becoming someone who fit their lives better. It had been my own choice. Coyotes are very adaptable.

I remember staring at the man's back and understanding that, although I must hide from everyone else, I could not hide from myself anymore. So I had Karen put the tattoo on the center of my body, where I could protect my secret and it could keep me whole. I'd finally started to enjoy being who I was instead of wishing that I were a werewolf or human so I'd fit in better.

'It's a coyote pawprint,' I said firmly. 'Not a wolf's.'

He grinned at me and stuck his head out the window again; this time his shoulders followed.

'You're going to fall out,' I told him.

12

'The pack is coming,' I told Samuel, as we cruised slowly by Warren's house for a look-see. 'I don't know how much you remember from while you were changing, but Warren called for help. Adam was sleeping and couldn't be woken up—' With Samuel safe, I could worry about Adam. 'Is that normal?'

Samuel nodded, and I felt a wave of relief. Clearing my throat, I continued, 'Since we can't trust the pack, I think Warren is going to try to keep them away from Adam – which would be fine except that Darryl is Adam's second.' Which meant a fight.

Samuel told me once that, despite all the physical benefits they gain, the average life span of a werewolf from his first Change until his death is ten years. People, like my old friend Dr Wallace, who had to be eliminated within their first year, accounted for some of that. But most werewolves died in dominance fights with other wolves.

I didn't want Warren or even Darryl to die tonight – and if one of them did, it would be my fault. Without my flash of intuition or paranoia that there was something wrong with the pack, Warren wouldn't have been trying to keep Darryl away from Adam.

Richland was quiet, but both sides of the street on Warren's block were solid with parked cars. I recognized Darryl's '67 Mustang as I passed it: the pack was already here. I parked a block away and jogged back with Samuel at my side.

A woman stood under the porch overhang in front of Warren's door. Her black, black hair was pulled back into a waist-length ponytail. She folded her sleekly muscled arms and widened her stance when she saw me. She was a chemistry teacher at Richland High and Darryl's mate.

'Auriele,' I said, climbing up the stairs until I shared the porch with her.

She frowned at me. 'I told him that you wouldn't do anything to hurt Adam, and he believed me. I told him you would not act against the pack. You have some explanations to give.'

As Darryl's mate, Auriele ranked high in the pack. Normally I'd have discussed the matter with her politely – but I needed to get past her and into Warren's home before someone got hurt.

'Fine,' I said. 'But I need to explain myself to Darryl, *not* you, and *not* right now.'

'Darryl is busy,' she said, not buying my argument. I'd noticed before that teaching classrooms of teenagers made Auriele hard to bluff.

I opened my mouth to try again, when she said, 'We keep the Silence.'

Wolves have little magic, as most people think of it. Sometimes there will be one, like Charles, who has a gift, but for the most part they are limited to the change itself, and a few magics that allow them to stay hidden. One of those is Silence.

I glanced around and saw four people (doubtless there were others if I cared to look) standing unobtrusively around Warren's duplex, their eyes closed and their mouths moving in the chant that brought Silence upon all that stood within their circle.

It was to keep the battle inside from disturbing anyone. It meant that the fight had already begun; the pack would not willingly break the Silence and let me through.

'This fight is without merit,' I told her urgently. 'There is no need for it.'

Her eyes widened. 'There is every need, Mercy. Darryl is second, and Warren defies him. It cannot go without answer. You can talk after he is through disciplining that one.' Her mobile brows drew together as she stared at Samuel. In a completely different voice, she asked, 'Who is that? There were strange wolves dead at Adam's house.'

'This is Samuel,' I said impatiently starting up the stairs. 'I'm going in.'

She'd started forward to intercept me, then hesitated as she took in Samuel's unusual coloration. 'Samuel who?' she asked.

Twice a year the Alphas met with Bran in Bran's corporate headquarters in Colorado. They sometimes brought their seconds or thirds – but never the women. Part of that was practicality. Alphas are uncomfortable outside their own territory, and they interact badly with other Alphas. With their mates beside them, all of that discomfort and territorialism had a greater tendency to turn toward violence.

That meant Auriele had never met Samuel, but she'd heard of him. White wolves named Samuel are not very common.

'This is Dr Samuel Cornick,' I told her firmly. 'Let us through. I've got information about the people who attacked Adam.'

I was tired and worried about Warren – and Darryl; otherwise, I wouldn't have made such an obvious misstep: I doubt she heard anything except my command.

She wasn't stupid; she knew I was not Adam's mate, no matter that he'd claimed me before the pack. I was not werewolf, not pack, not her dominant, and she could not listen to me and keep her place.

All hesitation left her manner, and she closed with me. I was a fair bit taller than she, but it didn't slow her down. She was a werewolf, and when she put her hands on my shoulders and pushed, I stumbled back three or four steps.

'You are not in charge here,' she said in a voice I'm certain worked very well in her classrooms.

She tried to push me again. Her mistake. She was a lot stronger than I, but she didn't have any experience in fighting in human shape. I moved aside, letting her momentum do most of my work. I helped her fall down the stairs with only a gentle push to keep her off-balance and make her lose control of her landing. She landed hard on the sidewalk, hitting her head on a stair.

I didn't wait around to make sure she was all right. It would take a lot more than a header down the stairs to slow a werewolf down much. The wolf closest to me started to move, but had to stop because it would have ruined the spell of Silence.

The door wasn't locked, so I opened it. Samuel brushed past me. The sound of Auriele's enraged snarl sent me scrambling in after him.

Warren's living room was a mess of scattered books and bits of broken furniture, but both Warren and Darryl were in human form. It told me that Darryl was still trying to keep the fight from being a fight to the death – and so was Warren. Werewolves in human form might be very strong, but they weren't half as deadly as the wolf.

Warren took one of his dining-room chairs and broke it over Darryl's face. The sound of the blow was absorbed by the pack's spell casting, so I could only judge the force by the size of the pieces the chair broke into and by the spraying blood.

In a move so quick my eyes couldn't quite catch it, Darryl had Warren on the ground with a lock on his throat.

Samuel darted in and closed his mouth over Darryl's wrist – then danced back out of reach. The unexpectedness of it – Darryl hadn't heard us come in – loosened Darryl's hold, and Warren broke out of it, scrambling away to get some room.

That meant Samuel could take up a position between both of them. Warren, breathing hard, sagged against a wall and wiped blood out of his eyes. Darryl had taken two swift steps forward before he recognized Samuel and almost fell over backward to keep from touching him, an expression of absolute astonishment on his face.

As soon as I was certain neither Darryl nor Warren was going to continue the fight, I tapped Samuel on the shoulder to get his attention. When he looked at me, I pointed to my mouth and ears. There wasn't a chance in hell that the werewolves outside would listen to me and stop their chanting – and we all needed to talk.

I expected Samuel to go outside, but he did something else. His power rushed through the house with the force of a firestorm after some idiot opens a door to let oxygen into a room that has been smoldering for hours. The air filled with him, with his scent and power; it popped and crackled until I felt as though I was breathing the sparklers that children play with on the Fourth of July. Discharges of power sparked on my skin until it felt raw, loosening my control of my extremities. I fell helplessly to my knees. My vision began to sparkle, too. Black swirls and bright snapping lights made me drop my head on my knees as I fought to keep conscious.

'Enough, Samuel,' said a voice I dimly recognized as Adam's. 'I think you made your point, whatever it was.'

I left my head on my knees. If Adam was here, everything else could wait until I caught my breath.

Footsteps came down the stairs with the light, quick movements I associated with Adam – he had been doing some rapid healing. I raised my head too soon and had to put it

218

back down. Adam rested his hand on the top of my head, then moved away.

'What was this about?' he asked.

'We've been looking for you for two days, Adam.' Darryl's voice sounded a little distorted. 'All we had was a message on Elizaveta Arkadyevna's answering machine that she told us was from Mercy – and your wrecked house with three dead werewolves that no one could put names to. You, Jesse, and Mercy were all missing. We've been watching your house, but it was sheer dumb luck that one of the pack saw Mercy riding around with Kyle earlier. When I called Warren, he wouldn't admit you were here, but he didn't say you weren't either, so I called the pack and came over.'

I looked up again, and this time the world didn't spin. Darryl and Warren were both kneeling on the floor, near where they'd been fighting when I'd last seen them. I saw the reason for the odd enunciation problem Darryl was having – a nasty cut on his lip was visibly healing.

'I couldn't lie to Darryl,' explained Warren. 'You were in a healing sleep, and I couldn't wake you up. I couldn't let any of the pack up there while you were vulnerable.'

Samuel sat beside me and licked my face, whining softly. 'Ish,' I said, thrusting him away. 'That's just gross. Stop it, Samuel. Didn't Bran teach you any manners at all?'

It was a deliberate distraction, designed to give us all a chance to decide how to handle the situation without more bloodshed.

'Warren was acting under my orders,' said Adam slowly.

'I see,' said Darryl, his face becoming carefully expressionless.

'Not against you.' Adam waved his hand at chest height – *don't feel hurt*, the gesture said, *it wasn't personal*.

'Then who?'

'We don't know,' I told him. 'There was just something that bothered me.'

'Tell them what happened that night,' Adam said.

So I did.

To my surprise, when I told them that I'd had a bad feeling about calling in the pack, Darryl just nodded, saying, 'How did they know where Adam lived? Or when the meeting was over? How did they know he didn't have an army at his house like some of the Alphas do? Jesse's not stupid. When she heard the sound of the tranq guns firing, she wouldn't have screamed – but they knew where she was anyway.'

I thought about that. 'There was just the one human they sent up after her – and he went right to her room.'

Darryl made a sweeping gesture. 'I'm not saying that there are not explanations other than a betrayal by one of the pack – but you made the right choice.'

It shouldn't have made me feel good – but I'm as much a sucker for a pat on the back as the next woman.

'Go on, Mercy,' said Adam.

So I continued the explanation as succinctly as possible – which meant I left out any details that weren't their business, such as my past relationship with Samuel.

The rest of the pack filtered in while I talked, taking up seating on the floor – moving broken furniture out of the way as necessary. It wasn't the whole pack, but there were ten or fifteen of them.

Auriele sat next to Darryl, her knee just brushing his. She had a nasty bruise on her forehead, and I wondered if she would continue to treat me with the cool courtesy she'd always extended to me – or if she, like the females in Bran's pack, would consider me an enemy from now on.

Warren, I thought, with Adam's support, had just cemented his place in the pack – at least with Darryl, whose body language told the rest of the pack that Warren was not in disgrace. Darryl valued loyalty, I thought, suddenly certain it wasn't Darryl who had betrayed Adam.

Who then? I looked out over the faces, some familiar, some less so; but Adam was a good Alpha, and other than Darryl, there were no wolves dominant enough to be Alphas themselves.

I got to our decision to bring Adam to Warren's, saying only that we thought it would be a better hiding place than his house or mine, and stopped because Darryl was all but vibrating with his need to ask questions.

'Why did they take Jesse?' he asked, as soon as I quit speaking.

'Warren tells me there haven't been any ransom calls,' Adam said. He'd begun pacing sometime during my story. I couldn't see any sign he'd ever been hurt, but I suspect some of that was acting; an Alpha never admits weakness in front of the pack. 'I've been thinking about it, but I honestly don't know. One of the wolves who came to my house was someone I once knew – thirty years ago. We were both turned at the same time. His experience was . . . harrowing, because he Changed without help.' I saw several of the wolves wince. 'He might bear a grudge because of it, but thirty years is a long time to wait if revenge is the only reason for taking Jesse.'

'Does he belong to a pack?' Mary Jo asked from the back of the room. Mary Jo was a firefighter with the Kennewick FD. She was small, tough-looking, and complained a lot because she had to pretend to be weaker than all the men on her team. I liked her.

Adam shook his head. 'David is a lone wolf by choice. He doesn't like werewolves.'

'You said they had humans with them, and new wolves,' Warren said.

Adam nodded, but I was still thinking about the lone

wolf. What was a man who had been a lone wolf for thirty years doing running in a pack of new wolves? Had he Changed them himself? Or were they victims like Mac had been?

Samuel laid his muzzle on my knee, and I petted him absently.

'You said they used silver nitrate, DMSO, and Ketamine,' said Auriele, the chemistry teacher. 'Does that mean they have a doctor working for them? Or maybe a drug pusher? Ketamine isn't as common as meth or crack, but we see it in the high school now and then.'

I straightened up. 'A doctor or a vet,' I said. Beside me Samuel stiffened. I looked at him. 'A vet would have access to all of those, wouldn't he, Samuel?'

Samuel growled at me. He didn't like what I was thinking.

'Where are you going with this?' asked Adam, looking at Samuel, though he was talking to me.

'Dr Wallace,' I said.

'Carter is in trouble because he can't accept being a werewolf, Mercy. It is too violent for him, and he'd rather die than be what we are. Are you trying to say that he is involved in a plot where young wolves are held in cages while experiments are performed upon them? Have you ever heard what he has to say about the animal experimentation and the cosmetics industry?'

For a moment I was surprised Adam knew so much about Dr Wallace. But I knew from the reactions of the people in Aspen Creek that Adam had spent time there. I suppose it only made sense that he would know about Dr Warren's troubles. From the murmurs around us, the rest of the pack didn't, though.

Adam stopped arguing with me to explain to everyone who Dr Wallace was. It gave me time to think.

'Look,' I said when he'd finished. 'All these chemicals for the drug they shot you with are readily available – but who would think to combine them and why? Who would want to be able to tranquilize a werewolf? Dr Wallace is in danger of losing control – I saw it myself this week. He is worried about his family. He wouldn't have developed a way to administer drugs to werewolves in order to kidnap Jesse, but he might have developed a tranquilizer for people to use on him – in case he lost all control, and his wolf attacked someone.'

'Maybe,' Adam said slowly. 'I'll call Bran tomorrow and have him ask Dr Wallace about it. No one can lie to Bran.'

'So what do they stand to gain with Jesse?' Darryl asked. 'Money seems ridiculous at this point. It seems that this attack was directed at the Columbia Basin Pack's Alpha rather than at Adam Hauptman, businessman.'

'Agreed.' Adam frowned at him. 'Possibly someone wants control of the pack? There isn't much I would not do for my daughter.'

Control of the pack or control of Adam, I wondered, *and is there a difference between the two?*

'Whoever it is and whatever they want, we should know before dawn. We know where they are staying,' I said, reaching into the pocket of my jeans and pulling out the paper the vampires had given me and handing it to Adam.

'Zee's informant said that our enemies paid the vampires almost ten thousand dollars to leave them alone while they were here,' I told Adam.

Adam's eyebrows shot up even though he clutched the paper with white fingers. 'Ten thousand is way too much,' he said. 'I wonder why they did that?'

He glanced at the paper and looked around the room. 'Darryl? Warren? Are you up to another adventure tonight?'

'Nothing's broken,' Darryl said.

'Not anymore,' agreed Warren. 'I'm up for it.'

'Samuel?'

The white wolf grinned at him.

'We can take my van,' I offered.

'Thank you,' said Adam, 'but you are staying here.'

I raised my chin, and he patted my cheek – the patronizing bastard. He laughed at my expression, not like he was making fun of me, but like he was really enjoying something . . . me.

'You are not expendable, Mercedes – and you are not up to facing a pack war.' By the time he'd finished speaking the smile had left his face, and he was watching the people in the room.

'Listen, buddy,' I said. 'I killed two werewolves – that makes my kill sheet as high as yours this week – and I didn't do so badly getting that address from the vampires either.'

'*You* got the address from the *vampires*?' said Adam, in a dangerously soft voice.

'Patronizing bastard,' I muttered, driving my van through the empty streets of East Kennewick. 'I am *not* pack. He does *not* have the right to tell me what to do or how to do it. He has no right to yell at me for talking to the vampires. He is *not* my keeper.'

He was, I'd finally had to concede, right about how little help I'd be in a fight with another pack of werewolves. Warren had promised to call me when they were through.

I yawned and realized I'd been up for nearly twenty hours – and I'd spent that last night tossing on a strange motel bed, alternately dreaming of Mac dying because of something I hadn't done and of Jesse alone and crying for help.

I pulled into my driveway and didn't bother parking the van in its usual place, safe in the pole-built garage. I'd clean out the wrappers and the socks in the morning and put it away. Zee's dagger, which I'd put back on before I left Warren's to make certain I didn't just leave it in the van, got tangled in my seat belt. I was so tired I was in tears by the time I finally was free.

Or maybe I was crying like the kid who gets picked last for the softball team at school – and is told to go somewhere and not get in the way while the rest of them played ball.

I remembered to get the guns out of the van and to grab my purse. As I started up my steps, I realized that Elizaveta Arkadyevna hadn't gotten around to cleaning the porch yet because I could still smell Mac and the distinctive scents that accompany death.

No, I decided, my lips peeling back from my teeth in a snarl, I was crying because I wanted to be in on the kill. These people had come into my territory and hurt people I cared about. It was my duty, my right, to punish them.

As if I could do anything against a pack of werewolves. I brought my hand down on the safety rail and snapped the dry wood as easily as if it had been resting on cinder blocks at the dojo. A small, soft presence rubbed against my ankles and welcomed me with a demanding mew.

'Hey, Medea,' I said, wiping my eyes before I picked her up and tucked her under the arm that wasn't holding my guns. I unlocked my door, not bothering with the light. I put the guns away. I set my cell phone in its charger beside the regular phone, then curled up on the couch with a purring Medea and fell asleep waiting for Warren's call.

The sun in my eyes woke me up. For the first few moments I couldn't remember what I was doing sleeping on the couch. The clock on my DVD player read 9:00 A.M., which meant it was ten in the morning. I never reset it to account for daylight savings.

I checked my messages and my cell phone. There was a call from Zee asking me to check in, but that was it. I called Zee back and left a message on *his* machine.

I called Adam's home phone, his cell phone, and his pager. Then I called Warren's home number, too. I looked Darryl's phone number up in the phone book and called him, writing down the other numbers his machine purred at me. But he wasn't answering his cell phone either.

After a moment of thought I turned the TV onto the local station, but there were no emergency broadcasts. No one had reported a bloodbath in West Richland last night. Maybe no one had found the bodies yet.

I took my cell, got in the Rabbit, and drove to the address the vampires had given me – I might have given Adam the paper, but I remembered the address. The house was completely empty with a FOR SALE sign on the front lawn. I could smell the pack faintly around the perimeter of the building, but there was no sign of blood or violence.

If the address had been false, where was everyone?

I drove to my shop before I remembered it was Thanksgiving and no one would be bringing in cars for me to fix. Still, it was better than sitting home and wondering what had happened. I opened one of the big garage doors and started to work on my current project.

It was difficult getting anything done. I'd had to take off my phone so I didn't break it while I was working, and I kept thinking I heard it ring. But no one called, not even my mother.

An unfamiliar car drove up and stopped out front, and a tiny woman dressed in red sweats and white tennis shoes got out. She met my gaze, nodded once, and, having acquired a target lock, walked briskly over to me.

'I am Sylvia Sandoval,' she said, extending her hand.

'You don't want to shake my hands just now,' I said with a professional smile. 'I'm Mercedes Thompson. What can I do for you?'

'You already have.' She put her hand down and nodded

back at her car, a been-there-done-that Buick that was, despite rust spots and a ding on the right front fender, spotlessly clean. 'Since your Mr Adelbertsmiter fixed it, it has been running like new. I would like to know how much I owe you, please. Mr Adelbertsmiter indicated that you might be interested in exchanging my son's labor for your time and trouble.'

I found a clean rag and began rubbing the worst of the grease off my hands to give myself time to think. I liked it that she had taken time to learn Zee's name. It wasn't the easiest name to wrap your lips around, especially if your first language was Spanish.

'You must be Tony's friend,' I said. 'I haven't had time to look at the bill Zee prepared – but I am shorthanded. Does your son know anything about fixing cars?'

'He can change the oil and rotate the tires,' she said. 'He will learn the rest. He is a hard worker and learns fast.'

Like Zee, I found myself admiring her forthright, determined manner. I nodded. 'All right. Why don't we do this. Have your son come' – When? I had no idea what I was going to be doing for the next couple of days – 'Monday after school. He can work off the repairs, and, if we suit, he can keep the job. After school and Saturday all day.'

'His school comes first,' she said.

I nodded. 'I can live with that. We'll see how it works.'

'Thank you,' she said. 'He'll be here.'

I watched her get into her car and reflected that Bran was lucky she wasn't a werewolf or he might find himself having trouble keeping his place as Alpha.

I paused and stared at my dirty hands. Last night someone had asked what the kidnappers wanted. They didn't need Adam's place in the pack, not if they had their own pack. If they wanted money, surely there were easier targets than the Alpha's daughter. So there was something special about

Adam. Among the werewolves, it is a matter of safety always to know where you rank in the pack. In the hierarchy of the Marrok it was not so important – as long as everyone remembered that Bran was on top. But people kept track anyway.

I had a very clear memory of my foster father crouching in front of my chair and naming off names on my fingers when I was four or five. 'One is Bran,' he said. 'Two is Charles, and three is Samuel. Four is Adam of the Los Alamos Pack. Five is Everett of the Houston Pack.'

'One is Bran,' I said now. 'Two is Charles, and three Samuel, both Bran's sons. Four is Adam, now of the Columbia Basin Pack.'

If there was something special about Adam, it was that – other than Bran's sons, he was the nearest challenger for the title of Marrok.

I tried to dismiss it at first. If I wanted to get Adam to fight Bran, I certainly wouldn't start by kidnapping his daughter. But maybe they hadn't.

I sat down in the Bug's driver's seat, and the old vinyl cracked under me. What if they had come to talk to Adam rather than attack him? I closed my eyes. Suppose it was someone who knew Adam well like his old army buddy. Adam had a hot temper, explosive even – although he could be persuaded to listen, once he'd calmed down again.

Given that the enemy was a werewolf, he would be afraid of Adam, or at least cautious. That's the way the dominance game works. Meeting an Alpha on his home territory puts him in a superior position. Can't take a gun loaded with silver ammunition because that would be a declaration of war – he'd have to kill Adam or die himself. Suppose this enemy had on hand a drug, something to calm a werewolf down. Something to keep Adam from killing him if negotiations went poorly.

But things don't work out right. Someone panics and shoots the person who opens the door – less dominant werewolves would have a tendency to panic when invading an Alpha's home. Suppose they shoot him several times. A mistake, but not irreparable.

Except that then Adam attacks. So they shoot Adam, too, and chain him so they can hold him until he listens. But Mac dies and Adam is not in any mood to listen. He begins to break free, and when you have enough drug in him to stop that, he is too far under to discuss anything.

They are panicking. They have to come up with a new plan. How can they get Adam to cooperate?

'Jesse's upstairs,' I said, snapping my fingers in a quick rhythm that answered the speed of my thoughts.

Take Jesse, then force Adam to listen. Or, if he won't listen, then threaten to kill Jesse.

It made as much sense as anything else. So where did Mac and the drug experiments come in?

I scrabbled out of the Bug and jogged into my office to locate a notebook. I had no proof of any of it, just instincts – but my instincts were sometimes very good.

On one page, I wrote down: *Drug experiments/buying new werewolves?* and on the next *Why replace Bran with Adam?*

I set a hip over a three-legged stool and tapped my pen on the paper. Other than the tranquilizers that had killed Mac, there was no physical evidence of any other drugs, but Mac's experiences seemed to indicate that there were more. After a moment I wrote down: *Were Ketamine/silver nitrate/DMSO the only drugs?* Then I wrote down the names of people likely to have knowledge of all the drugs. *Samuel, Dr Wallace*, and after a thoughtful pause I wrote *Auriele*, the chemistry teacher. With a sigh I admitted: *it could be anybody.* Then, stubbornly, I circled Dr Wallace's name.

He had the ability and a motive for making a tranquilizer

that would render him harmless to the people he loved. I quit playing with my pen. *Or would it?*

Wasn't the vampire's Kiss a tranquilizer? It was possible a submissive werewolf might have come out of it like any other tranquilized animal, groggy and quiet. Stefan had said that only some wolves became problematic. Samuel had come out fighting, with his wolf ready to attack, just as if he'd been trapped.

I thought of the broken manacles Adam had left behind in his house. He'd put his reaction down to Jesse's kidnapping – but maybe that was only part of it. But, that was a side issue for now.

I looked at the second page. *Why replace Bran with Adam?*

I brushed my finger over the words. I wasn't certain that was the motive, but it was the kind of motive that would leave bodies on the ground without discouraging the perpetrators. They left Adam alive when they could easily have killed him, so they wanted something from him.

Bran had been Marrok for almost two centuries. Why would someone get desperate to change the way things ran just now?

I wrote down: *want change*.

Bran could be a bastard. He was a ruler in the old-fashioned despot sense – but that was something the werewolves seemed to want. Under his rule the werewolves in North America had prospered, both in power and numbers – while in Europe the wolves waned.

But would Adam be any different? Well, yes, but not in any way that I could see would benefit anyone. If anything, Adam would be more despotic. Samuel said that Bran had considered using Adam as the poster child for the werewolves – but it would never have worked. Adam was too hot-tempered. Some reporter would shove a camera in his face and find himself flattened on the pavement.

That was it.

I sucked in my breath. It wasn't change that someone wanted – it was *to keep everything the same.* Bran was planning on bringing the wolves out.

Suddenly it didn't seem so odd that one of Adam's wolves might have betrayed him. (I wasn't as confident that my instincts were right as everyone else seemed to be.) But I could see how one of Adam's wolves could feel that aiding the enemy had not been a betrayal. They were preparing the way for him to take power. No harm was supposed to have come from their raid on Adam's house – but they wouldn't be discouraged by the deaths there. Werewolves die – and their wolves had died for a cause. A wolf like Mac, who wasn't even pack, wouldn't be a great loss when measured by what was at risk.

The betrayer could be anyone. None of Adam's pack had any personal loyalty to Bran.

I took out the card Bran had given me and called the top number. He picked up on the second ring.

'Bran, this is Mercy.' Now that I had him on the phone I wasn't certain how much to tell him – far too much of what I'd put together was pure speculation. Finally, I asked, 'Have you heard from Adam?'

'No.'

I tapped my toe. 'Is . . . is Dr Wallace still there?'

Bran sighed. 'Yes.'

'Could you ask him if he developed a tranquilizer that works on werewolves?'

His voice sharpened. 'What do you know?'

'Nothing. Not a damn thing, including where Adam and your son are right now. Just when are you considering bringing the werewolves out in public?'

'Samuel's missing?'

'I wouldn't go that far. The whole pack is with them – they just haven't bothered to check in with me.'

'Good,' he said, obviously not surprised that they hadn't seen fit to keep me updated. 'In answer to your previous question – I believe it is something that must be done soon. Not this week nor next, but not a year from now either. My contacts in the FBI laboratories tell me that our existence is an all-but-open secret right now. Like the Gray Lords, I've come to the conclusion that since coming out is inevitable – it is imperative to control how it is done.'

See? Werewolves *are* control freaks.

'How many people . . . how many *wolves* know about this?' I asked.

There was a pause. 'This is pertinent to the attack on Adam?'

'I believe so, yes.'

'Most of the wolves here would know,' he said. 'I haven't been keeping it a secret. Next month at the Conclave I am going to make a general announcement.'

He didn't say anything more, just waited for me to tell him what I'd been thinking. It was pure speculation, and I was opening myself up to ridicule by saying anything at all. I sat on that stool and realized that I had my loyalties, too. I was not a werewolf, but Bran was still my Marrok. I had to warn him.

'I have no proof,' I told him. 'Just a theory.' And I told him what I thought had happened and why.

'I don't have any idea who it is,' I told the silence at the other end of the line. 'Or if I'm right.'

'If it is a werewolf who is unhappy about revealing himself to humans, it seems odd that there would be humans working with him,' Bran said, but he didn't say it like he thought my theory was stupid.

I'd almost forgotten about the humans. 'Right. And I don't have much of an explanation about the drug tests that Mac told us about either – other than maybe they were worried about dosage or side effects. Paying for new-made werewolves seems like a lot of risk with very little benefit.'

'When two wolves are fighting, having one of them drugged could greatly influence the outcome,' said Bran. 'I like your theory, Mercedes. It isn't perfect, but it feels like you're on the right trail.'

'He wouldn't have to worry about the loyalties of humans,' I said, thinking out loud.

'Who?'

'Adam says that one of the wolves who attacked his house was someone he knew, a wolf who shared his rebirth.'

'David Christiansen.'

'Yes.' It didn't surprise me that the Marrok would know who I was talking about. Bran managed to give the impression that he knew every werewolf anywhere personally. Maybe he did.

'David works with humans,' Bran said slowly. 'But not with other werewolves. I wouldn't have thought he would ever be a part of a plot that included rape – Changes like that experienced by your Alan MacKenzie Frazier. Still it is something to consider. I'll call Charles and see what he makes of it.'

'He's still in Chicago?'

'Yes. You were right; it was Leo. Apparently his salary wasn't enough to support the kind of living he wanted to enjoy.' Bran's voice sounded neutral. 'He didn't know the wolf he sold the young victims like your Alan MacKenzie Frazier to – there were six of them altogether. He didn't know what they wanted the young ones for, either. Stupid of him. The Alpha's second is the one who set up the deal, but Charles is having difficulty getting any more information out of the second because he has left town. It may take us a while to find him. The rest of the pack seems to have been unaware of what was going on, but we are breaking them up anyway.'

'Bran? If you hear from Samuel or Adam, will you tell them to call me?'

'I'll do that,' he said gently and hung up.

13

I was in no mood for working on the Beetle after talking to Bran, so I closed up shop and went home. Bran had thought my ideas had merit, which was all well and good, except it did not answer the tightness in my belly that told me I should have gotten a call by now. My nose had told me that Adam hadn't found Jesse at the empty house in West Richland, but it didn't tell me where they'd gone afterward.

I paused again on my porch at the smell of death that still lingered there. I decided Elizaveta Arkadyevna was punishing me for not telling her what was going on. I'd have to clean the porch myself or be reminded of Mac's death every time I walked in my house for the next few months.

I opened the door, still thinking of Mac, and realized what else my senses had been trying to tell me a moment too late. All I had time to do was drop my chin so that the man who'd been standing behind the door didn't get the choke-hold he'd gone after, but his arm was still tight around my head and neck.

I twisted around sharply in his grip until I faced him, then threw everything I had into a short, sharp punch into the nerve center on the outside of the big muscle of his thigh. He swore, his grip loosened, and I pulled free and started fighting in earnest.

My style of karate, Shi Sei Kai Kan, was designed for soldiers who would be encountering multiple opponents – which was good because there were three men in my living room. One of them was a werewolf – in human form. I didn't have time to think, only react. I got in some good hits, but it rapidly became apparent that these men had studied violence a lot longer than I.

About the time I realized the only reason I was still up and fighting was because they were being very careful not to hurt me, the werewolf hit me once, hard, square in my diaphragm, then, while I was gasping for air, tossed me on the floor and pinned me there.

'Broke my f—'

'Ladies present,' chided the man who held me in an implacable grip that was as gentle as a mother holding her babe. His voice had the same soft drawl that sometimes touched Adam's voice. 'No swearing.'

'Broke my *freaking* nose then,' said the first voice dryly, if somewhat muffled – presumably by the broken nose.

'It'll heal.' He ignored my attempts to wriggle out of his hold. 'Anyone else hurt?'

'She bit John-Julian,' said the first man again.

'Love nip, sir. I'm fine.' He cleared his throat. 'Sorry, sir. It never occurred to me that she'd have training. I wasn't ready.'

'It's water under the bridge now. Learn from it, boy,' my captor said. Then he leaned down and, in a voice of power that vibrated down my spine, said, 'Let us chat a little, hmm? The idea is not to hurt you. If you hadn't struggled, you wouldn't even have the bruises you do now. We could have hurt you much worse if we had wanted to.' I knew he was right – but it didn't make him my best friend.

'What do you want?' I asked in as reasonable a tone as I could manage, flattened, as I was, on the floor beneath a strange werewolf.

'That's my girl,' he approved, while I stared at the floor between my couch and end table, about two feet from my left hand, where Zee's dagger must have fallen when I went to sleep last night.

'We're not here to hurt you,' he told me. 'That's the first thing you need to know. The second is that the werewolves who have been watching your house and the Sarge's have been called off – so there's no one to help you. The third is—' He stopped speaking and bent his head to take a deeper breath. 'Are you a were? Not a werewolf. You don't smell right for that. I thought it might just be the cat – never had a cat – but it's you that smells like fur and the hunt.'

'Grandpa?'

'It's all right,' the werewolf answered, 'she's not going to hurt me. What are you, girl?'

'Does it matter?' I asked. He'd called Adam 'Sarge' – as in 'Sergeant'?

'No,' he said. He lifted his weight off me and released me. 'Not in the slightest.'

I rolled toward the couch, and grabbed the dagger, shaking it free of sheath and belt. One of the intruders started forward, but the werewolf held up a hand and the other man stopped.

I kept moving until I was crouched on the back of the couch, the dagger in my hand and my back to the wall.

The werewolf's skin was so dark the highlights were blue and purple rather than brown. He knelt on the floor where he'd moved as soon as he let me up. He wore loose khaki pants and a light blue shirt. At another gesture, the two men backed up farther, giving me as much room as they could. They were lean and tough-looking and like enough to be twins. Like the werewolf, they were very dark-skinned. Between skin tone, general build, and that 'Grandpa,' I was betting that they were all related.

'You're Adam's army buddy,' I told the werewolf, trying to sound relaxed, like it made me think he might be on my side, like I didn't know that he'd been involved in the debacle at Adam's house. 'The one who was Changed with him.'

'Yes'm,' he said. 'David Christiansen. These are my men. My grandsons, Connor and John-Julian.' They nodded as he said their names. John-Julian was rubbing his shoulder where I'd gotten a good grip with my teeth, and Connor was holding a wad of tissue to his nose with one hand while the other held my Kleenex box.

'Mercedes Thompson,' I told him. 'What do you want?'

David Christiansen sat down on the floor, making himself as vulnerable as a werewolf could get.

'Well, now, ma'am,' he said. 'We've gotten ourselves into something of a fix, and we're hoping you can help us out of it. If you know who I am, you probably know I've been a lone wolf by choice since the Change.'

'Yes,' I said.

'I never finished high school, and the military was all I knew. When an old buddy recruited me for a mercenary troop, I was happy to go. Eventually I got tired of taking orders and formed up my own troop.' He smiled at me. 'When my grandsons resigned their commissions and joined us, I decided to quit fighting other people's wars for them. We specialize in extracting kidnapped victims, ma'am. Businessmen, Red Cross, missionaries, whatever, we get them out of the hands of the terrorists.'

My legs were getting tired, so I sat down on the back of the couch. 'What does this have to do with me?'

'We find ourselves somewhat embarrassed,' the werewolf said.

'We're on the wrong side,' said the man who'd answered to John-Julian.

'Gerry Wallace came to you,' I whispered, as if a loud noise would destroy my sudden comprehension. It was David's talking about being a lone wolf that had done it. Lone wolves and Dr Wallace meant Gerry, the Marrok's liaison with pack-less wolves. 'He told you that Bran intended to tell the world about the werewolves.' No wonder Gerry was too busy to spend time with his father.

'That's right, ma'am,' agreed David. He frowned at me. 'You aren't a werewolf, I'd swear to it, so how do you know so much about us—' He broke off his speech as a look of sudden comprehension came into his face. 'Coyote. You're the girl who turns into a coyote, the one raised by the Marrok.'

'That's me,' I said. 'So Gerry talked to you about Bran's decision to bring the werewolves out into the public?'

'Bran is abandoning the wolves to the humans, just like the Gray Lords did their people,' said Connor of the bloody nose. My strangeness evidently took second place to his indignation toward Bran. 'He's supposed to protect his people. *Someone* needed to challenge him before he could do it.'

'So you suggested Adam?'

'No, ma'am.' David's voice was mellow, but I bet if he'd been in wolf form, his ears would have been pinned against his skull. 'That was Gerry. He wanted me to come talk to him, one old friend to another.'

'Bran is not one of the Gray Lords. He would never abandon his wolves. I suppose it never occurred to you to call Adam on the phone and talk to him – or even Bran, for that matter,' I said.

'We were just back from a mission,' David said. 'We had the time. Some things just work better in person.'

'Like kidnapping?' I asked dryly.

'That was unplanned,' Connor said, a touch of heat in his voice.

'Was it?' murmured David. 'I've been wondering. The whole thing came off so badly – with four of Gerry's wolves dead – that I can't help but wonder if it was planned that way.'

'Three of his wolves dead,' I said. 'Mac was ours.'

David smiled, more with his eyes than his lips. 'Yes, ma'am. Three of his wolves died, then, and one of Adam's.'

'Why would he want to kill his own wolves?' asked Connor.

'We'd have to look at the wolves who died.' David looked thoughtful. 'I wonder if they were dominant wolves. I didn't know any of them well – except for Kara. *She* wouldn't have liked taking orders from Gerry for long. The boy, Mac, betrayed him by going to Adam for help.'

'You make Gerry sound like a psychopath,' said John-Julian. 'He didn't strike me as crazy.'

'He's a werewolf,' David told him. 'We're a little more conscious of the chain of command than humans. If he wants to stay in control, he'd have to get rid of the wolves who were more dominant – and, eventually, the wolves who betrayed the pack.'

I looked at David. 'I don't know Gerry well, but if I were to guess, I'd say you were dominant to him, too.'

David grimaced. 'I have my people. I don't want Gerry's, he knows that better than anyone. He's watched me for years.'

'So he felt safe calling you in,' I said tentatively. 'Knowing you wouldn't challenge his leadership.'

'Gerry told Grandpa that Adam didn't want to challenge Bran, but he might listen to an old friend,' said John-Julian mildly. 'He offered to fly us out here to talk, so we agreed. It didn't take long before we realized matters were a little different than presented.'

'I'd made inquiries.' David took over the narrative. 'I called friends and found out that Bran really does intend to tell the Alphas at the December meeting that he is going to take us public. So we came here to talk to Adam. I didn't think it would do much good. Adam likes the Marrok too much to challenge him.'

'But matters weren't quite as they were presented,' said Connor. 'Gerry never told us he was assembling an army of mercenaries and werewolves.'

'An army?' I said.

'A small army. Two or three of the lone wolves like Kara, who couldn't find a pack of their own,' John-Julian explained. 'And a small group of mercenaries, loners he apparently offered to turn into werewolves.'

'I should have put a stop to it when the damn fool armed a bunch of frightened idiots with tranquilizer guns.' David shook his head. 'Maybe if I'd realized Gerry'd come up with something that could hurt a werewolf . . . Anyway, from that moment on it was a classic SNAFU.'

'Adam said they shot Mac when he opened the door,' I said.

'Gerry'd gotten them so worked up about how dangerous Adam was that before they even checked to see who it was, they shot him.' John-Julian's voice held only mild regret – and I had a feeling that was mostly for the stupidity of the shooting rather than Mac's death.

'Did you know Mac?' I asked, looking down at Zee's dagger because I didn't want them all to know how angry I was. But, of course, the werewolf knew.

'No, they didn't,' David said. 'We flew in last Monday afternoon.' He gave me an assessing look. 'We were there when one of Gerry's mercenaries, a human, came in thoroughly spooked.'

'The man said someone killed his partner,' said John-Julian looking at me, too. 'A demon.'

'No demons.' I shrugged. 'It doesn't take a demon to kill an untrained, newbie werewolf who was too stupid to live.'

I swallowed my anger – it wasn't their fault they didn't know Mac. I looked at them and hesitated. Maybe they should.

My inclination was to trust them. Part of it was that their story rang true – though I didn't know them well enough to tell for sure. Part of it was remembering Adam's voice as he talked about David Christiansen.

'Let me tell you about Mac, the boy who died on my porch,' I said, then told them about his Change, the Chicago Alpha who sold him to Gerry, and the drug experiments.

'All we saw were the tranq guns,' said John-Julian, slowly. 'But two shots killed the young wolf – and they shot Adam with five before he was doped enough they could bind him.'

'Our metabolisms are put out of commission by the silver while this DMSO carries the drug more quickly into our blood system?' asked David. 'Does that mean someone could just substitute something else for the Ketamine?'

'I'm not a doctor,' I told him. 'It sounded like something like that would work, though.'

'Maybe that's what it sounded like to Gerry, too, and he was testing it out,' said David. 'With a real pack, it wouldn't have worked, but with this mix of lone wolf deviants and new wolves born of mercenaries who also have to work alone – there's no one who would feel it necessary to protect the prisoners.'

That was nature's balance to the role of the dominant wolf. As strong as the instinct of wolves to follow those who were dominant, was the instinct of dominants to protect those weaker than themselves.

'All lone wolves aren't deviants,' protested Connor.

David smiled. 'Thank you. But werewolves need packs. It takes something stronger to keep them away. A few are like me, we hate what we are too much to live within a pack. Most of them, though, are outcasts, men the pack wouldn't accept.'

His smile changed, grew bleak. 'I have my pack, Connor. It's just not a pack of werewolves—' He looked at me. 'I left the other members of our team with Gerry to keep an eye on the situation there. There are six of us. A small pack, but it works for me. Most wolves who live very long outside of a pack go a little crazy. Mercenaries are a little the same way. A mercenary who only works alone usually does so because no one else will work with him because he's stupid or crazy – and the stupid ones are mostly dead.'

'Not someone I'd want to meet as a werewolf,' I said, as my phone rang. 'Excuse me a minute,' I said, and fished around in my pockets for my cell, which had miraculously escaped damage.

'Happy Thanksgiving, Mercy!'

'Happy Thanksgiving, Mom,' I said. 'Can I call you back? I'm a little busy right now.'

'Your sister has just told us she's engaged . . .' said my mother, blithely ignoring me. So I sat and listened to her chatter about my siblings and my stepfather while three mercenaries sat in my living room and watched me.

'Mom,' I said, when she showed signs of slowing down. 'Mom, I have company over.'

'Oh, good!' she said. 'I was worried about you all alone on Thanksgiving. Is it Warren and that nice young man of his? I hope he keeps this one. Do you remember the last one? Easy on the eyes, I must say, but he wasn't someone you could have a conversation with, was he?'

'No, Mom,' I said. 'These are new friends. But I have to go, or they're going to feel like I'm ignoring them.'

I hung up the phone gently a few minutes later.

'I forgot today was Thanksgiving,' David said, but I couldn't tell if it bothered him or not.

'I've been thinking about these drug experiments, sir,' said Connor. 'Most men who are trying to assassinate a ruler intend to set themselves up instead.'

'These are werewolves,' his grandfather said. 'Not humans. Gerry could never be Marrok. Oh, he's a dominant – but I doubt he'd ever be strong enough to be Alpha of any pack, let alone all the packs. He knows that.'

'But does he like it?' asked Connor. 'Have you watched him among his wolves? Did you notice that the mercenaries he has who are still human show signs of being dominant? He tells them that he can't risk losing them right now — but I think he's being cautious. He doesn't like it when you give his wolves orders and they obey.'

'He can't change what he is,' said David, but not like he was disagreeing.

'No, sir. But he has Adam under his control now, doesn't he? Between finding the right combination of drugs and Adam's daughter, he could have Adam under his control all the time.'

David tilted his head, then shook it. 'It wouldn't work. Not for long. An Alpha would kill himself fighting before he'd submit for very long. He'd defeat the drugs or die.'

I wasn't so certain. I don't think anyone knew exactly how the drug cocktails would work — not even Gerry, who had been experimenting with new wolves and not powerful ones like Adam.

'It doesn't matter what we think. Could Gerry believe they would work on Adam?' asked John-Julian.

For some reason, they looked at me, but all I could do was shrug. 'I don't know Gerry. He didn't spend much time with the pack, and he traveled a lot with his job.' I hesitated. 'Bran wouldn't put a stupid person in a position like that.'

David nodded. 'I never thought Gerry was stupid before this. But that bloodbath has had me rethinking my opinions.'

'Look,' I said. 'I'd love to discuss Gerry, but why don't you tell me what you are doing here and what you want from me first.'

'I still don't like what Bran's doing,' David rumbled. 'Not at all. But I like what Gerry is doing even less.'

'Gerry asked us to deliver the boy's body to your doorstep,' explained John-Julian. 'He said that you needed a warning to stay out of wolf business. We met him back at the house he was using for headquarters and that was when we found out that he'd kidnapped Adam's daughter and left three of his wolves to die.'

'You don't leave your men behind,' said Connor.

'You don't attack the innocents,' John-Julian told me. It sounded like a creed.

David gave me a half smile. 'And, though I think Bran needs to be brought up short, only a fool would think he could get Adam to move a step he doesn't choose to. I'd leave Gerry to learn his lesson, but our honor is at stake. We don't hurt the innocents – so we're getting Adam and his daughter away tonight.'

'They have Adam?' It wasn't really a surprise. What else could have kept the pack away from phones all day? It was even a relief to know because there had been a dozen other, worse things that had occurred to me.

What did come as a surprise was the door opening, though I hadn't sensed anyone on my front porch. Samuel, back in his human shape, let himself into my house. He was wearing only jeans. Even his feet were bare, and he limped a little as he came to me. 'They have Adam,' he confirmed.

I might not have heard him or smelled him, but David didn't look surprised. He'd made a subtle gesture that kept his men where they were – though I could see they were tense and ready to act.

'David Christiansen, meet Dr Samuel Cornick,' I said. 'Samuel, this is David, Adam's old army buddy. He's here to get Adam and Jesse out.'

'So I heard,' Samuel said, sitting down on the couch next to my feet.

'What happened to you?' I asked.

'We got to the address we had for the other wolves and found a few signs, but nothing definite. We wandered around quite a while before Darryl realized the reason Adam wasn't recalling us from the hunt was because he was gone, along with his car. Someone saw him with a cell phone – which he didn't have when we left Warren's house. Several wolves noticed the car drive away, but no one thought to question Adam.'

'Wait a minute,' I said, because I was getting a very bad feeling. 'Wait a minute. The vampires would have checked out the address – Bran says there's nothing more paranoid than a vampire. They'd have made certain there were wolves where they were supposed to be, don't you think? Even just to make certain that it was wolves who'd come. But when half our pack shows up, they can't find enough scent to track the others?' I looked at David. 'And when Mac's body was left on my porch, I couldn't scent anyone else who shouldn't have been there – I didn't smell you.' I hunched my shoulders. 'I should have realized it then, shouldn't I? It's not just Gerry, is it?' I saw Samuel stiffen and remembered he hadn't known. 'Gerry Wallace is working with our witch.'

There were a lot of witches who could sterilize a body so that not even the keenest nose, or the best-equipped, best-trained forensics team could find a clue. But Elizaveta Arkadyevna was one of the few witches who could have removed the scent of David and his men without removing the scent of Adam's house.

'There's a Russian witch,' David said.

'If the wolf packs come out into the open, witches will lose a lot of business,' I said. 'Staying hidden bears a high price – and the witches are some of the people who benefit.

I'm not even certain it would be a breach of contract, not as long as Gerry wants to make Adam the Marrok.'

'What?' Samuel's voice was so quiet it made me nervous.

'Gerry doesn't want the wolves to be made public,' I explained. 'He decided Adam is the only one who can prevent it – by killing Bran.'

He held up a hand, his eyes cool as they watched the other men. 'I think that Mr Christiansen should tell me what he believes is happening.' So Samuel could see if he was lying or not. Samuel was one of the wolves who could do that.

David knew it, too, I could see it in his smile. 'Gerry Wallace told me that Bran was abandoning his people. He asked me if I would speak to Adam and see if I could get him to object.'

'Meaning fight the Marrok for leadership,' clarified Samuel.

'Yes. To that end he flew me and my boys out here. I was *surprised* at the method he chose. I would not have brought armed men to confront an Alpha in his own home – but I could not object more strongly without a fight that would have left me in charge of Gerry's wolves – and a sadder bunch of wolves you've never seen. I knew that Adam was capable of defending himself, so I went along with it.'

David shrugged. 'Talking to Ms Thompson, we've pretty much decided that Gerry intended that blood be spilled because the wolves who died would have been trouble for him. I think he intended blackmail rather than talk from the beginning.'

Samuel inclined his head. 'He knows Adam. Adam wouldn't challenge my father – even if he disagreed with what Bran was doing. He doesn't want to be Marrok.'

'He doesn't know Adam very well if he thinks he can control him by threatening his daughter,' said David.

'I think you're wrong,' I said. 'I think Adam would do anything to save Jesse.'

'You all sound as if it is a given that Adam would kill my father.'

I considered that. 'Gerry's the one who believes it. Maybe he intends to do something to ensure Bran's death. He still thinks that he's the only one who knows about the tranquilizers.'

Samuel growled, and I patted him on the top of the head. The back of the couch wasn't as comfortable as the seat – but I liked being taller than the two werewolves. Samuel pulled my hand down to his shoulder and held it there.

'So why did you come here?' he asked David. 'Couldn't you find Adam's pack?'

'I wasn't looking for the pack,' David said. 'Gerry's got Adam drugged to the gills. I went in to talk to him and he almost tore through his chains. From what he said, he thinks he's got a traitor in his pack – I think he's right. I suspect that's how they took him. Even so, I think the drug is making him more paranoid. Getting him out safely with his human child is going to require his cooperation.

'He doesn't trust me – and I'm sorry to say he has reason.' He looked at Samuel. 'I don't think he'll trust you either – not another male when his daughter is there.' He turned back to me. 'But you have his scent all over your van, and he has a picture of you in his bedroom.'

Samuel gave me a sharp look. 'In his bedroom?'

It was news to me, too. But I was more worried about Adam and Jesse than a picture.

'All right,' I said. 'Where are they holding him?'

With two exceptions, Samuel didn't seem to have a problem letting David make all the plans. First, Samuel insisted on calling in the wolf pack – though he agreed they were only to be backup, waiting a few minutes away. Only Darryl would know what was up, until the very last minute.

He also insisted on calling his father and telling him what we knew.

'Adam won't fight him,' Samuel told David's frozen face. 'I know he doesn't like coming out, but he understands my father's reasons.' He sighed. 'Look, none of us are happy about it, not even the Marrok. But my father has had several wolves report that one of the government agencies is threatening them with exposure if they won't cooperate.'

Some expression crossed David's face too quickly for me to read, but Samuel nodded. 'I wondered if someone had talked to you, too. The others were all military. We've become an open secret – and that's not safe. Frankly, I'm surprised that Bran's managed to keep us hidden this long. I thought that once the public accepted the fae they'd discover all of us.'

'They didn't want to know,' I said. 'Most of them like their safe little world.'

'What will your father do to Grandpa?' asked Connor.

Samuel raised his eyebrows. 'I can't think of anything he's done wrong. He's sworn no oaths to Bran or anyone else – nor done anything to betray our secrets. Just the opposite.'

My cell phone rang again – it was Bran. That werewolf was uncanny. 'Mercedes, let me speak to my son.'

I looked at Samuel, and said, 'He's not here. I told you earlier that I haven't heard from him since last night.'

'Enough games,' Bran told me. 'Give the phone to Samuel.'

Raising my eyebrows at David Christiansen and his men, I handed the phone over and listened to Samuel explain matters. Bran had probably heard the lie in my voice when I told him Samuel wasn't here. Probably. But David, who had heard both sides of the conversation, was going to be forever convinced that the Marrok *knew* that Samuel was sitting beside me.

I hid my satisfaction. The more powerful the wolves believed Bran, the safer he was.

14

We rode with Christiansen and his grandsons for most of the way, me as human and Samuel in wolf form. He'd shifted again at my house because other wolves can sense the change.

David dropped us off about a mile from the site with directions on how to get there. The idea was for me and Samuel to sneak up on our own. Then I'd see if I could wriggle my way through a hole in the side of the warehouse where Adam and Jesse were being kept, and Samuel would rendezvous with Adam's pack and wait until they were called in.

Adam and Jesse were being held at a tree farm, nestled in the rolling lands just south of Benton City, a small town about twenty minutes outside of Richland.

Though the tree farm was closed, there were still acres of trees unharvested. I recognized various maples and oaks as we passed, as well as a few pines.

A huge pole building, obviously the warehouse David had told me about, was nestled well behind the manufactured home. The house was boarded up, and there was a Realtor's sign beside it proudly proclaiming it SOLD.

Samuel at my side, I crouched in a ditch surrounded by a thicket of Russian olive and gave the place a good looking over. From where I sat, I couldn't see any vehicles, so they were probably all parked on the other side of the warehouse.

Christiansen had told us that the tree farm had been purchased by a local winery that intended to use the land to grow grapes. Since they wouldn't plant until the coming spring, the whole thing – house and warehouse – was supposed to be empty until then.

The Realtor's sign told me that one of Adam's wolves had indeed betrayed him and gave me a name.

I pulled out my cell phone and called Darryl's number. By this time, I had it memorized.

'Have you gotten in touch with John Cavanaugh, yet?' I asked. John Cavanaugh was one of the wolves I didn't know very well – he'd been at Warren's for our council of war.

'We haven't been able to locate him.'

I heaved a sigh of relief that Darryl ignored, still lost in his irritation at not being told exactly what we were doing. He wasn't happy at having to follow Samuel's orders, either.

'As *instructed*, I'm not leaving messages on answering machines. That means we are going to be short a lot of people.'

'I'm looking at John Cavanaugh's name on a Realtor's sign outside of the tree farm where they're holding Adam,' I told him.

There was a long pause.

'I see,' he said thoughtfully, and hung up. Not one for long good-byes, our Darryl, but a smart man. John Cavanaugh wouldn't be called for this rescue – or any other. Maybe it should have bothered me more that I had just signed a man's death warrant, but I'd wait and see how Adam and Jesse came out of it before I felt sorry for Cavanaugh.

Beside me, Samuel whined softly.

'All right,' I told him, and began disrobing. It was cold out. Not as cold as Montana, but too chilly to do anything but fling clothes off as fast as I could – while being careful not to stick myself on the Russian-olive thorns. I folded my clothes, somewhat haphazardly, and turned off my cell phone.

'You don't have to wait for me to get in,' I told him again.

He just stared at me.

I heaved a put-upon sigh, then I shifted. Delightfully

warm again, I stretched, wagged my tail at Samuel, and headed out for the warehouse. It was still daylight, so I took a circuitous route to avoid being seen. I was aware of Samuel trailing me, though I never saw him. Quite impressive considering his coloring – white is good for a Montana winter, but winter in eastern Washington is usually gray and brown.

One corner of the aluminum side of the warehouse was bent up, just a little, right where Christiansen had told me it would be. I had to work at it, but I got inside at the cost of a little fur. My nose told me that another coyote and several smaller critters had used the same route within the past few months. If Gerry or one of his wolves caught my scent, hopefully they'd just think another coyote had gotten in.

The interior of the warehouse was cavernous and no warmer than it had been outside. Somehow, though Christiansen had said I wouldn't have any problem finding a place to hide, I'd expected it to be empty. Instead it was filled with hundreds, maybe thousands of crates, pallet-sized with three-foot-tall plywood sides, warped by moisture and wear. The crates were stacked three high on racks that reached to the ceiling, maybe thirty feet over my head.

The air smelled musty. As I looked around, I saw there was a sprinkler system set up and drains in the floor. It made sense, I suppose. When the warehouse was full of trees, they would have had to keep the plants moist somehow until they shipped them.

I found a stack whose bottom crate bore a sheet of paper that said '*Hamamelis Virginiana – Witch Hazel 3'–4'*.' It was empty, but the astringent smell of the shrub still clung to the gray wood. I could have hidden inside the top crate, but I'd be easy to see while I was jumping in or out. Instead, I curled up on the cement between the bottom crate and the metal exterior wall, as safe as I could be under the circumstances.

The plan was for me to wait for one of David's sons to come and get me. They were going to 'do the extraction' (David's words) at night, which was still a few hours away.

Gerry had been having problems with Adam. Even with the tranquilizer, they'd found that having guards in the room they were keeping him in made him too agitated. They remembered the way he'd broken through their restraints at his house, so they did their best to keep him calm: that meant most of the time he and Jesse were alone with a guard outside the room. Gerry's scent bothered Adam enough that he'd had to stay out of the warehouse entirely.

Although we weren't getting Jesse and Adam out for a few hours, I could go in with them and do my best to get Adam ready to be rescued.

We'd argued about that. David had wanted me to wait until his man was on guard duty near dusk, but I didn't want to leave Adam and Jesse alone any longer than they had to be. David thought the risk of discovery was too high.

Samuel settled the argument. 'Let her go. She's going to do it anyway, and this way we can reduce the risks.'

David hadn't been happy, but he'd bowed to higher authority – and better judgment. Samuel was right. I wasn't about to let Adam and Jesse wait around without protection when I could be there with them. Gerry was the only wolf who would know my scent, and he was staying away from the warehouse. All the other wolves would just assume I was a coyote, and there were lots of coyotes around.

I still had to wait for escort, though, which might be a long time coming, but it was safer than having me wander around looking for where they were hiding Adam and Jesse.

It is impossible to stay in the state of readiness while

waiting motionless. Eventually I fell into a light doze that lasted for maybe an hour before the newly familiar smell of John-Julian woke me.

I crept out cautiously, but he was alone, with my pack over one shoulder. He didn't talk to me, just turned and threaded his way through the crates to a section of the warehouse that looked as though it had been offices. Like the crates, they were stacked one atop the other, three high.

He climbed the stairs to the middle tier, where the far door had a bright and shiny dead-bolt lock that made it stand out from the others. When he turned the bolt and opened the door, I darted inside and stopped.

No wonder Gerry left them with only one guard at a time. There was no chance either Jesse or Adam would escape on their own.

Jesse was lying on a bare mattress. Someone had wrapped duct tape around the lower half of her face, covering her mouth, hair, and neck. Getting it off was going to be nasty business. Handcuffs held her wrists together, and a climber's rope secured the handcuffs to the two-by-four bed frame. Her ankles were bound together and tied to the foot of the bed, making it impossible for her to do much more than wiggle.

She stared at John-Julian with dull eyes – and didn't seem to notice me at all. She was wearing pajamas, probably what she'd been wearing when they'd taken her, those soft cottony plaid things with a T-shirt top. On the white underside of her left arm was a bruise so dark it appeared black rather than purple.

Adam was seated in a chair obviously made by the same style-impaired carpenter who'd thrown together the bed frame. It was crude, made of two-by-fours and lag bolts, though I don't suppose they were worried about style. Heavy manacles, just like something you'd expect in a wax museum or medieval torture chamber – held his wrists onto the chair arms and a second set held his ankles to the chair legs. But even destroying the chair wouldn't free him because there were enough silver chains wrapped around him to have funded the local school system for a year.

'Gerry won't come here,' said John-Julian to me. Adam opened his eyes, just a bare fraction, and I saw that his irises were yellow gold and blazing with rage. 'His presence has the same effect on Adam that my grandfather's does. Not even the drugs are enough to keep Adam calm – so Gerry will stay away. Our man is only on guard for another five minutes. The next one is the enemy; but after that, Shawn, one of our men, takes over for a two-hour shift.'

John-Julian continued giving me information I already knew, repeated to make sure I understood. 'Shawn'll come in to help you as he can. The guards are supposed to stay downstairs, except when they first come on shift. But you need to leave both of them bound until Shawn takes over guard duty in case they don't. There's one guard watching the prisoners, and there are four men on patrol over the property. One of those is supposed to just walk around the outside of the warehouse. There's electricity and satellite TV in the house, so most of them are in there when they're not on duty. No one really expects Adam's pack to find them this soon, so they're not on high alert.'

David's men were doing the lion's share of guarding the prisoners because Gerry didn't have many people he could trust with a helpless fifteen-year-old girl – that not being a talent much in demand in the world of crazy mercenaries and lone wolves. David said that Gerry had paid them to stay and work guard duty. Gerry seemed to believe that David wouldn't work against him as long as he was paying them.

While John-Julian was talking, I glanced around the

room, which wasn't exactly bursting with places to hide. As long as they didn't come all the way in, I could conceal myself behind the door or in the big, sliding-door closet – some clichés are clichés because they work. There was no reason for the guards to search the room as long as Adam and Jesse were still there.

Jesse finally stirred as she realized he wasn't talking to her. She twisted awkwardly until she got a good look at me, then made a harsh noise behind her gag.

'Shh,' he told her, then said to me. 'You've got about four hours. We'll create a diversion – not my job, but you'll know it when you hear it. Your job is to get these two down the stairs and into the room nearest the big garage door. Grandpa will find you there, and we'll escort you out.'

I nodded, and he set the pack he carried on the floor.

'Good luck,' he said quietly, and left, locking the door behind him.

I shifted as soon as the door closed and opened the pack, pulling out underwear, a dark T-shirt, and a pair of old sweats. I dressed, put on my shoulder harness and slid my SIG into it. It was chambered and ready to go. I'd brought my foster-father's Smith & Wesson, too. It was too big for a shoulder harness, and I couldn't fire it as often, but the .44 magnum bullets packed more punch than the 9mm. If everything went right, I wouldn't have need for either.

I heard someone coming up the stairs and realized that I hadn't heard John-Julian go down – which was pretty good for a human. Assuming that this was the new guard, I grabbed my pack and hid in the closet, the SIG back in my hand. The closet had a sliding door, but I left the side farthest from the door open, just as it had been.

I could see Jesse jerk against her ropes as someone turned the bolt and threw open the outer door.

'Hey, pretty thing,' said the guard. I could smell the garlic he'd eaten recently, and something unhealthy and sour. He wasn't a werewolf, but he wasn't anyone I particularly wanted around Jesse either. 'I'm here to take you to the bathroom. If you're nice to me, I'll even let you eat something. I bet you're hungry by now.'

He walked over to Jesse and I had a perfect shot at his back. The temptation to take it was made stronger by the panic in Jesse's eyes and the smell of fear that washed off her.

Adam snarled, and the guard drew his gun and turned toward him. He pulled the trigger and Jesse made a horrible, disbelieving sound. I had my gun out and was tightening my own finger when I realized that the gun had made a soft pop rather than a bang – it was an air-powered tranq gun. If he'd had a werewolf's hearing, I'd have had to shoot him anyway because I couldn't help the gulp of air I'd taken when he shot Adam.

'That'll keep you for a while,' he said, presumably to Adam. He holstered the gun and bent over to work on the knots at Jesse's feet. If he'd turned around, he could have seen me – just as Jesse did.

I shook my head at her and touched my eyes, then pointed at the guard. She got the point because she quit looking at me – staring fixedly at the ceiling instead.

He didn't seem to hear it, but someone was jogging up the stairs – possibly drawn by the sound of the gun's discharge, soft as it had been. The door was hanging open so the second man came right in. This one was a werewolf. I couldn't see him, but I could smell him just fine.

'Smells like animals in here,' he said, in a voice that echoed in a bass so low that it sounded muffled.

At first, I was sure he was talking about me.

The guard I could see jerked around, obviously caught by surprise. If he'd shifted his eyes ten degrees, he'd have been staring right at me, but the second guard held his attention instead.

'You an animal, Jones?' the second man asked with a soft eagerness in his voice. 'I am.'

Jones backed up until the bed caught him behind the knees and he sat down, half on top of Jesse. I could have told him that was stupid. You don't back away from predators – it gives them the wrong idea.

When Jones didn't say anything, the werewolf laughed. 'I thought the boss told you he didn't want you anywhere near this child. Am I right?'

I don't know what the werewolf was doing, but it must have been frightening because Jones was making small noises. The werewolf moved at last, a big redheaded man with a dark beard cut close to his face. He grabbed Jones, a hand on each shoulder of his shirt, and picked him up off the bed with a grunt of effort. He turned toward the door and tossed the lighter man across the room. I didn't see Jones hit the floor, but I heard him gasp.

'Go,' the werewolf said.

I heard Jones scramble down the stairs, but I wasn't certain that it was an improvement. The man who was left was far more dangerous. He'd made that remark about animals. Had he scented me? Or was he just taunting Jones?

I stood motionless, except for a slight tremor I couldn't control, and tried to think good thoughts. Fear is a strong scent, and while Jesse was scared enough for the both of us, I was hoping to stay unnoticed.

'All right, Angel, let's get you untied,' the werewolf said to Jesse in a gentle voice that might have been more reassuring if I hadn't been able to smell his lust. Jesse was unable to do so, and I saw her relax fractionally.

His big hands made short work of the knots, and he helped her sit up like a gentleman, giving her time to work

259

out the stiffness in her shoulders and back. She, smart girl that she was, positioned herself so that his gaze was away from the closet.

He gave her a gentle boost so she could stand, then steadied her with light hands as she walked out of my view and out the door. I leaned against the wall, closed my eyes, and prayed I'd made the right decision, that he wasn't going to do anything more than take her to use a rest room.

In the meantime, I needed to check on Adam.

The dart was still stuck in his neck, and I pulled it out and dropped it on the floor. He opened his eyes when I touched him, but I don't think he saw anything.

'It's all right, now,' I told him, rubbing gently at the bloodstain on his neck. 'I'm here, and we're going to get you and Jesse out. We know who at least one of the traitors is, and the rest won't be able to cause any harm.'

I didn't tell him who 'we' encompassed. I wasn't sure he was hearing me anyway, but I wanted to soothe him rather than rile him. There was another dart tangled in the sleeve of his right arm, and I pulled it out, leaning across his body to do so. His head dropped forward until his face was buried between my shoulder and my neck. I couldn't tell if it had been a purposeful move on his part or if I'd bumped him, but I could hear his breathing deepening.

'That's right,' I told him. 'You sleep and get rid of this poison.'

I stayed there, holding him against me until I heard someone start up the stairs again. I rearranged Adam until he looked like he had when they'd left, minus the darts, then scrambled quietly back into my hiding place.

I waited, worried, as a single set of footsteps came back up the stairs. It wasn't until he came into my view again that I realized the guard was carrying Jesse. She was stiff in his arms and staring at the wall.

'Sorry, Angel,' he crooned, as he tied her up efficiently. 'I'd have given you privacy if it were up to me, but we couldn't chance it, could we?'

He was a dead man, I thought, memorizing his features and the way he moved so I'd know him again – even if Gerry happened to have two six-foot-plus redheaded giants in his pack. I'd heard the satisfaction in his voice, and I'm certain Jesse did as well. He wanted to scare her.

Adam stirred. I could hear it, though he was out of my range of vision. 'Mercy,' he said, his voice a hoarse rasp.

The guard laughed. 'Mercy, is it. You'll find none of that around here.' He reached down and patted Jesse's face. 'Until next time, Angel.'

Adam called her Angel, I remembered, feeling a little sick. The door shut, and the bolt slid home. I waited until he'd gone back down before I moved out of the closet. Jesse was still staring at the wall.

Adam's head had fallen forward again, and I couldn't help but touch him again to make sure he was still breathing. Then I went to his daughter.

She hadn't altered her position since the guard had retied her. Two hours before it was safe to release them, I thought, even while I was digging in the pack for something to cut Jesse's ropes. There was no way I could leave her like this for two more hours.

I don't know why I brought Zee's dagger with me, or why I reached for it instead of the pocketknife I'd also packed, but it came into my hand like it belonged there.

Jesse jerked when I put a knee on the bed, so I touched her shoulder. 'It's me, Mercy. No one's going to hurt you anymore. We've got to wait, yet, but we're going to get you out of here. You need to be quiet. If you can do that for me, I'll get this rope off you and see what I can do about the duct tape.'

She'd gone from being utterly passive to shivering as if

she were frozen as soon as I began talking to her. It was chilly in the room, and they hadn't covered her, so I supposed that might have been part of the problem. But she was sucking in air as hard as she could – a difficult task, since she could only breathe in and out of her nose.

I touched the edge of the dagger to my thumb. It was sharp, but not sharp enough to make cutting through climbing rope very easy. I slid the blade between a strand of the rope and the bed frame and almost stabbed myself when I pulled back and there was no resistance. I thought at first that the dagger had slipped out from under the rope – but the rope was clean-cut.

I gave the dagger a look of respect. I should have realized that any dagger Zee carried about as personal protection would have some surprises in store. I cut the rope at her feet, and she pulled her knees up to her chest and tucked her arms around her middle. Tears slid down her face, and I rubbed her back for a minute. When she seemed to be calming a little, I went back to the pack and pulled out a small, travel-sized can of WD-40.

'Next to vinegar and baking soda, WD-40 is the miracle discovery of the age,' I told her. 'Right now we're going to use it to loosen up this duct tape.'

I wasn't certain it would work, although I had used it to clean up duct tape residue on cars. But as the oil worked into the edge of the tape I was able to peel it slowly off her skin. When enough of the tape was loose, I slid Zee's dagger against the tape and cut through it close to her ear. I wasn't worried about freeing her hair just now – I only needed to get it off her face.

It came up as nicely as any of the stuff I'd peeled off cars. It didn't take very long before her mouth was free, and I sliced the remaining tape so that all she had was a strip stuck in her hair.

'That tastes terrible,' she said hoarsely, wiping her mouth with the bottom of her shirt.

'I don't like it either,' I agreed, having gotten the oil in my mouth a time or two when I forgot I had it on my hands. 'How long since you had something to drink?'

'When they brought Dad in,' she whispered to her knees. 'When I talked, he kept rousing from whatever they keep injecting him with, so they gagged me. I thought werewolves were impervious to drugs.'

'Not this drug,' I told her as I went back to my pack and pulled out the thermos of coffee. 'Though I don't think it's working as well as they want.

'I should have thought to bring water,' I told her, holding a thermos cup filled with the noxious-smelling black stuff near her face. I know that most people like the smell, but for some reason I can't stand it.

When she didn't move I snapped, 'Come on now, you don't have time to wallow. Tonight, when you're home, you can go catatonic if you want to. You need to help me get your father up and running.'

I felt like I was beating a whimpering dog, but she sat up and took the small metal cup in a trembling hand. I'd been expecting that, and only filled the cup halfway. She grimaced at the taste.

'Drink it,' I told her. 'It's good for what ails you. Caffeine and sugar. *I* don't drink it, so I ran over to your house and stole the expensive stuff in your freezer. It shouldn't be that bad. Samuel told me to make it strong and pour sugar into it. Should taste sort of like bitter syrup.'

She gave me a small smile, then a bigger one, and plugged her nose before she drank it all down in one gulp. 'Next time,' she said in a hoarse voice, 'I make the coffee.'

I grinned at her. 'That's it.'

'Is there any way to get the handcuffs off?' she asked.

'We've got a conspirator coming in a couple of hours,' I told her. 'He'll have keys.'

'Okay,' she said, but her mouth trembled. 'But maybe you could try to pick them. These aren't the good ones, like cops have, but more like the ones you find at BDSM stores.'

'Jessica Tamarind Hauptman,' I said in a shocked voice. 'How would you know about that?'

She gave me a watery giggle. 'One of my friends has a pair he got at a garage sale. He locked himself in and couldn't find a key. He was pretty panicked until his mom picked the lock.'

I took a good look at the keyhole. It looked suspiciously clumsy to me. I didn't have any handy bobby pins or wire hangers, but Zee's dagger had a narrow point.

I took one of the cuffs and tried to insert the narrow end of the dagger. First I thought it wasn't going to fit, but with a little pressure it slid in just fine.

'Ow.' Jesse jerked her arms.

I pulled the dagger back and looked at the scratch on her wrist. Then I looked at the cuff where the dagger had slid through the metal almost as easily as it had the rope.

'Metal mage indeed,' I murmured.

'What kind of a knife *is* that?' Jesse asked.

'A dagger. A borrowed one.' I set it against the chain between the cuffs and watched the chain melt away from the edge of the dark gray blade. 'Hmm. I suppose I'm going to ask more questions next time I borrow something from a fae.'

'Can it cut all the way through the cuffs?' Jess held up the damaged one, which was already half sliced through.

I held it away from her bruised skin and cautiously slid the dagger between her wrist and the cuff. It looked like some bad special effect as the metal parted from the blade.

A filmmaker would have added sparks or a bright red glow – all I could detect was a faint whiff of ozone.

'Who did you borrow it from?' she asked, as I cut through the second cuff. 'Zee?' I saw his status rise from crusty old friend to intriguing mystery. 'How cool.' She sounded almost like herself, and it was a painful contrast to the purpling bruise down one side of her face and the marks around her wrists.

I didn't remember seeing the bruise on her face before the werewolf took her downstairs.

'Did he hit you just now?' I asked, touching her cheek and remembering the sight of the guard carrying her while she tried to be as small as possible.

She withdrew, the smile dying and her eyes growing dull. 'I don't want to think about him.'

'All right,' I agreed easily. 'You don't need to worry about him anymore.'

I'd see to it myself if I had to. The veil of civilization fell away from me rather easily, I thought, taking the empty cup and twisting it back on the thermos. All it had taken was the sight of that bruise, and I was ready to do murder.

'You really ought to have more of this,' I told her. 'But I need the caffeine for your father. Maybe Shawn will bring something with him when he comes.'

'Shawn?'

I explained about David Christiansen and the help they had promised in getting us all out in one piece.

'You trust them?' she asked, and when I nodded, she said, 'Okay.'

'Let's go take a look at your father.'

Once I'd freed Jesse, there was little benefit to leaving Adam in chains, and all that silver couldn't be helping him any. I brought Zee's dagger up to bear, but Jesse caught my hand.

'Mercy?' she said in a small voice. 'When he starts coming out of it, he's . . . .'

'Pretty scary?' I patted her hand. I'd thought a time or two that her experience with werewolves had led her to think of them like pets, rather than dangerous predators. It looked as though that wasn't going to be a problem. I remember David saying that Adam had gone crazy when he'd come into the room, and I remembered the ruins of Adam's living room. Maybe the veil had been ripped from her eyes a little too thoroughly.

'What did you expect when he's helpless in the hands of his enemies?' I said reasonably. 'He's trying to defend you as best he can. It takes a tremendous amount of will to overcome the stuff they've been pumping into him. You can't expect the results to be pretty.'

I had been going to start with one of the chains, but Jesse's concerns made me realize that I was a little worried about completely freeing Adam, too. That would never do. Not if I was going to get him up and mobile. If I was afraid of him, it would rouse the predator.

Resolutely, I pressed the knife against the heavy manacle that held his left wrist. I had to be careful because the manacles fit his wrists tighter than the cuffs had fit Jesse. There was not enough space between his skin and the metal to slide the dagger in without cutting him. Remembering how the blade had reacted to cutting Samuel, I thought that might be a bad thing. So I let the knife rest on the metal without adding any force so I could pull it away as soon as it was through.

At first I thought it was the heat of my hands warming the haft, but as the blade broke through the manacle, I had to drop it because it had grown too hot to hold. Adam's hand slid off the chair arm to rest in his lap.

It took almost an hour to cut away the rest of the manacles

and chains. Each time the knife heated up, it did so more quickly and took longer to cool off. There were scorch marks on the linoleum floor and a few blisters on my hand by the time Adam was finally free of the silver chains.

Jesse helped me to gather all the chains together and heap them on the bed. We had to be careful not to drag them on the floor because the sound of metal on hard surfaces tends to carry.

We were just dropping the last of it when I heard the sound of the guard's footstep on the stair. I dropped Zee's dagger on the bed with the silver, pushed Jesse toward the closet, and drew my gun. I aimed it about six feet up the door, and froze, waiting for the bolt to turn on the lock.

He whistled as he inserted the key and I steadied my grip. I planned on hitting him in the middle of his chest first, then two shots into his head. If he wasn't dead after that, he'd be incapacitated so I could finish him off. It would rouse everyone, but I had no options: I had neither time nor inclination to rebind the prisoners.

As I drew in a breath I heard a man's voice, distorted by the door and by distance so I couldn't quite make out what he said. But I heard the man outside our door. If I had to kill someone, I was happy it would be the one who'd hit Jesse.

'Checking on the prisoners,' he said. 'It's about time to shoot Hauptman again.'

The second man said something else.

'I don't need orders to watch the clock,' he said. 'Hauptman needs more of the drug. He's not going to kick the bucket over a little silver. Hang what Wallace says.'

I sucked in my breath as power crept up the stairway. Not Adam's or Samuel's caliber, but power nonetheless, and I guessed that the man talking to our guard was David Christiansen.

The guard growled, but he pulled the key out of the door and tromped down the stairs. I heard the sound of a short, nasty little argument, and when no one came back up the stairs I decided Christiansen had won his point and put my gun away again.

'Well,' I told Jesse as I tried to steady my breathing, 'wasn't that fun.'

She'd curled up in the bottom of the closet. For a moment I thought she was going to stay there – but she was tougher than that. She gathered her courage and got to her feet.

'Now what?'

I looked at Adam. He hadn't moved.

I crossed the room and put my hand against his face. His skin was cool to my touch, which was bad. Because of their high metabolisms, werewolves usually feel warmer to the touch. I wondered how much of that silver they'd pumped into his system.

'I need to get some of that coffee into him,' I told Jesse. 'And I have some food, too – which should help.'

She stood by me and looked at him, then looked at me. 'Okay,' she said finally, 'I give. How are we going to get him to drink coffee?'

In the end, we dragged him out of the chair and propped his head up against Jesse's thigh. We dribbled the coffee, which was still hot, into his mouth. Neither of us could figure out how to make him swallow, but after a few dribbles, he did it on his own.

After the third swallow, he opened his eyes, and they were night-dark velvet. He reached up and grasped Jesse's hand where it lay on his shoulder, but his eyes were on me.

'Mercy,' he mumbled. 'What the *hell* did you do to my French Roast?'

I had a moment to believe all my worries had been for nothing when he dropped Jesse's hand and his spine curled backward, throwing his head farther into her lap. His skin went gray, then mottled, as his hands clenched. His eyes rolled back until all I could see were the whites.

I dropped the coffee and grabbed Jesse under the shoulders and dragged her away from Adam as far and as fast as I could.

'He'll hit his head,' she said, beginning to struggle as she realized, as I had, that he was having a seizure.

'He'll heal a cracked skull, but you can't,' I told her. 'Jesse, he's a werewolf – you can't go anywhere near him when he's like this. If he hits you, he'll break bones.' I thanked the dear Lord sincerely that he'd let go of Jesse's hand before he crushed it.

As if it had been awakened by the same demons that were causing his convulsions, I felt the sweep of power arise from him – as would any other werewolves in the area. Which, if Christiansen's figures were accurate, numbered twelve.

'Can you shoot?' I asked her.

'Yes.' Jesse didn't look away from her father.

I pulled the SIG out and handed it to her.

'Point this at the door,' I said, digging to the bottom of the pack for the .44. '*If* I tell you to shoot, pull the trigger. The first pull will be a little stiff. It's loaded for werewolf. We have allies here, so wait until I tell you to shoot.'

I found the revolver. There was no time to check it, but I'd loaded it before I put it in the pack. That would have to do. The Smith & Wesson was a lot heavier than the SIG, and it could do a lot more damage.

'What's wrong?' Jesse whispered, and I remembered she was human and couldn't feel the song of the Alpha's strength.

The music grew, abruptly doubling, and the focus faded until I couldn't tell that it was coming from Adam anymore. Light feet ran up the stairs and the bolt turned on the door.

Jesse was still looking at me, but I had my revolver up and aimed as the door opened.

'Don't fire,' I said, raising my gun and putting my hand on top of hers so that the automatic's nose stayed on the ground. 'He's one of ours.'

The man who stood in front of the door had skin the color of hot chocolate, a green T-shirt that said DRAGONS KILLED THE DINOSAURS, and hazel eyes. It was the shirt that told me he was David's man. He was standing very still, giving us time to decide he was on our side.

'I'm Shawn,' he said, then he saw Adam.

'Damn,' he said, stepping into the room and shutting the door quietly. 'What's going on?' he asked, his eyes on Adam, who was flat on his back, his arms and legs doing a strange, jerky sort of dance.

'I think he's changing,' Jesse answered.

'Convulsions,' I said. 'I'm no doctor, but I think that too much of the silver has worked its way into his nervous system and damaged something important.'

'Will he be okay?' Jesse's voice shook.

'He's tough,' I told her, hoping she wouldn't notice I hadn't answered the question. How much silver did it take to kill a werewolf? Usually it was a function of power – but there were some werewolves who were more sensitive to it than others.

'I was switching guard duty with Hamilton when the captain picked a fight with Connor and gave me the high sign to get my ass up here,' Shawn said. 'I hadn't taken three steps when every werewolf on the place was converging on the captain. I take it that something about this fit called them all?'

I nodded and explained to both of them as best I could. 'I don't know how Christiansen is doing it,' I told him, 'but he's pulling Adam's power and muddying it. I bet everyone will think it's him.'

'Because of the fight,' Shawn said in an 'ah-hah' voice.

But I'd lost interest in how quick off the mark Christiansen had been, because Adam quieted and lay limp. Jesse would have gone to him then, but I held her back.

'Wait,' I said, using the opportunity to take the automatic back from her so that she didn't fire it by accident. 'Make sure he's finished.'

'He's not dead?' she asked.

'No. I can hear him breathing.' It was faint and shallow, but steady.

I stowed the Smith & Wesson on the top layer in my pack and put the SIG back in its holster. Thanks to Christiansen we weren't going to have a pack of wolves converging on us – but that might change at any time.

Adam hadn't moved, but his breathing grew deeper. I started to tell Jesse that it was all right, when Adam abruptly rolled on his side and jerked into a fetal position with a low groan.

15

'*Now* is he shifting?' asked Jesse.

'That would be bad,' said Shawn. 'We don't want him changing until he's kicked off the effects of the drugs. I talked to some of the men who were in your house when he broke free. He was tranqued up then, too.'

'Stop scaring her,' I snapped. 'He'll be all right. Besides, I don't think he's changing.' Actually, that werewolfy feeling of power had died to nothing. I had no idea what he was doing.

The dress shirt Adam wore, dirty, torn, and stained with drops of blood, looked more gray than white. A lot more gray. He'd broken out into a sweat, and the fabric began to cling to him, outlining the taut muscles of his shoulders and back. I could even see the bumps of his spine. The shirt shimmered a little under the cold fluorescent lights as he shivered miserably. I couldn't tell if he was conscious or not.

I holstered the revolver and walked slowly toward him.

'Adam,' I said, because he had his back to me. It is never a good thing to startle a werewolf. 'Are you all right?'

Unsurprisingly, he didn't answer.

I crouched and touched the wet fabric, and he grabbed my wrist – his movement so fast that he was just suddenly there, on his back. I don't remember seeing him roll over. His eyes were yellow and cold, but his grip was light.

'You're safe,' I told him, trying to stay calm. 'Jesse's here, and she's safe, too. We're going to get you on your feet in fighting shape, then we're getting out of here.'

'It's the silver,' said Shawn, awed. 'That's why the shirt

272

is turning gray. Fu— I mean, damn. *Damn*. He's sweating silver. Damn.'

Adam didn't look away from me, though he flinched subtly at the sound of Shawn's voice. His blazing gold eyes held mine, somehow hot and icy at the same time. I should have looked away — but it didn't seem like a dominance contest. It felt like he was using my eyes to pull himself up from wherever the drugs had forced him. I tried not to blink and break the spell.

'Mercy?' His voice was a hoarse whisper.

'*C'est moi, c'est moi*, 'tis I,' I told him. It seemed appropriately melodramatic, though I didn't know if he'd catch the reference. I shouldn't have worried.

Unexpectedly, he laughed. 'Trust you to quote Lancelot rather than Guinevere.'

'Both of them were stupid,' I told him. 'Arthur should have let them marry each other as punishment and gone off to live happily on his own. I only like *Camelot* for the music.' I hummed a bit.

The mundane talk was working. His pulse was less frantic, and he was taking deep, even breaths. When his eyes went back to normal we'd be out of trouble. Except, of course, for the small matter of a warehouse full of enemies. One trouble at a time, I always say.

He closed his yellow eyes, and momentarily I felt cut adrift and abandoned until I realized he was still holding my wrist as if he were afraid I'd leave if he let go.

'I have the mother of all headaches,' he said, 'and I feel like I've been flattened by a steamroller. Jesse's safe?'

'I'm fine, Dad,' she said, though she obeyed the urgent signal I made with my free hand and stayed where she was. He might have sounded calm, but his scent and the compulsive way he was holding on to my wrist contradicted his apparent control.

'Bruised and scared,' I said. 'But otherwise unhurt.' I realized that I actually didn't know that and gave Jesse a worried glance.

She smiled, a wan imitation of her usual expression. 'Fine,' she said again, this time to me.

His sigh held relief. 'Tell me what's been going on.'

I gave him a short version – it still took a while to tell. Except for when I told him about David Christiansen's invasion of my home, he kept his eyes shut as if it hurt him to open them. Before I finished he was twisting uncomfortably.

'My skin is crawling,' he said.

'It's the silver that's bothering you.' I should have thought of that earlier. Touching his shirt with my free hand, I showed him the gray metal on my index finger. 'I've heard of sweating bullets before, but never silver.' I started to help him remove his shirt when I realized he couldn't run around naked with Jesse here. 'I don't suppose you have any extra clothes, Shawn? If that silver stays against his skin it'll burn him.'

'He can have my shirt,' he said. 'But I can't leave to get clothes; I'm on guard duty.'

I sighed. 'He can have my sweatpants.' The T-shirt I was wearing hit me halfway down my thighs.

Shawn and I stripped Adam as quickly as we could, using the shirt to wipe most of the silver off his skin before covering him in my sweats and Shawn's green T-shirt. Adam was shivering when we finished.

The thermos cup had dumped its sticky contents all over the floor when I dropped it, but both it and the thermos had survived. I had Jesse pour hot coffee down her father as fast as he'd drink it, and, with something to focus on, she steadied. When the coffee was done, she fed him the raw roast from the Ziploc bags without turning a hair.

I was worried because Adam was so passive, not a state I'd ever seen him in before. Samuel had said prolonged exposure to silver increased sensitivity. I thought about Adam's headache and the seizures and hoped lycanthropy was enough to allow him to heal.

'You know,' said Shawn thoughtfully, 'for someone who wants this one to fight the head wolf in a month, Gerry's not taking very good care of him.'

I was frowning at him when I heard the door open.

'Hey, Morris,' said the stranger as he opened the door, 'the boss wants to see you and—' His eyes traveled to Adam and Jesse and he stopped speaking and went for his gun.

If I had been alone, we'd have all been dead. I didn't even think to pull my weapon, just stared in shock, belatedly realizing that Shawn hadn't bolted the door when he'd come in. Shawn's gun popped quietly three times in rapid succession, putting a neat triangle of red over the intruder's heart, making little more noise than someone opening a can of pop. He was shooting a small-caliber automatic with a silencer.

The wounded man fell slowly to his knees, then forward onto his face. I pulled my SIG at last and took aim.

'No,' Adam said. 'Wait.' He looked at his daughter. 'You told me you weren't hurt – is that true?'

Jesse nodded resolutely. 'Just bruises.'

'All right, then,' he said. 'Mercy, we're going to try to leave as many alive as possible – dead men tell no tales, and I want to know exactly what's been going on. We'll be gone before this man heals enough to be a danger. Leave him be.'

'He's not dead?' asked Shawn. 'The captain says you can kill werewolves with lead.'

Not being in the habit of taking on werewolves, Christiansen's men hadn't had silver ammunition, and my supply was limited. Silver bullets are expensive, and I don't go out hunting werewolves on a regular basis. Only Connor had had a gun that could use any caliber I had anyway. I'd given him a half dozen of my 9mm bullets.

'You have to take out the spinal column if you want to kill a werewolf without silver,' I told him. 'And even then . . .' I shrugged. 'Silver ammo makes wounds that don't heal as fast, gives them a chance to bleed out.'

'Damn,' Shawn said, with a last look at the bleeding werewolf he'd shot. He took out a cell phone and dialed in several numbers.

'That'll let everyone know we're on the move,' he told me when he'd finished, tucking the small device back into his pants pocket. 'We've got to get out of here now. With any luck they'll assume someone's out on the range and won't pay attention to my shots. But someone's going to miss Smitty, and we need to be out of here when they do.' Then he got down to business and organized our retreat.

I put the SIG back in its holster and took out the .44 magnum. I didn't have a holster for it so I'd just have to carry it. I shoved the extra magazine for the SIG into my bra because I didn't have any better place to store it.

We dragged the wounded werewolf out of the doorway, then Shawn and Jesse got Adam to his feet. Shawn because he was the strongest of us, Jesse because I knew how to shoot a gun. I went out the door first.

This part of the warehouse was set apart from the main room. The offices had been set into a section half the width of the building, and below me was a bare strip of cement wide enough for two trucks to drive side by side. Leaning over the railing to check beneath the stairway, I could tell that there was no one nearby, but I couldn't see very well into the rest of the building because of the racks of giant crates.

As soon as the others were out of the room and onto the landing, I ran down ahead of them to the second-floor landing, where I could guard their descent. Shawn's plan was that we were going to try to get Adam to the cars. One of Gerry's men drove a classic Chevy truck that Shawn said he could hot-wire faster than he could put a key in the ignition.

I tried to control my breathing so I could listen, but the warehouse was silent except for my comrades coming down the stairs and the ringing in my ears that could have obscured the movements of an army.

There was a garage door right next to the offices, the kind that is double-wide and double-high so a semi can drive through it. Shawn told me it was kept padlocked from the outside, and Gerry had shot the motor that opened it when he'd decided to keep Jesse in one of the offices here where he could control who had access to her. We'd have to make our way back toward the other side of the warehouse and go out a person-sized door, which was the only one unlocked.

As I waited at the bottom of the stairs, trying to see into the warehouse past the impossible maze of crates that could conceal a dozen werewolves with a host of hiding places to spare, I thought about what Shawn had said at last. He was right. If Gerry wanted Adam to kill Bran, he'd need him in a lot better shape. It wouldn't take Bran more than a few seconds to kill Adam in his present condition.

Gerry wasn't stupid, Samuel had told me. So maybe that was the result he intended.

It occurred to me that there were an awful lot of things that didn't make sense if Gerry wasn't stupid – and Samuel was a pretty good judge of character. David seemed to think that the bloodbath at Adam's house had served to rid Gerry of some unwanted competition – but it had also drawn the Marrok's attention. And it would have drawn Bran's eye, even if I hadn't taken Adam to him. An attack at an Alpha's home was important. Then there was that payment to the vampires. I might have found out about it sooner than expected, but if Bran had come sniffing around, I was pretty sure he'd've discovered it, too.

If I were trying to get someone to challenge for Marrok, I wouldn't make my candidate hate me by kidnapping his daughter. If I were going to use underhanded methods to force a challenge I wasn't certain my candidate would win, I would make sure to cover my tracks so Bran would never find out – and Bran had a deserved reputation for finding out everything.

Gerry had all but painted a billboard that said, 'Look at what I'm doing!' and, if he wasn't stupid, he'd done it on purpose. Why?

'Mercy.' Shawn's whisper jerked me back to the present. They were down the stairs, and I was blocking their way.

'Sorry,' I said in the same soundless whisper.

I took point, walking a few steps ahead and looking around the crates as we passed. It was slow going. Adam was having problems with the leg he'd damaged in the first attack, and Jesse was too short to be a good crutch when paired with Shawn, who was nearly six feet tall.

I'd heard something, or thought I had, and I stopped. But when the sound didn't repeat, I decided it was still the ringing in my ears, which was coming and going a little. I hadn't taken but three steps when power ran through me like a warm, sweet wind.

'The pack's here,' said Adam.

I'd never felt them like that before, though I suppose I'd never been in a situation where they were all coming together with one purpose. That might have been all it was, or it might have been because I was standing so close to the pack's Alpha.

Adam stopped and closed his eyes, breathing in deeply. I could almost see the strength pouring into him, and he straightened, taking all of his own weight.

Jesse was watching her father, too. Only Shawn kept his mind and his eyes on the job, and it was the widening of his eyes that had me spinning back around.

If the werewolf had been after me, I'd have been dead. But he had picked out the most dangerous of us and brushed by me like a cannonball, knocking me into a crate. The Smith & Wesson flew out of my hand, but didn't go off when it hit the ground. I heard my upper arm crack and felt a wash of pain as the force of his passing continued to spin me until I landed on the floor facing Adam as the wolf jumped on him.

Jesse screamed. Shawn had emptied his gun without slowing down the wolf. He drew a wicked-looking knife and closed in to use it, but the werewolf caught him with one of those quick catlike sideswipes that no canid should have the lateral motion to do. Like me, Shawn hit a crate and collapsed on the floor.

I struggled to my feet and took out Zee's dagger with my left hand. I don't know why I didn't draw my SIG except that the shocking speed of the attack had left me dazed. This week aside, I usually kept the violence in my life controlled and confined to a dojo.

I started forward, and something red rushed past me in a blur of motion. Another werewolf. I had time to believe that we were out of luck, when it grabbed the first wolf by the scruff of the neck and tossed it back down the aisle, away from Adam.

The red wolf didn't pause there, but was on the gray-and-tan animal almost before it landed. Adam was covered in blood, but before I made it to him, the wounds closed in a rush of power that was pack-scented. He rolled to his feet, looking better than I'd seen him since Monday night.

I, rather belatedly, remembered I had another gun, and dropped Zee's knife so I could draw the SIG, waiting for the two wolves to separate enough that I could shoot. With a little perspective I could see that the red animal was taller and leaner than usual, as if he'd been bred for running rather than fighting.

'I don't want them dead if I can help it,' Adam said, though he didn't try to take the gun from me.

'This one needs to die,' I said, because I'd recognized his scent. He was the one who had slapped Jesse's face.

Adam didn't have the chance to argue with me because the gray-and-tan wolf came out on top of the wrestling match and I pulled the trigger three times. It wasn't the .44, but even a 9mm does a lot of damage when it hits the back of a skull at under fifteen feet.

Adam was saying something. I could see his mouth move, but my abused ears were roaring with a sound as big as the seashore. One of the downsides of good hearing is sensitive ears – something the wolves, with their healing abilities, don't have to worry about much.

He must have realized I was having trouble hearing him because he tapped my gun and raised an eyebrow, asking me a question. I looked at the crumpled werewolf, then at Jesse. Adam followed my gaze, and his face grew cold and hard. When he held out his hand, I gave him the SIG.

He stalked to the werewolves, no trace of a limp in his stride. He reached down and grabbed the dead wolf with one hand and hauled him off the other one, who rolled to his feet then stood still, head down, looking dazed. Adam cupped a hand under the red wolf's jaw, checking for damage. Apparently satisfied, he turned to the defeated opponent and emptied the gun into the body.

I saw him snap his fingers, and the red wolf shook his whole body as if he'd just come out of a swimming pool, then came to sit at Adam's heel, just like a well-trained dog. Jesse picked up the dagger and sheathed it for me as Shawn got slowly to his feet. He put a fresh magazine in his gun, then put a hand on my broken arm.

I must have made a noise, but the next thing I remember is being on my knees with my head low and a big, warm hand on the back of my neck. Adam's scent, rich and exotic, was all around me, giving me the strength to calm my queasy stomach. I don't think I lost consciousness completely, but it was a near thing.

When I lifted my head, the red wolf stuck his nose in my face and ran a long tongue over my cheek before Adam cuffed him lightly. I got to my feet with Adam's help, but stood on my own.

Adam reloaded the automatic when I handed him a fresh clip – though he grinned when I took it out of my bra. I think I was glad I couldn't hear well enough to decipher what he said. He put the SIG in my holster, picked up my revolver, and handed it to me. Then he turned his attention to Shawn, who waved away Adam's concern.

The werewolf at our side was more reassuring than the loaded gun I carried as we walked toward the door. It wasn't that he was more effective than the .44, but his presence meant that the pack was near. All we had to do was join them, and we were safe.

I glanced at Adam. He looked healthy, as if he'd never been hurt. I'd heard that the Alpha could take strength from his pack; but I didn't know why it had worked here, when it hadn't had the same effect at Warren's house.

Shawn went through the door first, the red wolf at his heels. It was night, and the waxing moon was high in the sky. Adam held the door open for Jesse and me, then walked out into the field of parked cars like a man walking into his own living room.

At first I could see no one, but then a shadowy form emerged from behind a car, then another one, and another. Silently Adam's pack formed around him. Most of them were in wolf form, but Warren and then Darryl came as humans. They wore dark clothing and both of them were armed.

Warren looked at the red wolf, our rescuer, and raised an eyebrow, but he didn't break the silence. He examined Adam and then touched Jesse's bruised cheek.

'Warren.' Adam spoke in a soft voice that wouldn't carry far. 'Would you take my daughter and Mercedes to safety, please?'

Another time I would have argued with Adam. After all, who had rescued whom? But my arm was throbbing brutally and I'd done my killing for the day. The only good thing was that my ears had quit ringing. Let Adam and his people finish this, I was ready to go home.

'I don't want to leave you,' said Jesse, taking a firm grip on her father's borrowed T-shirt.

'I'll take her to my house,' Warren said, with a reassuring smile at Jesse. 'You can stop and pick her up on the way home.' In a softer voice, he said, 'I'll stay with you until he comes. You'll be safe with me.'

'All right.' Jesse nodded in a quick, jerky motion. I think she'd just figured out that her father wanted her out of the way before he dealt with the people who'd kidnapped her.

'I don't have a car here, though,' Warren told Adam. 'We ran about three miles as the crow flies to get here.'

'Shawn?' I said, trying to keep my voice as quiet as everyone else's had been. 'You told me that there was an old truck around here somewhere that was easy to hot-wire? If you can tell me where to look for it, I can hot-wire it so Warren can get us out of here.'

'On the far side of the warehouse, away from everyone else's cars,' he said.

I started off alone, but Warren and Jesse were soon on my heels. The truck was the only car on the far side of the warehouse. Parked in the center of the pale illumination of one of the warehouse's exterior lights, was a '69 Chevy, painted some dark color that glittered. Someone was going to be very unhappy to see his toy missing – if he survived Adam's wrath.

But that wasn't my problem. My problem was how to hot-wire a car when my right arm was broken. I'd been keeping it tucked against my side, but that wasn't going to be enough for much longer. The pain was steadily getting worse and making me light-headed.

'Do you know how to hot-wire a car?' I asked Warren hopefully, as we approached the truck.

'I'm afraid not.'

'How about you, Jesse?'

She looked up. 'What?'

'Do you know how to hot-wire a car?' I asked again, and she shook her head. She smelled of fear, and I thought of how she had clung to her father.

'That guard tonight,' I said.

She looked puzzled for a minute, then flushed and hunched her shoulders.

'He's not going to bother anyone ever again.'

'He was the dead werewolf?' I couldn't read the expression on her face. 'That's why you killed him?' She frowned suddenly. 'That's why Dad shot him like that. How did he know? He was unconscious – and you didn't say anything to him.'

'I didn't need to,' I answered, and tried to explain that moment of perfect understanding, where a gesture had told Adam everything he needed to know. 'He saw it in my face, I suppose.' I turned to Warren and handed him the .44 so I could do my best with the truck.

Hot-wiring the truck with one hand took me longer than the keys would have, and the awkward position I had to take in order to strip the housing off the steering wheel and touch wires had me bumping my injured arm. But the engine roared to life at last – something bigger than the original power-house rumbled underneath its hood – and I realized my hearing had cleared up completely.

'I've never heard you swear before,' said Jesse, sounding a little better. 'At least not like that.'

'Power words. Without which mechanics the world over would be lost.' Warren's tone was light, but his hands were gentle as they helped me extract myself from the cab. He handed me my gun and, when I fumbled, took it back and made sure it was at half-cock before he handed it to me again.

He opened the passenger door and helped Jesse inside and then held his hand out to me. I took a step toward him, then something attracted my attention.

At first I thought it was a sound, but that was only because I was tired. It was magic. It wasn't wolf magic or fae magic.

And I remembered Elizaveta.

Samuel knew about her, I told myself. But I knew that I couldn't leave. None of the werewolves could feel her magic, not until it was too late, and Samuel might not know how important it was that Adam know that Elizaveta was working with Gerry.

Elizaveta Arkadyevna Vyshnevetskaya was not just any witch. She was the most powerful witch in the Pacific Northwest.

I had to warn Adam.

'Get Jesse to your house,' I told him. 'Feed her, make her drink gallons of orange juice, cover her with a blanket. But I have to stay.'

'Why?'

'Because if Bran brings the wolves out in the open, Adam's witch on retainer loses her income.'

'Elizaveta?'

284

A gun went off, echoed by a second and third crack.

'Get Jesse out of here, I have to warn Adam. Elizaveta's here and she's working on some sort of spell.'

He gave me a grim look. 'How do I turn off the truck?'

Bless him. He wasn't going to argue.

'Just pull the wires apart.'

There was gunfire from the other side of the warehouse, four shots. They sounded like they were coming from somewhere near the boarded-up house.

'Be careful,' I told him. He kissed me on the forehead without touching my poor sore body, then hopped in the cab.

I watched him back out, turn on the lights, and drive away. Jesse was safe.

I've always been able to sense magic of all kinds, be it werewolf, witch, or fae – and I know that isn't usual. Charles, when he found out, told me to keep it secret – in light of the vampire's reaction to finding out what I was, I could see that there was more to Charles's advice than I'd thought.

From what Stefan had told me, I was somewhat immune to the vampire's magic, but I wasn't such a fool as to assume the same was true of witchcraft. Once I found her I had no idea what I was going to do with her – but I try not to worry about one impossible task until I've completed the first.

Turning in a slow circle gave me a direction. The pulse of magic felt like a warm wind in my face. I took two steps toward it . . . and the spell drifted away into nothing. All I knew for sure was that Elizaveta was here, and she was somewhere in front of me. The best thing to do was to find Adam and warn him, so I walked back around the warehouse.

Things had changed since I left. Adam, the red wolf still sitting at his feet, had only a handful of wolves with him. Shawn, David's grandsons, and a couple of other humans I didn't know, held guns on a group of men who were stretched out on the ground in a spread eagle.

As I approached them, David and Darryl escorted another man out and sent him sprawling by the other men.

'That's all the humans, Sarge,' David said. 'We left a couple dead in the house. But the wolves have scattered, and I couldn't pick up Gerry's trail, though, not even when I started from the last place I saw him. His scent just fades away.'

'Adam,' I said.

He turned to look at me and the red wolf suddenly leaped into the air as a shot rang out. It wasn't a particularly loud shot; it sounded like a small caliber.

'Get down!' barked David as he dropped to the ground. His men crouched, still holding their guns on their prisoners.

The wolf beside Adam stood for just a moment longer, then collapsed, as if it had listened to David as well – but I could see the dart dangling on his side and knew he'd been hit by one of the tranquilizer guns.

Adam didn't drop. Instead he closed his eyes and canted his face upward. For a moment I wondered what he was doing, then I realized the light on his face came from the moon, which rose above us almost exactly half-full.

Darryl, low to the ground, surged over the distance between Adam and him. He stopped beside the downed wolf, jerked the dart out.

'Ben's okay,' Darryl said, raising his gun so he'd be ready to shoot as he scanned the darkness surrounding us.

Ben was the red wolf. It had been Ben, the psycho-killer from London, who had saved us. Saved Adam twice.

Another shot fired. Adam moved his hand and the dart fell to the ground to roll harmlessly against his feet. His eyes were still closed.

'Sarge, Mercy,' hissed David. 'Get down!'

I realized then that I was still standing, too, leaning a little toward Adam as he called down the moon. I might have knelt then, if only because David told me to, but Adam threw back his head and howled, a wolf's song rising from his human throat.

For a moment the eerie sound rose, echoed, and died away into silence, but not an empty silence. More like the deadly quiet that precedes the start of the hunt. When he howled again, he was answered by every werewolf within hearing distance.

I could feel a song surging into my throat, but like my wild brethren, I knew better than to sing with the wolves.

When Adam called a third time, Darryl and David both dropped their weapons and began to change. The moon's call sang through the trees and I could feel it catch the rest of the wolves and force them into their wolf form. I could hear cries of agony from those who fought it and groans from those who didn't.

Adam stood in the moonlight, which seemed somehow brighter than it had been moments ago. He opened his eyes and looked at the moon's face. This time he used words.

'Come,' he said.

He didn't speak loudly, but somehow his voice, like his song, spread through the abandoned tree-farm like a roll of thunder, powerful and unavoidable. And the wolves came.

They came by ones or twos. Some came with joyful dancing steps, others with feet dragging and tails low. Some were still changing, their bodies stretched and hunched unnaturally.

The warehouse door banged open and a man staggered out, one hand clutched to his chest. It was the guard Shawn had shot. Too weak to change, he still answered the power of Adam's call.

I wasn't immune. I took a step forward without watching the ground and stumbled over a stick. I caught my balance, but the jerky move set off the pain in my arm – and the pain cleared my head like a dose of ammonia. I wiped my watering eyes with the back of my wrist and felt the unmistakable surge of witchcraft.

Heedless of Adam's magic and my arm, I started running, because, in the night air, thick with power, I felt the spell gathering death and it bore Adam's name.

I couldn't take the time to find the witch; the spell was already set in motion. All I could do was throw myself in front of the spell, just as Ben had thrown himself in front of the dart.

I don't know why it worked. Someone told me later that it shouldn't have. Once a spell is given a name, it's sort of like a guided missile rather than a laser beam. It should have moved around me and still hit Adam.

It hit me, brushed through me like a stream of feathers, making me shiver and gasp. Then it paused, and, as if it were a river of molten iron and I a magnet, all the magic flowed back into me. It was death-magic and it whispered to me, *Adam Hauptman*.

It held a voice. Not Elizaveta's voice, but it was someone I knew: a man. The witch wasn't Elizaveta at all – it was her grandson Robert.

My knees bowed under the weight of Robert's voice and under the stress of taking upon myself Adam's name so that the magic stopped with me. My lungs felt as if I were breathing fire and I knew that my interference couldn't last for long.

'Sam,' I whispered. And as if my voice had conjured him from thin air he was suddenly in front of me. I'd expected him to be in wolf form like everyone else, but he wasn't.

He cupped my hot face in his hands. 'What's wrong, Mercy?'

'Witch,' I said and I saw comprehension in his eyes.

'Where is she?'

I shook my head and panted. 'Robert. It's Robert.'

'Where?' he asked again.

I thought I was going to tell him I didn't know, but my arm raised up and pointed at the rooftop of the boarded-up house. 'There.'

Samuel was gone.

As if my gesture had somehow done something, the flow of magic increased fivefold. I collapsed completely, pressing my face against the cold dirt in hopes of keeping the fire burning inside of me from consuming my skin. I closed my eyes and I could see Robert, crouched on the roof.

He'd lost something of his handsomeness, his face twisted with effort and his skin mottled with reddish splotches.

'Mercedes.' He breathed my name to his spell and I could feel it change like a bloodhound given a different handkerchief to sniff. 'Mercedes Thompson.'

Mercedes, whispered the spell, satisfied. He'd given death my name.

I screamed as pain rushed through me, making the earlier agony from my arm pale in comparison. Even in the consuming fire, though, I heard a song. I realized there was a rhythm to Robert's spell, and I found myself moving with it, humming the tune softly. The music filled my lungs, then my head, banking the fire for a moment while I waited.

And then Samuel stopped the magic for me.

I think I passed out for a little while because suddenly I was in Samuel's arms.

'They're all here, but for one,' he said.

'Yes.' Adam's voice still held the moon's power.

I struggled and Samuel set me down. I still had to lean against him, but I was on my feet. Samuel, Adam, and I were the only ones on our feet.

There couldn't have been as many as it looked like. The Columbia Basin Pack is not that big, and Gerry's pack was much smaller – but all of them were sitting on the ground like a platoon of Sphinxes awaiting Adam's order.

'Two of the lone wolves, older and more dominant, ran when you first called,' Samuel said. 'The rest answered. They're yours now. All you have to do is call Gerry.'

'He won't come,' Adam said. 'He can't leave. That much I can do. But he's not a lone wolf. He belongs to the Marrok.'

'Will you let me help?'

The moon caught Adam's eyes and, although he was still human, his eyes were all wolf. I could smell his reaction to Samuel's question. A low growl rose over the waiting were-wolves as they smelled it, too. Wolves are territorial.

Adam stretched his neck and I heard it pop. 'I would appreciate it,' he said mildly.

Samuel reached out his hand and Adam took it. He straightened and lifted his face to the moon once more. 'Gerry Wallace of the Marrok Pack, I call you to come and face your accusers.'

He must have been very close, because it didn't take him long. Like Samuel, he had stayed in human form. He paused at the edge of the wolves.

'Gerry, old friend,' said Samuel. 'It's time. Come here.'

The gentle words didn't hide their power from me – or from Gerry. He dropped to his hands and knees and crawled through the motionless wolves, his head down submissively. He wasn't fighting anymore.

He stopped when he neared us. I thought he'd be angry – as I would have been if someone had forced me against my will. Or maybe frightened. But I'm not a werewolf. The only emotion I could catch was resignation. He'd lost and he knew it.

Adam crouched until he sat on his heels and put his hand on Gerry's shoulder.

'Why?'

'It was my father,' Gerry said. His face was calm and his voice dreamy, firmly held in the moon's call. 'He was dying. Cancer, they said. I talked and talked. I begged and pleaded. Please, Papa, being a wolf is a wonderful thing. I think he was just tired of me when he agreed. Bran did it — because I couldn't bear it. And at first it was perfect. The cancer went away, and he could run.'

'I heard,' Adam said. 'He couldn't control the wolf.'

'Wouldn't.' It was eerie hearing that peaceful tone while tears slid down Gerry's face. 'Wouldn't. He had been a vegetarian, and suddenly he craved raw meat. He tried to set a bird's wing, and it died of fear of the thing he'd become. Bran said being a werewolf was breaking my father's heart. He couldn't — wouldn't — embrace what he was because he didn't want to be a predator. He didn't want to be like me.'

Adam frowned at him. 'I thought you were trying to keep Bran from exposing us to the humans.'

Gerry wiped his face. 'Bran said if my father was not so dominant, he would not have been able to resist the wolf. But the more he resists, the less control he has. He almost killed my sister.'

'Gerry.' Samuel's voice was firm. 'What does this have to do with Adam?'

Gerry lifted his head. He couldn't meet Samuel's eyes, or Adam's, so he looked at me. 'When you fight,' he said, 'the wolf and the man become one. It would only take once. Just once and my father would be whole.'

'He didn't want Adam to fight Bran,' I said suddenly. 'Did you, Gerry? That's why you weren't concerned with all the silver your men were pumping into him. Did you want to kill him?'

He looked at me with his father's eyes and said, 'Adam had to die.'

'You don't care about Bran's decision to expose the were-wolves, do you?' asked Samuel.

Gerry smiled at him. 'I've been arguing for it ever since the fae came out. But I needed money to set my plan up, and there are a lot of wolves who don't want to come out in public view – and they were willing to pay for it.'

It was suddenly clear. And Samuel was right. Gerry wasn't stupid: he was brilliant.

'Buying new werewolves from Leo in Chicago, the drug experiments, the attack on Adam's house; they were all intended to do two things,' I said. 'To show Bran that you were behind them all, and to prove to your father that you weren't.'

He nodded.

'Adam had to die,' I said, feeling my way. 'But you couldn't kill him. That's why you left him to the mercies of your werewolves when he was still drugged. That's why you stayed away from the warehouse, hoping that your men would pump enough silver into Adam to kill him.'

'Yes. He had to die and not by my hand. I had to be able to look my father in the eye and tell him that I hadn't killed Adam.'

I was shivering because it was cold and my arm, which had been surprisingly quiet for the past few minutes, began to hurt again. 'It wasn't Adam you wanted to fight Bran, it was your father. You were counting on Bran going to your father as soon as he figured out what you were doing.'

'My father called me this afternoon,' Gerry said. 'Bran had asked him about the tranquilizer and told him that I might be behind the attacks on Adam. My father knows I want the wolves to quit hiding. He knows how I feel about animal experimentation and the way some Alphas exploit some of our new wolves. He knows I'd never try to kill Adam.'

'If Adam died, my father would tell yours before he came here to kill you,' Samuel said.

Gerry laughed. 'I don't think so. I think Bran would have come here and killed me for my crimes. I hoped he would. I have killed too many innocents. But when he told my father what I had done, my father wouldn't believe him.'

'Believing the Marrok had you executed for something you didn't do, Carter would challenge him.' Samuel sounded almost admiring. 'And my father couldn't refuse the challenge.'

'What if Bran talked to Dr Wallace first?' I asked.

'It wouldn't have mattered.' Gerry sounded certain. 'Either to protect me or avenge me, my father would challenge Bran. Even before he was wolf, my father was the Marrok's man. He respects him and trusts him. Bran's betrayal, and Dad would see it like that, could have only one answer. Only Bran could unite my father, wolf and man, against him – Dad loves him. If Dad and his wolf face Bran in a fight, they will do it as one being: Bran told me that it would only take that one time for my father to be safe.'

'If Dr Wallace challenged Bran, Bran would kill him,' said Adam.

'Witches are expensive,' whispered Gerry. 'But there are a lot of wolves who want to hide and they gave me money so they could keep their secrets.'

'You were paying Robert, Elizaveta's son. He'd do something to ensure your father's victory.' I'd thought Robert was doing it for money. I just hadn't realized he would be getting it so directly.

'They'd be looking for drugs,' said Gerry. 'But no one except another witch can detect magic.'

'I can,' I told him. 'Robert's been taken care of. If your father challenges Bran, it won't be Bran who dies.'

He sagged a little. 'Then, as a favor to me, Samuel, would you ask Bran to make certain my father never finds out about this? I don't want to cause him any more pain than I already have.'

'Do you have any more questions?' Samuel asked Adam.

Adam shook his head and got to his feet. 'Is he your wolf tonight or mine?'

'Mine,' said Samuel stepping forward.

Gerry looked up at the moon where she hung above us. 'Please,' he said. 'Make it quick.'

Samuel pushed his fingers through Gerry's hair, a gentle, comforting touch. His mouth was tight with sorrow: if a submissive wolf's instinct is to bow to authority, a dominant's is to protect.

Samuel moved so fast that Gerry could not have known what was happening. With a quick jerk, Samuel used his healer's hands to snap Gerry's neck.

I handed Adam my gun so I had a hand free. Then I took out Zee's dagger and I handed it to Samuel.

'It's not silver,' I said, 'but it will do the job.'

I watched as Samuel made certain Gerry stayed dead. It wasn't pleasant, but it was necessary. I wouldn't lessen the moment by looking away.

'I'll call Bran as soon as I have a phone,' he said, cleaning the dagger on his pants leg. 'He'll make sure that Dr Wallace never knows what happened to his son.'

A few hours later, Bran and Carter Wallace took a run in the forest. Bran said the moonlight sparkled on the crystals of the crusted snow that broke beneath their dancing paws.

They crossed a frozen lake bed and surprised a sleeping doe, who flashed her white tail and disappeared into the underbrush as they ran by. He told me that the stars covered the sky, so far from city lights, like a blanket of golden glitter.

Sometime before the sun's first pale rays lit the eastern sky, the wolf who had been Carter Wallace went to sleep, curled up next to his Alpha, and never woke up again.

Samuel hadn't killed Robert, so we turned him over to his grandmother: a fate he did not seem to think was much of an improvement. Elizaveta Arkadyevna was not pleased with him. I wasn't altogether sure that she was unhappy with his betrayal of Adam or with his getting caught.

Samuel decided to stay in the Tri-Cities for a while. He's been spending most of his free time on the paperwork involved in getting his medical license extended to Washington. Until then, he's working at the same Stop And Rob where Warren works – and he seems to like it just fine.

Bran didn't, of course, throw his wolves to the world and abandon them there. He is not one of the Gray Lords to force people out of hiding who don't want to come. So most of the werewolves are still staying hidden, even though Bran found his poster child.

You can't turn on the TV or open the newspaper without seeing a picture of the man who penetrated a terrorist camp to find a missionary and his family who had been kidnapped.

The missionary and his wife had been killed already, but there were three children who were rescued. There's a color photograph that made the cover of one of the news magazines. It shows David Christiansen cuddling the youngest child – a little blond-haired toddler with the bruise of a man's fingers clearly visible on her porcelain skin. Her face is turned into his shoulder, and he is looking at her with an expression of such tenderness that it brings tears to my eyes.

But the best part of the picture is the boy who is standing beside him, his face pale, dirty. When I first saw it, I thought he just looked numb, as if his experiences had been too great to be borne, but then I noticed that his hand is tucked inside of David's and the boy's knuckles are white with the grip he has on the man's big fingers.

16

Because there isn't much a mechanic with a broken arm can do besides get in the way, Zee sent me to the office to work on my paperwork. I didn't get much done there either, but at least – as Zee put it – I wasn't whining at him.

He wouldn't tell me anything about his dagger or who Adelbert was and why he needed smiting – and I hadn't been able to find it on the Internet, either. When I got persistent, Zee told me he liked the modern era, with its steel and electricity, better than the old days because there was more for a *Metallzauber*, a gremlin, to do than build swords to kill other folk. Then he exiled me to the office and went back to fixing cars.

I am right-handed, and it was my right arm that was broken. I couldn't even use it to hold a piece of paper still because the doctor at the emergency room insisted I wear my arm strapped to my side. I even had to type on my computer using one hand – which made it painstakingly slow to do any work. So I used the computer to play Vegas-style solitaire and lost two thousand dollars of imaginary money, instead.

It was probably not the best moment for Gabriel Sandoval to show up. I'd forgotten I'd told his mother to send him over Monday after school.

He had to wait until I typed in their bill, then an hourly wage that looked fair to me. It would give him twenty hours to work off, though, and that seemed too much to me. So I added a couple of dollars an hour, until the time looked better.

I printed it out and handed it to him. He looked it over and crossed off the salary and replaced it with the original one. 'I'm not worth that yet,' he said. 'But I will be by the end of the first month.'

I reassessed him. He wasn't tall, and he'd never be a big man, but there was something solid about him, as young as he was.

'All right,' I said. 'It's a deal.'

I showed him around the office, which took all of five minutes. Then I sat him down at the computer and ran him through my inventory program and my billing system. When he seemed to have the hang of it, I gave him my stacks of paperwork and left him to it.

I walked back into the shop and tilted my thumb at the office when Zee looked up.

'I think I've found Tad's replacement,' I told him. 'I gave him my paperwork, and he didn't even growl at me.'

Zee raised his eyebrows. 'Tad never growled at you.'

'"Damn it, Mercy, can't you remember to give me the bills the day you get them?"' I quoted in my best crabby-Tad voice.

'You'd think someone raised around werewolves would know the difference between growling and swearing,' Zee observed. He put down his wrench and sighed. 'I'm worried about that boy. You know he got that scholarship so they could have their token fae to tow around and point out.'

'Probably,' I agreed. 'They'll never know what hit them.'

'You think he's all right?'

'I can't imagine a place where Tad wouldn't be all right. Nothing scares him, nothing bothers him, and he's frighteningly competent at whatever he chooses to do.' I patted Zee on the back. I enjoyed watching him play nervous father. This was a conversation we'd been having since Tad left for Harvard. I kept track of them and e-mailed Tad with a count once a week.

I heard the office door open and waved Zee to silence so we could listen to how my new office lackey dealt with customers.

'Can I help you?' he said in a smooth, dark voice that surprised me. I hadn't expected him to flirt.

But then I heard Jesse say, 'I'm here looking for Mercy – she didn't tell me she had someone new working for her.'

There was a short pause, then Gabriel said in a sharp voice, 'Who hit you?'

Jesse laughed and said lightly, 'Don't worry. My dad saw the bruise, and the person who hit me is dead now.'

'Good.' Gabriel sounded as though he wouldn't have minded if it had been the truth. Which it was.

'I have someone waiting for me in the car,' she said. 'I'd better go talk to Mercy.'

She came into the shop with a thoughtful look on her face. 'I like him,' she said.

I nodded. 'Me, too. Nice haircut.'

We'd stopped by Warren's house after cleanup at the tree farm to find Jesse minus the duct tape that had still been stuck to her hair – and also minus most of her hair. Warren had looked . . . well, he ought to have looked ashamed, but there had been amusement in his eyes.

Jesse rolled her eyes at me. 'Who'd have thought a gay man couldn't cut hair.' She ran her fingers through the inch-long strands that had been tipped with a glittery gold color. She looked like a flapper from the 1920s wearing one of those beaded caps.

'He told you he didn't know how to give haircuts,' I said, as she walked over and kissed Zee on the cheek.

'I got it fixed the next day.' She grinned at me, then she

lost her smile. 'Dad called Mom yesterday and told her what happened. Everything that happened.'

I knew her mother. She and Adam had only been divorced four years, and Adam had lived behind me for almost seven. 'What did she say?'

'That he was to fly me back to Eugene on the first flight home and never darken her doorstep again.' She touched her lips. 'She does it on purpose, you know. Tries to make him feel bad, like he's an animal. If that doesn't work, she brings up her four miscarriages as if they didn't hurt him as much as they hurt her. As if everything is his fault. And he buys it every time. I knew what she was going to do, so I made them let me listen in on the extension. I think he was just going to agree with her and send me back, so I said some things that maybe I shouldn't have.'

I didn't ask, just waited. She could tell me if she wanted to. Apparently she did.

'I told Dad about her boyfriend who tried to climb into bed with me when I was twelve. And the time two years ago, when she left for a weekend in Vegas without telling me she was going anywhere. It got pretty ugly.'

'I'm sorry.'

She lifted her chin. 'I'm not. Mom agreed to let me stay here for the rest of the school year, then they'll talk. Anyway, Warren's out waiting for me in the car – Dad said it would be a long time before he could contemplate leaving me alone – at least a week. I have a request for you.'

'What did'ja need?' I asked.

'Dad asked me to stop in and see if you'd come to dinner. Somewhere expensive, 'cause we owe you.'

'I'll close up here so you can go clean up,' Zee said a little eagerly. I hadn't been *that* whiny. Really.

'All right,' I said. 'You can pick me up at—' I started to twist my right wrist, winced and remembered I'd put my watch on my left wrist that morning. It was almost four. 'Six-thirty.'

'He'll be there,' she said, and waltzed back into the office to flirt with the help.

'Go,' said Zee.

It wasn't that easy, of course. I introduced Gabriel and Zee, then puttered around getting things finished until nearly five. I grabbed my purse out of the safe and started out the door when my undercover friend pulled up in the parking lot driving a black and shiny eighties convertible Mustang.

'Tony,' I said.

He was still in his ubermacho guise, I noticed, as he sprang out of the car, over the door. The opaque black sunglasses disguising his eyes made him look menacing and sexy.

'Your engine is missing,' I told him.

'Funny' – he gave his car an implacable look – 'it was here just a minute ago.'

'Ha-ha,' I said. My arm hurt, and I wasn't in the mood for stupid jokes. 'Get someone to check your engine.'

'What did you do to your arm?' he asked.

I remembered Jesse's method of telling the whole truth, and said, 'I got knocked into a bunch of wooden crates by a werewolf while I was trying to rescue a young girl from the clutches of an evil witch and a drug lord.'

'Ha-ha,' he said in the exact same tone I'd given his joke. 'Must have been something stupid if you won't tell the truth.'

'Well,' I said, considering it, 'maybe "drug lord" was too strong a word. And maybe I should have mentioned the girl's handsome and sexy father. What do you think?'

'Mercy,' he said, taking my good arm and turning me around so we were walking back into the office. 'We need to talk.'

'Can't talk,' I said. 'I've got a date.'

'Nice try. But you haven't had a date since I met you.' He opened the door and escorted me inside.

Gabriel looked up from my . . . *his* paperwork and the pleasant smile on his face went away.

'What are *you* doing here?' he said, standing up and coming around the corner. 'Let her go. Now.'

Great, I thought. *Just what I need, another macho male in my life trying to take care of me.*

Tony dropped my arm and collapsed onto one of the uncomfortable chairs I use to encourage my customers to find something else to do rather than wait around while I fix their cars. He buried his face in his hands and either started laughing or crying. I figured he was laughing.

When he raised his head, he'd done one of those amazing changes — partially helped, I have to admit, by losing the sunglasses. But it was body language and facial expression, as much as anything. He just suddenly looked ten years older and, except for the earrings, much more respectable.

'Tony?' said Gabriel, obviously stunned.

'I've been working undercover at Kennewick High right under his nose,' Tony told me. 'He never even noticed. I told you most people can't recognize me.'

'I've never argued with that,' I said. 'I think you're a good undercover cop.'

Tony shook his head. 'Hey, Gabriel, would you give us a minute alone? I have some questions for Mercy.'

'Sure.' Gabriel shook his head and started off. He turned around once on his way out to the shop, as if to make sure that Tony was still sitting there.

'I've been giving him a really hard time at school,' Tony said, once we were alone. 'But he can take care of himself.'

'I really do need to get home,' I told him. 'What did you need?'

He lifted up one hip and pulled a folded piece of paper

out of his back pocket. 'That kid you had helping you,' he said. 'I've got some more information on him.'

I took the paper and unfolded it. It was a grainy black-and-white picture of Mac with 'MISSING' written across the top in capital letters. It gave his vital statistics – he had been sixteen – but gave no more information.

'Alan MacKenzie Frazier,' I read.

'They traced him here from a phone call he made to his family last week.'

I nodded, handing the paper back and continued to lie to Tony with the truth. 'He asked if he could make a long-distance call the last day he was here – a week ago today. He worked all that day, but I haven't seen him since.'

I'd talked to Bran about Mac. He said he'd see to it that a hiker would find Mac's remains in the spring so that his parents wouldn't have to wait by the phone forever. It wasn't much, but it was the best I could do.

It took some scrambling and a fair bit of help, but I managed to be dressed, clean, and beautiful for dinner with Adam and Jesse. Which turned out to be dinner with just Adam because Jesse told him she wasn't feeling well. He left her home watching a movie with Darryl and Auriele because Warren was out on a date with Kyle.

Under the mellowing influence of good food and good music, Adam relaxed, and I discovered that underneath that overbearing, hot-tempered Alpha disguise he usually wore was a charming, overbearing, hot-tempered man. He seemed to enjoy finding out that I was as stubborn and disrespectful of authority as he'd always suspected.

He ordered dessert without consulting me. I'd have been angrier, but it was something I could never have ordered for myself: chocolate, caramel, nuts, ice cream, real whipped cream, and cake so rich it might as well have been a brownie.

'So,' he said, as I finished the last bit, 'I'm forgiven?'

'You are arrogant and overstep your bounds,' I told him, pointing my cleaned fork at him.

'I try,' he said with false modesty. Then his eyes darkened and he reached across the little table and ran his thumb over my bottom lip. He watched me as he licked the caramel from his skin.

I thumped my hands down on the table and leaned forward. 'That is *not* fair. I'll eat your dessert and like it – but you can't use sex to keep me from getting mad.'

He laughed, one of those soft laughs that start in the belly and rise up through the chest: a relaxed, happy sort of laugh.

To change the subject, because matters were heating up faster than I was comfortable with, I said, 'So, Bran tells me that he ordered you to keep an eye out for me.'

He stopped laughing and raised both his eyebrows. 'Yes. Now ask me if I was watching you for Bran.'

It was a trick question. I could see the amusement in his eyes. I hesitated, but decided I wanted to know anyway. 'Okay, I'll bite. Were you watching me for Bran?'

'Honey,' he drawled, pulling on his Southern roots. 'When a wolf watches a lamb, he's not thinking about the lamb's mommy.'

I grinned. I couldn't help it. The idea of Bran as a lamb's mommy was too funny. 'I'm not much of a lamb,' I said.

He just smiled.

Time to change the subject again, I thought, taking a quick sip of ice water. 'Warren tells me you've accepted our favorite serial rapist as a permanent member of the pack.'

'He wasn't responsible for the rapes in London.'

He sounded certain, which meant that he'd asked Ben for the truth and gotten it. Still, I could hear the irritation in his voice and I couldn't help but push a little bit more. 'They stopped when he left.'

'He came to the rescue twice, and the second time it was only chance that he intercepted a tranquilizer rather than a bullet. Gerry's men carried silver ammunition,' he snapped impatiently.

I smiled at him and he balled up his napkin in disgust. 'Point to you,' he said.

'I bet you wouldn't let him date Jesse,' I told him smugly.

When he drove me home, he got out of the car and walked around to open the door for me. Maybe it was because I couldn't open the door with my broken arm, but I thought it might be the kind of thing that he always did.

He walked me to my front porch and cupped his hands around my face. He stood there for a moment, then glanced over his shoulder and up at the moon, which was nearly full. When he turned back, his eyes had yellow streaks running through the brown.

His lips were soft as they feathered over mine tentatively until I leaned against the pressure of his hands, trying to get closer. Then he laughed, a low, chest-deep sound, and really kissed me.

With my broken arm strapped between us, there was no body language involved, just mouth and hands. He wore cologne. Something rich and subtle that blended with his exotic scent.

When he drew away from me, I left my hand on his cheek, enjoying the faint scratchiness of his beard and the pounding of my heart. Silence grew between us, silence and something tentative and new.

Then the door opened and my new roommate looked out with a grin. 'Hey, guys, are you through yet? I made some hot cocoa because I figured Mercy wasn't wearing much – but I guess you took care of any chill from the weather.'

Samuel had been savage when I came home from the garage and told him that I was going out to dinner with

Adam. I'd had to remind him forcefully that he had no claim on me, not anymore. He was staying with me until he could find an apartment of his own, and that didn't give him the right to dictate who I went to dinner with.

If I'd realized that it was going to be a real date, I'd have been kinder. I knew that Samuel was still interested in me – and part of me still loved him.

When Jesse the Matchmaker called me to tell me that her father was on his way over, and not to worry about her because she was just fine, Samuel'd stalked off to sulk in his room, the bigger of my spare bedrooms. But when I'd started trying to put on my dress, he barged into my room to help. I could have done it myself. I wasn't making pained noises, no matter what he said. But, I had to admit, maneuvering clothes, the myriad of mysterious, but businesslike, Velcro straps that grew off the brace the hospital doctor had given me to keep my arm immobilized, and my broken arm was easier with three hands rather than only one.

He hadn't been happy when I left, but I refused to let guilt decide who I would date. I don't play games with people I care about, and I won't let them play games with me. I promised him that I wouldn't have sex with Adam any more than I'd have sex with Samuel. Not until I knew what I felt and what they felt. But that was as far as I was willing to go.

I'd known that giving him the evening to think about it had been a mistake. I probably should have told Adam that Samuel was still staying with me as soon as I realized he didn't know – but what we'd been experiencing tonight had still been too fragile for that.

So Adam got blindsided by Samuel The Live-in Lover.

'Not kind, Samuel,' I said, then turned to Adam. 'He is staying here until he gets an apartment.' I looked at Samuel. 'It should be really soon now.'

'I thought you had a practice in Montana, Dr Cornick,' said Adam. He'd released me when the door opened, but then he'd put a hand low on my back – one of those staking-claim gestures that guys do around other guys.

Samuel nodded and stepped back, holding the door so that we'd all come inside. As soon as they were both in the enclosed space of my living room, I could smell the power rising from both of them.

'I was working at a clinic in rotation with three other doctors,' he said, leading the way into the kitchen. 'They won't suffer. I left Aspen Creek a while ago, and I've found now that I've returned I can't settle in. So I thought I'd try someplace closer than Texas.'

Adam accepted a steaming cup and blew on it thoughtfully. 'You mean you are petitioning to join my pack?'

Samuel's smile, which hadn't left his face since he opened the door, widened even farther. 'I wouldn't dream of it. I'm going lone wolf – you'll probably get the official letter informing you of that from Bran sometime this week.'

I left them to it. They weren't paying any attention to me anyway. I couldn't get the dress off easily without help, but I pulled a pair of sweats on over the top of it. A loose sweatshirt covered my broken arm, strap-bearing torture device and all. Shoes were harder, but I found an old pair of tennis shoes that I hadn't untied and pulled them on my feet over a pair of ankle socks.

When I went back out to the living room, both men were still involved in one of those pleasant but deadly conversations that usually ended up badly. They stopped speaking when I opened the front door, but as soon as I closed it behind me, I heard them start up again.

I was driving the van, because my Rabbit didn't have power steering. I had to pull over a few miles from home so I could use the cell phone.

'Stefan,' I said. 'Your parts are here. I've got a broken arm, so you'll have to do all the work – but I can talk you through it.'

'How did you break your arm, Mercy?' he asked.

'A werewolf tossed me against a giant packing crate while I was trying to rescue a frightened young girl who'd been kidnapped by an evil witch and a drug lord.'

'It sounds interesting,' Stefan said. 'I'll meet you at your garage.'

See. Some people believe me.

extras

www.orbitbooks.net

extras

about the author

Patricia Briggs lived a fairly normal life until she learned to read. After that she spent lazy afternoons flying dragonback and looking for magic swords when she wasn't horseback riding in the Rocky Mountains. Once she graduated from Montana State University with degrees in history and German, she spent her time substitute teaching and writing. She and her family live in the Pacific Northwest, and you can visit her website at www.patriciabriggs.com

Find out more about Patricia and other Orbit authors by registering for the free monthly newsletter at: www.orbitbooks.net

interview

The Mercy Thompson books are fast-paced, enjoyable and varied. Do you have any tips on how to sustain tension and interest to keep readers hooked throughout a series?
I only know how to keep me interested <grin>. I need characters I care about, which means I have to understand and believe in their motivations so they feel real. That means that the events of a story have to have an impact on the characters, an impact that might carry over from one book to the next. I need a plot that makes sense and one with an outcome that is important to the main characters. I need a world that is consistent and believable.

How did Mercy Thompson and her world come into being for you?
When my editor called to ask me to write an urban fantasy (she knew I loved them because we'd been exchanging reading lists for a long time) she told me they wanted the story to focus on vampires and werewolves with a "strong female protagonist who had a complicated love life", a love life that had something to do with vampires and werewolves. So that was set for me as was the convention that these stories would take place in our world as it would be if the things that go bump in the night were real.

Oddly enough, Mercy's name was the first thing that came

to me. The pun (that she was a VW mechanic named Mercedes) was purely unintentional, though I took advantage of it.

I like shifters, always have. And I knew that I wanted an underpowered character because they are more fun to write about. A coyote just seemed the perfect answer to the were-wolves – and since the coyote is a North American native species it was obvious that Mercy had to be at least part Native American. And since by that time I already knew she'd be caught between worlds, human and preternatural, it seemed proper to have her half Native American and half white so she'd straddle those worlds as well.

Once I had Mercy, I played with various locations to put her stories in. I am tolerably familiar with Spokane, Washington; Seattle, Washington; Portland, Oregon; and even Chicago. But then I started thinking about the Tri Cities (where I was living). It just fit the bill. It was someting a little different with lots of interesting people: Hispanic, Indians (both Native Americans and India Indians), Russians, Laotians, Japanese, Chinese and a host of other people. There are some cool places: The Hanford Nuclear Power Plant, Pacific Northwest Laboratories, and a huge winery/beer industry. And it was all in my own back yard (until we moved again <grin>).

Your book seems to incorporate a number of different mythological traditions (Mercy herself being American-Indian, and the fae Zee being of Germanic origin, to name some strands). Do you have to do much research for your books?
Absolutely. I grew up with my sister reading fairy tales to me every night: The Brothers Grimm, Lang's colour fairytale collections, Hans Christian Andersen and all the rest, I was the only one in my elementary school class who knew who Dick Whittington was. I bought Katharine Brigg's Encyclopedia of Fairies twenty-five years ago (when my sister took hers with her). So I'm fairly comfortable with

Celtic/British and Northern European fae folk, which gave me a good solid starting place.

I've also read a lot of American Indian folktales. But when I was reading them as a kid, I didn't pay attention to which tribes the stories came from. So when I started the Mercy books, I did a lot of work brushing up my knowledge of Indian folklore. Again, so I'd have a place to start writing from.

When I get to specifics I do more research. I don't use the folklore like a blueprint, but more as a suggestion or jumping off point.

I noticed that you have taught Greek and Roman mythology, did this develop from your interest in fantasy fiction, or was it a simultaneous/independent development?
Ah, that sounds so much more . . . sophisticated than what it was – I taught a bunch of eleven and twelve year olds (sixth graders for those of you who know the US school systems). It was a lot of fun, but hardly needed an expert.

My interest in mythology, like many of my interests, started with horses – in this case, Pegasus. Once I read Pegasus I had to figure out who Medusa was and . . . This happened when I was about seven or so. For most of the next three or four years I read horse stories (I still have large portions of Black Beauty memorized), fairytales (including Greek mythology, which I considered part of the same genre), and Robin Hood stories. It was only later I put Greek and Roman mythology together with the actual Greeks and Romans. I did a little more research on them in college, but when I set out to teach what I knew to a bunch of innocent kids who would take what I said (when they were listening) as gospel, I did a lot more reading and studying.

How do you manage to fit your writing routine around your life? With a busy home-life it must be hard to juggle the unpredictability of family with work. . .
Sometimes it gets pretty difficult. Right now I have an office

in town, and that helps a lot. I take my youngest to school in the morning and work until she gets out. But I'm a wife and mother first and a writer, second. Sometimes that means I'm writing at two in the morning when everyone is asleep.

Again on a theme of writing/writers, you have been a published author for over ten years now with a large number of books to your name. Has the craft become any easier over time? Or not?!

Some things are a lot easier. I know how to write conversations (or at least I think I do!), transitions and room descriptions that don't bog down the story. I can tell when a story takes an odd turn if it is worth following, or if I should haul it back to follow the track I planned on. I can write faster and write better.

What is harder is trying not to rewrite a story I've written before, or develop themes I've already pounded into the ground. Sometimes the most logical path for a plot to take is a repeat of a scene I used in the last book so I have to figure out something different.

How extensively do you plot your novels before you start writing them? Do you plot the entire trilogy/series before you start writing or do you prefer to let the story roam where it will?

I don't do a lot of plotting ahead of time. There are two reasons for that. First, I find if I know where the story goes, I don't have any motivation for writing it. I'm ready to find a new story to play with. The second is that when I do sit down and plot out a story, that plot/outline is only good for a few days of writing before the story changes anyway.

The only exception to that was the Raven duology (Raven Shadow and Raven Strike). Those I plotted out. Partially because it was the first time I wrote a real proposal. (Dragon Blood was also written on spec, but I didn't know I was writing a proposal when my editor asked for a synopsis so I just wrote something off the top of my head and sent it to her.) That's when I discovered that books are much more fun to write when I don't know exactly what's going to happen.

So I start with a character in a place and give them a problem to work on. Usually I have some idea where I want the story to end up, but I'm not too unhappy if it doesn't work out that way. Writing like this means that my edits are extensive, especially the first couple when I have to take out parts from the beginning that are no longer important. But I like the way the story turns out better, it's less predictable and more fun for me.

Your website is great – packed with interesting information about yourself and your books. I feel one matter in need of further investigaton is the name of your cat – any particular reason why he is called Roadkill?!
Yes. He was a big cat and, once he'd gotten past his kitten phase, lazy. He'd lie around with both front feet stretched in front of him and his head tucked under his chest. He was the old-fashioned Siamese-type (bulky) so he looked liked he'd died and had a few days to bloat.

And on a more serious note, to find out more about Patricia and her books, (almost!) everything you might want to know can be found at www.hurog.com

if you enjoyed
MOON CALLED
look out for

BLOOD BOUND

also by

Patricia Briggs

if you enjoyed

MOON CALLED

Patricia Briggs

1

Like most people who own their own businesses, I work long hours that start early in the morning. So when someone calls me in the middle of the night, they'd better be dying.

'Hello, Mercy,' said Stefan's amiable voice in my ear. 'I wonder if you could do me a favor.'

Stefan had done his dying a long time ago, so I saw no reason to be nice. 'I answered the phone at' – I peered blearily at the red numbers on my bedside clock – '*three* o'clock in the morning.'

Okay, that's not exactly what I said. I may have added a few of those words a mechanic picks up to use at recalcitrant bolts and alternators that land on her toes.

'I *suppose* you could go for a second favor,' I continued, 'but I'd prefer you hang up and call me back at a more civilized hour.'

He laughed. Maybe he thought I was trying to be funny. 'I have a job to do, and I believe your particular talents would be a great asset in assuring the success of the venture.'

Old creatures, at least in my experience, like to be a little vague when they're asking you to do something. I'm a businesswoman, and I believe in getting to the specifics as quickly as possible.

'At three in the morning you need a mechanic?'

'I'm a vampire, Mercedes,' he said gently. 'Three in the morning is still prime time. But I don't need a mechanic, I need you. You owe me a favor.'

He was right, darn him. He'd helped me when the local Alpha werewolf's daughter was kidnapped. He had warned me that he'd be collecting in return.

I yawned and sat up, giving up all hope of going back to sleep. 'All right. What am I doing for you?'

'I'm supposed to be delivering a message to a vampire who is here without my mistress's permission,' he said, getting to the point. 'I need a witness he won't notice.'

He hung up without getting an answer, or even telling me when he was coming to pick me up. It would serve him right if I just went back to sleep.

Muttering to myself, I threw on clothing: jeans, yesterday's T-shirt complete with mustard stain, and two socks with only one hole between them. Once I was more or less dressed, I shuffled off to the kitchen and poured myself a glass of cranberry juice.

It was a full moon, and my roommate, the werewolf, was out running with the local pack, so I didn't have to explain to him why I was going out with Stefan. Which was just as well.

Samuel wasn't a bad roommate as such things go, but he had a tendency to get possessive and dictatorial. Not that I let him get away with it, but arguing with werewolves requires a certain subtlety I was lacking at — I checked my wristwatch — 3:15 in the morning.

For all that I was raised by them, I'm not a werewolf, not a were-anything. I'm not a servant of the moon's phases, and in the coyote shape that is my second form. I look like any other *canis latrans*: I have the buckshot scars on my backside to prove it.

Werewolves cannot be mistaken for wolves: weres are much bigger than their non-preternatural counterparts — and a lot scarier.

What I am is a walker, though I'm sure there once was another name for it — an Indian name lost when the Europeans devoured the New World. Maybe my father could have told me what it was if he hadn't died in a car wreck before he knew my mother was pregnant. So all I know is what the werewolves could tell me, which wasn't much.

The 'walker' comes from the Skinwalkers of the Southwest Indian tribes, but I have less in common with a Skinwalker, at least from what I've read, than I do with the werewolves. I don't do magic, I don't need a coyote skin to change shape – and I'm not evil.

I sipped my juice and looked out of the kitchen window. I couldn't see the moon herself, just her silver light that touched the nighttime landscape. Thoughts of evil seemed somehow appropriate while I waited for the vampire to come for me. If nothing else, it would keep me from falling asleep: fear has that effect on me. I'm afraid of evil.

In our modern world, even the word seems . . . old fashioned. When it comes out of hiding briefly in a Charles Manson or a Jeffrey Dahmer, we try to explain it away with drug abuse, an unhappy childhood, or mental illness.

Americans in particular are oddly innocent in their faith that science holds explanations for everything. When the werewolves finally admitted what they were to the public several months ago, the scientists immediately started looking for a virus or bacteria that could cause the Change – magic being something their laboratories and computers can't explain. Last I'd heard Johns Hopkins had a whole team devoted to the issue. Doubtless they'd find something, too, but I'm betting they'll never be able to explain how a 180-pound man turns into a 250-pound werewolf. Science doesn't allow for magic any more than it allows for evil.

The devout belief that the world is explainable is both a terrible vulnerability and a stout shield. Evil prefers it when people don't believe. Vampires, as a not-random example, seldom go out and kill people in the street. When they go hunting, they find someone who won't be missed and bring them home where they are tended and kept comfortable -- like a cow in a feedlot.

Under the rule of science, there are no witch burnings allowed, no water trials or public lynchings. In return, the average law-abiding, solid, citizen has little to worry about from the things that go bump in the night. Sometimes I wish I were an average citizen.

Average citizens don't get visited by vampires.

Nor do they worry about a pack of werewolves – at least not quite the same way as I was.

Coming out in public was a bold step for the werewolves; one that could easily backfire. Staring out at the moonlit night, I fretted about what would happen if people began to be afraid again. Werewolves aren't evil, but they aren't exactly the peaceful, law-abiding heroes that they're trying to represent themselves as either.

Someone tapped on my front door.

Vampires *are* evil. I knew that – but Stefan was more than just a vampire. Sometimes I was pretty sure he was my friend. So I wasn't really afraid until I opened the door and saw what waited on my porch.

The vampire's dark hair was slicked back, leaving his skin very pale in the moon's light. Dressed in black from head to heels, he ought to have looked like a refugee from a bad Dracula movie, but somehow the whole outfit, from black leather duster to silk gloves, looked more authentic on Stefan than his usual bright-colored T-shirt and grubby jeans. As if he'd removed a costume, rather than put one on.

He looked like someone who could kill as easily as I could change a tire, with as little thought or remorse.

Then his mobile brows climbed his forehead – and he was suddenly the same vampire who'd painted his old VW bus to look like Scooby's Mystery Machine.

'You don't look happy to see me,' he said with a quick grin that didn't show his fangs. In the dark, his eyes looked more black than brown – but then so did mine.

'Come in.' I backed away from the door so he could; then,

because he'd scared me I added snappishly, 'If you want welcoming, try stopping by at a decent hour.'

He hesitated on the threshold, smiled at me, and said, 'By your invitation.' Then he stepped inside my house.

'That threshold thing really works?' I asked.

His smile widened again, this time I saw a glint of white. 'Not after you've invited me in.'

He walked past me and into the living room and then turned like a model on a runway. The folds of his duster spread out with his turn in an effect nearly cape-like.

'So how do you like me *à la Nosferatu*?'

I sighed and admitted it. 'Scared me. I thought you eschewed all things gothic.' I'd seldom seen him in anything other than jeans and T-shirts.

His smile widened even more. 'Usually I do. But the Dracula look does have its place. Oddly enough, used sparingly, it scares other vampires almost as well as it does the odd coyote-girl. Don't worry, I have a bit of costuming for you, too.'

He reached under his coat and pulled out a silver-studded leather harness.

I stared at it a moment. 'Going to an S&M strip club are you? I didn't realize there was anything like that around here.' There wasn't, not to my knowledge. Eastern Washington is more prudish than Seattle or Portland.

He laughed. 'Not tonight, sweetheart. This is for your other self.' He shook the straps out so I could see that it was a dog harness.

I took it from him. It was good leather, soft and flexible with so much silver that it looked like jewelry. If I'd been strictly human, no doubt I'd have been taken aback at wearing such a thing. But when you spend a good part of your time running around as a coyote, collars and the like are pretty useful.

The Marrok, the leader of the North American werewolves, insists that all of the wolves wear a collar when they run in the cities, with tags that identify them as someone's pet. He also insists the names on the tags be something innocuous like Fred or Spot, no Killers or Fangs. It's safer that way — both for the werewolves and the law-enforcement people who might encounter them. Needless to say, it's as popular with the werewolves as the helmet law was with the motorcyclists when it first went into effect. Not that any of them would dream of disobeying the Marrok.

Not being a werewolf, I'm exempt from the Marrok's rules. On the other hand, I don't like running unnecessary risks either. I had a collar in my kitchen junk drawer — but it wasn't made of nifty black leather.

'So I'm part of your costume?' I asked.

'Let's just say that I think this vampire might need more intimidation than most,' he answered lightly, though something in his eyes made me think there was something more going on.

Medea wandered out from wherever she'd been sleeping. Probably Samuel's bed. Purring furiously, she wound her small self around Stefan's left leg and then rubbed her face against his boot to mark him as hers.

'Cats and ghosts don't like vampires,' Stefan said staring down at her.

'Medea likes anything that might feed or pet her,' I told him. 'She's not picky.'

He bent down and scooped her up. Being picked up isn't Medea's favorite thing, so she yowled at him several times before going back to purring as she sank her claws into his expensive leather sleeve.

'You aren't cashing in your favor just to appear more intimidating,' I said, looking up from the soft leather harness to meet his eyes. Unwise with vampires, he himself had told me so, but all I saw was opaque darkness. 'You said you wanted a witness. A witness to what?'

'No, I don't need you in order to appear intimidating,' Stefan agreed softly after I'd stared at him for a few seconds. 'But *he'll* think intimidation is why I have a coyote on my leash.' He hesitated, and then shrugged. 'This vampire has been through here before, and I think that he managed to deceive one of our young ones. Because of what you are, you are immune to many vampiric powers, especially if the vampire in question doesn't know what you are. Thinking you a coyote, he's probably not going to waste his magic on you at all. It is unlikely, but he might manage to deceive me as well as he did Daniel. I don't think he'll be able to deceive you.'

I'd just learned that little tidbit about being resistant to vampiric magic. It wasn't particularly useful for me since a vampire is strong enough to break my neck with the same effort I'd put into snapping a piece of celery.

'He won't hurt you,' Stefan said when I was silent for too long. 'I give you my word of honor.'

I didn't know how old Stefan was, but he used that phrase like a man who meant it. Sometimes he made it hard to remember that vampires are evil. It didn't really matter, though. I owed him.

'All right,' I said.

Looking down at the harness I thought about getting my own collar instead. I could change shape while wearing a collar – my neck wasn't any bigger around as a human than as a coyote. The harness, suitable for a thirty-pound coyote, would be too tight for me to regain human form while I wore it. The advantage of the harness though, was that I wouldn't be attached to Stefan by my neck.

My collar was bright purple with pink flowers embroidered on it. Not very *Nosferatu*.

I handed the harness to Stefan. 'You'll have to put it on me after I change,' I told him. 'I'll be right back.'

I changed shape in my bedroom because I had to take off my clothes to do it. I'm not really all that modest, a shapeshifter gets over that pretty fast, but I try not to get naked in front of someone who might misread my casual nudity for casualness in other areas.

Although Stefan had at least three cars that I knew of, he had apparently taken a 'faster way,' as he put it, to my house, so we got in my Rabbit to travel to his meeting.

For a few minutes, I wasn't certain he was going to be able to get it started. The old diesel didn't like getting up this early in the morning any more than I did. Stefan muttered a few Italian oaths under his breath, and at last it caught and we were off.

Never ride in a car with a vampire who is in a hurry. I didn't know my Rabbit could peel out like that. We turned onto the highway with the rpms redlined; the car stayed on all four wheels, but only just.

The Rabbit actually seemed to like the drive better than I did; the engine roughness I'd been trying for years to get rid of smoothed out and it purred. I closed my eyes and hoped the wheels stayed on.

When Stefan took us over the river on the cable bridge that dropped us off in the middle of Pasco he was driving forty miles an hour over the speed limit. Not slowing noticeably, he crossed through the heart of the industrial area to a cluster of hotels that sprang up on the far edge of town near the on-ramp to the highway that headed out toward Spokane and other points north. By some miracle – probably aided by the early hour – we weren't picked up for speeding.

The hotel Stefan took us to was neither the best nor the worst of them. It catered to truckers, though there was only one of the big rigs parked in the lot. Maybe Tuesday nights were slow. Stefan parked the Rabbit next to the only other car in the lot, a black BMW, despite the plethora of empty parking spaces.

I jumped out of the car's open window into the parking lot and was hit with the smell of vampire and blood. My nose is very good, especially when I'm a coyote, but like anyone else, I don't always notice what I'm smelling. Most of the time it's like trying to listen to all of the conversations in a crowded restaurant. But this was impossible to miss.

Maybe it was bad enough to drive off normal humans, and that's why the parking lot was nearly empty.

I looked at Stefan to see if he smelled it, too, but his attention was focused on the car we'd parked beside. As soon as he'd drawn my attention to it, I realized the smell was coming from the BMW. How was it that the car could smell more like a vampire than Stefan the vampire did?

I caught another, more subtle, scent that caused my lips to draw away from my teeth even though I couldn't have said what the bitter-dark odor was. As soon as it touched my nose it wrapped itself around me, clouding all the other scents until it was all I could smell.

Stefan came around the car in a rush, snatched up the leash and tugged it hard to quiet my growl. I jerked back and snapped my teeth at him. I wasn't a damn dog. He could have asked me to be quiet.

'Settle down,' he said, but he wasn't watching me. He was looking at the hotel. I smelled something else then, a shadow of a scent soon overcome by that other smell. But even that brief whiff was enough to identify the familiar smell of fear, Stefan's fear. What could scare a vampire?

'Come,' he said turning toward the hotel and tugged me forward, out of my confusion.

Once I'd quit resisting his pull, he spoke to me in a rapid and quiet voice. 'I don't want you to do anything, Mercy, no matter what you see or hear. You aren't up to a fight with this one. I just need an impartial witness who won't get herself killed. So play coyote with all your might and if I don't make it out of here, go tell the Mistress what I asked you to do for me — and what you saw.'

How did he expect me to escape something that could kill him? He hadn't been talking like this earlier, nor had he been afraid. Maybe he could smell what I was smelling — and he knew what it was. I couldn't ask him though, because a coyote isn't equipped for human speech.

He led the way to a smoked glass door. It was locked, but there was a key-card box with a small, red-blinking, LED light. He tapped a finger on the box and the light turned green, just as if he'd swiped a magnetic card through it.

The door opened without protest and closed behind us with a final sounding click. There was nothing creepy about the hallway, but it bothered me anyway. Probably Stefan's nerves rubbing off on me. *What would scare a vampire?*

Somewhere, someone slammed a door and I jumped.

Either he knew where the vampire was staying, or his nose wasn't hampered by the scent of that otherness like mine was. He took me briskly through the long hallway and stopped about halfway down. He tapped on the door with his knuckles, though I, and so presumably Stefan, could hear that whoever awaited us inside the room had started for the door as soon as we stopped in front of it.

After all the build up, the vampire who opened the door was almost anticlimatic, like expecting to hear Pavarotti sing Wagner and getting Bugs Bunny and Elmer Fudd instead.

The new vampire was clean shaven and his hair was combed and pulled back into a tidy, short, ponytail. His clothes were neat and clean, though a bit wrinkled as if they'd been in a suit-case — but somehow the overall impression I got was disheveled and filthy. He was significantly shorter than Stefan and much less intimidating. First point to Stefan, which was good since he'd put so much effort into his Prince of Darkness garb.

The stranger's long-sleeved, knit shirt hung on him, as if it rested on skeleton rather than flesh. When he moved, one of his sleeves slid up, revealing an arm so emaciated that the hollow between the bones of his forearm was visible. He stood slightly hunched, as if he didn't quite have the energy to straighten up.

I'd met vampires other than Stefan before: scary vampires

with glowing eyes and fangs. This one looked like an addict so far gone there was nothing left of the person he had once been, as if he might fade away at any moment, leaving only his body behind.

Stefan, though, wasn't reassured by the other's apparent frailty – if anything, his tension had increased. Not being able to smell much around that unpleasant, pervasive bitterness was bothering me more than the vampire who didn't look like much of an opponent at all.

'Word of your coming has reached my mistress,' Stefan said, his voice steady, if a little more clipped than usual. 'She is very disappointed that you did not see fit to tell her you would be visiting her territory.'

'Come in, come in,' said the other vampire, stepping back from the door to invite Stefan through. 'No need to stand out in the hallway waking up people who are trying to sleep.'

I couldn't tell if he knew Stefan was afraid or not. I've never been quite sure how well vampires can scent things – though they clearly have better noses than humans do. He didn't seem intimidated by Stefan and his black clothes, though; instead he sounded almost distracted, as if we'd interrupted something important.

The bathroom door was shut as we walked past it. I pricked my ears, but I couldn't hear anything behind the shut door. My nose was useless. Stefan took us all the way to the far side of the room, near the sliding glass doors that were all but hidden by heavy, floor-to-ceiling, curtains. The room was bare and impersonal except for the suitcase, which lay closed on top of the chest of drawers.

Stefan waited until the other vampire had shut the door before he said in a cold voice, 'There is no one trying to sleep tonight in this hotel.'

It seemed an odd remark, but the stranger seemed to know what Stefan meant because he giggled, cupping a hand coyly over his mouth in a manner that seemed more in keeping with a twelve-year-old girl than a man of any age. It was odd enough that it took me a while to assess Stefan's remark.

Surely he hadn't meant it the way it sounded. No sane vampire would have killed everyone in the hotel. Vampires were as ruthless as the werewolves in enforcing their rules about not drawing unwanted attention to themselves — and wholesale slaughter of humans would draw attention. Even if there weren't many guests, there would be employees of the hotel.

The vampire dropped his hand from his face leaving behind a face empty of amusement. It didn't make me feel any better. It was like watching Dr Jekyll and Mr Hyde, the change was so great.

'No one to wake up?' he asked, as if he hadn't reacted in any other way to Stefan's comment. 'You might be right. It is still poor manners to keep someone waiting at the door, isn't it? Which one of her minions are you?' He held up a hand. 'No, wait, don't tell me. Let me guess.'

While Stefan waited, all of his usual animation completely shut down, the stranger walked all the way around him, pausing just behind us. Unconstrained by anything but the leash, I turned to watch.

When he was directly behind Stefan, the other vampire bent down and scratched me behind my ears.

I usually don't mind being touched, but as soon as his fingers brushed against my fur I knew I didn't want him touching me. Involuntarily, I hunched away from his hand and into Stefan's leg. My fur kept his skin away from mine, but that didn't keep his touch from feeling filthy, unclean.

The scent of him lingered on my fur and I realized the unpleasant odor that had been clogging my nose was coming from him.

'Careful,' Stefan told him without looking around. 'She bites.'

'Animals *love* me.' The remark made my flesh crawl it was so inappropriate coming from this . . . creeping monster. He crouched on his heels and rubbed my ears again. I couldn't tell if Stefan wanted me to bite him or not. I chose not, because I didn't want the taste of him on my tongue. I could always bite him later if I wanted to.

Stefan didn't comment, nor did he look anywhere except straight in front of him. I wondered if he would have lost status points if he'd turned. Werewolves play power games, too, but I know the rules for them. A werewolf would never have allowed a strange wolf to walk behind him.

He left off petting me, stood up, and walked around until he faced Stefan again. 'So you are Stefan, Marsilia's little soldier boy. I *have* heard of you – though your reputation is not what it once was, is it? Running away from Italy like that would soil any man's honor. Somehow, still, I expected more. All those stories . . . I expected to find a monster among monsters, a creature of nightmares who frightens even other vampires – and all I see is a dried-up has-been. I suppose that's what happens when you hide yourself in a little backwater town for a few centuries.'

There was a slight pause after the other vampire's last words.

Then Stefan laughed, and said, 'Whereas *you* have no reputation at all.' His voice was lighter than usual, sounding almost rushed, as if what he was saying was of no moment. I took a step away from him without meaning to, somehow frightened by that light, amused voice. He smiled gently at the other vampire and his tone softened further as he said, 'That's what happens when you are newly made and abandoned.'

It must have been some sort of vampire super-insult because the second vampire erupted, reacting as if Stefan's words had been an electric goad. He didn't go after Stefan, though.

Instead, he bent down and grabbed the bottom of the king-sized box spring and jerk-lifted it and everything above it over his head. He swung it toward the hall door and then around so that the ends of the box spring, mattress, and bedding were balanced for an instant.

He shifted his grip and threw them all the way through the wall and into the empty hotel room next door, landing on the floor in a cloud of Sheetrock dust. Two of the wall studs hung splintered, suspended from somewhere inside the wall, giving the hole in the wall the appearance of a jack-o-lantern's smile. The false headboard, permanently mounted into the wall where the bed had been, looked forlorn and stupid hanging a foot or more above the pedestal of the bed.

The vampire's speed and strength didn't surprise me. I'd seen a few werewolves throw temper tantrums, enough to know that if the vampire had been truly angry, he wouldn't have had the control it took to manage the physics of swinging the two unattached mattresses together through the wall. Apparently, as in werewolf fights, battles between vampires have a lot of impressive fireworks before the main show.

In the silence that followed, I heard something, a hoarse mewling noise coming from behind the closed bathroom door – as if whatever made it had already cried out so much it could only make a small noise, but one that held much more terror than a full-throated scream.

I wondered if Stefan knew what was in the bathroom and that was why he'd been afraid when we were in the parking lot – there were things that even a vampire ought to be afraid of. I took a deep breath, but all I could smell was the bitter darkness – and that was getting stronger. I sneezed, trying to clear my nose, but it didn't work. Both vampires stood still until the noise stopped. Then the stranger dusted his hands lightly, a small smile on his face as if there had not been rage just an instant before.

'I am remiss,' he said, but the old fashioned words sounded false coming from him, as if he were pretending to be a vampire the way the old vampires tried to be human. 'You obviously do not know who I am.'

He gave Stefan a shallow bow. It was obvious, even to me, that this vampire had grown up in a time and place where bowing was something done in Kung Fu Theater movies rather than in everyday life. 'I am Asmodeus,' he said grandly, sounding like a child pretending to be a king.

'I said you have no reputation,' Stefan replied, still in that light, careless voice. 'I didn't say I didn't know your name, Cory Littleton. Asmodeus was destroyed centuries ago.'

'Kurfel, then,' said Cory, nothing childlike in his manner at all.

I knew those names, Asmodeus and Kurfel, both, and as soon as I realized where I'd heard them, I knew what I had been smelling. Once the idea occurred to me, I realized the smell could be nothing else. Suddenly Stefan's fear wasn't surprising or startling at all. Demons were enough to scare anyone.

'Demon' is a catchall phrase, like 'fae,' used to describe beings who are unable to manifest themselves in our world in physical form. Instead, they possess their victims and feed upon them until there is nothing left. Kurfel wouldn't be this one's name, any more than Asmodeus was: knowing a demon's name gave you power over them. I'd never heard of a demon-possessed vampire before. I tried to stretch my mind around the concept.

'You are not Kurfel either,' said Stefan. 'Though something akin to him is allowing you some use of his powers when you amuse him well enough.' He looked toward the bathroom door. 'What *have* you been doing to amuse him, sorcerer?'

Sorcerer.

I thought those were just stories – I mean, who would be dumb enough to invite a demon into themselves? And why would a demon, who could just possess any corrupt soul (and to offer yourself to a demon sort of presupposes a corrupt soul, doesn't it?) make a deal with anyone? I didn't believe in sorcerers; I certainly didn't believe in vampire sorcerers.

I suppose somone raised by werewolves should have been more open-minded – but I had to draw the line somewhere.

'I don't like you,' Littleton said coolly, and the hair on the back of my neck stood up as magic gathered around him. 'I don't like you at all.'

He reached out and touched Stefan in the middle of the forehead. I waited for Stefan to knock his hand aside, but he did nothing to defend himself, just dropped to his knees, landing with a heavy thud.

'I thought you'd be more interesting, but you're not.' Cory told him, but the diction and tone of his voice was different. 'Not amusing at all. I'll have to fix that.'

He left Stefan kneeling and went to the bathroom door.

I whined at Stefan and stretched up on my hind feet so I could lick his face, but he didn't even look at me. His eyes were vague and unfocused; he wasn't breathing. Vampires didn't need to, of course, but Stefan mostly did.

The sorcerer had bespelled him somehow.

I tugged at the leash, but Stefan's hand was still closed upon it. Vampires are strong, and even when I threw my whole thirty-two pounds into it, his hand didn't move. If I'd had half an hour I could have chewed through the leather, but I didn't want to be caught here when the sorcerer returned.

Panting, I looked across the room at the open bathroom. What new monster was waiting inside? If I got out of this alive, I'd never let anyone put a leash on me again. Werewolves have strength, semiretractable claws, and inch-long fangs – *Samuel* wouldn't have been caught by the stupid leather harness and leash. One bite and it would have been gone. All I had was speed – which the leash effectively limited.

I was prepared for a horrifying sight, something that could destroy Stefan. But what Cory Littleton dragged out of that room left me stunned with an entirely different sort of horror.

The woman wore one of those fifties-style uniforms that hotels give their maids; this one was mint green with a stiff blue apron. Her color scheme matched the drapes and the hallway carpets, but the rope around her wrists, dark with blood, didn't.

Other than her bleeding wrists, she seemed mostly unharmed, though the sounds she was making made me wonder about that. Her chest was heaving with the effort of her screaming, but even without the bathroom door between us she wasn't making much noise, more of a series of grunts.

I jerked against the harness again and when Stefan still didn't move, I bit him, hard, drawing blood. He didn't even flinch.

I couldn't bear to listen to the woman's terror. She was breathing in hoarse gulping pants and she struggled against Littleton's hold, so focused on him that I don't think she saw Stefan or me at all.

I hit the end of the leash again. When that didn't work I snarled and snapped, twisting around so that I could chew on the leather. My own collar was equipped with a safety fastening that I could have broken, but Stefan's leather harness was fastened with old-fashioned metal buckles.

The sorcerer dropped his victim on the floor in front of me, just out of reach – though I'm not sure what I could have done for her even if I could get within touching distance. She didn't see me; she was too busy trying not to see Littleton. But my struggles had drawn the sorcerer's attention and he squatted down so he was closer to my level.

'I wonder what you'd do if I let you go?' he asked me. 'Are you afraid? Would you run? Would you attack me or does the smell of her blood rouse you as it does a vampire?' He looked up at Stefan then. 'I see your fangs, Soldier. The rich scent of blood and terror: it calls to us, doesn't it? They keep us leashed as tightly as you keep your coyote.' He used the Spanish pronunciation, three syllables rather than two. 'They demand we take only a sip from each when our hearts crave so much more. Blood is not really filling without death is it? You are old enough to remember the Before Times, aren't you, Stefan? When vampires ate as we chose and reveled in the terror and the last throes of our prey. When we fed truly.'

Stefan made a noise and I risked a glance at him. His eyes had changed. I don't know why that was the first thing I noticed about him, when so much else was different. Stefan's eyes were usually the shade of oiled walnut, but now they gleamed like blood-rubies. His lips were drawn back, revealing fangs shorter and more delicate than a werewolf's. His hand, which had tightened on my leash, bore curved claws on the ends of his elongated fingers. After a brief glimpse, I had to turn away, almost as frightened of him as I was of the sorcerer.

'Yes, Stefan,' said Littleton, laughing like the villain in an old black and white movie. 'I see you remember the taste of death. Benjamin Franklin once said that those who give up their freedom for safety deserve neither.' He leaned close. 'Do you feel safe, Stefan? Or do you miss what you once had, what you allowed them to steal from all of us.'

Littleton turned to his victim, then.

Enter the monthly

Orbit sweepstakes at

www.orbitloot.com

With a different prize every month,
from advance copies of books by
your favourite authors to exclusive
merchandise packs,
**we think you'll find something
you love.**